Monuments to Murder

Margarite St. John

Monuments to Murder

Other Books by Margarite St. John

FICTION:
Face Off
Murder for Old Times' Sake
The Girl With A Curl

NON-FICTION:
Finding Mrs. Hyde:
Writing Your First Popular Novel

Our Loyal Readers Say About:

Face Off

"I really enjoyed *Face Off*. It is far better than James Patterson, Patricia Cornwell & Stuart Woods I also read over the past few months. I have recommended it to friends!"
- Jamie

"*Face Off* is easy and enjoyable reading. . . . The pace compelled me to read just one more chapter. . . . A good mystery with an explosive beginning and end."
- A fan, Marco Island

"*Face Off* is well-written and fast-paced. It's kind of a twisted romance as well as a murder mystery. The characters are thoroughly fleshed out, which is different from a lot of mystery novels. . . . I like the way the books ends. Surprising and very exciting."
- Anne-Marie

"The author has given us interesting characters involved in a compelling story line. An easy comfortable writing style keeps you involved and draws you on, chapter to chapter. I'm left wishing for more!"
- pageturner

"Couldn't put the book down! Extremely well-written with a suspenseful plot and interesting characters. Each chapter ended with a hook, so I couldn't wait to start the next one! All of the requirements of a great suspense novel were woven into the book with great thought. A definite must-read! I can't wait to read more from this author!"
- Heather

Monuments to Murder

"It took me only two days to read this book. It was funny, disturbing, educational, enlightening, and ended with a good twist. I'm hooked on this author."
- Anne-Marie

"This is the second book from this author that I have read and I absolutely loved it!! Suspenseful, interesting characters with whom it was easy to identify, and a plot that was both intriguing and yet easy to follow. I literally could not put down my Kindle for 2 days until I finished it! I would say that this author has exactly what it takes to please the suspense novel fan and keep them coming back for more! Can't wait to read her next novel."
- Heather

Murder for Old Times' Sake

"The characters are very interesting, the story compelling, and the who-done-it suspense kept me reading to the funny and fitting end. The author fleshes out the good guys, bad guys, and the somewhere in-betweens, as people the reader can sympathize with and understand their motivations and mindsets. I am looking forward to the fourth book."
- Anne-Marie

"Third book from this author that I have read and just a wonderful suspense novel all the way around! Very interesting characters combine with an exiting plot to keep the reader coming back for more. Details are woven in carefully giving the reader the sense that they "are there" as things are happening. Just loved it!"
- Heather

Finding Mrs. Hyde: Writing Your First Popular Novel

"I am a fan of Margarite St. John. She's written three mystery novels in the past year and I have enjoyed every one of the stories (see my reviews). This short guide for women writers is funny and on the mark. The book takes you on a short and sweet step by step process through the stages of writing a good mystery story. Read this before you write."
- Anne-Marie

Table of Contents

Part One

Part Two

Part Three

Part One

"You must all know half a dozen people
at least who are no use in this world,
who are more trouble than they are worth."

Quote from George Bernard Shaw in a clip from
The Soviet Story, May 5, 2008

For where you have envy and selfish ambition,
there you find disorder and every evil practice.

James 3:16

1

A Nest of Worms
Friday, April 7, 2006

Verlin Dootz Grubbs was a simple man with simple pleasures, a man of few words. Some people even called him simple, though because he somehow knew the Latin names of herbs and flowers, others called him an idiot savant. The sound of those words, "simple" and "idiot," the tone of voice in which they were said, hurt him. Even he had to admit, however, that it was strange the way he struggled to find the everyday words he needed, yet his brain was stuffed with names like *Origanum vulgare* and *Salvia officinalis 'Icterina.'* Latin words wriggled around in his head like a nest of worms.

His sister, Jerry Lee Beaudry, was a very smart woman but not always nice to him. True, she let him live in an apartment over the carriage house in a far corner of her estate in Naples, Florida, where he could work in her magnificent walled garden any time he pleased. But she warned him that he couldn't leave the garden unless somebody went with him. He didn't like that, but he was too afraid to disobey her because her punishments were harsh.

Verlin's favorite retreat was the little stone, ivy-covered potting shed attached to the greenhouse. There he had appropriated a tall wooden cabinet for his treasures. In the heat of the day, he retreated to a discarded wicker chair in the cool, shady depths of the aromatic shed, where he could examine his treasures, one by one.

With the money his sister occasionally gave him, he bought second-hand coffee-table books with beautiful photo spreads of the world's greatest gardens. By contrast, the herb books he collected were often homely, illustrated with black line drawings and marred by mysterious stains and smudges. Every day he perused at least one of the garden books for ideas about the best arrangements of shrubs, herbs, and flowers. And every day he also studied the herb books, wishing he had the means to make the meads and wines for which recipes were given. Fortunately, drying and grinding herbs into powders that could be used in tisanes and infusions was well within his power. From one beam of the garden shed hung an assortment of fresh herbs drying upside down. From another beam hung a row of neatly labeled gauze bags filled with seeds and powders.

The cabinet also held an array of Mason jars, some filled with found objects, some with souvenirs -- buttons, belt buckles, jewelry, coins. Many of the objects once belonged to people who no longer walked the earth. He knew where their bodies or ashes were kept but not where their souls had gone. Perhaps their souls hadn't flown away yet. In fact, he was pretty sure their souls had been detained and resided in his souvenir treasures. As a caretaker of souls, Verlin took good care of the souvenirs against the day the souls left forever to be reunited with their bodies.

Once again, on a Friday night in early April, he found himself unable to sleep. When he couldn't sleep, he opened a little cigar box near his single bed, removed a special herb cigarette, descended the stairs of the carriage house, and wandered out into the garden. Jerry Lee's boyfriend, Phil Coker, supplied him with special cigarettes he called 'cannablis,' telling him they'd soothe his troubled mind. When Verlin tried to correct Phil's pronunciation, Phil just laughed and said it was a joke. For the life of him, Verlin couldn't understand why getting a Latin name wrong was funny. He thought that a man as famous as Phil was, as devoted to *Cannabis sativa* as he was, should call his favorite herb by its proper name.

That night, the garden was lit only by a half moon. When

Verlin found his favorite bench, he lit the hand-rolled cigarette and gazed at the loveliest marble monument in the garden, an angel with the face of a girl who disappeared many years ago. One of his most beautiful treasures was the silver locket she once wore, engraved with her initials -- NSD, for Nicky Sue Darling. Some nights he was troubled about what might have happened to her almost twenty years ago after Jerry Lee told him to return to Charleston alone, but tonight he was in a different mood. He simply admired her pretty face. The statue, which Jerry Lee said was a goddess, not an angel, stood on a long marble plinth, where the girl was entombed. It was comforting to know where Nicky Sue was. He realized she was probably just hair and bones now, but at least she wasn't ashes.

The tall urns flanking the statue caught his attention. The strongly scented *Jasminum nudiflorum* spilling out of them was in serious need of pruning. He needed to attend to that.

Before getting up to return to bed, he once more looked proudly at the *Datura stramonium* that marched all the way around Nicky Sue's plinth, softening its hard edges. Visitors called the beautiful yellow flower Angel's trumpet, a name far more fitting than they knew, for in the right dose it gave them heavenly visions. In the wrong dose, they actually heard the angel's final trumpet, as Nicky Sue surely had. He sometimes wondered what that would sound like. He hoped the place to which souls flew was a garden like this one, but with all the dead people alive again, graced by lovely new bodies.

In that new and better garden, he'd be like everyone else. He'd be able to talk the way he wanted. He'd be handsome and wouldn't need glasses. There would be no troubling secrets. He'd be safe and respected, maybe even admired for his special knowledge of herbs. That would be a welcome change because so long as he was confined to Jerry Lee's garden, he had to be discreet, she said. Nobody could know that with herbs he had the power of life and death.

2

Gilt Trip

Saturday, April 8, 2006

Molly Standardt, flanked by her husband, Carl, and her best friend, Sara Bancroft, surveyed the room at The Owl and the Pussycat where in an hour she would start autographing her first true-crime book, *Gilt Trip.*

She felt lucky that The Owl and the Pussycat still existed. It was one of the last independent bookstores in Naples, Florida, owned for fifty years by Irv and Dalia Silverman, an eccentric couple in their seventies. They barely made a living any more, but they weren't about to quit educating the world. As devoted bibliophiles, with hundreds of loyal customers who depended on their recommendations, they were too stubborn to give in to Barnes and Noble or Border's. They enjoyed hosting book clubs and still published popular book reviews in *The Naples Daily News.* But their favorite event was a book signing, especially when the author was a local celebrity with a best-seller on her hands.

Molly had come by her celebrity very suddenly. Last year, when she was still the pseudonymous author of a gossip column called *Shots in the Dark* for a Marco Island newspaper, she had a small part in uncovering the dark past of a successful and very rich plastic surgeon whose true character was exposed only after an accident involving his cigarette boat, *Face Off.* The guilt of those who knew and loved his wives but failed to protect them, together with the gilt-edged life the surgeon's wives had unknowingly created for him, melded into the title of her book. *Gilt Trip* was now number three on the non-fiction best-seller list. Molly was famous and, if not yet rich, well on her way.

Her husband, Carl, an orthodontist on Marco Island, where they still lived, slipped his arm around Molly's waist and kissed her cheek. He was several inches shorter than his lovely wife. "You'll be the most beautiful woman in the room, darling."

She bent down to kiss his cheek. "Thank you." She looked at the long walnut table, scuffed with years of hard use. On it, her books were stacked in neat piles. She couldn't imagine selling all of them.

"I just hope we get enough customers for all those books. Otherwise, I'll never hold my head up again."

"Then I'll buy all of them," Sara said, kissing her friend on the other cheek. "I plan to send one to every friend I have anyway."

Carl smiled at Sara. "You've taken all this very gracefully. If Molly hasn't already said so, we thank you for letting her invade your life this way . . . and remaining our friends."

Sara returned Carl's smile. "It isn't my favorite way to come to public attention, I'll give you that, but facts are facts, and Molly did as tasteful a rendition of them as she could, given the awkward circumstances."

The circumstances were undeniably awkward for Sara Bancroft. For many years, the plastic surgeon who was the subject of Molly's book had been her husband Bob's partner in a well-regarded medical practice, and then for a few months he was her brother-in-law as well after marrying her sister, Lily Anderson, in a hasty civil ceremony in Miami. Once Sara and her husband recognized Dr. Bruce McPhee Blackburn for the man he really was, they did their best to protect Lily, who, bless her heart, barely escaped with her life.

"It's the happy ending that tempers the notoriety," Sara said, patting her friend's hand.

"What happy ending?" Lily asked as she walked up behind them.

"Getting my book published," Molly said, hastily changing the subject. No use opening up old wounds. "Getting a book signing gig at The Owl and the Pussycat. That's all we were talking about."

"How do you think the room looks?" Lily asked. She'd done all the planning, all the publicity. Despite the immense wealth she now had, and despite having married the ambitious, good-hearted detective who saved her, she'd begun life anew as an event planner, working six days a week, sometimes seven. Her company, Tiger Lily Events, was growing so rapidly she'd had to hire a secretary, an office manager, a scheduler and booker, an etiquette specialist, a publicist, and a bookkeeper. Simon Diodorus, an acquaintance she'd made last year at the Marco Island Golf and Racquet Club, consulted on high-end projects whenever his friend Arachne 'Nee-Nee' Spanopoulos excused him from serving as her walker.

"Perfect," Molly said. "The sherry and crumpets table is a nice touch, and the azaleas are fabulous."

"I don't want to be pushy, but you might want to seat yourself now," Lily said, handing Molly a beautiful gold pen. "There are simply floods of people already streaming through the doors."

"Oh, gosh, you're right. Well, here goes."

For the next four hours, Molly autographed book after book, occasionally stopping to chat with an old friend or accept a stranger's compliment. Every forty-five minutes, Irv Silverman had to send his grandson to the storeroom to retrieve more tomes.

It was almost closing time when a woman handed Molly a book and said to make it out to Jerry Lee Beaudry. As Molly began writing the name, she suddenly recognized it. She looked up. The woman, now in her late sixties, her skin tight as a mask, glared back. "Remember me?"

"Of course. From Charleston."

"No. A suburb of Charleston. Remember Poppy?"

"Your daughter. I haven't seen her in ages. Is she still as beautiful as she was then?"

"More beautiful than you ever were."

Molly, her face growing hot as if she'd just been slapped, returned to signing the book. This was no time for a scene about

8

Poppy. Jerry Lee was famous for her scenes, especially when it came to Poppy, whom she protected like a lioness with cubs facing a snarling hyena.

But before Molly could add her signature, Jerry Lee grabbed her wrist. "Sign it 'Judas.'"

The woman's grip was like the claw of a wild animal. Molly pulled away. "Get your hand off me."

Jerry Lee removed her hand and with the other slapped down a newspaper folded in threes. "You did this."

Molly glanced at the newspaper. "Did what?"

"Exposed my daughter."

Molly looked up at her accuser. "Exposed? What are you talking about?"

"The abortion," she hissed, her face contorted with rage.

Bernie Katzenbaum, a local detective who worked for Lily's new husband, Tom Lawton, had been standing a few feet behind Molly, not expecting trouble but always prepared for it. Built like a linebacker, she was dressed in a navy pantsuit that was tight across the shoulders and resembled a police uniform. "What's going on here?" she asked, giving Jerry Lee a hard look.

In a small voice, Molly said, "This woman's accusing me of something I know nothing about."

Bernie moved around the table to stand inches from the woman with the big mouth. "What's her name?" she asked, directing her question to Molly while staring at the troublemaker.

"Jerry Lee Beaudry. I knew her years ago."

"Well, Jerry Lee Beaudry, it's time for you to step outside. Now."

"I want my book. I paid for it."

Bernie handed her the book. "You want to walk out on your own power or have my help?"

"I'm leaving." When she was a few yards from the front door, Jerry Lee turned and screamed at Molly. "I'm not done with you, Judas."

"Maybe not, but you're done for tonight," Bernie said, wishing she could kick the harridan out on her ass.

9

After Molly signed books for the last of the stragglers and some of them were still gathered around the sherry table, she put her head in her hands. Sara, who had been sitting beside her, handing over books open to the frontispiece and answering customers' questions, picked up the newspaper. "Do you know what that woman was talking about?"

"I might. I saw something yesterday about Ferrin McBride's wife, how years ago she had an abortion. I didn't know anything about it until I saw the article."

"Ferrin McBride. The Congressman running for a second term? His wife?"

"Yes. Poppy Beaudry -- that was her name before she married Ferrin. They're very pro-life, so a secret abortion is big news."

"Not so secret if it's in the papers."

"She called me Judas. She must think I spilled the beans."

"But you said you didn't know about it."

"I didn't. Twenty years ago she also thought I cheated Poppy out of the Miss South Carolina title."

"Did you?"

Molly looked shocked. "Of course I didn't."

"I'm only teasing," Sara said. "The woman sounds like a paranoid she-devil."

"She said she's not done with me."

"When's the last time you talked to her daughter?"

"I can't even remember, it's so long ago."

"Were you friends despite the competition for the title?"

"Of a sort, yes. Friendships at that age, in that situation, aren't the best, but, yes, we were kind of friends."

"Maybe it's time for you to talk to Poppy."

3

He's a Hypocrite, Straight Up
Sunday, April 9, 2006

On Sunday morning, the day after the book-signing, Molly was sitting on her screened lanai in Roberts Bay. She was drinking coffee and reading the papers with her husband and mother.

Dee Applegate, who was visiting her daughter for a couple weeks, with the stipulation that she wasn't baby-sitting the twins, told Molly for the fifth time how much she liked the new furniture on the lanai. Also for the fifth time, she recalled sailing to Europe on an ocean liner with the same style of Twenties deck chairs. Carl joked that he hoped his wife hadn't been too much influenced in her decorating choices by the *Titanic*. Dee rejoined that when he heard an orchestra playing, he might want to leave.

Dee tolerated her son-in-law but never bothered to conceal her lack of enthusiasm for him. Her gorgeous daughter could have done so much better. For his part, Carl found his mother-in-law amusing. So far as he could determine, the only person she'd ever loved was Molly, and since they both loved the same woman, he could put up with her a few weeks a year.

When Molly located the article Jerry Lee Beaudry found so offensive, she called for quiet and read it aloud to her husband and mother.

At a fund-raiser on Thursday, Myron Mullett, former Collier County Commissioner and now the progressive candidate to represent the 14th Congressional District in the U.S. House of Representatives, told a wildly cheering audience that Congressman Ferrin McBride, a Republican, is the worst kind of hypocrite. McBride, Mullett's conservative opponent, who holds the advantage of being the incumbent, is staunchly pro-life.

Mullett brandished the latest issue of *Marie Claire*, a popular Canadian magazine for women. That issue features an exposé of the lives of Far Right political wives, alleging that McBride's wife, Poppy, had an abortion before they were married as she was preparing to compete for the title of Miss South Carolina in 1989. Mrs. McBride, then known as Poppy Jo Beaudry, the daughter of Jonah Beaudry, a prominent mortician in a Charleston, South Carolina suburb, finished as first runner-up, losing to Molly Applegate, now Mrs. Carl Standardt.

[The Standardts are Marco Island residents. Mrs. Standardt, a contributor to this paper, just published a best-selling true-crime novel about a man who was once her good friend. See Review of *Gilt Trip* on p. 7.]

In a press conference yesterday, Harley Wangle, Mullett's long-time press secretary and formerly the first black Director of the Florida Department of Highway Safety and Motor Vehicles, told reporters that the 14th District cannot afford to elect a man like McBride. He's "a hypocrite, straight up" who would deny all women other than his wife and daughter the right to choose.

Wangle then explained Mullett's proposed taxpayer-funded program to help "mature" drivers comply with new restrictions on license renewal. The restrictions are contained in a law Mullett backed. In response to critics,

Mullett estimates the law will only cost the State of Florida ten million dollars a year, a cost he says is well worth it. "Everybody knows that Florida highways are the most dangerous in the world. Seniors, of course, have the right to drive so long as they don't endanger others. Nothing is more important than highway safety," he said, "so we'll spend what we have to spend. Opponents just want people to die in accidents."

Wangle ducked questions about allegations that Mullett is hiding in off-shore accounts the fortune he inherited from his late father, Buddy Mullett, who founded a national chain of senior living centers called Mullett Village. Mullett's own mother-in-law lives at a center called Mullett Village at Naples. All Wangle would say was that Mullett is current on all back taxes and penalties.

Rep. Ferrin McBride, who was formerly Attorney General for the State of Florida, is a long-time proponent of fiscal responsibility. At the time this paper went to press, he could not be reached for comment.

Molly snorted. "'Good friend' indeed. I was never Bruce's *good* friend." She bent down to adjust the gold ankle bracelet, graced with a Leo disc, a gift from Carl in honor of making the best-seller list. "At least they spelled my name right."

"So the abortion -- that's the issue for Jerry Lee, is it?" Dee Applegate asked.

"Do you know, Mom, whether Poppy ever actually had an abortion?"

Dee, now a widow who was born and raised in Charleston and still lived there, explained that she was never friends with Jerry Lee Beaudry but remembered both her and Poppy very well. "In those days, remember, Jerry Lee ran a school called Crowning Glory for pre-teen girls competing in beauty pageants. I never let you go there because I didn't want you to be like Poppy. We all felt sorry for the poor girl. She hardly had any childhood at all, she was so over-scheduled with voice lessons and pageants."

"So," Molly said, used to her mother's digressions but mildly irritated by them, "did she have an abortion or not?"

"There was a rumor going around her senior year in high school that she did because she was suddenly hospitalized and almost died."

"From an abortion?"

"Her classmates were told it was a burst appendix, followed by septicemia. She damn near died from it."

"A burst appendix is not an abortion."

"The rumor was that it wasn't her appendix at all. She wouldn't have been the first girl to cover up an abortion. Some girls had as many appendixes as toes."

"Mom, how'd you get so cynical?"

"It wasn't me started the rumors."

"But, Mom, abortions were legal then. Why would anybody lie about having one?"

"People did. In Poppy's case, maybe it was her mother who was lying. Poppy couldn't be the pageant queen of Sweetgrass Weavers and Hog Farmers, let alone Miss South Carolina, if she was known to be promiscuous."

"How come you never told me this about Poppy before?"

"You were young when it happened, the same age as Poppy. I didn't want you to get any ideas."

"Mom!"

"Anyway, the abortion rumors began because, just before she was hospitalized, her boyfriend disappeared. What was his name again?" Dee closed her eyes and tapped her fingers on the arm of her chair. Each finger was adorned with a ring set with diamonds and a rainbow of semi-precious stones, the nails painted bright red. Finally, she opened her eyes. "Dewey Betz. That was his name. Minnie and Burley's youngest son. They were hog farmers, you know."

"Disappeared? You mean that literally?"

"Poof -- gone! There one day, gone the next."

"He ever turn up anywhere?"

"Not that I heard."

"So, do you have a theory about who told the *Marie Claire* reporter about Poppy's abortion. If it was an abortion?"

"Anybody who knew the Beaudrys in Charleston and heard the rumors might have speculated about it, but the only people who'd have any facts, I suppose, would be Poppy, her mother, or the doctor who attended her."

"Not her father?"

"He died a year or two before that. Sudden heart attack or stroke or something while he was embalming some poor stiff." She laughed. "You might say he became a stiff before he was done with the stiff he was working on." Dee finished her cup of coffee. "Everybody was very stiff that day. Which usually isn't a bad thing in a man."

Carl snorted a laugh.

"So the article got that wrong too. It makes it sound like her father's still alive."

Dee cackled and threw her head back, miming the dead. "She isn't the daughter of a prominent mortician. She's the daughter of a completely dead mortician."

"Mom. Your sense of humor is downright creepy."

Dee, a tiny woman with a feisty temper and an unedited mouth, was adorned with so much jewelry that she rattled when she walked, like a dog carrying too many collar tags. She stood up and waltzed -- rattle, rattle -- over to the buffet to pour herself more coffee. She turned around dramatically, adjusting her wig and batting her false eyelashes like a Broadway stage actress. She swayed a little on her mile-high wedges. "Not as creepy as real life."

Carl couldn't help it. He laughed so hard coffee shot out of his nose.

4

We Shouldn't Be Enemies
Wednesday, April 12, 2006

It took three days and several voice-mail messages before Poppy Beaudry McBride returned Molly's call.

"Poppy, I'm so glad you called back. Your mother came to my book-signing Saturday night and accused me of something concerning you. She's wrong -- completely wrong."

"I don't doubt that. What did she accuse you of?"

"Being the source of a very bad bit of gossip about you, something I swear I never knew anything about until that newspaper account of Mullett's fund-raiser. I'd like to talk to you about it, clear the air. My husband and I support Ferrin, you know. We've contributed to his campaign."

"Thank you for that."

"We shouldn't be enemies."

"I have plenty of enemies, but you're not one of them."

"Thank goodness, Poppy." She caught herself. "I don't mean it's good to have lots of enemies, I just mean . . . ."

"I know what you mean. You don't have to apologize for my mother. Even I don't do that."

Pleading a heavy schedule, Poppy finally agreed to meet her old rival, but only if Molly could drive up to Port Royal.

On Wednesday, when Molly arrived in Port Royal, she marveled at the beauty of the McBrides' blindingly white Italianate palazzo, lent importance by its sheer size, the colonnaded terrace enveloping the entire structure, and the lush green formal grounds cascading to Treasure Cove. The only color was supplied by tropical flowers spilling from giant mossy urns that looked like they'd been imported from Italy hundreds of years ago. For a man who'd been in public service most of his life, Ferrin McBride had done very well for himself. *How do politicians manage to get so rich?* Molly wondered as she made her way to the imposing front door.

Poppy greeted Molly with a firm handshake, then led her down a long marble-tiled hall illuminated by sunlight spilling through the French doors lining the terrace. Finally, they reached a conservatory on the south end of the palazzo. The intense sunlight streaming through the dome was filtered through the leaves of huge tropical plants. It smelled divine.

Molly noted with admiration that Poppy was as slender as ever, still very pretty, conservatively dressed. But somehow the pizzazz of Poppy's early years was gone. Once, she'd had sparkling eyes, a brilliant smile, long brown shiny hair. Now the eyes were guarded, the smile fleeting, the hair a medium-length highlighted blondish bob swept away from her pretty little ears.

After they were seated in Louis XV chairs and each had a glass of sweetened ice tea in hand, Molly broke the silence. "I read the horrible article after Jerry Lee gave me the newspaper. My mother's visiting Carl and me, and even she didn't know about the abortion . . . if there ever was one."

"It wasn't an abortion, exactly."

"I'm not prying. I don't need to know anything. I just want you to know from me that I didn't tell anybody anything, despite your mother's accusation. I didn't know anything to tell a reporter and, even if I had known, I wouldn't have said a word."

"But somebody did, didn't they?"

Molly didn't know what to say.

"Jerry Lee," Poppy said, "probably assumes you're the source of the leak because you're now a famous investigative reporter. Congratulations by the way."

"A bit of luck, really. Not so lucky for my friend Lily, but fortunate for me."

"You were always modest."

"I had a lot to be modest about," Molly said, an engaging smile lighting up her face. "Remember that baton twirling stunt I did at the pageant? I was all ass and fire."

Poppy's eyes sparkled with amusement. "Do I ever! Those were the first fire batons I ever saw."

"You were a trained singer, I was a fire-baton twirler, for heaven's sake."

"But you held it together after Nicky Sue disappeared. I fell apart."

"Well, she was your roommate. I'd have fallen apart too," Molly said. "I'm sure she'd have won, don't you agree?"

"No doubt in my mind. When she played *Für Elise*, you could hear a pin drop. The judges tried to hide the fact they were in love with her, but it was plain enough to me." Poppy shifted in her chair. "You don't happen to remember the question I was asked, do you?"

"No. I barely remember mine."

"It was about world hunger, something to the effect of what my solution for it was. I'd prepared for it, but everything I'd learned went right out of my head. All I could think about was Nicky Sue. I babbled incoherently about victory gardens and bringing back DDT and reducing caloric intake in rich countries and how the expanding deserts were diminishing arable land and the world needed more irrigation. Then I dissolved into tears. I think I actually sobbed." She hiccuped, on the verge of tearful laughter. "I know I actually sobbed. The only thing I felt good about afterwards is the big words I used, like arable and caloric. I thought my vocabulary might impress the judges so much they'd overlook the incoherence."

"Don't feel so bad, Poppy. Didn't I ramble on about world peace or something? I was definitely for it." She paused. "Wasn't I? Please tell me I was for world peace."

They looked at each other and smiled. Then they laughed. The conservatory rang with their laughter.

"The last thing I ever expected to do was win," Molly said, wiping her eyes. "You and Nicky Sue were prettier and more talented. Well, you still are prettier, and who knows? Nicky Sue might be too, wherever she is. *You* had better clothes than I did, that's for sure. You didn't need as much practice as I did walking in my gown, pirouetting just so, not stepping on the hem."

"I'm sure somebody'll find the archival footage of my babbling and run it on an endless loop. If they do, the reaction will probably be harsher than to the *Marie Claire* article. After all, what's worse in this era when everybody's famous for fifteen minutes: supposedly having an abortion or making a fool of yourself in public?"

"I haven't seen that article, by the way. I don't read *Marie Claire.*"

"Who does? I'll give you a copy of the magazine. Jerry Lee bought at least a dozen, heaven knows why. More tea?"

After Poppy had refilled their glasses, she resumed. "I was a very troubled girl twenty years ago. You probably never knew, but my dad died suddenly while I was still in high school and my boyfriend disappeared before the pageant. Add Nicky Sue to that equation and I was almost done for. I even thought about suicide."

"You're right, I never knew any of that. How did you keep all those secrets?"

"Guilt."

"Guilt? What guilt?"

"Survivor's guilt at living. At not disappearing. Everybody I loved or liked kept dying or leaving. I figured I was a living curse. If anybody got near me, poof -- something bad happened to them. So talking about my life was tantamount in my mind to admitting I deserved bad luck because I was the cause of other people's bad luck."

"I didn't know you had a high school boyfriend until Mom mentioned it yesterday. Have you ever heard from him?"

"Not a word. He disappeared when I told him I was pregnant. That was a shock, because he said he was ready to marry me. A day or two later, he was nowhere to be found. He never called, never wrote. Once I accepted that he'd lied about wanting to get married, I never expected to hear from him again."

"You really were pregnant then?"

"I really was. I'd secretly scheduled an abortion with Planned Parenthood, but before my appointment, I suddenly started hemorrhaging and convulsing. It was so bad, I almost died." She looked out toward the cove. "So, you see, I didn't have an abortion, but I intended to have one, so calling me a hypocrite isn't all wrong. Since then, I've changed my mind about things."

"Haven't we all?"

"I sympathize with women who want a choice, but choosing to take another person's life doesn't seem right. How is it any different from child sacrifice?"

Molly nodded. "Did you ever see that PBS program where cameras were inserted into women's uteruses? You could see the baby was a baby right from the start, not just a lump of tissue."

"For me, understanding DNA settled it for all time," Poppy said. "The only thing that fertilized egg can ever be is a human being. Once I got that straight in my head, I understood abortion is the murder of the innocent."

"Even so, I wouldn't ban it for a girl who's been raped."

"I go back and forth about making abortion illegal myself. God lets us choose our sins. Speaking of choosing our sins, every night, I thank God for his mercy in not letting me get to the abortion clinic. And in letting me live through those convulsions."

"You had convulsions?"

Poppy nodded.

"Did you ever find out what caused them?"

"No. My uncle Verlin gave me my afternoon tea, I lay down for a nap, and the next thing I knew I was in the hospital, Jerry Lee standing over me. I was temporarily paralyzed too, you know."

"My God, you were lucky to live, weren't you?"

"I was."

"Not to change the subject, but it's strange how you call your mother by her first name."

"We have a complicated relationship, Molly."

"I have the same with my mom. She thinks I could have done

a lot better than Carl Standardt because he's not tall and handsome or rich. Sometimes she embarrasses me because when she gets started on a subject, you never know where she'll end up or what'll come out of her mouth. She dresses like a teen-ager, wears too much jewelry and makeup. But, still, I love her, and I don't call her Dee."

Poppy laughed. "I remember your mother, a little bit anyway. She was always mending your clothes and talking about what a good student you were. I can't even picture her without pins in her mouth, kneeling to adjust your hems. I was so envious."

"Of what?"

"How much she loved you without making a fuss about it. Not like Jerry Lee, the stereotypical stage mother . . . always hovering, always critical, always adjusting a strap or my hair because I simply couldn't get it right, then saying ridiculously proud things about me. I know onlookers thought she was a good mother, but she wasn't. I felt like a puppet, too valuable to be left lying around, unprotected and uninsured, but basically unloved."

"I'm so sorry. But tell me about Ferrin. How's he doing?"

"Right now? He's huddling with his handlers, trying to figure out how to respond to this latest shot across the bow. He wants to hire somebody to find the leaker."

"I know just the man. Tom Lawton. He's a detective here in town. If you've read my book -- and by the way, I brought you an autographed copy -- then you know how great he is."

Poppy took the book Molly handed her without looking at it. "You need to talk to Ferrin. Maybe he'll interview this Tom Lawton . . . or somebody on his staff will."

"I'd like the chance to prove your mother wrong about me. What about letting Carl and me sponsor a fund-raiser?"

"You'd do that?"

"Of course. I'm not guilty of anything, but I feel that way. I want to do something nice for you."

"What I really need is somebody to write a sympathetic piece about me. Not untrue, mind you, but something that proves I'm not a total hypocrite. I'm a repentant sinner."

"I can do that too. In fact, I'd love it."

For the first time that afternoon, Poppy glowed with happiness and affection. "This means so much to me, Molly. You can't imagine what it's like to be a politician's wife, always under the microscope, the darkest spin put on every mistake . . . with no power to do anything about it."

"Sounds lonely."

"Like the outer reaches of hell sometimes." Poppy slapped her own cheek. "Oh, stop me. That's a little dramatic, isn't it? Forgive me for the self-pity." She stood up. "Thank you for coming to talk to me. That took courage."

Molly insisted on a hug before she left. "Why didn't we stay in touch after the pageant? What a lot of time we've wasted."

5

Run from Fear, Fun from Rear
Thursday, April 13, 2006

Phil Coker returned from Los Angeles to Jerry Lee's estate in Naples just in time to take delivery of his latest art acquisition, two green panels by Bruce Nauman called *Run from Fear, Fun from Rear*. They were so simple anyone could have painted them, but only Bruce Nauman did.

The crude words across the top of the panels, providing the title, suited him. In fact, without those words, the pictures wouldn't have excited him at all. Phil Coker, after all, was crude in the sophisticated way of Hollywood's most deranged element, and he'd spent the last thirty-five years of his life proving that to be true. Thirty-five years in which, after his first big success, he'd made only another dozen or so movies, mostly box-office bombs.

The secret regret of his life was that he'd been replaced by Michael Douglas in a thriller that -- as his bad luck would have it -- turned out to be a huge money-maker, for which Douglas had reportedly taken a percentage of the gross. Phil thought it was cool in those days to ignore direction, play the scene the way he wanted. He wanted James Dean's reputation as a rebel, and he got it. Unfortunately, he didn't have Dean's talent or Michael Douglas' either. After one particularly vital scene in *Midnight Caller* was shot eighty-seven times without his accepting direction, Phil was fired.

He couldn't wait to explain to Jerry Lee that Nauman was

part of the Sixties funk art movement in California. The most hilarious thing about Nauman was that, like Ferrin McBride, he was originally from Indiana, proving that not every Hoosier was a loser. His untutored but very rich mistress would grimace at the insult to Ferrin, though she readily agreed that Indiana was the pits. She'd pretend to understand what he was talking about, that funk art was good and Bruce Nauman was special. She'd say she knew just the wall to hang the panels on. Every once in a while she'd comment on how much she liked that shade of green or compliment him on his exquisite taste.

If there was an adjective he hated, it was exquisite. Funky, weird, macho, super-cool, rebellious, unreliable, insolent, bizarre, bad boy, anti-establishment, street-smart -- those were the words he wanted to hear about himself.

His favorite picture, however, was not the Bruce Nauman panels but one he'd acquired a decade earlier, Jean-Michel Basquiat's *Man from Naples,* a work of graffiti depicting block-letter text and an animal mask on unprimed canvas. It was so messy and primitive a first-grader might have done it to escape nap-time. The kid would surely have earned a slap upside the head and a failing grade. What Phil liked most was the fact that Basquiat started out life vandalizing buildings and subway cars in New York. Phil had done a lot of rebellious things in his life, but he'd never yet had the guts to spray-paint somebody's building.

Another thing: He wished he was part-black like Basquiat. Anything not white -- or not quite white -- had caché in his overlapping circles of New York art and Hollywood film. Andy Warhol might have been a better friend if Phil could have claimed a Haitian father. As it was, Phil slipped into Jerry Lee's tanning bed at least twice a week. In his mind, his chiseled face, his hooded eyes, and his growing expanse of forehead looked so much more intimidating with a deep tan than with the dead white complexion he was born with.

Conventional as Jerry Lee was, she was a godsend to Phil. He'd met her in a Chelsea art gallery six years earlier. She kept returning to a Jim Dine picture called *The Valiant Red Car*, a pop art piece with a graffiti edge he liked but couldn't afford. He persuaded her to buy it. The way he did it was to dazzle her with a true story about how he was present at a "happening" at the Reuben Gallery in New York when Dine, in costume, explained his picture titled *Car Crash*. Phil imitated Dine's over-dramatic recounting of the car accident, interrupted by schizoid pleas for help that alarmed the spectators as to his real state of mind.

Phil watched Jerry Lee's rapt face as he told her the story. She was easily impressed. When she put her right hand to her face in pretended shock, he noticed the magnificent diamond. Her mild southern accent, calling him *Shugah*, amused him. She was pretty in the buttoned-up way of the upper-class. The fact that she was a little older was a plus; older women, he'd found, were grateful for his company. Often, they were rich and not averse to supporting a boyfriend. And they didn't get pregnant.

When Jerry Lee hesitated, saying she wasn't sure she liked the picture enough to buy it, she'd sleep on the matter, Phil pushed hard. Right then and there, he had to see if she could really pay the ridiculous price. He didn't buy anything that day, having run out of credit, but after she completed the purchase, he took her to the Waldorf, where he was pretty sure a woman from the provinces would be impressed.

A month later, after visiting her every weekend, racking up credit card bills he couldn't pay, he moved into her Naples estate. All he owned in those days, besides his magnificent wardrobe, a Rolex watch, the remnant of an art collection he'd started selling off, and a Harley that was no longer drivable, was a La-z-boy recliner that he purported to love because it was so ugly and comfortable, as ugly and comfortable as the bourgeoisie he despised. In Phil's mind, the recliner was so amusingly awful it was chic. Jerry Lee promptly gave it to Goodwill.

On Thursday, two days before taxes were due -- an obligation Phil had avoided for years -- Jerry Lee told him she was holding a fund-raiser for her son-in-law, the red-faced political hack he despised for his conservative views. What decent person could oppose abortion or gay marriage? Who didn't think world government would end war? Why shouldn't confiscatory taxes be used to level the playing field?

Phil caught himself before he objected to her plan. He liked to pull her chain, but why waste an opportunity to strut the stage? So he said, that was fine with him, he'd use the opportunity to give everybody the experience of a lifetime -- a tour of his famous art collection.

"Maybe another time, Shugah. I don't want these people shocked into holding onto their money. For Poppy's sake, I want them to give until it hurts, so maybe you should stay out of sight that night, do something else. Go to the Club."

"All this time we've been together and you still don't have a clue," he said, smiling condescendingly and patting her behind. "People like Ferrin's uptight friends love being shocked. I'm the most fascinating zoo animal they'll ever meet. You're so naïve."

She made a face. "You're street-smart, everybody else is naïve, is that it?"

"So right, old girl," he answered, without a trace of irony. He cocked his head as if reading the stars. "No, I'm definitely staying. We'll auction off a lunch with me and five bidders, to be held at the Club, followed by a screening of *The Ho Chi Minh Trail*."

"That old thing?"

"An oldie but a goodie. I looked sexy then, didn't I?"

"You're stuck in the Sixties, Phil." Jerry Lee was in no mood for reminiscing about his Hollywood past. "Poppy called yesterday, said Ferrin's thinking about hiring some guy to find the leaker."

"What leaker?"

She made a face. "About Poppy's supposed abortion. There was no abortion, you know."

Phil walked away from her, toward the new Nauman panels, which were propped against the wall of the gallery leading to the living room, or as Jerry Lee called it, the parlor. Really, who cared about abortions? He was eternally grateful that several of his girlfriends had agreed to them. "You said that woman who just wrote a book did it. She's the leaker."

"Molly Standardt? She's a thief, a *poseur*. She should never have won the pageant title."

"Let it go," he said, not bothering to hide his irritation with a subject he'd long ago grown sick of.

"Don't get mad at me. I'm not the one who wants to find the leaker."

"Liar," he said, throwing her a teasing smile.

"I *know* who the leaker is. Ferrin's wasting his money." She pointed at the new pictures. "Speaking of money, what did you use to buy those?"

He gave her a smug look. "Somebody made me a deal I couldn't refuse. One of these days, I can start making payments on what I owe you."

"It'd have to be an awfully good deal to make even a dent."

He took her in his arms. The fact that she was nine years older than he was never slipped his consciousness. She was damned lucky to have a younger man in her bed, a famous one at that. One way or another, he never let her forget it. "Don't I give you what you want?"

Jerry Lee pulled away, *so* not in the mood for what he had in mind. She'd just had her hair and makeup done and was dressed for dinner at the Club. "No secrets now. What's the deal you couldn't refuse?"

"Virgil Goldstein is going to back the movie I pitched. I'm writing the screenplay with a little help, and I'm directing with no help at all. I'll have a role in the movie -- a minor one, but I'll get another Oscar nomination for it."

"Isn't Goldstein the big Hollywood muckety-muck who raised a lot of money for the Clintons?"

He play-slapped her face. "Stay on the subject, my beautiful Southern belle."

She play-slapped him back. "When did you have time to write a screenplay?"

"You're not listening. I haven't written it yet." He tapped his temple. "The treatment's in my head."

"So what's the movie about, Shugah?"

He decided to poke the dragon. "Your fire-eating son-in-law.

His hypocrisy. Poppy's little slip-ups."

"I ought to slap you for real."

"But you won't."

"Ferrin will sue."

"You think he'll recognize himself when I'm done with the character? No way in hell. The son-of-a-bitch is so clueless I could make him the actor in the story of his own life and he'd never know that he was playing himself. He's clueless, I tell you. When he looks in the mirror, he sees a saint, not the devil he is."

"He wasn't my first choice for Poppy, but he's not a devil, Phil. Ferrin's a thousand times better than that farmer's boy she was going to marry. And you say one bad thing about Poppy . . . ."

"Or what?"

She glared at him. "I'll kill you myself."

Tough as Phil Coker was, when Jerry Lee got that look in her eye, he retreated. Poppy was the Virgin Mary and Jerry Lee was her guardian angel.

He moved out of reach. "Jerry Lee, sometimes I wonder about you. You'll fall for anything. The movie isn't about your kid and her slimy husband. They're the world's most boring people, bar none, naïve Bible-thumping -- ."

"That's enough," she said. She didn't read the Bible herself, but she was superstitious about denigrating it.

He fished a hand-rolled cigarette out of a silver case he carried in his jacket pocket. "Back to my movie. It's another story about a disillusioned vet, but updated."

"Like *The Ho Chi Minh Trail?* The one that made you famous?"

"That's it. Brilliant, huh?"

"The disillusioned vet kills himself again?"

"Nah. This time he's a gay Gulf War vet, suffering from mysterious headaches, and he wins all his battles, on and off the field of war. When he gets back from the Gulf, the right-wingers deny they deliberately poisoned their own soldiers. Then he flies into a rage and mows down a whole platoon of soldiers on an army base in Texas. The military tribunal that follows exposes the indifference of the Defense Department to its wounded, its coverup of chemical weapons, its intolerance toward gays, the lack of -- ."

She cut him off, unwilling to let him finish his list of dreary complaints. "You sure that's a winning formula?"

"I've got feelers out to Tom Cruise."

"Really?"

"I think I'll call it *Run from Fear, Fun from Rear.* What do you think?"

"You call it that, Tom Cruise will run from fear to Tibet. Sean Penn: that's who you should put feelers out to. He likes playing gay men. He'll embrace the story."

"Any other helpful comments?"

"I think if you don't throw tantrums this time, piss off everybody involved, you might actually make a movie."

Before he could respond, Jerry Lee turned on her heel and said it was time to leave for dinner, which they couldn't do until he put that leather jacket away and found a sport coat. And, just this once, please, please, pretty please, leave the funny cigarettes at home.

6

Beaudry Hall
Friday, April 14, 2006

Late on Friday, when Poppy drove into her mother's vast brick courtyard and parked, Lily, sitting in the passenger seat, stared in surprise at the long red-brick building in front of her. It was four stories high, with a tall cupola rising from the roof.

"I've driven by here before but never imagined what kind of building lay beyond the outer walls. What an unusual house for Florida."

"That's Jerry Lee. You might not have noticed, but on the brick wall on the east side of the entrance, there's an inset stone carved with the name 'Beaudry Hall.'"

"I saw that."

"Pretentious, wouldn't you say?"

"Well . . . ."

"Go ahead, say it. Jerry Lee's nothing if not pretentious. She not only lives in a *faux* plantation house, named as if it were the real thing, but she likes to say we're from grand old Southern stock. If she gets an opening, she'll tell you we're descended from distant cousins of the Draytons who own the Magnolia Plantation near Charleston."

"You are?"

Poppy laughed as she got out of the car. "Her maiden name was Grubbs, so what do you think? Ferrin grows livid every time she says something about the Draytons."

The three women -- Poppy, Lily, and Molly -- together with Simon Diodorus stood in front of the grand staircase to the double entrance door on the second floor, where a deep veranda wrapped around the entire house. The ground floor was dedicated to garages. The third floor was adorned with balconies, the fourth with dormer windows.

"What am I looking at?" Simon asked, distaste evident in his tone. "The House of the Seven Gables?"

"Magnolia Plantation, gussied up and scaled down, without the live oaks and Spanish moss."

"What century is it inside?"

Poppy laughed. "Modern, more open than the original, but it has beautiful moldings and fireplace mantels, pocket doors, twelve-foot ceilings. *En suite* bedrooms. A huge kitchen worthy of *House Beautiful.* When you're inside the house, you'd never guess that the facade is antebellum."

They mounted the stairs to the entrance. Jerry Lee, standing behind her butler, said "Welcome to Beaudry Hall, y'all," exaggerating her accent. She greeted her daughter with a hug, and though she smiled at the other guests, she didn't offer to shake hands. At the sound of the woman's accent, Simon put a silk handkerchief to his nose, as if blocking a bad smell.

After they'd stepped inside and Poppy made the introductions, Jerry Lee looked at Molly. "My daughter swears you had nothing to do with that vile article."

"I didn't."

"She says I have to apologize to you for saying what I did."

So, are you apologizing or not? I'm waiting.

After an awkward silence, Jerry Lee said, "We'll let bygones be bygones."

That's your apology, you old bat?

"I told Ferrin that if there's going to be a fund-raiser, it's going to be here, even if you're sponsoring it. I don't imagine your house is anything like this."

"Oh, it isn't." Molly looked toward the rooms leading off

either side of the two-story entrance hall featuring a spiral staircase. "I can't imagine a more magnificent setting."

Simon started to laugh, then pretended to sneeze.

"You have a sinus problem or something?" Jerry Lee asked him.

He nodded, his face screwed tight to keep from laughing uncontrollably. To him, the house was as pretentious as its owner. "It affects my sense of taste -- er, taste buds, you know. Can't taste a thing. No taste at all." He pretended to blow his nose.

After giving him a puzzled look, Jerry Lee led her four visitors to a sitting room at the back of the house, overlooking her gardens. She served them some sort of fragrant herbal tea and passed around a plate of cheese straws she said were made from an old family recipe. After they'd talked awhile about the fund-raiser, they split up so they could see the gardens before it got dark.

Lily and Simon took the stairs down to the garden, where they would decide the locations of various tables and service stations for the fund-raiser. Since about two hundred people were expected to attend, at a thousand dollars a plate, they needed to find a big open space to set up twenty round dining tables, with service stations nearby.

About fifty feet from the back of the house, they came across a huge terraced square. The fountain in the middle was a giant bronze mermaid with an open mouth spewing water ten feet into the air. The water fell back into a round stone basin embellished with mythical sea creatures. Some sort of ground creeper surrounded the basin.

"Better hope there's no wind that night or the diners will be drenched -- some of them anyway, depending on which direction the spray goes." When Simon walked closer to the basin and looked at the water, he screamed and backed away. "Oh, dear, would you look at that?"

Having moved closer and spotted what he'd seen, Lily put her hand to her mouth. "What is it?"

He looked at her with horrified eyes. "A muskrat? It's all bloated and everything. I think I'm going to puke."

She put her arm around his narrow shoulders. "Calm down and get that hankie out, Simon. Notice the ears? the tail? It's a rabbit."

"That doesn't make things better. Rabbits are rodents, aren't they? And it's dead."

"I'll find the gardener and make sure the fountain is clean for the fund-raiser." She turned and looked at the house. "Why don't you inspect the kitchen so we know whether it's adequate for the caterers? I'm going to have a look around."

Though the terraced garden was vast, it was laid out in orderly squares separated by long slate walkways. Each square held a statue, usually a lovely maiden but sometimes a beautiful boy, whose Greek or Roman name appeared on a brass plaque at the base. Most of the squares had a viewing bench, and some contained an urn-topped Greek column wrapped in grapevines. Except for ubiquitous ferns, the shrubs and flowers changed from square to square. The only trees she recognized were banana trees, magnolias, and palms; the only shrubs she recognized were spreading yews.

As she neared the back of the garden, she spotted a greenhouse and a pretty little stone shed attached to it. Behind them stood a carriage house and a short drive leading to a side street. The door to the shed was open. She couldn't see anybody, so she stepped inside, where it was cool and dark. The scent of lavender perfumed the air.

A shelf of books in a tall cabinet caught her eye. She could never resist a book. She was flipping through one, noting how old and dog-eared it was but admiring the garden layouts, when a noise behind her made her look around. A thin, little man stood in the doorway, staring at her through thick tinted glasses. Dressed in overalls, a rope tied around his waist, he had a tonsured head and the air of an old monk. He was carrying a giant pruning shears and a canvas bag slung across his chest.

"Oh, my goodness, you scared me. Are you the gardener?"

"You like my books?"

"These are yours? Oh, I'm sorry, I didn't -- ."

"You like my books?"

"I do. I love books." She returned the book to its shelf. "Next time I come, I'll bring you a new one."

"Really?" He carefully locked the shears and placed them on a potting table. He shrugged out of the canvas bag and hung it on a hook.

"I promise. So, are you the gardener?"

"I'm Verlin. Jerry Lee is my sister. She lets me take care of the garden. Who are you?"

"Lily."

He smiled for the first time. "*Lilium*."

He cut her off when she started to correct his pronunciation. "*Lilium regale*. You look like a princess. So that's your real name."

"Isn't that Latin?"

"All flowers have Latin names. I don't know why everybody doesn't know them. Poppy's name, you know, is *Papaver*. Some people don't have a Latin name, like my sister. People like that aren't special."

"But Poppy's special, isn't she?"

He nodded vigorously. "I love Poppy because she's nice to me, like you. Sometimes I call her *Papaver somniferum*."

"Meaning what?"

"Opium poppy. I call her that because once upon a time, long ago, she went to sleep and I didn't know if she'd wake up."

"What do you mean, she went to sleep?"

He rubbed his hands down his trouser legs. "The tea I gave her."

"You gave her opium?"

He shook his head vigorously and pointed above her head to the gauze bags she hadn't noticed before. "I make powders from the herb garden. My sister puts them in tea."

"What do the teas do?"

"All kinds of things. *Digitalis purpurea* for the heart. You probably call it foxglove." He pronounced the Latin names with care, as if speaking to a moron. "*Opuntia engelmannii* for a hangover -- prickly pear. *Taxus baccata*, English yew, to get rid of a baby."

Lily stared at him in shock. Molly had told her about the nap-time tea that preceded Poppy's miscarriage. "Is that what you gave to Poppy that time she got so sick she had to go to the hospital?"

Verlin realized he'd said too much. "No, no, no. I just gave her peppermint tea for her nap." He walked closer to the cabinet. "Did you see my collections?"

Lily willed herself to calm down. "What collections?"

"All kinds of things. My favorite is buttons." He held up a Mason jar filled a few inches from the top with a variety of colorful buttons.

"You buy them at antique shops or something?"

Verlin looked horrified. "Never. I find buttons. They don't mean anything unless I find them."

"By the way, I meant to ask if you would clean the fountain before Jerry Lee's party. There's a rabbit in there, I think."

His head drooped a little. "I must of forgot."

"Forgot what?"

He took her hand and walked her to a corner of the shed. "See that steel trap? I have lots of them. I catch the chipmunks and rabbits. Then, using that long rope, I lower the trap into the fountain and let it sit there awhile. Then I dump the animal out and set the trap again. I just forgot to take the rabbit out last night."

"You mean they're still alive when you drop them in and they drown?"

He looked at her like she'd lost half her brain. "Yes. When they stop bubbling, it's time to take them out. Otherwise I'd have to wring their necks. If you don't kill them, they eat half the garden. They're pests, you know."

Lily was horrified at the idea of drowning rabbits. "My first pet was a rabbit. My dad nicknamed me 'Bunny.'"

"You're not Bunny, you're *Lilium*."

"Verlin, did you ever hear the story of Peter Rabbit? His buttons got caught in Mr. McGregor's net. But eventually he got away."

"A rabbit with buttons?" He looked at his button jar. "Oh, I wish I'd found him. Then I'd know where his soul was."

"I don't think rabbits have souls."

"I don't either because they don't have any buttons."

She gave him a puzzled look.

"The souls are in the buttons." Verlin was making an effort to be patient. "But that Peter Rabbit -- if he had buttons, he must have had a soul."

Having no idea what he meant and feeling very creeped out, Lily walked to the door. "I have to go now, Verlin, but I'll be back in a few days. I'll bring you a new book."

"Only if it has Latin names. Okay?"

"Okay." She turned to scan the vast garden. "What's the shortest way back to the fountain?"

"I'll show you. Can I hold your hand again?"

Lily paused, willing her heart to soften while keeping her mind on full alert. "Yes, of course."

Before they reached the fountain, they spotted Molly and Poppy in one of the shaded squares, sitting on a bench and gazing at a lovely statue of a winged maiden. "That's my favorite," Verlin said, pointing at it. He looked at the two women with troubled eyes. "And that's my bench they're sitting on."

"Who is this?" Molly asked, standing up and smiling at Verlin.

"Verlin. Jerry Lee's brother. He takes care of the garden. Don't you, Verlin?"

"Verlin's a master gardener," Poppy said, walking over to give him a hug. He stood still without hugging her back. He never hugged anyone.

"My garden," he replied as if they were arguing about ownership.

Lily returned her attention to the statue. "What a pretty face she has."

"It's Nicky Sue," Verlin said, still holding Lily's hand.

"I guess there's a resemblance, but that's not what the plaque says," Molly said, bending down to push the Angel's trumpet aside. The plaque read:

Nike, Goddess of Victory, Daughter of Styx

"Did Nike really have wings?" Poppy asked.

Molly stood up. "What I know about Greek goddesses you could put in a tea cup and still have room for tea."

"See the biggest letters?" Verlin asked, unwilling to give up. Sometimes people just didn't seem to hear him. "N - S - D. Nicky Sue Darling." He pointed to the long plinth. "She's in there, you know."

"I think the letters are out of order," Molly said.

"But they're the *same* letters," Verlin said stubbornly. Visitors could be so blind.

Jerry Lee, who'd quietly come up behind her brother, unhooked his hand from Lily's, and spun him around like a top. "Please, Verlin, you're going to be the death of me with your nonsense."

"Jerry Lee," Poppy said. "Let Uncle Verlin talk. He hardly ever gets a chance." She moved to give him another hug but he backed away.

"He talks way too much," Jerry Lee said sharply. "He doesn't have any idea what he's saying. Ever since that poor girl disappeared, he thinks he's found her . . . in the clouds, in a statue, in the shape of leaf. But we all know she's gone for good. Don't we?" she asked, play-slapping Verlin's cheek. Adopting a voice that almost sounded kind, she said, "Now go back to the shed and take your medicines. Later I'll bring you some tea." She turned back to the women. "Honestly, I don't know what to do with him."

As they watched him walk away but while he was still within earshot, Jerry Lee smiled at her visitors. "He's simple, you know. I've put up with him all his life, since he was a baby. If it wasn't for me, he'd have been put in an institution long ago."

Suddenly, she put her hand over her chest. "Oh, I think I'm fainting." Without warning, she crumpled to the ground. Molly screamed. Lily instinctively sank to her knees to help the woman, whose eyelids were fluttering. Poppy, unmoved, standing only a few feet away, simply watched.

"My heart. I'm having palpitations," Jerry Lee whispered to Lily. "Fetch my nitroglycerin tablets."

Lily looked up at Poppy, expecting her to run to the house.

Instead, Poppy moved to stand over her mother, a faint smile on her face. "Oh, Jerry Lee, stop it. You don't have anything wrong with you."

"Ungrateful girl," she whispered through gritted teeth. "I'm dying. There's an iron weight on my chest. I can hardly breathe." She panted to emphasize her words. "Be a good girl, call an ambulance."

"Stand up. We'll get you into the house."

To Lily's surprise, Jerry Lee struggled to her feet and leaning on her daughter made her way to the stairs. Their progress was slow, as if they were wading through sand, interrupted every few steps when Jerry Lee signaled that she had to stand still a second to clear her vision. They were almost at the stairs when suddenly Jerry Lee stumbled and fell hard against Poppy, sending both to the ground. Lily, who was only a few steps behind, helped them up. They climbed awkwardly to the second floor veranda in silence. Once inside the house, Jerry Lee staggered to a sofa in the sitting room and lay down, a hand over her eyes. "Somebody get me a cold cloth."

Poppy wet a towel in the kitchen sink and returned with it, handing it to her mother instead of laying it across her eyes.

After a few minutes when nobody knew what to do, Jerry Lee waved her hand. "Time for y'all to go now."

Lily looked at Poppy. "Do you think we need to call the EMTs?"

Poppy shook her head. "I'll go find Phil. He'll know what to do." When she reached the door to the dining room, she turned to her mother. "Feel better. See you soon."

7

People Like Him
Friday, April 14, 2006

Before the women reached Beaudry Hall's front door, which Niall, the butler, was holding open, Phil spotted them. Simon, standing nearby, mouthed "Help" to Lily.

She returned an inquiring look.

"Phil Cocker here -- ."

"Coker." Phil cut him off, his tone huffy. He didn't like people messing with his famous name. Getting his name wrong suggested that people didn't know who he was or had forgotten him.

"Coker." Simon's self-correction was elaborate. "Coker here has been showing me his *fabulous* art collection. Apparently everybody but me knows about it."

"Come over here," Phil said, beckoning to the women. "I'll show you my newest acquisition -- *Run from Fear, Fun from Rear.* Your friend here doesn't like it. I thought people like him would think it was funny."

"People like who?" Lily asked, catching Simon in the act of stuffing his finger down his throat.

"You know, people like Simon."

"Art lovers, you mean. You do love art . . . right, Simon?"

"So right. I love *art.*"

"I was just about to show Simon my most expensive piece."

Phil waited until the women had dutifully gathered round him, Poppy hanging back a little. They looked at a tan canvas filled with black scribbles and a few geometric shapes.

"The painting is called *Bolsena.*"

The name meant nothing to anyone.

"What's Bolsena about it?" Molly asked, thinking the unfamiliar word might be an adjective.

Before Phil could answer, Poppy spoke up. "To me, it looks like my math worksheets in high school."

Phil glared at Poppy. "Bolsena's a town in Italy, the town where the artist painted this."

"And the artist is . . . ?" Molly asked, still trying to be polite.

"You don't recognize this?" he asked. He looked at the women as if they were members of a long-lost New Guinea tribe. "Cy Twombly."

"Oh, cwap," Simon blurted out. "I should have known."

"Please don't tell me, girls, you've never heard of Twombly."

"Twombly's twash?" Simon asked, unable to stop himself. In a dramatic gesture, he slapped his hand over his mouth. "Did I say that out loud? Oh, bad boy. Vewy bad boy."

"You think it's cw -- crap?" Phil asked, sneering. He trained his closely set eyes on Simon. "I thought you at least would have some taste. I depend on guys like you for my wardrobe."

"I don't do Ché t-shirts."

"Well, you should."

"I told your mother I don't have any taste. I lost it when I first saw the house." This time, to stop a gob of howling laughter from spewing out of his mouth, he ate his handkerchief.

"We have to get going, Phil," Poppy broke in. "You might want to look in on Jerry Lee. She's having an attack in the sitting room."

"Serious?"

"Yes, very. She wants her nitroglycerin tablets and an ambulance."

"What happened this time?"

"Something somebody said in the garden, I guess. Having to

send poor Uncle Verlin to the woodsh . . . er, potting shed. He may need more help than she does."

"I'm not done with the tour."

"Sorry, but we don't have all night." She checked her watch. "We're going to be late for dinner if we don't hustle out of here. See you later."

All the way to the Club, Simon regaled his delightful women friends with hilarious tales of the tour he'd just had, imitating Phil's manner of speech in his own gay timbre.

When there was a brief lull in the laughter, he directed an apology to Poppy. "Sorry to say this, my dear, but Phil's a complete asshole."

"Don't I know it? Thank God my mother had the good sense not to marry that washed-up, third-rate, rat-faced, drug-addicted piece of shit . . . if you'll excuse my French."

"Oh, girl, don't hold back. Tell us how you really feel."

"How I feel is strictly off the record."

All through dinner, the women kept encouraging Simon to retell his stories about the art tour. Hearing Simon, in his fruitiest voice, imitate Phil's pretentious utterances, his indignation and wounded masculine pride, sent them into paroxysms of laughter. It was almost too cruel -- but not quite -- and it was definitely too funny. When Simon ran out of the real thing, he made up even funnier stuff. By the time dessert was over, their cheeks hurt from constant laughing and they were all the best of friends.

8

I'll Have Somebody's Head
Friday, April 14, 2006

While his wife was touring Jerry Lee's *faux* plantation, Tom Lawton was, for the first time, meeting Poppy's husband, Ferrin McBride, the conservative Congressman running for reelection on family values, fiscal responsibility, and a strong national defense, all the while distancing himself from President Bush. They were alone in Ferrin's office in the Port Royal palazzo. A bodyguard with an earpiece sat in the hall outside the paneled door; another stood on the terrace. There were daily death threats, often conveyed in left-wing blogs, so the protection was as constant and thorough, and almost as expensive, as if he were running for president.

McBride's office was actually a suite of rooms on the north end of the house, paneled in dark wood. The furnishings were solid, like the man himself. The row of French doors along the terrace faced Treasure Cove. After leading Tom to leather club chairs with a view of the water, Ferrin offered his visitor a mint julep in a silver cup, then a cigar from a humidor. They chatted awhile. Tom realized he was subtly being probed for experience and character. Ferrin McBride, a man who measured his words, was politeness itself.

"Let's get right to the point, Tom. My chief of staff has already vetted you, so I'm not going to waste your time or mine on the details of your resumé. I want to find the son-of-a-bitch who talked to that Canadian reporter about my wife."

"You have a theory about it?"

"So far as I can find out, nobody knew about the so-called abortion. I sure as hell didn't."

"No?"

"No. As you can imagine, it's caused some trouble between Poppy and me, her keeping a secret like that. I told her I can deal with anything so long as I know about it, but what am I supposed to do with secrets?"

"Is that a husband speaking? Or a politician?"

Ferrin smiled. He had the well-groomed look of a man prepared twenty-four/seven to face the press. His wavy reddish gold hair was cut short, his ruddy face freshly shaven. His light blue eyes were penetrating, his posture military. The only jewelry he wore was a simple gold band on his ring finger and a gold watch on his right wrist, meaning he must be left-handed. Ferrin McBride carried himself with the steely, easy confidence of a fighter pilot landing his jet on a carrier in high seas at night -- which he did during the first Gulf War, having been recalled to duty from the reserves.

"Both," he said. "I'm a husband first, a politician second, but in both capacities I have to see the enemy coming."

"You have a theory about who we're looking for?"

"No more than a dozen." He laughed grimly. "But no theories that make a lot of sense." He carefully rolled the ash off his cigar. "Poppy says she never told anyone about being pregnant or having a miscarriage. Her mother and uncle knew because they found her convulsing. The emergency room doctor might know something, but by the time she was hospitalized, there was no baby and she never admitted what happened. The story her mother gave out to her friends was acute appendicitis."

"If your wife didn't tell anyone, then it has to be her mother or uncle who talked to the Canadian reporter."

"Or the guy who got her pregnant."

"Know anything about him?"

"Dewey Betz. Her high school sweetheart. A farmer's boy

about to enlist in the Marines. A good mechanic. Handsome and smart but poor as dirt, apparently. Now you know everything I know about him."

"What about the hospital records?"

"We haven't seen the records, but as I said, I don't know that they would actually reflect what happened before my wife reached the hospital. I'll have Poppy give you a letter authorizing you to see them, if they still exist."

"I'm told your wife was runner-up for the Miss South Carolina title."

"That's how I met her, by the way. I saw her on television and arranged an introduction. We had some friends in common. I don't know about you, but I believe in love at first sight."

"Strangely, that was my experience with my wife. She married somebody else first, but now she's mine." In other circumstances, Tom wouldn't mind exchanging their stories, but this wasn't the time or place. "You sure she never told any of the other girls or a roommate -- anyone -- at the pageant? I don't know anything about beauty pageants, but I know something about women and they confide a lot in each other."

"She swears she didn't." Ferrin shifted in his chair. "You heard about Jerry Lee making a scene at Mrs. Standardt's book-signing?"

"I was there. My wife arranged the event. She and Molly are good friends."

"Poppy met with Mrs. Standardt a few days later. Even she didn't know a thing about Poppy's . . . Poppy's mishap. As a politician and a former prosecutor, I'm a pretty good judge of character, and as a husband, despite this one secret, I know my wife well enough to know she's not lying. She trusts Mrs. Standardt, so I think we can assume she's in the clear."

"Anybody on your staff you think might be a problem?"

"Everybody's been with me for years, except for my driver, but another background check on him and a couple of other people wouldn't hurt."

"You have any enemies?"

Ferrin laughed. "About half the people in the State. I'm a

44

Republican. I was a prosecutor, then the Attorney-General. Since then I've been in Congress for two years. So what do you think?"

"Anybody in particular?"

"Other than Myron Mullett and his aide Harley Wangle? Yes. I'll get a list in your hands by Monday. But for now I want you to concentrate on the libelous abortion story."

"Do you think you might sue whoever it turns out to be?"

"Never say never, but for now I'm saying no. A lawsuit would only add fuel to the fire and nothing would be resolved anyway by the time of the election." Ferrin let his gaze wander to the Cove. "As I said, concentrate on the abortion story. But don't lose sight of the big picture. There's more outside money in the race this year than ever before -- I mean by a factor of ten at least."

"Outside money? Really?"

"Left-wing money from all over the country has been flooding into Mullett's campaign in quantities I've never seen before, mostly from bundlers, many of them on the West Coast. This campaign might seem local and unimportant, but the liberals see every campaign these days as national, a duel to the death."

"Strong words."

"Strong forces, dark times." Ferrin chuckled grimly. "Conservatives know local campaigns mean more than they used to, but they haven't quite woken up yet, and they're confused about the change they want, so the money's scarce by comparison. What I want you to keep your eye on is the big picture. Question Jerry Lee -- go ahead." He waved his hand dismissively. "Check out the Charleston doctor -- go ahead with that too. Find Dewey Betz. If you can get that magazine reporter to say anything, good for you."

"Will do."

Ferrin leaned forward, wagging his finger. "But keep your eye on the background, the way the Secret Service does. Somebody's lurking out there who wants to bring me down. Somebody a lot bigger and more dangerous than the obvious candidates for leakage." He stood up to signal the end of the interview. "I think we're looking for somebody who wants to bring down, not just me, but every conservative running for office."

Tom stood up too.

"By the way, Tom, are you a registered voter?"

"Never missed an election. Maybe a couple of primaries, but not an election."

"And your political views?"

"Conservative. Strange to say, I never thought about politics much -- or religion or history or anything other than making a living -- until I met Lily. I'll make a bet that she's more conservative than you are. I've been influenced, you might say. As a former cop, I was already on what I'd call the right side, so all she's had to is nudge. She's very good at nudging."

Ferrin smiled. "My guess is that all good wives are skilled at nudging. Anyway, I like what you said about being on the right side. It's true on so many levels. I ask about your politics because I don't want any traitors in the camp. The stakes are too high." He stepped out onto the terrace, Tom following, then said something to the bodyguard Tom couldn't catch. Before Tom turned to walk to his car, Ferrin held out his hand. "Good to meet you, Tom Lawton. You have my full support. Tell my staff what you need and you'll get it or I'll have somebody's head."

Tom's healthy skepticism of all politicians was still intact, but he liked this man personally. In some other context, they might have been friends. "I'll do my best."

9

Always Stoned
Saturday, April 15, 2009

Late Saturday afternoon, Molly and Lily's sister, Sara, arrived at Lily's new house in Naples without their husbands, both of whom were still on the golf course with Tom on Marco Island. Molly and Sara came early to inspect the "story boards," as Simon Diodorus called them, for the decorating he was doing for Lily. Half the enormous house Lily and Tom had bought six months ago was still closed off with big plastic sheets. The gutting and rebuilding from the inside out felt like it would never end. The habitable half of the house was sparsely furnished with the bachelor furniture Tom had moved from his apartment on Fifth Avenue.

Simon greeted the women at the door with "Hi, girls" and dramatic gestures of welcome as if he lived there. The four of them then spent the next hour sipping wine and talking about the fabrics, the furniture, the rugs, the lamps, the art work that Simon was proposing. He was in his element, the center of attention, playing house. The women had lots of comments on his proposals.

They couldn't help it -- the conversation eventually returned to Jerry Lee, her boyfriend, her estate, and her fake heart palpitations. For the first time, Lily recounted her tour of the gardens with Verlin, the idiot savant who knew more Latin than English. "In case you didn't know, my real name is *Lilium regale*. Poppy's is *Papaver somniferum*, I think."

"So what's mine?" Simon asked.

Lily laughed. "You don't have a flower name, my dear, so you're not special."

He slapped both his cheeks. "What was my mother thinking, not naming me Delphinium? I could be Delphi Diodorus."

"I'd stick with Simon if I were you."

"No, I'm serious. I'll come out with a bedding line called 'Linens by Delphi.' If Nate Berkus can do it, so can I. All I have to do is get on Oprah."

"Add something about how you're New Age," Sara interjected, "and you'll probably succeed in that endeavor."

"Anyway, Lily, your tour was better than mine," Simon continued. "You at least met the idiot savant. I met the idiot asshole." Simon got up and looked around. "Where's my briefcase, by the way?"

"Over there," Lily said, pointing to the half-finished granite island in the kitchen.

"I've got something for you girls. It's absolutely delicious." He sat back down, tucking one leg under his butt. He held up an issue of *Rolling Stone* so the women could see the cover, then turned to an inside page. "Let me read you something I'll bet you haven't seen. The article is called 'Shock and Awe.' That tells you something right there, I think. Anyway, here goes."

Phil Coker, Hollywood's bad boy who hasn't made a picture in over ten years, is back on the A-list. Virgil Goldstein, the award-winning director of docudramas about Viet Nam, Nixon's disgrace, the Kennedy assassination, and Enron corruption, just signed Coker to reprise his 1963 hit, *The Ho Chi Minh Trail*. The advance on the contract is rumored to be in the millions. Coker's screenplay -- working title, *Rear Action* -- is set in Kuwait during the first Gulf War and will star Tom Cruise. No shooting schedule has been announced. A spokesman for Cruise, who is currently vacationing on the Italian Riviera, said the actor hadn't been approached by either Coker or

Simon looked up at his audience. "Do you believe that? A washed-up, empty-pocket blowhard wearing Ché t-shirts, smoking dope, and living off an old, rich woman in Florida gets millions in advance to make another movie only fourteen people will ever see. How do some people do it?"

"I never saw that 1960s movie you mentioned," Lily said. "When this house is done -- if it ever is," she said, throwing Simon a warning look, "we'll have to watch it."

Simon ignored the look. "*Rolling Stone,* or as I call it, *Always Stoned,* just can't get out of the Sixties, so of course it loves the drug-addled icons of the past."

"What I don't get," Molly said, "is why the first Gulf War would excite anybody. We've moved on: Bosnia, Afghanistan, Iraq, the stand-off with Iran. So what's being reprised exactly?"

After dropping his head on his shoulder and pretending to snore, Simon theatrically snapped to attention. "Frankly, I don't believe a word of that squib. I'll bet it's Coker's PR machine at work."

"He has a PR machine?" Sara asked. "Paid for with whose money?"

"Well, not his," Simon said. "He hasn't made a picture in at least ten years, and except for that early movie about Viet Nam, he never had another hit. Remember that guerilla movie back in the Seventies? Set in Africa, something about silver mines, what was its name? *Silver Back,* I think. Anyway, Phil-the-Pill got a serious back injury trying to do his own stunts, got addicted to painkillers, and then was in and out of rehab for years."

"How in the world do you know all that?" Sara asked.

"You don't get the Hollywood trades, I suppose," he responded, pretending to mock Sara. "Or *Vogue* or *W.* You probably subscribe to *Coastal Living* and read books like *War and Peace,* stuff called literature." He laughed, pleased with himself. Every group of girlfriends needed a comedian like him.

Sara laughed. "Well, not *War and Peace,* but otherwise you have me dead to rights."

"After seeing that Joker yesterday, I'd advise him to get back on drugs. Seriously, I mean it. He used to be interesting. Now he's just a pompous bore."

Molly grabbed *Rolling Stone* off of Simon's lap. "Is there more about Goldstein in here?"

"Goldstein is Verbena's dad, right?" Sara asked.

Lily raised her eyebrows, signaling there was to be no mention of the actress' parentage in Simon's presence.

"Verbena," Simon said, looking at each woman quizzically. "Verbena Cross? You know her? You know her well enough to call her by her first name?"

"Tom met her over a year ago," Lily said.

"How? Doing what?"

Lily looked at him, pulling a zipper over her mouth. "My husband's a private detective, remember? The key word being private."

"You know Hollywood royalty, girlfriend?" He bobbed a little in his chair.

The three women couldn't help a burst of laughter. Simon looked at them, visibly irritated at the notion that some inside information was being withheld from him. "Why are you all laughing?"

"Hollywood royalty," Lily said, stalling for time and hoping to obscure the reference. From Tom's work for Verbena, she and her friends knew that the actress was not Hollywood royalty at all. She was illegitimate, born to an uneducated Tennessee teen-ager and secretly adopted by Virgil Goldstein and his actress-wife Ellen Matter, who since then had carried out an elaborate charade that Verbena was their blood daughter. "Simon, think about it. Who in Hollywood is really royalty -- other than Zsa Zsa Gabor's husband?"

This time, even Simon laughed. "Oh, I get you."

The women repressed their snickers. He *so* didn't get it.

"Anyway," Lily continued, "we don't know a lot about her father other than he's very rich, very left wing, and recently hosted a fund-raiser with Barbra Streisand for an obscure politician from Chicago, named Oback Barama or something like that. A foreign name I can never remember. You know who I mean, the street organizer who came out of nowhere and gave that big speech at the Democratic presidential convention about there being no red or blue states, only one color-blind America."

"So tell me more about Verbena," Simon insisted. Politicians were *so* boring.

"It's her father we're interested in, his association with Coker."

Something clicked over in Molly's mind. "You don't suppose Jerry Lee ever told Coker about Poppy's so-called abortion, do you?"

Sara looked at her friend. "The same thought just crossed my mind."

"Meaning Coker gave the information to Goldstein?" Lily asked.

"Gave?" Molly asked skeptically. "I don't think so. Meaning Coker traded Poppy's embarrassing secret for a movie deal with Goldstein."

The four of them just looked at each other.

"That's so paranoid," Simon finally said. "For this gossip, I think we need another bottle of wine. Mind if I open a fresh one and pour?"

"Go right ahead," Lily said, waving in the direction of the kitchen, where a little white mini-fridge did duty until the new stainless steel appliances arrived.

Just as Simon was refreshing his friends' glasses, the men walked through the front door. "Ah, Rhett Butler," Simon called out in Tom's direction. The three men were carrying pans of food from Campiello.

"And I'm Scarlet O'Hara," Lily said, getting up to greet her husband.

"And I'm Prissy," Simon said in his prissiest, blackest voice.

"Of course you are. Who else would you be?" Tom laughed.

The party of seven retired to the unfinished patio where an assortment of plastic chairs, soon to be discarded, had been assembled around a rusted wrought iron table.   Simon couldn't wait to return the conversation to Hollywood. "Anyway, as I was saying, Tom, when I was so rudely interrupted, maybe Coker sold Poppy's secret to Goldstein. Maybe that's what the millions are really for."

Tom glanced at Simon, amused. "I'm afraid I lost the script. What page are we on?"

Simon and the women recounted the last hour of their conversation and gave him the *Rolling Stone* article. Tom said only that they might be onto something.

Before the party broke up very late Saturday night, Tom and Molly agreed to coordinate their trips to Charleston, Tom to follow up on his new assignment to find the leaker, Molly to get background information for her piece on Poppy. After that, since they were all invited to the premiere of Verbena Cross' new movie, *Bonaventure Blues* -- all except Simon, who begged to be included and had to be satisfied with a promise that Tom would do his best -- they'd meet in Savannah for a long weekend.

At the door, Simon hugged Lily. "When you have a kid, you better make me the godmother."

Lily laughed. "Protestants don't do godmothers, my dear, and you'll notice there's no nursery in this house. Maybe later. So go get your beauty rest." She tapped his chest. "Seriously, Simon. I mean it. Rest up. You've got to get on the stick because if I don't get a functioning kitchen soon, not to mention a laundry room, I'm going to have to take your wine away."

"Oh, cwap, not my wine." He blew her kisses all the way to his car, a little BMW coupe Nee-Nee let him use. Lily winced every time she saw it. It was so like the one her first husband bought her, the one that was meant to kill her.

10

Scarlett and Rhett

Saturday, April 15, 2006

Tom loved his wife's parties but loved even more the time he had alone with her, especially after everybody went home and they could recount the best lines of the evening, punctuated with lots of laughter.

"Oh, lawsy, Scarlett, the wine isn't chilled," he said, returning to the patio, stacked at one end with wooden forms and bricks yet to be laid. Having draped a paper napkin over his arm, he offered her a fresh bottle of warm wine in the manner of a Las Vegas sommelier condescending to a table of Kansas hicks. "I think this one will suit you, though. Very elegant and supple, with a crisp note of belladonna and a finish of warm, unwashed socks. So how about it?"

"Have at it, Rhett." Lily waved her empty glass. "And don't just pour an inch in here because I'm not sniffing and swirling it around. I want this glass topped off now. By the time I go to bed, I wanna know I had some wine."

"Well, it won't be the first time I've carried you to bed, Scarlett, so, frankly, I don't give a damn. Knock yourself out." He turned off the outside lights so they were completely in the dark.

Having been influenced by Bob Bancroft, his brother-in-law, a cigar fancier, Tom had finally taken up the habit except that, unlike Bob, he limited himself to one treat a night just before bed. Tonight he lit a *Cohiba Red Dot Robusto*, sat back, and contemplated his world, so much richer than a year ago. It was a night with almost a full moon. A bit of wind had come up. Staring out to the dark, choppy Gulf, focusing on a streak of moonlit water, he asked, "You know how much I love being married to Lily Claire Anderson?"

"No. Tell me again, Thomas Underwood Lawton. How much?"

He stretched out his arms like a child. "This much."

"Me too."

"I have never given a party amidst so much construction debris as tonight."

"You gave parties before we were married? I never got invited to one."

"*Touché.* I never gave a party until I married you. But my point is, will this house ever be done? Or is that too much to ask?"

"It'll never be done if Simon has anything to do with it. He'd live here if he could."

"Have you checked any of those boxes stacked in the garage? I swear I saw one of them moving on its own."

Lily laughed. "When he left tonight, I watched him all the way to his car for fear of that very possibility."

"I can't tell you how much I miss simple things like a refrigerator and washing machine. That mini-fridge barely holds a bottle of wine."

"Simon can't make up his mind about appliance brands, but he assures me they have to be foreign and expensive with unpronounceable names or they won't be good enough, so prepare yourself. I think it's going to be awhile."

"I can just see him handing us manuals translated from the French by a street person who's lived in the sewer for the last twenty years." He adopted a nasal accent. "To get l'ectro for l'appliance, shove strongly la trois-pronged masculine thing (illustratione X-334y) into the girly wall holes and -- ."

Lily laughed so hard she spit wine onto her clean white blouse. "Stop, stop. I don't have another clean shirt. And I don't have a washing machine."

"I like a girl who looks a little dirty."

"I didn't know that about you. Every day, another surprise."

"So what do you think of Poppy McBride?"

"She's lovely. From what Molly told me, she was pregnant but never had an abortion. She miscarried before she ever got to the clinic. Strangely, she was paralyzed for awhile. That doesn't sound normal to me."

"So who knew about the miscarriage? Did she say?"

"The usual suspects: her mother and her uncle. Verlin probably doesn't have anybody to tell the secret to, but I'm thinking, wouldn't Jerry Lee be likely to say something to Phil? That movie deal he's just gotten from Goldstein . . . maybe he got it in return for some information harmful to Ferrin. I'm just thinking."

"Thinking like a detective, my dear."

"It's contagious."

"I think I'll give Verbena a call about her father."

"Tom, do you know how much I hate that name Verbena Cross? If I hadn't seen that *National Enquirer* article claiming you were going to marry her, I'd never have married . . . him." Neither Lily nor Tom ever mentioned Bruce's name. That ghost had to be put to rest.

"If I hadn't slipped up with Amy, you wouldn't have believed anything anybody said about me. Or if I'd told you what I knew about . . . about him, you might have backed off in time. So . . . ," he sighed, "we both made big mistakes."

"But in the end we got it right."

"We did that." Tom took his wife's hand. "Do you remember that lunch at Campiello when I gave you the book you'd been reading in the airport when we met?"

"*Pride and Prejudice?* The special old edition. How could I ever forget it? It's my favorite book, bar none, and if I ever get a bedside table, it'll always rest there, near at hand when I need a refresher."

"More precious than the first edition he gave you?"

"Yes." She was going to sell the first edition of *Pride and Prejudice* that Bruce had given her, but when Tom found out about it, he urged her to keep the book because it was so rare.

"That afternoon when I gave you the book, Lily? I wished so much we were going home together afterwards. Watching you walk away after lunch, my heart actually hurt."

"But it's all healed now, right?"

"It is." He watched a cloud slide over the moon. "So back to the McBrides. Ferrin's quite a guy, very military, very polite. He has wavy hair like mine, only red -- probably the bane of his existence. A few times, I think he almost called me 'sir.' I like him. But I can't get out of my mind a question about where he made all his money. He was in the Air Force and then in government, so how does all that add up?"

"It'll take Bernie about five seconds of Googling to find that out. My question is a little different. Is he as conservative as he makes himself out to be?"

"You'd have to be the judge of that. We really didn't talk about politics, other than a few questions about whether I voted and which way. Apparently, I passed the test."

"He talks a good game, and of course I'm not voting for a liberal like Mullett, you understand, but I have my reservations about McBride. Every politician who gets elected to high office falls in love with high office and wants more and more of our money to spend as he pleases. All for our good, of course."

"While I was on the golf course, I got a text from someone on Ferrin's staff that I'm interviewing Jerry Lee on Monday. It's all set up."

"The person you've really got to meet is Uncle Verlin, the idiot savant. But I'd brush up on my Latin if I were you. And you might not want to mention rabbits. By the way, he said something very strange to me."

"Only one strange thing?" She'd already told him about the rabbit souls and buttons.

"I asked him what the dried herbs were for. One of them was for getting rid of babies, which I took to mean in the womb rather than after birth."

"Remember what that one was?"

"Not the whole Latin name, just the word *taxus*. But I remember that the common name is English yew. He said his sister puts the herbs in teas. He also said how Poppy once fell asleep and he wasn't sure she'd wake up. That's why he calls her opium poppy, in Latin, of course. I asked if that's what happened to Poppy, meaning when she miscarried. He said no, he'd just given her peppermint tea. I didn't mention abortion or anything like that, yet he seemed to know what I was talking about."

"So what's your conclusion about Uncle Verlin and English yew?"

"Not a firm conclusion, but do you think Jerry Lee might have used an herb-spiked tea to cause a miscarriage in a daughter she didn't want to remain pregnant while preparing for the Miss South Carolina title?"

"I thank my lucky stars that's not my part of the assignment. I just have to identify a leaker, or at least eliminate several candidates for the honor."

"Tomorrow, after Easter services, I want to spend some time with the Silvermans to find a book about herbs . . . identified by their Latin names, of course. I promised Uncle Verlin a new book, and I need an education myself."

She held out her glass for more wine. "By the way, how's your golf game coming?"

Tom cleared his throat. He'd agreed to learn the game of golf to bond with Bob and Carl. Bob claimed he'd find it relaxing and help him network with clients. So far, it wasn't relaxing, and if he didn't get better soon, clients would laugh at him. "For hating it as much as I hated baths when I was eleven? Fantastic."

Lily giggled. "Don't hold back. Give me the details."

"Well, today I stayed under 200. Bob was impressed. You might say he was gleeful. The golf cart I was driving didn't turn over. As you know, I have a carefully crafted slice, but this time I didn't smash Carl in the head, wing a pelican in mid-air, or break a window, so I did nothing to jack up my insurance rates or get a call from the wildlife service. No need whatsoever for you to call our insurance agent. Best of all, I started out with a dozen Bridgestone e6+ balls and, though I lost every last one of them, I returned with the two that have been mine from birth."

Lily laughed.

"Probably a small thing to you, Scarlett, but I'm pretty proud."

"Congratulations, Rhett. You're going to beat the stuffing out of me the next time we get to the links."

"I doubt that very much, my dear, but thanks for the encouragement. Someday, you're going to be able to take me to almost any golf club in the country and not want to hide in the club freezer. I think."

11

Do Yourself a Favor
Monday, April 17, 2006

On Monday morning, Tom found himself in Jerry Lee's sitting room overlooking her gardens. His hostess was sitting on the very same green couch Lily had described as the scene of the woman's recovery from a dramatic fainting spell. He asked her how she was doing.

"Better. I've had these spells forever, Tim."

"Tom."

"Oh, forgive me. Tom. My heart just isn't what it used to be."

"Ferrin probably told you why I'm here."

A look of distaste passed over her face for a fleeting second. "What do you think of my famous son-in-law?"

Tom was prepared to ask the questions but not answer them. "He seems to be a very . . . a very solid man."

"Did you know he's twelve years older than my Poppy?"

"That makes your daughter about what . . .?"

"Thirty-six. She was only twenty when he asked for her hand, like a gentleman, but a man in the Air Force . . . well, as you can imagine, I was reluctant to give my permission. I wasn't planning on her marrying a military man. But at least he was ambitious."

"He seems to have done pretty well for himself."

"He wasn't a pig farmer, like that boy who got her pregnant, or an enlisted man, which that boy would have become if he'd gotten

59

in the Marines. And Ferrin's father was a respectable businessman, or claimed to be. They were nothing to be proud of, though."

"Why not?"

"They owned trailer parks. Still do."

"I never guessed that."

"The McBrides are from Indiana. You ever been there?"

You ask like Indiana is a foreign country. "I graduated from Indiana University in Bloomington. My parents were professors there."

"They're still there?" she asked, as if he'd left them in a Russian prison.

"No. They escaped years ago."

"Well, that's good. Anyway, the McBrides are in the manufactured-home industry. Old Jake McBride -- I only met him once, at the wedding -- didn't call them trailers or mobile homes. Oh, no. They were manufactured homes." Her tone was contemptuous. "Not content with fleecing people one way, old Jake had them coming and going. He made his real money when he started buying up farmland and leasing the ground for the homes he manufactured. He made the farmland into landscaped, gated communities with club houses, swimming pools, tennis courts, and golf courses. The leases and fees made him rich. Now the family company, McBride Communities, owns some gated communities in central Florida. Can you imagine?"

What a strange woman you are, lady, saying the manufacture of something valuable is equivalent to fleecing. But Tom stayed on point. "I wondered how McBride became so wealthy."

"The developments always have pretentious Irish names -- if that isn't an oxymoron. 'Limerick Lakes,' 'Dublin Downs,' 'Galway Gardens.' There's a scam for you -- making the lower middle class feel wealthy, helping them get above their station. Give me a break."

"Is Ferrin's father still alive?"

"Killed years ago in a plane accident, left Ferrin and Seamus, his older brother, with fortunes. Seamus runs the business now. Jake, the old fool, flew his own Piper Cub, got caught in a cross-wind, flipped it over on his own air-strip, burned to a crisp. That's what happens to hicks who make money -- they become over-confident, think they can do anything. Ferrin's the same way. Before he started running for Congress, he used to fly himself everywhere too. I told Poppy not to get in a plane with him, but she never listened. They still have a Gulfstream, but it's not big enough for his bodyguards, so it's sitting idle somewhere."

"If I were you, I wouldn't worry much about your daughter's safety with Ferrin. Isn't he an experienced Air Force pilot?"

She ignored his question. "Are you married, Tim?"

"Tom. Yes, to Lily Anderson, last year." He never used her former married name.

"You aren't *that* Lily's husband, are you? The pretty blonde who was here with Poppy?"

"I am that very Lily's husband." He was proud of being her husband. He'd worked hard for the honor.

"Sure you don't want any tea?"

"No. I'm sure, thank you. I know it's painful, but I don't want to waste your day and I'd like to hear about your daughter's abortion."

"I'm so tired of that word, Tim. It wasn't an abortion," she said testily. "She miscarried. She was taking a nap and started having convulsions."

"While she was napping?"

"Yes."

"You just happened to look in on her or something?"

Jerry Lee's eyes narrowed. "She was having a migraine, so I sat in a chair in the corner. I was a very attentive mother. I hardly ever left her alone."

"Forgive me for being so blunt, but you must have left her alone, at least long enough for her to get pregnant."

"She was sneaking out with that farmer's boy, Dewey Betz. He was about to enlist in the Marines. He wasn't a good enough student to go to college."

"Whatever happened to Dewey Betz?"

"I don't know. He just left town."

"Because Poppy was pregnant?"

"I'm not sure he even knew she was pregnant, but probably."

"Did his parents know?"

"I have no idea. We didn't run in the same social circles, so I never met them."

"Who knew about her pregnancy?"

"No one except me."

"What about your brother?"

"He might have heard something but neither Poppy nor I ever said anything directly to him. We told him it was appendicitis. He's simple you know."

"What else was going on about the time she miscarried?"

"She was getting ready for the Miss South Carolina pageant."

"That was 1989?"

Jerry Lee nodded. "She couldn't be pregnant, or she'd have had to drop out."

"So the miscarriage was convenient?"

"In every possible way," she said without a trace of guilt or shame.

"Do you remember the name of the emergency room doctor?"

"Collin Lindstrom."

"What a memory you have."

"I remember everything about that time. Later that ridiculous Molly Standardt won instead of my gorgeous daughter. Have you ever seen that woman?"

"Yes. She's a friend of my wife's."

"Well, sorry to say anything bad about a friend, but she doesn't hold a candle to Poppy, does she? Admit it. She could stand to lose a little weight." Jerry Lee put her teacup down with a sharp clink. "More than a little, in my informed opinion."

Tom was saved from having to answer when Phil Coker shambled in, rubbing his eyes. He was wearing a gray and red Mao t-shirt and a pair of very wrinkled blue plaid boxer shorts. "Got any coffee?"

"Find Maria," Jerry Lee said. "She'll make you some."

Phil looked at Tom as if seeing him for the first time. "Oh.

Didn't know you had company."

"Phil, this is Tim."

"Tom." Tom stood up and held out his hand. "Tom Lawton. And you're Phil Coker, I presume."

Phil backed up a step, gesturing as if batting away a bumblebee. "Hold your fire, man. Too early for niceties."

"Is that a political statement, that t-shirt?"

Phil looked down at his chest. "Aren't we all revolutionaries these days?" He laughed as he headed toward the kitchen. "At least the man could read, not like our current president. What's Molly Ivins call him . . . the Shrub?"

He returned a few seconds later and took a chair kitty-cornered from Tom's. "Is my Southern belle here telling you the story of her daughter's miscarriage? The wrongs done to Poppy by every man who ever crossed her path? The loss of the pageant crown? The sneaky reporter up north?"

Jerry Lee looked embarrassed. "Phil! That isn't nice."

"I take it Jerry Lee told you about Poppy, Phil. You ever tell anybody else?"

"What kind of question is that?"

"Phil wouldn't tell my secrets." Jerry Lee's voice was edgy. "Would you, Phil?"

Phil just smiled.

"Speaking of secrets, it's no secret," Tom said, "that Ferrin wants to find out who made up the story about the abortion."

"Ferrin," he spit. "That hypocrite? He doesn't even work for a living."

And you do? "Politics is work, don't you think?"

"No, man, it's horse shit. Every mealy-mouth politician is just like every other one. I'm waiting for an iron man to mount the world stage, impose some order on the riffraff." He lit a cigarette. "Where's Mussolini when we need him, huh? He knew how to run things."

"Phil!" Jerry Lee exclaimed.

Tom watched a lot of World War II documentaries with Lily. "I think Mussolini ended up hanging upside down from a meat hook under a bridge with his mistress, didn't he?"

"He wore great uniforms, though. Give him that."

Tom wanted to bring Jerry Lee back into the conversation. "How did you two ever meet, you're from such different backgrounds?"

Though Tom had directed his question to his hostess, Phil answered. "In an art gallery in New York. You collect art?"

"Can't say that I do."

"Well, you've probably heard I have a famous collection, mostly funk and pop, outsider art, graffiti, counter-culture stuff. I was friends with Andy Warhol, you know."

"I didn't know that."

"I was going to buy a Jim Dine picture when this lady here" -- he winked at Jerry Lee -- "stole it from right under my nose. So I took her to the Waldorf, see if I could buy it off her."

"And did you?"

"No, man. She ended up buying me. I was irresistible." He sat back and patted his chest. "When you got it, you got it."

"You were my style, Phil, but the picture wasn't. You said I should buy it, told me a funny story about the artist, so I gave in. My real passion is glass." She pointed to a complicated spiky glass sculpture, predominately blue and green, hanging over the back of the sofa dividing the sitting room from the kitchen. "That's Dale Chihuly. I'm sure you recognize his work."

"Not original to the period of the house, I presume."

Jerry Lee reacted without a shred of humor. "I'm not that provincial." She walked over to a built-in pickled maple cabinet filled with glass vases and sculptures, most of which looked liked they'd morphed into monstrous fungi only Hieronymus Bosch could love. "I like modern things, museum pieces. They appreciate faster than oil stocks. That's what Phil says anyway."

Tom's eyes wandered to the floor. More pickled wood. From the associations with this house alone, he was quickly developing a number of intense new aversions -- to pickled wood, tea, glass sculptures, and Mao t-shirts.

Suddenly Jerry Lee clutched her chest.

"Now, Jerry Lee, don't go having another of your spells." Phil looked around as a dark-haired woman wearing a white uniform entered. "Maria, it's about time, babe. I'll take that coffee by injection, if you please. And bring me the pot while you're at it."

Jerry Lee made her way back to the green sofa. "You think you're the only one with heart problems?"

"I don't have heart problems," Phil said testily.

"One more angina attack and I'm going to start calling you Dick Cheney."

Phil looked at Tom. "Don't believe a word this woman says. I don't have heart problems. I just said so on some insurance forms Goldstein made me fill out, so don't make me a liar."

"You probably swore you're off drugs, too. Right? Including pot?"

He glared at his Southern belle. "Who doesn't smoke pot? It should be the national symbol: an eagle with one claw grasping some weed, the other grasping a wad of dollar bills." He turned to Tom. "Weed and wad, the stuff of life. Don't you agree?"

Tom wasn't getting into that discussion. "My wife tells me you're going to make a new movie."

Phil thrust his chin in the air, as if Tom had just challenged him to a duel. "Yeah, *Rear Action*. I want Tom Cruise, my sweetheart here wants Sean Penn. Who would you go for?"

"A question like that -- way above my pay grade. The only connection I have with Hollywood, and it's a very slight one, is that I happen to be acquainted with Verbena Cross."

"Goldstein's daughter?" Phil frowned. "I'm impressed. He's the guy backing my picture. How do you know Verbena?"

"Long story. And believe me, it's only a slight acquaintance, nothing worth talking about. So let's get back to your new picture. When are you going to start shooting?"

"Oh, man, I can see your modesty about Hollywood is well-earned. You know nothing about the place, I can tell. Lucky you. Tons of arrangements have to be made first. All the fucking suits, the guys with money, have to gather in a room and make speeches. After pulling their thumbs out of their ass, they hold them in the air to check which way the wind is blowing. Then they start checking their traps for suckers who'll spend a fortune to be listed as a producer."

"You have no idea what the suits, as you call them, do," Jerry Lee said scornfully from a supine position, still clutching her chest. "You just think somebody's printing money in a back room somewhere."

"Isn't that exactly what they do?"

"My poor husband worked like a dog making sure I can live like this."

"Embalming corpses. Making dead people look alive."

She smiled wickedly. "Not so different from acting, when you think about it."

"I'm going back out there," Phil said, pointing in the general direction of California, "to see Goldstein and the suits in a week or two. I'll give you a little education when I get back."

"How about giving me a little money? I haven't seen a dollar of those millions you supposedly got from Virgil," Jerry Lee said.

He made a face at her. "Not in front of the help, sweetheart." He threw a shit-eating grin at Tom. "No offense, man. Southern belles don't talk about money. At least, they're not supposed to."

"No offense taken." It wasn't the first time a Hollywood figure had referred to Tom as "the help." Verbena Cross did it when she hired him to find her stalker and then pressured him into acting as her date at her New Year's Eve party in Malibu.

"So, has this lady's popinjay son-in-law really hired you to find the bastard who leaked the story about Poppy?"

"Stop it, Phil. He's not a popinjay. And at least he's not a tinpot revolutionary like you, who'd confiscate my money for welfare cheats and rain forest parks in Iowa. If I have to pay one more dime in taxes, I'll be broke and you'll have to sell a few of those masterpieces instead of buying more."

"You're right about the money but wrong about everything else. With Ferrin-the-fool in power, the rich like you will just get richer and richer. The poor like me will die in the streets. Ferrin *is* a revolutionary, whether you believe it or not. If he gets the chance to get real power, he'll turn this country upside down. The son-of-a-bitch will make Sunday school mandatory. Meanwhile, he'll be festooning the coast with oil rigs. He'll starve the poor and send his own wife to jail for having an abortion."

"If I hear that word one more time, I'm going to scream. She didn't *have* an abortion."

"No. You just had your brother slip her a little tea, the old-fashioned way. You're just lucky she didn't die, like that other girl . . . what was her name?" He looked at Tom, a wicked smile on his face. "You know about my Southern belle's famous teas? You know about the troll in the garden, the one that grinds all those herbs into powder?" He looked at the table beside Tom. "Smart man. I see you refused a cup of tea. I stick with coffee. It's safer."

Jerry Lee abruptly stood up. "I've had enough, Phil. You're as sick in the head as Verlin." She turned to Tom, who at her signal had gotten to his feet. "Don't listen to Phil *or* Verlin. They don't know what they're talking about. Do yourself a favor. Find Dewey Betz or Collin Lindstrom. And don't forget your friend Molly. I don't trust that nosy upstart further than I can throw her. Better yet, take that stupid magazine reporter to the Star Chamber and grill her. I know Canada's a frozen wasteland, but she shouldn't be that hard to find. Look for a den of wolves."

Suddenly recovered, Jerry Lee started for the door opening onto the veranda. "Come along, Tim. I'll take you through the garden, let you meet my brother."

12

Nothing's Ever What It Seems
Monday, April 17, 2006

As soon as Tom returned to his office, he placed a call to Verbena Cross, the Hollywood actress who'd hired him the year before to find her stalker. Ten minutes later, she called back.

"So, how's my favorite detective? Married, I hear."

"Has it been that long since we talked?"

"You heard I'm marrying Bordon?"

"No. He got back from The Czech Republic, I take it."

"In one piece, more or less."

"He'll be at the premiere of *Bonaventure Blues* then?"

"If his schedule holds, he will. Speaking of the premiere, my assistant booked you three double rooms, veranda level, at The Marshall House on Broughton Street. The hotel used to be an old yellow fever hospital, if you're a history buff. The whole of Savannah is practically booked up, so she had to drop a few names, like mine, pull a few strings, like Dad's."

"Speaking of your dad . . . ."

"What's the old socialist up to this time?"

"I'm told he's backing a picture Phil Coker will direct."

"Oh, that. Don't believe a word. By the way, where'd you hear it?"

"A friend of my wife's read it in *Rolling Stone.*"

"My assistant showed me that gaseous puff-piece too. What a

laugh!"

"So there's no connection between Virgil and Coker?"

"Oh, there is, but my dad's not stupid enough to hire that miscreant as a gofer, much less back him to write, direct, and act in another picture about a war nobody gives a crap about. Did you ever hear how Coker lost the biggest part of his life to Michael Douglas? He showed up late, wouldn't take direction, propositioned every woman that walked by, smoked dope on the set."

"Hard to get a picture made that way."

"Worse, do you know what happens to the insurance costs when your star is as unreliable as Coker? Eight, ten percent of the deal. No, dad wouldn't risk a dime on that has-been."

"You said there is a connection, though."

"I know Coker's been out here a few times, taking meetings with some of Dad's people." She laughed. "We take meetings out here, you know. We have people. Do you have people?"

It was Tom's turn to laugh. "We're on the wrong coast to take meetings or have people."

"Dad used to collect the same kind of art Coker does, funk, pop, that sort of stuff. In fact, Dad just gave him a couple of old funk art pieces he didn't want any more, something with a gay title. Can't remember exactly. I collect Andrew Wyeth myself. You collect art?"

"That's the second time I've been asked that today. I'm beginning to feel like a hick."

"Don't. You collect secrets, sort of like a priest. Anyway, not to get off the subject, Dad's working on a couple of projects, but he's really more interested in politics right now than movies. Al Gore is his latest BFF, so he's working with a bunch of very powerful people on global warming. They're putting together a climate exchange in Chicago, some way to make lots of money from the world's misfortune."

"You ever hear of a Florida politician named Ferrin McBride?"

"No. Should I?"

"Probably not. His wife was just libeled in an article claiming she had an abortion. From what I've found out so far, she had a miscarriage when she was a teen-ager but not an abortion. She's a good woman, humiliated, and her husband is livid. The McBrides are pro-life so even a hint that she had an abortion is a scandal. Might even force McBride out of the Congressional race."

"Why are you telling me this?"

"McBride hired me to find the source of the libel. Coker lives with McBride's mother-in-law. McBride's a rich conservative. Coker's a revolutionary in need of money, so the two men don't like each other. Your dad funds liberal causes. He might like getting some dirt on a conservative. Every election these days, however local, is treated like a national election, or so I'm told. And dirty secrets are valuable. Money's flowing to McBride's opponent from California liberals. You don't suppose -- ?"

"The dime just dropped."

"You'd be doing me a big favor if you kept your ears open. I'm not trying to start a family fight, or anything, but if you hear anything about what Coker's been telling your father, or where your dad's millions are really going -- and if you feel inclined to pass the news along -- I'd be eternally grateful."

"I'll do better than that. Let me do a fund-raiser for your client. What's he running for, by the way? And what are his politics exactly?"

"Congress and conservative, in that order. But I'd be willing to bet you're not a conservative."

"No, but I am a rebellious daughter, remember? And I feel sorry for any woman who has a secret that would ruin her life if it floated to the surface. As you well know. As it happens, I've never had an abortion but when I was young I was glad to have the option, so I can't go along with your client's politics. However, I have my own reasons for hating Coker, so if I can stick a fork in him, I'm ready."

"Speaking of secrets, how's Gi working out?"

"Still on her meds, never misses a session with her therapist, acts like she's nothing more than my body double. I never thought your solution to my stalker twin would work, but it did. Cross your fingers and spit into the wind."

"They're crossed. Both hands. No wind, though."

"So, what about that fund-raiser?"

"Hate to break it to you, Verbena, but California wouldn't be a good venue for McBride. My wife's planning a big fund-raiser for him here in Naples a few days after your premiere. It'll be held in the gardens of the estate where Coker lives with Mrs. McBride's mother."

"Gosh, Tom, let me think about that." A split second later, she spoke again. "Just kidding. No thinking necessary. I've never done anything this impulsive in my life, other than marrying my first husband. Give me the date, and if I can be there, I will. I'll get back to you this afternoon."

"If you do that, I'm not sure we can find a big enough venue."

"That's not a bad problem for a politician to have now, is it?"

"No."

"You don't think I'd be a liability, do you?"

"I'm no politician, but I'll get back to you on that."

"Can we talk at three this afternoon? Let's not waste time exchanging messages."

"I'll make sure I'm available."

"Don't you love life, Tom? Nothing's ever what it seems." She hung up before he could respond.

Brimming with news and needing a break, Tom then called his wife.

"I just got off the phone with Verbena."

"My favorite person. How is she?"

"She wants to attend McBride's fund-raiser."

"You sure that's all right with the campaign?"

"No, but I'll let you know. I think you can at least double the size of the party if she comes."

"There's no room for a sit-down dinner in that case, so everything will have to change. Did you just fall in love with Beaudry Hall?"

"About that. There will be no pickled wood in our house. None whatsoever. Nor any glass sculptures or funk art, and don't serve me herbal tea. No garden full of Greek statues. If I see Mao's face anywhere, I'll break something. And if you have an uncle like Verlin, keep him hidden, I beg you. I want a contract to that effect."

Lily laughed. "I'm dying to hear the story of your morning at Beaudry Hall blow-by-blow. So what else is new?"

"My heart's broken over this, but Simon won't be joining us in Savannah. Everything's booked up. Fortunately, we have rooms at a hotel that used to be a yellow-fever hospital, which pleases me no end. Changing the subject here, but did you know Phil Coker has heart problems?"

"Not surprised. He was a drug addict for years."

"Remember those green panels with the dirty name Coker showed you? He didn't buy them. Goldstein gave them to him. If Coker got an advance of millions for his new war picture, they haven't shown up, at least not in Jerry Lee's pocket. And he knows all about Poppy's miscarriage."

"Pillow talk."

"Pillow talk's my favorite, but Jerry Lee swore nobody knew about Poppy except her and maybe the emergency room doctor. When you see Verlin tomorrow to give him the herb book, you might ask if any strangers have been around digging for secrets."

"I don't get you."

"Mullett's men. I think Phil was the leaker, but I want to eliminate the troll if I can. Maybe he said more than he knew to the wrong people."

"The troll?"

"That's what Phil calls Verlin. As Verbena so aptly said, nothing's what it seems."

13

Jonah Was Old School
Tuesday, April 18, 2006

Betty Darling, Nicky Sue's mother, greeted Molly and her mother warmly, more than happy to get the chance to talk about her lovely daughter after so many years. She said it was a relief to talk about the girl openly. Most people avoided the subject as if Nicky Sue had committed a crime or something.

Betty ushered the women to a shady little screened porch jutting off the side of her old Queen Anne style house in Little Gap, a small town in the foothills of the Smokies. The house needed painting. Betty used a kitchen towel to wipe off the dusty wrought iron guest chairs and brought them sweet tea in jelly glasses. Molly shuddered at the spider webs festooning the corners of the porch, which canted a little toward the front yard. Every once in awhile a car passed on the narrow street. The only other sounds were bird chatter. On a round table beside Betty's chair was a dog-eared pamphlet, *The Upper Room*. Molly didn't know how people lived such quiet, lonely lives.

After giving her hostess an autographed copy of *Gilt Trip* and talking about that awhile, Molly told the story that had surfaced about Poppy Beaudry. "I'm getting some background for a story about Poppy, make her human, you know. So I'm starting with you."

"But I never really knew Poppy very well. Or that mother of

hers. I heard things but I didn't see them myself. If Nicky Sue was here, she could probably tell you quite a bit."

"What do you remember about Jerry Lee?"

"Poppy and Nicky Sue were roommates and Poppy's mother was their chaperone. She was pushy, and I didn't like her. When she spoke to the girls, she sounded like an Army sergeant talking to raw recruits. Soon as they got to their room, before they'd even moved in their stuff, she chose the best bed for her daughter, tried to commandeer most of the closet for her. Every moment I was ever in that woman's presence, I had to remind myself to act like a Christian. That's about it."

"What do you remember about the pageant?"

"My daughter had more points than either of you girls -- don't mean to hurt your feelings, but that's the truth -- even though she had less pageant experience than you did. Nicky Sue was there to get some money for college. My husband ran a Texaco station, but with five kids, there was never enough money. It practically broke us just paying for the piano lessons, buying her clothes and makeup, paying the pageant fees."

"I remember that cream silk evening gown," Dee said. "Nicky Sue looked like a Greek goddess."

"I made that. On an old treadle machine, if you can believe that. The silk was so fine I had to buy special needles and thread, keep adjusting the bobbin. Almost drove me crazy. I still have that Singer upstairs if you want to see it. The dress too, for that matter." Betty patted her curly white hair as if getting control of bad memories. "Makes me sad she never got to wear it except during rehearsal. It still smells a little like her, though."

"Have you heard from her since then?" Molly asked.

"No. There've been sightings from time to time, and we've followed up every last one of them. You'd be surprised how many look-a-likes a person has, everywhere from New Mexico to Maine. Our best lead was she was supposed to be working at a dry cleaners in Georgia, but that turned out to be another dead end. We got our hopes up for nothing. My husband's dead now, so it's just me doing it. I haven't heard anything in several years, though, so it's no burden."

"Did the police investigate?"

"Nicky Sue was considered an adult who might have just left on her own, so it was days before they took any interest, and then the only person they ever questioned was her boyfriend, poor boy, 'cause he was the last to see her."

"Why do you say 'poor boy?'"

"There's been a cloud over Paul's head ever since."

"He saw her the night before the final day of the pageant?"

"He admitted she snuck out to see him. They went to a movie . . . *Indiana Jones*, I think. They walked back to the hotel, but Paul said they went their separate ways a couple blocks from a back door to the hotel because she wanted to sneak into her room without anybody seeing that she'd been with a man. That was strictly forbidden. Nobody ever saw her again."

"Well, somebody must have," Dee said, repressing the dark thought that if the girl was murdered, which seemed likely, somebody did see her again, and that somebody was probably a crazed pervert still running loose.

"Do you suspect the boyfriend of anything?"

"No. I knew Paul from the time he was in diapers. Nicest family you ever met. I like to think Prince Charming found Nicky Sue and took her to his castle. Sometimes, I think I feel her presence."

"What do you remember about Poppy?"

"Very quiet but nice, not like her mother. Generous, too. She let Nicky Sue wear a pair of her shorts when Nicky Sue spilled Coke on hers. I don't know if you remember, but that sparkly butterfly pin Nicky Sue wore in her hair during the rehearsal for the evening gown competition? That was Poppy's. My girl must have been wearing it the night she left to see Paul, because Jerry Lee demanded it back and nobody could find it. How is that old hag, by the way?" Looking apologetic, she put a hand over her mouth. "I shouldn't call her that, should I?"

Molly ignored the apology. In private, she'd called Jerry Lee much worse. "Living in Naples, Florida in a big plantation house.

She lives with an actor you might have heard of: Phil Coker."

"Phil Coker," she mused, closing her eyes for a second. "Is he the sleazy guy that made that Viet Nam movie so many years ago? My husband, God rest his soul, served over there. He hated that movie, said it was a bunch of lies."

Dee nodded. "Coker's not exactly like her poor old husband, Jonah, huh?"

"What Poppy told Nicky Sue about Jonah, he was old school, honest as the day is long, a strict father. He liked his bourbon and cigars but he was a church-goer. I never met the man, but Poppy confided in Nicky Sue, the way roommates do late at night. She said her dad didn't like her being in pageants. He objected to all the makeup, the scanty outfits, the sexy moves. Her parents fought a lot about that, and her dad finally said his daughter was going to stop doing pageants, concentrate on her studies so she could get into a good college. But he never got his wish because suddenly he died."

"Of what? The stress of living with that harridan?" Dee rattled an armload of bracelets for emphasis.

Betty smiled. "He was a big man, I'm told, very overweight. I never seen him myself. He was actually embalming somebody when he had a massive stroke. He was gone," Betty said, snapping her fingers, "just like that. Anyway, that's what Poppy told my daughter."

"I heard the same thing," Dee said.

"He couldn't have been very old, could he?" Molly asked, a little miffed that Poppy had never confided in her at the pageant.

"Oh, I think he was a lot older than his wife. Did you know Jerry Lee grew up a few towns over?"

"No."

"Her dad was a farmhand, often out of work, living in a shack in the woods. They didn't have a pot to . . . well, you know. Dick -- my late husband -- didn't like to see them come to the gas station because the Grubbs stole things."

Molly was on alert. "You mean Jerry Lee didn't grow up in a wealthy family in Charleston?"

Betty looked stunned. "Jerry Lee Grubbs? Are we talking about the same woman?"

"I think so."

"Jerry Lee Grubbs grew up poor as dirt with a very mean mother. Her mother, can't remember her name, never got beyond the third grade because her own step-mother made her stay home and raise her half-brothers and -sisters. Jerry Lee's dad was mean too, especially when he was drunk, which was most of his waking hours."

"How in the world did Jerry Lee escape to Charleston?"

"Well, she was pretty and smart, so that helped. And luck was with her. She was working in a dime store, jerking sodas." Betty paused and looked at Dee. "Remember when dime stores had soda fountains?"

Dee nodded. "Those were the days."

"Well, anyway," Betty resumed, "that's where Jonah ran into Jerry Lee. He was a widower with money, lonely, no kids. He was just passing through when he stopped for a soda. He must have thought he'd found the woman of his dreams. I don't think Jerry Lee had even graduated from high school when Jonah ran into her."

"Dreams, my ass. More like his nightmares," Dee said. Catching her daughter's look, she slapped her hand over her mouth. "'Scuse my language."

"You know a lot more about Jerry Lee than you let on at first," Molly said.

"It comes back, you know, when I'm forced to think about it. I try never to think about nasty things. I'd go crazy if I did. Do you read the Psalms?"

"The only one I know is the 23rd."

"You should try them. I read one every night, gets me through the dark places. You know the one that says 'the ransom for a life is costly, no payment is ever enough?'"

Both Molly and Dee shook their heads.

"Those nights when I think the worst? I read that Psalm, then I pray that if somebody did something bad to my precious daughter, they'll find out what the payment really is, not just up there" -- she pointed to the bead-board ceiling -- "but right here."

Molly and Dee fell silent.

Molly hesitated to ask her final question. "Do you have any idea what happened to your daughter?"

Betty looked away. "No. I keep asking the Lord to tell me, but He just says to wait, I'll find out in due time. He has His own plan, you know."

"Considering everything, Mrs. Darling, it was very nice of you to let us visit you like this."

"You know who you should talk to?" Betty stood up, adjusting her faded dirndl skirt. "Paul Rossetti. He lives on Hilton Head, owns a golf shop there. I don't think he ever married."

Molly looked at her mother. "Why not go see him? It might be useful. And I love Hilton Head. You up to it?"

Dee looked out to the street, where her silver Mustang was parked. "I'm up for anything, so let's go for a ride." She smiled at Betty. "But not until I see that cream silk evening gown you made for Nicky Sue and the old Singer treadle . . . if that's all right with you."

It was more than all right with Betty.

★ ★ ★ ★ ★

Before Molly and her mother headed east to catch I-95 for the long drive to Hilton Head, they detoured into the country, following Betty's directions, to get a look at the house Jerry Lee had grown up in. Molly had to see it for herself. After getting lost and stopping for help at a gas station, they finally found what they were looking for a few yards off a dirt road.

Molly gasped. The place was dreadful, something out of a National Geographic pictorial on Third World living conditions. Even when it was occupied, it couldn't have been called a house. It was a shack, nothing more.

In total, the structure wasn't as large as her lanai on Marco Island. How had it ever held four people? A little pitched roof over the front entrance was hanging at a crazy angle, and a lean-to had almost detached itself from north side of the shack. The little windows on either side of the doorless front entrance no longer held even shards of glass. A cottonwood was growing up through the caved-in roof. The chimney on the south side had lost most of its bricks. Kudzu looked like it was eating the remains.

Molly switched her gaze to the surroundings. Some old tires were barely visible through the weeds, and a rusting machine she couldn't identify lay across what must once have been the path to the front door. A section of wire fence had fallen toward the road, propped up at one end by a half-rotted wooden post that probably once held a mailbox.

"Can you believe this, Mom? I'm going to get out and take a picture. I bet Poppy hasn't ever seen this."

"Watch out for snakes and poison ivy."

When Molly got back in the driver's seat, she asked, "So what do you think?"

Dee rattled her bracelets. "I think if I'd grown up in this hellhole, I'd pretend I was something else too. Makes me feel almost sorry for Jerry Lee."

14

You Can Take That to the Bank
Wednesday, April 19, 2006

Tom's interview of Dr. Collin Lindstrom yielded some interesting new information but not the identity of the leaker, except by elimination.

On a rainy April day, they met in a Charleston suburb of handsome houses and well-kept lawns. The doctor's home office was large and messy. His desk was weighed down by stacks of papers, the bookshelves loaded with thick textbooks bearing titles like *Electronic Resources for Healthcare Professionals* and *Triage Procedures.*

"I'm updating a textbook for RNs," he explained, adjusting his bow tie. "Retirement was killing me, so I'm an adjunct professor in the College of Nursing at the Medical University of South Carolina. All this paper," he said, sweeping his arm above the desk, "is the result of writing and teaching."

After thanking his host for taking the time to meet with him and introducing himself, Tom handed him Poppy's authorization waiving her privacy rights in regard to her medical history.

Dr. Lindstrom looked up from the letter. "So what can I do for you, Mr. Lawton?"

Tom told his host about the *Marie Claire* abortion story and McBride's campaign for Congress. "We're trying to find out who put that story around. Very damaging, as you can imagine, especially because Mrs. McBride claims it isn't true, that she miscarried instead. Poppy's mother said you were the treating physician in the emergency room."

Dr. Lindstrom briefly glanced at the window, then back at Tom. "Ordinarily, I wouldn't remember a case that old, but the circumstances were so odd it stands out. All signs were that the girl had been pregnant but there was no fetus by the time I saw her, so I can't say what happened before she arrived in my emergency room. What stands out is the shape she was in: unconscious, having seizures, then temporarily paralyzed. And her mother! Now there's a woman I won't soon forget. She demanded that I write nothing down, even gave me a false name at first. I didn't stand for that, of course."

"So there was no abortion."

"As I said, none after she was admitted to my emergency room. She'd been pregnant, that we verified. But I can't say what happened before I saw her, whether somebody aborted her or she just miscarried. All I can attest to is that no abortion occurred in my emergency room. First rule of medicine, you know: do no harm."

"You ever figure out what caused those strange symptoms?"

"No. We were thinking something neurological, maybe a brain tumor, even some kind of very severe food poisoning."

"What about household poisons?"

"That was one of many possibilities in the back of my mind, but I didn't connect the symptoms with anything I'd encountered before, like arsenic or anti-freeze. Blood tests were done, of course, but you have to know what you're looking for when it comes to poisons. Thankfully, she recovered, mostly with time and, maybe, divine providence. Sometimes that's all that stands between life and death, you know. Keeps mortal men like me humble."

"Do you think I could see the records?"

"I'm afraid you've hit a dead end, Mr. Lawton. There was a fire in the records room years later. There might be some duplicate records somewhere, but good luck finding them." Dr. Lindstrom rubbed his head again. "They wouldn't tell you anything more than I already have anyway."

When Tom started to stand up, Dr. Lindstrom held out his hand like a school crossing guard with a stop sign. "Hold on. I just remembered something. There was a strange little man with the women. I remember him for a couple of reasons. He was wearing thick, tinted glasses, looking very agitated. His gestures were jerky and awkward. I thought he might be retarded." He paused. "We could say 'retarded' in those days without rebuke. Anyway, at one point, when I stepped away for a second, he tugged on my sleeve, saying he wanted to tell me something. He whispered a couple of words. The only one I caught was 'Texas.' But before I could figure out what the poor little guy was trying to say, the girl's mother hustled him out of there, screaming at him to go back to the car and wait for her. Though I felt sorry for the little bugger, being screamed at like that, I was glad the girl's mother hustled him out because we had enough chaos without him pulling at me. I've always wondered, though, what the poor little guy wanted to tell me."

"Texas? Sounds like *Taxus.*"

The doctor cocked his head, waiting for Tom to elaborate.

"The strange little guy who tugged on your sleeve might have been Poppy's uncle, Verlin Grubbs. He knows a lot about herbs, and you wouldn't know by looking at him, but he knows all their Latin names. Recently he told my wife that English yew gets rid of babies. He gave her the Latin name, but all she could remember was *Taxus.* Which sounds like Texas if you don't know the context."

"You don't say? *Taxus* means toxin. Hold on, I have a dictionary of natural medicines and poisons." He got up and looked through several shelves before he found the book he was seeking. He consulted the table of contents, then opened the book and flipped through, finally running his finger down a page until he found what he was looking for.

"Here it is. 'English yew, or *Taxus baccata*, is a primitive conifer. Except for the berries, all parts contain taxine, which depresses cardiac function. Before birth control was available, apothecaries would dry the leaves and stems and grind them to a powder. Administered in a liquid in minute, very dilute quantities, the resulting potion acted as an abortifacient, causing convulsions, sometimes paralysis, and even death. There is no known antidote, and because the proper dosage is difficult to regulate, the toxin is not used in modern medicine.'"

He put the book down. "Well, well, well. A very old mystery solved, just like that. The difference between a medicine and a poison, you know, is typically nothing more than dosage. Whoever gave her that potion almost killed the poor girl. If they didn't want her dead, they were damn lucky."

"Just thinking aloud here, but that person, whoever he or she is, is very unlikely to have told a reporter because they'd be incriminating themselves. Certainly, they didn't tell you."

"Well, maybe the odd little man tried, but he didn't get to finish his thought and at the time I wasn't focusing on poisonous herbs, I can tell you that. As I said, I was thinking more along the lines of some neurological disorder."

"I take it, then, that no reporter from *Marie Claire* ever contacted you."

The doctor sat back, steepling his hands, his face showing no emotion at all. "I know what you're getting at."

"Sorry, but I have to be sure."

"In my day, doctors never needed a federal law to keep a patient's secrets. I don't know what's happened to this country, the government sticking its nose into everything, treating professionals like naughty children who spend their days tattling, but I don't like it." He picked up his pen and twirled it. "I can assure you, Mr. Lawton, that no reporter has ever contacted me about that girl and even if he had I wouldn't have said a word. I'd have booted him out of this office."

He stood up, pointing his pen at Tom. "I've never said a word about that case to anybody but you, and then only because the patient wanted me to. My ethics are intact. You can take that to the bank."

15

Ball in Play

Wednesday, April 19, 2006

It was Wednesday afternoon before Molly and Dee could get a look at Paul Rossetti.

They arrived in Harbour Town on Hilton Head Island late Tuesday and found the golf shop he owned. It was cool and quiet and smelled like good leather. Vintage golf lithographs hung on dark-paneled walls. One side of the store was devoted to fine sports clothes and expensive gifts, the other to golf equipment of every description. After looking around a bit, the women were told that the owner had taken some visitors out on his yacht and wouldn't be back until Wednesday.

Molly decided to buy something for Carl, who was having to take care of the twins after a hard day's work. She pulled out a white silk dinner jacket to examine it.

"Who's that for?" Dee asked.

"Mom! For Carl, of course."

Dee took hold of the sleeve. "Size 44 short." She looked at her daughter. "You need to put that man on a diet. Put him on a rack too, stretch out him out a ways."

"Stop it. Carl's just fine the way he is."

"If you say so."

After Molly had completed the purchase, the pair spent the rest of the evening strolling along the waterfront, getting manicures in an Asian salon, and driving to the Café St. Tropez for dinner, where they feasted on veal paprikash in pastry shells. They ended the night back in Harbour Town, sitting in rocking chairs to watch the seagulls and comment on the other tourists, few of whom were up to Dee's sartorial standards.

Finally, on Wednesday, they completed their mission. When they entered the Hilton Head Links Shop after lunch, they were told by a clerk that the boss was in his office, meeting with a salesman. When he finally emerged, Molly was startled. A man of medium height but a good twenty pounds overweight, Paul Rossetti looked a decade older than his forty-some years. The sun appeared to have smoked him like a brisket, cratering deep lines around his eyes and mouth, rendering his bald pate almost as dark as the fringe of hair encircling it. She noticed there was no ring on his left hand.

When they were seated on the patio of a nearby restaurant, sipping lemonade, Molly explained her assignment for the McBrides and the conversation they'd just had with Nicky Sue's mother. At the mention of his old flame, Paul's face softened.

"I'm sure this isn't your favorite subject," Molly said.

"Yes and no. There's hasn't been a day in the last seventeen-eighteen years I haven't thought about Nicky Sue. But the subject is too painful to talk about." He pushed his chair back as if ready to leave.

Molly stretched out her hand. "Please, hear me out. Nicky Sue was Poppy's roommate at the pageant. We both remember her fondly. All I want is some background for the piece I'm going to write. It was Nicky Sue's disappearance that brought Poppy to her knees. The only reason I won was that Nicky Sue disappeared and Poppy fell apart."

"Go on."

"Nicky Sue would have beaten both of us, you know, hands down, if she hadn't left before the last day."

"And I would have married her if she hadn't left."

"You've never gotten a hint, then, of what happened or where she is? Both Poppy and I would love to find her."

"No more than I would. The police fingered me as the culprit. They never charged me with anything, but as you can imagine, my life was never the same."

"Betty Darling says you left her a couple blocks from the hotel."

"Against my better judgment, I might add. But she didn't want anybody to know what she'd been up to. Not that we did anything bad. We just watched a movie, that's all, sat on a park bench awhile."

"*Indiana Jones*, Betty said."

"*Indiana Jones and the Last Crusade*, to be precise. I haven't been able to watch a Harrison Ford movie since then."

"What do you think happened?"

"I *know* what happened. I told the cops a dozen times, but they never believed me. I stood and watched her walk back. About a block from the hotel, a car pulled up alongside the curb, right under a streetlight. I could see heads in both the driver's and passenger's seats. I thought a man was driving but I couldn't be sure. Nicky Sue got in, without any hesitation so far as I could see, so she must have known the people. The car pulled away. That's the last time I saw her."

"Did you see the car well enough to describe it?"

"A Chevrolet Impala hardtop, 2-door, 1959, big fins, dual exhaust, reddish color with a lot of chrome. I say 'reddish' because the streetlights distort color. One taillight was out. I couldn't see the license plate."

"That's pretty specific. Why couldn't the cops find it?"

"Wouldn't you think they could have found the car if they'd looked hard enough? For Pete's sake, it was already old in 1989. I know a lot of Impalas were made, but how many of that particular model were still on the road thirty years later?" Paul lit a cigarette. "My parents thought the cops never really considered any suspect but me. I was convenient and they couldn't be bothered looking elsewhere."

"How did you happen to be in Greenville? Were you attending the pageant?"

"No. I was attending North Greenville University, getting a master's in business, concentrating in sports management." He gave her a rueful look. "I was going to be a big-time sports agent in those days, maybe make the professional golf circuit for a few years first. Anyway, Nicky Sue and I grew up a few blocks from each other in Little Gap, so the fact that she happened to be in Greenville for a week was a godsend. We couldn't pass up the opportunity to see each other." He paused. "Little Gap. I take it's that where you were yesterday if you were talking to Betty."

"Right. Mrs. Darling still lives there, in the same house Nicky Sue grew up in."

Paul signaled the waitress for another round of lemonades. "How is that sweet old thing?"

"Sweet and old but dusty too," Dee said. "Immersed in Bible stuff."

"Mom. She wasn't dusty."

Paul smiled for the first time. "The whole town is a little dusty. The school we attended was tiny, only about eighteen kids a class, everybody in the same building from K through senior high school, one of the last of its kind, I suspect. The school building had been constructed by some special agency of the Roosevelt administration in the Thirties, complete with a quotation from John Dewey carved above the door. 'Arriving at one goal is the starting point to another.' As a kid, I was puzzled by that dreary idea. Still am.

"Anyway, every year the school sponsored a talent show. Nicky Sue probably wasn't more than twelve years old when she played a piano piece that was just sensational. She won the contest, of course, and I fell in love just listening to her play. She was a joy to look at too, sweet as pie. We had our first date a few years later. Neither of us ever dated anybody else."

"Now, that's a love story."

"Once I had the golf shop up and running profitably, I hired a detective but nothing ever came of it. I even posted a reward for information." Paul held up his left hand to show that he wore no rings. "Nothing ever came of the other relationships I've had since then. I didn't make the golf tour and I didn't go into sports management."

Molly searched for comforting words. "But your golf shop looks like a winner."

"It is. You might say at least one thing in my life worked out."

"For a hundred different reasons, I want to find Nicky Sue, but I don't know where to go from here."

"You've got my support, Molly, whatever you do. I'd like to clear my name once and for all." He looked out at the harbor. "Tell you what, ladies. If you're staying another day, I'll take you for a tour of the island on my boat. We can talk some more. Maybe I'll remember something that will help." He winked at Dee. "You can meet my dad. He's been divorced forever, but he still has an eye for the ladies."

Dee adjusted the clutch of beads and chains hanging to her waist. "What's your boat called?"

"*Ball in Play*."

She winked back at Paul. "Sounds promising." Without checking with her daughter about staying another day, she answered for both of them. "Nothing we'd like better, Paul."

16

Where's My Money?

Wednesday, April 19, 2006

On Wednesday night, Phil told his Southern belle he was going out for an hour or so to buy some vino at a high-end wine shop having a tasting of half a dozen rare California vintages. He'd return in an hour or so.

He backed Jerry Lee's Cadillac out of one of the six garages situated on the ground floor, idled a minute in the courtyard, then pulled out onto the street. Instead of heading downtown, he made an immediate right turn onto a side street, and stopped a few yards beyond the side drive to Jerry Lee's carriage house. He only had to wait a few minutes until the Russian joined him. They then drove to a nearby public park and pulled into a parking space. Phil left the motor running because it was too hot turn off the air conditioner.

The first words out of Phil's mouth were, "Where's my money?"

The muscular man in the passenger's seat threw up his hands. "Nothing doing with me."

"Goddamn it, man, I gave Virgil everything he wanted."

"What can I say? Boss wants more."

"More what?"

"Dirt on McBride Communities. Or McBride. He ever do an affair, maybe with a man? Do an arms deal? Make a baby with some chick?" The Russian mimed tippling from a bottle. "Maybe drink a lot? Boss want something like that."

"Hell, you're in a better position than I am for that kind of dirt."

"So far, nothing." He spread his hands wide. "Every second, I watch, believe me. My ears I keep open."

They argued for a half hour. No money changed hands. When Phil dropped the man off back at the gate outside the carriage house, neither man realized two people were watching the Russian make his way to a bike chained to a lamp post.

Verlin, who had been polishing the old Impala in a far corner of the carriage house, idly wishing Jerry Lee would let him drive it again, stepped toward the gate for a breath of fresh air, curious if he'd see again what he'd seen every other Wednesday night at this time for the last five or six weeks. He stood in the shadows where he could see the street without being seen. He had a special cigarette in his pocket but took his time lighting it.

Jerry Lee was laying some flowers on the steps of the mausoleum where her husband's coffin occupied a niche. It was the nineteenth anniversary of his death. For the first few years, she performed the ritual because that was the kind of things grieving widows did. Lately, however, she felt some emotion because she rather missed Jonah. In life, she'd resented his strong opinions, which often differed sharply from hers, but at least he supported her instead of siphoning off her wealth, the way Phil did. In widowhood, she longed for the security Jonah provided.

Phil's presence gave her a certain caché she wouldn't otherwise have, but it was growing tiresome. Though he thought of himself as an original, in fact his antics were predictable and boring. Every year he nattered on about a comeback; every year his inflated hopes came to nothing. Every year he racked up bigger bills on her credit cards; every year his promises to repay her came to nothing. If he didn't start repaying her soon, she'd have to sell the house. The only thing she had going at the moment was an LLC with her son-in-law to develop the acreage she'd once occupied with Jonah in South Carolina.

When she straightened up, she caught the scent of Phil's cigarettes on the breeze. Looking to her left, she spotted a figure in shadow standing to one side of the iron gate. Too short to be Phil. She crept toward the gate. It was Verlin. What in the world was he doing?

She walked softly within a yard of him. He turned when he heard her and put his finger to his lips.

"What's that you're smoking?" she whispered.

"Cannablis." Jerry Lee could barely hear him. "That's what Phil calls it."

"Really, you too . . . ." He was standing suspiciously close to the gate. "You aren't thinking of opening that gate, are you?"

He pointed to the side street. "Phil just dropped that man off again."

She had to lean into him to hear what he was saying. "What man?"

"See that bike? Watch."

They watched a very muscular man in black spandex, shaped like a human V, walk across the street. After donning goggles and a helmet and looking up and down the street but not in the direction of the carriage house, he unchained a bike from a lamp post and quickly rode away.

"Who is he?"

Verlin shrugged.

"You ever see his face?"

"No."

"You sure Phil dropped him off?"

"I'm sure, unless you let somebody else drive the Cadillac."

"And you've seen the guy on the bike before?"

"Every week, this time."

"For how long?"

"I'd have to check my diary, but at least since March."

"Come get me next week. We'll watch together."

When Phil returned without any wine, saying it was all moonshine and rot, nothing either of them would drink, Jerry Lee was uncharacteristically understanding. She studied him with narrowed eyes. "That's all right, Shugah. Bad luck happens."

She didn't accuse him of sneaking out to score some weed. Instead, she suggested he go down to the ground floor, where a state-of-the-art, temperature-controlled wine cellar had been constructed in a corner of the long garage, and bring up a bottle of the 1995 Heidsieck Blanc des Millénaires. She'd read it didn't age well, so who knew, if they didn't drink it now, when they'd get the chance?

17

Spy Run
Thursday, April 20, 2006

Tom discovered that Minnie and Burley Betz had moved from their small farm near Charleston to the outskirts of Beaufort, where they lived in a modest little bungalow on a small lot on a block of identical post-war houses constructed for returning GIs eager to leave the war behind and start a normal life. Burley, Minnie said, had already left for work at a downtown stable that housed horses for the carriage rides that were so popular with tourists.

"He leads tours, drives a carriage?"

"Oh, no. Burley's not good with words, won't wear a uniform, hates tourists." She explained that her husband was a genius with horses and knew more than a vet about their ailments. He could shoe a horse in minutes.

Minnie, a white-haired dumpling of a woman built for comfort, invited him to take an iron shell-back chair on their front porch. She said she'd back in a minute, make himself comfortable. She returned with sweet tea in heavy tumblers and a plate of misshapen chocolate chip cookies. They were the best chocolate chip cookies Tom had ever eaten. After Minnie took the twin to his chair, Tom sketched out his quest, just enough information to make it clear who he and his client were. He wanted to know something about her son, if she didn't mind.

"When Poppy got pregnant, Dewey said he wanted to marry

her. Burley would have gotten his shotgun out if our boy hadn't been willing."

"Did you ever meet Poppy?"

"No. We knew who her family was, of course, because they had a big red brick funeral home on the outskirts of town. The family lived on the second floor, and once driving by I saw Poppy's mother out in the yard. When Big Pop died -- that was Burley's dad -- Jonah Beaudry was the undertaker, so we met him face-to-face. But I never saw Poppy, except on the TV, or talked to her mother."

"So where is Dewey now?"

"Don't know."

"Tell me about that."

"One day he just done up and left without a word. We thought our boy might have changed his mind about getting married, run off to join the Marines, like he'd planned before the girl got pregnant. We waited to hear from him. Then we tried for a few months to find him but nothing ever came of it."

"No sightings, nothing?"

"Oh, one or two in the early years, but nothing since."

"Where do you think he is?"

"Hiding somewhere. As the youngest, he was always a little unsure of himself, very worried when he did anything bad, even the silly stuff boys do. He loved guns and knew how to use them but he accidentally shot a horse once. Burley gave him a good beating for that. I don't think the poor boy ever got over his mistake."

"But he must have loved you. Wouldn't you think he'd try to get in touch, even if he didn't tell you where he was?"

"No. He was a secretive boy."

"And you're okay with that?"

She wiped her brow with her apron. "No. But it's his life, ain't it?"

"How did you know that he was really gone for good?"

"He took his car one night and just didn't return the next day or the day after that. If we didn't see the car, we knew we wouldn't see him."

"Did you go to the police?"

"Heavens no. In those days, we were living out in the country. Burley had a little still in the corn shed, so he never wanted the police around."

"I didn't know anybody did that any more."

"His dad, Big Pop, was from the hills of West Virginia. He lived with us till he died. The Betz men didn't believe in buying what they could make themselves."

"Tell me about Dewey's car."

"Burley let him have an old '38 Plymouth that was Big Pop's. They fixed it up together. The transmission was never good, but they got it to running. Dewey spent every spare hour he had working on that old thing. He wanted to be a mechanic for the Marines. You ever learn to drive a stick shift?"

"Years ago, but it's too much work."

"Couldn't agree with you more. If you didn't adjust that clutch just right, the old Plymouth shuddered like a stallion in heat."

Tom was afraid he wouldn't get that image out of his head all day. After a long silence, Minnie gave him a worried look. "Poppy ever have that baby?"

"No."

"Not surprised. We thought maybe she was lying to Dewey so she could get married because nobody ever told us about a baby, asked us for money or anything like that. After Dewey hot-footed it out of here, I was pretty sure that's what happened. Dewey must have found out she was a liar and decided to start over somewhere else."

"Has a reporter ever talked to you about Poppy?"

"What might a reporter look like?"

Tom suppressed a laugh. "There isn't one look. They don't wear uniforms or badges. In this case, the reporter is a woman, but I can't tell you what she looks like. She'd have asked a lot of personal questions about your son. She'd probably try to get you to say Poppy had an abortion."

"Did Poppy do that?"

"No, I don't think so. . . . So, any encounters with a person like that?"

"Other than you?"

"Well, as I told you, I'm not a reporter. But, yes, has anyone else come around looking for information about Poppy?"

She shook her head. "No. Burley don't like outsiders much."

"If anybody contacts you, would you let me know? Or if you hear anything from your son . . . ."

"Sure thing. But don't hold your breath."

Before getting up, he handed her his business card. "I'm heading back to Charleston, but you can always get me on my cell phone."

"Well, then, let me wrap up some of them cookies for you and put some lemonade in a jar. It's a long, hot drive where you're going."

* * * * *

Tom reached Charleston just after noon and, using his new GPS system, found the suburban funeral home Poppy had grown up in -- or the remains of it. A wrecking ball was taking down the back wall when he arrived. In back of the funeral home, a silt fence surrounded acres of dirt being graded by large machines. He drove back to a Walmart he'd passed, bought some rubber boots and a couple bottles of water, and returned to the site.

"What's going on?" he asked of a man wearing a hard hat, standing near the machine with the wrecking ball.

The man pointed to a sign that read Coming soon. Spy Run Lake Villas. Lots Available. "We've got eighty acres here. The site's being developed."

"That was a funeral home you're taking down, right?"

"Right you are."

"Who's developing the site?"

"Don't know. I just work for the demolition company. You'll have to ask somebody else."

"Is it okay if I walk to the back?"

"None of my business. Just take that path over there so you don't get hurt."

Tom made his way through the mud to the back and watched the graders for awhile. Suddenly, one of them halted near a pond that was being drained. As he drew closer, he could see something metallic just sticking above the water.

Suddenly, half a dozen men got down from their machines and walked over.

"What is it?" Tom asked one of them.

"Looks like a car. We're going to have to close the site for awhile, call the Sheriff, get a crane in here."

Several hours later, the car was lifted out of the pond. It was an old Plymouth, so rusted he couldn't decide what the original color had been. Wondering if Dewey had been found at last, Tom waited until the Sheriff had inspected it. There was no body inside.

After finding out where the car was being taken, he wrote down as much of the license plate as was discernible and called McBride's office to see if they had enough leverage to get custody of it. After being transferred several times, Tom at last reached a man who seemed to know what he was talking about. "That's a McBride Communities project. Shouldn't be a problem."

Nothing surprised Tom any more. Who, after all, was more likely to develop Jerry Lee's property than her own son-in-law? As he returned to his car, he glanced at the sign again and smiled. At least the place wouldn't have one of those Irish names she so despised.

18

Closer to Home
Saturday, April 22, 2006

Once again, on Saturday, Tom found himself in Ferrin McBride's home office. This time, in honor of the weekend, his host was wearing a pair of jeans and a white button-down shirt open at the neck with the sleeves rolled up, revealing the thick neck of a former football player and the muscled forearms of a fighter pilot.

Ferrin spoke first. "We have the car from the new development site. The Sheriff thought it was just abandoned by the Beaudrys, but privately we asked Burley Betz to look at it. He identified it as his son's. Any theory as to why it was in that pond?"

"None, other than it looks suspicious."

"Or how long it had been there?" Ferrin asked

"According to his mother, the boy left home in 1989 and never returned, so a reasonable guess is seventeen years. Minnie Betz, by the way, thinks her son left town because he was ashamed either of getting Poppy pregnant or being lied to."

"I'm not following you."

"It's complicated. Since she never heard of any baby being born to Poppy, Minnie thinks your wife might have been lying just so Dewey would marry her. Then, when he learned there was no baby, he left town out of embarrassment."

Ferrin wrinkled his forehead. "But now they must realize he

didn't leave town because he left his car at the funeral home. Not unless he hitched a ride with somebody."

"I haven't talked to them since the car was found in the pond, so I don't know what the Betzes are thinking or what they know. But my money is on a different scenario. Dewey loved that car, so voluntary abandonment doesn't seem to me to be likely."

Ferrin looked thoughtful. He got up, grabbed a putter, walked over near the open doors to the terrace, and began practicing putts. "Don't mind me. I don't get enough time for golf."

"No problem. Suit yourself."

"You play golf?"

Tom laughed. "My brother-in-law insists I play with him and Carl, so I'm trying." He described his best day on the course when he shot below 200 and didn't wing a pelican.

"How about a round after we're done here? Call your brother-in-law, see if he and Carl can join us. I'll have André book us for a 2:30 tee time. We'll be done in time to take our wives to dinner." He smiled. "I don't know if that's your routine -- Saturday night date -- but it's Poppy's and therefore mine."

"Mine too. Wives have a way of ordering our lives, don't they?"

"That they do. So, back to your report."

"Since nobody's seen or heard from Dewey in seventeen years and the Betzes wouldn't talk to a reporter even if one showed up, they're not the leakers. Neither is Dr. Lindstrom, who was indignant at the very idea he might have betrayed a patient's privacy. That leaves Nicky Sue and her mother, Betty Darling, assuming Poppy might have told her roommate something. According to Molly, Betty Darling never talked to a reporter and Nicky Sue doesn't seem to be traceable. Molly, by the way, talked to Paul Rossetti, Nicky Sue's boyfriend and the last person to see her. He claims, however, that he wasn't the last to see her because she got into a '59 Impala with two other people before reaching the hotel."

"Doesn't look good, does it?" Ferrin said. "I mean, for finding the leaker."

"I have no reason to suspect that any story about an abortion could have come from Nicky Sue, her mother or former boyfriend, Dewey Betz, his family, or Dr. Lindstrom. I think we need to look closer to home."

"Jerry Lee is closer to home."

"But what would she have to gain?" Tom asked.

"My question exactly. Poppy is her idol. Did you know she has a shrine -- that's what I call it -- in an alcove off her bedroom dedicated to everything Poppy? Ribbons, tiaras, crowns, trophies, photos, that sort of thing. Even some Barbie dolls dressed in miniatures of Poppy's favorite pageant costumes."

"I hear some pageant mothers are like that."

"And did you know the only income Jerry Lee has other than from investments will come from the Spy Run development? Unless, of course, she starts selling some of the rare wines she's been amassing or those grotesque glass things she collects or anything else she has stashed away."

"No, I didn't know that."

"So, let's add this up. She adores Poppy and wouldn't betray her. She needs me for financial security, so I can't see her killing the goose laying golden eggs. Therefore, I can't see her as the culprit."

"As I said, I think we need to look closer to home."

Ferrin completed another putt before responding. "That leaves Verlin." He laughed. "Verlin Dootz Grubbs. How about that for a name?"

"Verlin Grubbs would have been enough, I think. Dootz is just piling on."

"My thought exactly."

"So, how would Verlin have leaked anything?" Tom asked. "Supposedly, he was only told that Poppy had appendicitis."

"Bear with me if I digress a little, Tom. Something you said about Paul Rossetti jogged my memory. Jonah Beaudry had a little collection of vintage cars. Maybe 'collection' isn't the right word. If old Jonah the mortician ever drove a car and liked it, he kept it rather than trading it in. Some of the cars were really old and all were in excellent condition. Did you know that?"

"No."

"Jerry Lee had me sell all of them except the Impala" -- he threw out his arm in a sweeping gesture -- "talking about Impalas. It was shipped here last year. I think it's a '59 hardtop."

"An Impala like the one Paul Rossetti described as the car Nicky Sue got into when he let her walk back to the hotel?"

"Can't be sure, but maybe. According to Poppy, Jonah let Verlin -- or the troll, as Jerry Lee so affectionately calls him -- drive it once in awhile when she needed to go somewhere and there was nobody else to give her a lift. Poppy needed a lot of rides because she took voice lessons, sang in the church choir, had fittings at a dressmaker's, that sort of thing, and sometimes she just couldn't ride a bike into town. Verlin spent a lot of time with Poppy, probably knew everything that ever happened to her."

"Speaking of Verlin, if anybody gave Poppy an herb to cause a miscarriage, it was he." Tom told Ferrin about his conversation with Dr. Lindstrom.

"Now there you might be wrong. Verlin might have known what to give her, but my bet is that it was Jerry Lee's idea and she administered it."

"It almost killed the poor girl."

"But it didn't. She lived to appear in the pageant and might have won if she hadn't been so upset over Nicky Sue going missing."

"I already thought of Verlin as an inadvertent leaker. My wife bought him a special gardening book. I suggested that she ask him if anybody had been around to talk to him."

"I like the way you think, detective."

"From what I've been told, Uncle Verlin wouldn't say much to a stranger about Poppy because she's the love of his life." Tom remembered something. "He did, however, tell the ladies that Nicky Sue was in that statue of Nike. Did you know that?"

"Yes. He thinks the garden is heavily populated with ghosts. Jonah's in the mausoleum, along with Jerry Lee's mother and father and Jerry Lee's older sister, who died in childhood. Nicky Sue's in the statue. Dewey Betz is the bronze pig in the herb garden."

"The bronze pig?"

"Notice I said he *is* the bronze pig, not that he's *in* the bronze pig. Verlin insists on that distinction. I'm told Dewey's dad was a hog farmer."

"I hadn't heard about the bronze pig before."

"Have you had a tour of Jerry Lee's gardens?"

"Yes. And I met Verlin, but I didn't see the pig."

"Well, we're going to arrange another visit. You need to see Dewey-the-pig. We'll get Jerry Lee out of the house and take a private tour with the troll so you can get a good look at the Impala too."

"I have to admit I didn't concentrate on Verlin as the leaker. When you gave me that list of employees, you said all of them had been with you a long time except for the driver. I had my assistant Bernie Katzenbaum start doing a background check on him since you said he's your newest employee. He turns out to be a very interesting man."

"How so?"

"Did you know he overstayed his green card and never applied for citizenship?"

"So he's not here legally."

"And his name isn't Alex Abrams. It's Alexie Abramova. And he wasn't born in Ohio. He was born in 1974 in Kyrgyzstan when it was still part of the old Soviet Union. He arrived in this country twenty-one years later."

"What's he doing here?"

"What he *was* doing was working part-time at a gym in Los Angeles. On the side, he did some driving for a guy connected with the Soros Documentary Fund, which makes left-wing documentaries. The leadership of the Fund was eventually turned over to Robert Redford's Sundance Institute. Virgil Goldstein made one of the Soros documentaries about how the war on terror is a fraud."

"Ah, the Goldstein connection. He sends me a driver. His rebellious daughter decides to stick one in his eye by supporting me."

"The fact that Verbena Cross is a headliner for the fund-raiser has caused attendance to soar, as I'm sure you're aware."

"I could have gone either way on that," Ferrin said, wiggling his hand, "but if she's telling the truth that she's not going to say anything incendiary, just going to show feminist support for a woman whose private secret has been outed, I guess it's poetic justice."

"Bernie, by the way, talked with the author of that article in *Marie Claire*. The reporter wouldn't reveal her sources, which was no surprise, but Bernie's convinced the woman talked to no one we've interviewed -- no one, that is, with direct knowledge. And the reporter, oddly enough, isn't Canadian at all, as we'd thought. She used to work for a talent agency in Hollywood. And she's not a woman either, strictly speaking. She's trans-gendered."

"Another Hollywood connection."

"I imagine your staff kept a copy of Alex-Alexie's passport. When you get a chance, could somebody get me a copy?"

"I'll also get you a copy of the glowing recommendation from Governor Schwarzenegger's office."

"Now that takes some chutzpah, falsifying a recommendation like that."

"You think it was ginned up so I'd think a fellow conservative recommended him?"

"Fellow conservative? I don't know a lot about politics, but Lily doesn't think the Austrian immigrant is very conservative."

"Touché. A RINO."

"A what?"

"Republican in name only."

"I'll remember that. I didn't know about the Governor's recommendation, but now that I've heard about it, I'd bet it's fake."

"Suspicious as all that may be, Alex-Alexie couldn't be the leaker because he doesn't know squat about my family. We can check the records, but he's never been past the waiting room in my downtown office. He waits in the car. And he's never been in this house. He shares an apartment nearby with a couple of other guys. Besides, he could look all day and all night for records about

Poppy's -- well, her medical condition -- but he wouldn't find a thing anywhere. There are no records that I know about -- even at the hospital, as you've confirmed."

"Does he know Jerry Lee?"

The two men looked at each other. Coming to the same realization simultaneously, they spoke in chorus. "Phil Coker."

"I know from my visit to Jerry Lee that Phil knows all about Poppy's miscarriage," Tom continued. "He also said something strange -- about how Poppy was given a special tea, like 'that other girl,' whoever that was. So there's been pillow talk."

Ferrin stood the putter in a corner and returned to his leather desk chair. "Pillow talk. There's an image that'll make you go blind."

"If Alexie Abramova knows anybody, it's Phil. If there are millions leaving Goldstein's pocket for Florida, it's not to make a movie with Coker but to smear you and support Mullett. And Phil's not paying whatever debt he owes to Jerry Lee, so whatever money is flowing from California, it isn't landing in Phil's pocket."

Ferrin looked at his watch. "You need to call your wife about this golf date?"

"Give me a few seconds."

"Tell you what. Ride with me and you'll get a good look at Alexie Abramova."

"Before we go, let's just sum up. As to the leaker, we've eliminated everybody but Jerry Lee's boyfriend and your Russian driver. As to the missing persons connected with your wife, we haven't found Dewey but we found his car in the pond behind the Beaudry Funeral Home. Nor did we find Nicky Sue, but we know Jonah owned and Verlin drove an Impala that sounds uncannily like the one Paul Rossetti saw Nicky Sue get into the night she disappeared."

"And Jerry Lee holds my Irish family in contempt!" He laughed. "I wonder if she'd be interested in flying lessons."

19

I Was Channeling Jonah
Saturday, April 22, 2006

At the same time that Tom was reporting to Ferrin McBride in Port Royal, Molly was reporting to Jerry Lee and Poppy. They were seated in cushioned wicker armchairs on the second-story veranda of Beaudry Hall, overlooking the gardens. Maria brought them sweet tea in vintage drinking glasses and a plate of homemade miniature sticky buns. Molly talked about inconsequential things for awhile: the long drive from Marco Island to Little Gap in Dee's Mustang, then the drive to Hilton Head, the waterside hotel room they found in Harbour Town, her mother's caustic comments about Carl, the background she'd gathered for a piece about Poppy. She left out the part about looking at the house where Jerry Lee grew up.

After filling in the details of her interviews with Betty Darling and Paul Rossetti and Tom's interviews with Dr. Lindstrom and Minnie Betz, she announced her conclusion. "Whoever told that *Marie Claire* reporter about a so-called abortion is still unknown to Tom and me. It wasn't anybody either of us met in South Carolina."

"I don't believe it," Jerry Lee said. "You just didn't ask the right questions."

"Jerry Lee, for goodness' sake." Poppy threw her mother a sharp glance. "Give the woman some credit."

"You'll never convince me you didn't do it," Jerry Lee said, aiming a kabuki smile at Molly. "You have everything to gain: a story to write, another book for the best-seller list, a little vacation with your mother at my son-in-law's expense." Her soft, half-joking tone and Southern accent did nothing to lessen the sting of the unfair accusation.

Poppy stood up. "We're going to leave if you keep talking like this."

"Sit down, Shugah. And that Impala Saul told you about."

"Paul."

"Whatever. You sure he saw the car he claimed to see?"

"I have no way of knowing," Molly said, "but he was very specific. 1959 two-door hardtop, big fins, reddish color, whitewalls. He saw two people in the front seat; he thought at least the driver was a man."

"That car sounds like one my husband owned. Jonah's was an Impala, a '58 or '59, only it wasn't redd*ish*. It was true red, Roman red they called it, with a white top. He'd kept several of the cars from his youth in perfect condition. Sometimes he took Verlin for a ride in them. My brother's very childlike about things like car rides, you know."

"Well," Poppy said, thinking aloud. "We know it wasn't Dad and Verlin in the car Paul saw because Dad died several years before the pageant."

"For God's sake, Poppy, I wasn't suggesting anything of the kind. The car Saul saw in Greenville couldn't have been Jonah's. That would be absurd. The coincidence is striking, though. And hearing about that lovely old Impala brought back memories, that's all."

"Did Verlin ever learn to drive?" Molly asked her hostess.

"No."

"Jerry Lee, he did so," Poppy scolded. "Whenever you and Dad were busy, Uncle Verlin drove me wherever I needed to go." She looked at Molly. "We lived more than a mile out of town, so unless I rode my bike, I needed a ride."

"I didn't mean Verlin never drove . . . just not often. And he's all done with that part of his life now. His eyes are so bad, I don't think he could pass a vision test any more."

"Did you go see the place where I grew up?" Poppy asked Molly.

"No, but Tom did. It's being torn down, as I'm sure you know."

"It is?"

"So that great husband of yours doesn't tell you everything." Jerry Lee looked inordinately pleased.

Poppy faced her mother. "I know the property's being developed but I thought the funeral home was going to be turned into a clubhouse or something."

"I told Ferrin I wanted it torn down to the ground, and he gave me no argument at all. It would have cost more to gut and modernize that old place than build something brand new, and it's situated wrong anyway, right where the main access road will be cut."

"So the carriage house and garage are gone too?"

Jerry Lee nodded.

"What did you do with Dad's old cars?"

"Sold most of them."

"But not all?"

"Well, speaking of the Impala . . . I kept that because Verlin had a fit about it. He always loved it. Now he polishes it every week. Keeps him busy."

"How about we go see it?"

"I'd like that," Molly said. "But there's one more car to tell you about."

"What car?" Jerry Lee frowned.

"While Tom was on the site, the grading crew found an old rusted car in the pond."

"What?" Poppy exclaimed. "A car in our pond?"

"Why in hell was anybody digging around in the pond, may I ask?" Jerry Lee's voice had risen an octave. "It's going to be the stormwater retention pond for the development, a lake feature."

"Tom said they were draining it so they could dredge it to

make it bigger and deeper. It'll be stocked with fish and be big enough that the residents can put paddle boats on it."

"Ferrin swore it wouldn't be touched." Jerry Lee's face burned bright red.

"Well, it was. When the pond was drained, they found a '38 Plymouth."

Poppy stared at her mother. "A '38 Ply- . . . you mean Dewey's car?"

"I don't believe it." Jerry Lee clutched her chest.

"I think Tom told Ferrin to get it back from the Sheriff if he could."

"Did he get it back?" Jerry Lee asked, her voice rising.

"I think so."

"Was there any . . . anything in the car?" Poppy asked.

"No," Jerry Lee blurted out before Molly could respond. "Nothing. Anyway, that's what I'm assuming."

"You mean like a body?" Molly asked, looking at her friend.

Poppy nodded.

"Not that I know of."

"Of course there wasn't a body," Jerry Lee said in a quieter voice. "You girls watch too many crime shows."

"How would Dewey's car end up in the pond?" Poppy looked at her mother.

"How would I know?" Jerry Lee turned on Molly. "When did the car get into the pond? Or how? Does anybody know?"

"You'd have to ask Tom. I've told you all I know."

"That stupid boy must have driven it, or pushed it, into the pond himself before he left town."

"But why, Jerry Lee?" Poppy was determined to get an answer.

"Maybe it was Dewey's parting gesture, like cutting off your nose to spite your face." Jerry Lee mimicked a boy's voice. "'If I can't marry your daughter, then see what you've made me do.'"

"Who told him that . . . that he couldn't marry me?"

Jerry Lee gave her daughter a hard look. "Are you going to sit here and tell me you're not better off married to Ferrin than Dewey?"

"I repeat: Who told him he couldn't marry me?"

"Jonah did."

"He was dead when Dewey left!" Poppy practically shouted.

"Hush your mouth, girl. I was channeling Jonah. He'd never want you to marry beneath yourself. Dewey was a farmer's son and was never going to amount to anything. Ferrin may not be all that, but at least he's ambitious, and his family has money. Even if it is trailer park money, it was worth waiting for."

"So you told Dewey he wasn't going to marry me, is that it?"

"I did what any mother would do."

"When did you get the chance to do that?"

"You expect me to remember that? For heaven's sake, it was almost twenty years ago."

"Did you put his car in the pond?"

Jerry Lee clutched her chest again. "How in the world would I do that, Shugah?"

"That's not an answer."

"No. I didn't put his damn car in the pond. How's that for an answer?"

"Where is Dewey? Where'd he go after you talked to him? Did you arrange something?"

"No, I didn't arrange anything. I hope he's in hell. But Molly says his own mother doesn't think he's dead, so if I had to guess, he was dishonorably discharged from the Marines and is living on the street somewhere, cadging money for booze and sleeping on grates, probably faking some war-related illness. That's my guess. What's yours?" Jerry Lee put her head down to her knees and took deep breaths.

"What's the matter?" Molly asked.

"Heart," Jerry Lee whispered. "Poppy, get my nitro."

After throwing her mother a doubtful look, Poppy got up and left the veranda. Jerry Lee raised her head high enough to watch her daughter enter the house. Then she suddenly stood up, but instead of following her daughter, she staggered toward the railing. Molly bolted out of her chair to steady the woman. Suddenly, Jerry Lee fell hard, with her full weight hitting Molly in her hip and shoulder, shoving Molly to the edge of the veranda. As Molly screamed and scrambled to get a purchase on the balustrade to right herself, she felt herself losing her balance. Just as she started to wrench herself upright, Jerry Lee fell against her again, this time so hard Molly lost her grip and fell over the railing.

* * * * *

She woke up hours later in the hospital. Poppy and Sara were sitting in the guest chairs. "Where's Jerry Lee?" Molly asked in a fearful voice.

"On a different floor," Poppy answered. "She's recovering from another of her so-called heart attacks. Her cardiologist is trying to decide what really happened to her."

Molly checked her hands; she still had her rings on. She checked her ear lobes. Her earrings were in place. Then she stuck out her swollen ankle. "Where's the ankle bracelet Carl gave me?"

Poppy got up to look.

"I don't know. Were you wearing it?"

"I was. I don't want to lose it."

"Maybe the EMTs took it off because your ankle was swelling. Or maybe it dropped in the hedge. I'll ask Verlin to look for it." Poppy stroked her friend's forehead. "That's the least of your worries, I'd say. Fortunately, you landed in the arborvitae hedge Verlin's so proud of. You missed a wrought iron stake by a couple of inches, just short of a slate walkway. But for that miracle of a perfect landing, you'd have had more than a few cuts and bruises. You were lucky, my friend."

Despite the circumstances, Molly smiled. "I used to be a cheerleader, you know. I know how to stick a landing."

"If you'd just been twirling a fire baton as you flew through the air, the judges would have been dazzled. As it is, you can put to rest forever the idea that you didn't deserve to win the beauty pageant."

They laughed until they cried.

20

The False Queen
Saturday, April 22, 2006

Verlin liked Zodiac signs, but he'd never found any before. This one was a gold disc with a stylized lion in relief, attached on either side to a fine gold chain. He'd found it on the woman who broke his hedges. So she was a Leo. That meant that the woman who'd worn it viewed herself as the king of the jungle. Well, not a king, but a queen. Jerry Lee wouldn't like her because she was a Leo too. His sister would never tolerate another queen in her kingdom. She'd view this woman as a false queen who needed to be driven out.

When he heard the woman scream, he was in the Nike garden, pruning the *Jasminum nudiflorum*. He dropped his pruning shears and ran towards the house to see what the screaming was about.

He noticed the cleft in the arborvitae hedge before he focused on the woman lying in it. He was very upset that his precious hedge was broken. But then he realized that the woman might be broken too because she was lying at an odd angle. Her eyes were closed and she wasn't moving. He put his ear to her chest. She was alive.

He wanted to get her out of his hedge, but she was too heavy for him to lift out and lower onto the ground, so he took her hand in his. He'd comfort her until help came.

Then he noticed the chain around her ankle. He was

mesmerized by the lion disc glinting in the sun. The other women were running around on the veranda, making loud, useless noises, paying no attention to him. From the name the women were screaming, he realized the woman in the hedge was called Molly. He'd seen her before.

He let go of Molly's hand, unhooked the ankle chain, and slipped it into the pocket of his overalls, before the women reached the garden. He could see the woman's ankle was swelling. He'd done her a favor. He was again holding the false queen's hand when the ambulance came.

That night, he marked his diary entry with his own hand-drawn version of Leo. His Mason jar of treasures was getting so full he'd have to find another.

Part Two

"O divine art of subtlety and secrecy! Through you
we learn to be invisible, through you inaudible;
and hence we can hold the enemy's fate in our hands."

Sun Tzu, The Art of War

"Enter through the narrow gate.
For wide is the gate and broad is the road
that leads to destruction, and many enter through it.
But small is the gate and narrow the road that leads
to life, and only a few find it."

Jesus speaking, Matthew 7: 13, 14

21

That's Our Story
Monday, April 24, 2006

Matt Bearsall relished his new assignment from his old friend Tom Lawton. Matt, the first black Chief of Detectives for the Marco Island Police Department, retired in 2005, having reached the age of 65. Before he moved to Marco, Matt had worked with Tom in Naples when both were plainclothes detectives. In those days, Tom was the junior officer whom Matt trained and mentored. Now that he was retired, Matt found himself in the anomalous position of answering to Tom when he was lucky enough to get the occasional assignment.

Not that he needed the money. His wife, Doris, a Spellman graduate whom he'd married a few months after graduating from Morehouse College in Atlanta, was very canny with money. Though they'd graduated in 1962 when black rebellion and far-left politics were all the rage, neither went that direction. Doris, a teacher, came to hate public schools for dumbing down the curriculum and paying useless administrators more than teachers. All three of their children were therefore sent to parochial school. When Doris left teaching, she began studying financial markets and investing their money. As a result of the tidy little fortune she had amassed, she opposed capital gains taxes, welfare programs, and big government spending. As a devoted Catholic, she also opposed abortion and gay marriage.

Matt's views of politics were more nuanced -- or, as Doris claimed, more conflicted. All his life he'd served in government, first in the Marines, then in various police departments. Government was essential to national defense and public order. Still, he'd seen enough abuse of power to distrust anyone who craved it. Reluctant to openly oppose the commonly accepted view that African-Americans must support liberal politicians, neither he nor Doris was politically active, though privately they listened to Walter Williams. Their occasional modest contributions to a senatorial, gubernatorial, or presidential campaign were therefore never advertised, even to family or friends.

The assignment to infiltrate the Myron Mullett Congressional campaign was, to say the least, intriguing. Posing as a liberal required no acting skills, for everyone, black and white, simply assumed Matt was liberal. He didn't have to say a thing. And working his way to the inside was no problem either, for Harley Wangle, Mullett's press secretary, was also a Morehouse alumnus, though seventeen years younger than Matt. Both had been firsts -- Matt as the chief of detectives for an important police department, Harley as the director of an important State agency. Both had served in the Marines, though Matt secretly harbored the disdain of a well-regarded officer for an enlisted man with a spotty record.

To arrange a meeting with Harley, Matt shamelessly invoked the brotherhood of Morehouse alumni who'd served in the Marines and dropped references to a powerful mutual friend in the state legislature. Matt hinted that he could serve the campaign in an unusual way: gathering intel on the conservative candidate.

Their first meeting was at Mullett's headquarters in a space Wangle called his office, a small, windowless area marked off from a big featureless room by two walls and a third formed of file cabinets and stacked boxes. Electronic gadgets littered Wangle's desk. Matt, a big man but still fit and trim who, except for a brief period in his teens, had always worn his hair closely cropped, noted with disapproval Harley's paunch, his disheveled appearance, and his glistening Jheri curl.

"Tell me about yourself, brother," Harley said. Matt wondered if he had ADD. Harley was constantly squirming, checking his BlackBerry, scribbling notes on a pad, glancing past the file cabinets, smiling inappropriately. His crossed leg bounced incessantly. It was all Matt could do not to bark an order to sit still, wipe the smile off his face, and pay attention.

When Matt gave the man a short history of his education and work experience, Harley smiled. "And your politics?"

"What do you think?"

"I hear you, brother." He tapped his pencil on the desk. "Tell you what. We hear a famous actress is supporting McBride. She's going to be appearing at his fundraiser in a couple weeks. Any chance you could attend? We'll pay the charge, which reportedly has risen to two thousand dollars a plate, to get you in. You married?"

"Yes."

"Take your wife, on us."

Matt nodded. "Who's the actress?"

"Ever hear of Virgil Goldstein?"

Matt pretended he hadn't.

"Makes great movies with the right slant, if you know what I mean. Remember *The Ho Chi Minh Trail?*"

"I do. Brings back memories of the Sixties." *Bad memories of a war I barely escaped.*

"Virgil makes documentaries for liberal causes. He has a a daughter, Verbena Cross. She's got a new movie coming out, something about the blues, can't remember the title. Anyway, Virgil's upset. He's helping us out a lot, doesn't like what his daughter is doing for McBride."

"So what can I do?"

"Get some dirt on her. Discredit her."

"I don't mean this disrespectfully, but why discredit her? Isn't she a pretty minor player, all things considered?" Matt studied Harley's face. He'd have to find out what kind of grade point average the character behind the desk had managed to maintain at Morehouse. Harley didn't seem to be the sharpest tool in the drawer. "And do you really believe Virgil wants to find dirt on his own daughter? Unless you talked to Virgil himself, I'd discount that part of the assignment."

"Hadn't thought of that." Harley stood up, shook himself, and sat back down. "Well, we've got to do something. Hollywood's our exclusive bailiwick. We don't want that shithead McBride connected with the film industry's glamor and influence. You can't believe how much the Hollywood crowd is giving campaigns like ours nowadays. Money, ads, PR, even people."

"People?"

Harley looked around as if ferreting out spies. "We've got a man right next to McBride, he doesn't even know it, the sanctimonious son-of-a-bitch."

"Really?" A look of disapproval stole across Matt's face. He was used to profanity, but hearing every other sentenced larded with it was more than he could stand.

"Hollywood and government are like this," Harley said, holding up crossed fingers. "You know much about international politics?"

Matt shook his head.

"Well, brother, you'll learn. Ever since the Soviet Union broke up, this country's been infiltrated with apparatchiks from the old USSR looking to transform this country into the liberal paradise they lost. They like unions and rough demonstrations. They cook elections. They make sure people vote early and often, Chicago-style. We use them."

"Is there somebody I should recognize as on"-- Matt hesitated, oddly reluctant to betray his own views so baldly -- "our side?"

"McBride's driver. He's our guy. You heard that story about his wife's abortion? Alexie got that, don't ask me how." He put his hands on either side of his mouth and said in a hoarse whisper, "Coker. You know who he is?"

"Hollywood actor."

"Lives with McBride's mother-in-law. He'd tell anything to get on Goldstein's good side. Wants to make a comeback. But you didn't hear that from me."

"Let me get this straight. Coker told McBride's driver who

told Goldstein about Mrs. McBride's abortion. Is that it?"

"Man, let's not spell it out. I thought getting something like that on Goldstein's daughter might be just the thing, but maybe you're right. Could backfire." Harley wiped his sweaty forehead. "Forget Verbena Cross. But how about McBride himself? He's a rich man, got to have done some dirty deals, wouldn't you say? He's been in Washington for two years, voted against every tax increase ever proposed. Does he pay his taxes? He preaches family values. Is there an intern with knee burns? What about his brother who runs the family company? Using non-union labor in their factories or constructions crews? They hiding all their money offshore?"

"I guess your man would know about that last one." Matt caught his error. Mullett was now nominally his man as well.

"Whoa, brother. Don't believe everything you hear. What Myron does is totally on the up-and-up." He laughed without humor and winked. "That's our story and we're sticking to it."

"Got you."

"You think you can get inside that Bible-thumper's campaign?"

"I wouldn't have offered my services if I couldn't."

"Mind telling me about your connection?"

"I would mind. With respect, the fewer people who know about my connections, the better for your . . . our man Mullett. But if you see me hanging around with the big-wigs in the opposition party, you'll look the other way, knowing that's what I've got to do to be effective."

Harley stood up and held out his hand. "Hate to cut this short, but I've got work to do. My assistant will get you set up."

Before Matt left the building, he found the restroom and washed his hands over and over as if he'd just touched carrion. When he looked in the mirror, the man staring back at him was James Armistead, the black Revolutionary War patriot who worked as a double agent for General Lafayette. Like Armistead, he was now in a dirty business. Heroes often were, though Matt didn't think of himself in that exalted company. He just wanted to stay as clean as he could.

22

One Foggy Night
Wednesday, April 26, 2006

Jerry Lee breathed a sigh of relief. She was feeling fine, having been discharged from the hospital Sunday morning. She hadn't had a heart attack after all, the cardiologist concluded. Probably another angina episode. There appeared to be no damage to her heart. Claiming that her old nitro had been reduced to powder, Jerry Lee wangled a new prescription for a fresh vial of pills.

Molly, she knew, had suffered no more than bruises, cuts, a chipped elbow, a sprained ankle and shoulder, and a broken thumb. Jerry Lee had wanted the woman dead. Unaccountably, Lady Luck had made her face to shine on that deceitful woman.

Of course, Jerry Lee reluctantly admitted to herself, it was just possible Molly and Tom were telling the truth, that no one leaked that story about Poppy except somebody very close to her. By the process of elimination, taking into consideration the risks and benefits to each potential leaker, she concluded that Phil was the culprit, and it might have something to do with the muscular man in spandex he secretly met on Wednesday nights outside the carriage house gate.

Time, then, to try another tack. On Wednesday night, she was ready. Everything was going as planned.

Phil was out of the way. He had taken her Cadillac around 10 o'clock, ostensibly to attend another unadvertised wine tasting at a specialty shop. She politely asked him if afterwards he would drive to the home of a Marco Island wine dealer who'd acquired a case of *premier cru* claret from Bordeaux. The dealer, who was secretive about how he'd acquired the valuable wine, refused to keep it in his shop; he'd only deliver it to her or Phil at his house. He asked that they pick up the wine after ten but before midnight Wednesday, cash in hand, no receipt. Jerry Lee did not inform Phil that there was no secretive wine dealer, there was no wine, and the address was false. The bastard deserved to waste his time.

As soon as Jerry Lee heard her boyfriend pull out of the garage, she ran upstairs to her dressing room, where she removed her makeup, slicked her hair into a tight bun, and donned a kangol like the one Phil affected when he was trying to be cool. She borrowed one of Phil's less inflammatory t-shirts and paired it with a pair of plain black trousers. Before she descended to the garage, she kissed one of Poppy's beauty pageant trophies, a good-luck ritual she'd engaged in for many years, and grabbed a bottle of water from the kitchen.

Once in the garage, she placed duct tape over the license plate on Phil's car. She despised Phil's Prius for its political correctness and lethargic performance, but tonight it was perfect. She drove around the corner and idled at the intersection with the palm-lined side street that ran alongside her house. Not seeing her Cadillac but spotting the bike under the streetlight, she then rounded another block to wait until the bike owner returned with Phil. She only had to wait about a half hour.

Once Phil had dropped off his passenger and moved on down the street, presumably on his way to find the non-existent wine dealer on Marco, she watched the spandex guy mount his ride and set off for parts unknown. She followed the biker at a discreet distance, keeping his red reflectors in sight. Eventually, she realized he was heading toward Port Royal, where her daughter lived. She looked briefly to heaven, thanking the gods of darkness for a ground-hugging fog and only a sliver of moon and for leading her to a part of town she knew like the back of her hand.

About a mile before reaching the McBride mansion, when

the street was clear of traffic, she flipped on her brights and sped up. When she was a few yards behind the biker, he turned around to glare at her, giving her the finger. She smiled mockingly at the futility of his rude gesture. He had no idea what he was in for. Without another thought, she gunned the engine, swerving sharply to clip the biker before he could head to the curb. The right front headlight shattered. The sound of breaking glass, crunching metal, and the impact of body on machine caused her heart to hammer in her chest. Some piece of the bike seemed to have attached itself to her car. She could hear it hitting the pavement.

She found herself almost out of breath. Hitting a living body was so much more personal than she anticipated. Poison was cleaner, more remote. She could pretend someone else had done it. When she reached for her purse, she realized she'd forgotten her nitro.

Fighting to regain her composure, she glanced in her passenger side mirror, seeing no more than a dark heap of man and machine splayed along the curb. It was too dark and foggy, and she was traveling too fast, to tell whether the man was moving or not. Then she glanced in her driver's side mirror, noticing, for the first time, a car following her about half a block behind. Thank God she'd obscured the license plate with duct tape.

After a moment of hesitation, she roared away. When she reached the bottom of Port Royal, she careened into a private drive as far as she could and doused her lights. Leaving the motor running, she got out to see if she could dislodge whatever had attached itself to the Prius, but in the dark she couldn't see it. She got back in the car. After a few minutes of waiting, her heart hammering, she made her way out of Port Royal by a route that allowed her to avoid Spyglass Lane. Even then, though no cars seemed to be following her, she took a circuitous route home, randomly turning corners, left, then right, then left again, as if still eluding the headlights she'd seen behind her. The clickety-click, clickety-click of the stowaway metal hitting the streets rattled her nerves.

After she parked in the garage as close to the back and

passenger-side walls as possible, she tore the duct tape off the license plate, then raced back upstairs. Since the damage to the car was on the front passenger side, Phil might not spot it until after he'd driven the car again. She'd claim it must have happened to him in a parking lot and rail against nasty drivers who didn't leave notes taking responsibility for their accidents.

After reapplying her makeup and letting her hair down, she swallowed an Ambien and crawled into bed so when Phil got home she'd appear to be asleep. In fact, she was so exhausted that she fell asleep immediately and didn't hear him come upstairs.

For Phil's part, when he reached the master bedroom, he was so furious at his fruitless errand that for a second he entertained the idea of beating his Southern belle to death in her sleep. He actually picked up one of Poppy's trophies and silently cocked his arm over his lover's head. He waited for her to move or say something, but she lay there like a dead woman. It took all his will power not to bring the trophy down on her skull. If she'd moved an inch, he'd have killed her.

Instead, after a few seconds of indecision, he took a deep breath and replaced the trophy. Knowing he needed to get out of there before he did something he couldn't undo, he crept back downstairs to the back garden to smoke a little weed, knock back a few Tequila shots, and cool off. He woke in the morning, stiff and hungover, on the bench in Nike's garden. His mouth tasted as if he'd eaten a laundry basket full of socks, and he was shivering. The nightmare in which he kept falling off the hill crowned with the famous Hollywood sign seemed to have played through his head all night long.

23

Trespass
Wednesday, April 26, 2006

Again on Wednesday night, Verlin left the carriage house, where he'd been sitting in the Impala, pretending to drive it, and walked to the gate. He saw the biker get into his sister's Cadillac. Since Phil drove the Cadillac on Wednesday nights, he wondered why Jerry Lee didn't come to the gate to watch with him. He'd reminded her that morning, just as she'd instructed last week, but in response she just said maybe it was time.

"Time for what?" he asked.

"Oh, never mind, Verlin. Go back to your buttons and books. I think it's time for me to stop dithering and start doing something."

He didn't know whether that meant she would join him or not at the carriage gate, but her tone alerted him that somebody was in trouble. He'd heard that decisive tone before when Jonah put his foot down about the pageants, when Poppy was sneaking out with Dewey, and when it was common knowledge Poppy would lose to the sweet little pianist from Little Gap.

So, after waiting a few minutes after the Cadillac disappeared, and without lighting his special cigarette, he made his way, very quietly, to the side of the house, where he could see the courtyard. When he saw Jerry Lee leave in Phil's car, wearing Phil's hat, he decided Phil must be in trouble.

With a key his sister didn't know he possessed, he opened

the side door to the garage, crept through the corridor running alongside the wine room, and reached the stairs to the kitchen. Once on the second floor, he crept to the narrow back staircase, the one used by the servants. He knew Maria had left for the day. Niall would be smoking a pipe in his garrett suite at the other end of the house, watching the shows he liked, the food network and reruns of his favorite soap operas on the BBC.

When he reached the bedroom floor, Verlin hurried down the corridor, hugging the shadows along the wall, to the master suite. The room was dark but he knew the way to Phil's dressing room. Once there, he turned on the overhead light and looked around. He knew it pretty much by heart, but Phil was a bit messy, so things were not always where they should be. He wanted a souvenir, something small and valuable.

He examined a set of onyx buttons for a tuxedo shirt, and though buttons were always attractive, he'd never seen Phil wear them. They meant nothing. Then he fingered a pair of gold cufflinks bearing Phil's sign of the Zodiac, Scorpio. He hadn't seen Phil wear those either, but *Arachnida* was very tempting. After mating, the female scorpion sometimes ate the male. The venom of some species was so toxic it could even kill humans. Legend had it that if a scorpion was cornered, it would sting itself to death with its own tail. Of course, Verlin thought, Phil would be a scorpion. The symbol was so riveting that he would draw it to mark the day's entry in his diary.

Before moving on to other treasures, Verlin took a moment to marvel at the unbelievable luck of finding two Zodiac signs in a couple of days. The lion and the scorpion. In a fight, which would win? He'd like to see that contest.

He put the links aside and moved on to the collection of campaign buttons. The slogans, however, meant nothing, and most of the faces were too scary for his taste. All but one that is. The face of Jimmy made him smile. It looked a bit like him. Even the sweater Jimmy was wearing resembled the beige cardigan Jerry Lee made him wear for dress-up. But the campaign button was plastic-coated, and the pin at the back was bent. It was old and yellowed, so it wasn't special. Still, he knew Phil valued this collection, so he set Jimmy aside with the Zodiac cuff links.

Finally, he came to a hook from which hung various pendants, some on leather cords, some on chains. Some of the cords showed a lot of sweaty wear, and some of the chains were tarnished. But one of the pendants was a bright silver medallion carved into a peace sign, a symbol he liked because it look like an upside-down, three-branched tree, or Neptune's trident. He had no idea why an upside-down tree or trident represented peace, but then many symbols he was familiar with, especially runes, made little sense.

He sniffed the braided leather cord. It smelled like Phil. He slipped the pendant around his neck and checked himself in a full-length mirror. Very nice. He'd never owned a necklace before. Even with his overalls, it made him look dangerously cool.

With a start, he caught sight of a little clock on a dresser and realized he'd been in the dressing room over an hour. He took off the pendant, scooped up the cuff links and campaign button, and slipped all three items into the pocket of his overalls. After turning off the overhead light, crossing the bedroom, and carefully closing the door to the master suite, he made his way through the hall, hugging the wall, to the servants' staircase. He hurried down the uncarpeted steps, wishing he'd worn sneakers, trying not to make noise. After a hasty detour to the kitchen, where he grabbed a beer out of the refrigerator, he returned to the ground floor, felt his way in the dark past the wine room, and left. But before he could lock the outside door, he heard a car entering the courtyard.

He crept around the side of the house, in time to see Phil's Prius return. The passenger headlight was out, the mirror hanging by a thread, the fender dented. Jerry Lee must have driven somewhere. Where had she been? What had she done? Why had she hurt the car?

He crept back to the side door, which he locked, and returned to the carriage house gate, but he knew he'd taken too long to see the drop-off of the biker in spandex. He was disappointed but not surprised to see that the bicycle was no longer chained to the lamp post.

His heart skipped a beat as it suddenly hit him how careless he'd been. Phil could have returned while he was still in the house. The dreadful idea that, by losing track of time, he might have been caught in the house made Verlin so nervous he didn't have the strength in his legs to make it all the way to the Nike garden. He sat down on a rock near the potting shed to smoke his special cigarette.

After awhile, he calmed down. From the shadows, he kept his eye on Jerry Lee's bedroom. Strangely, no lights came on. No lights came on anywhere in the house. His sister didn't come out to her bedroom balcony for a nightcap. He knew Jerry Lee liked the dark, but normally her light was on for an hour before she went to bed, and normally she sat on her balcony awhile before going to sleep. Fortunately, she was a creature of habit. He treasured habits because they made it easier to invade people's lives without their knowing it. The change in Jerry Lee's habits meant something important had happened.

Verlin allowed his mind to drift to the objects he'd found. They were his now. He put his hand in his pocket to cup them, mindful not to stick himself with the pin on the campaign button. He took deep satisfaction in having anticipated the actor's downfall. Though he didn't know what form the downfall would take, he knew that once Phil was gone from their life, there might not be a way to retrieve a suitable souvenir, something where the man's soul, when it finally left his body, could reside until the last trumpet sounded.

Just before he was ready to go in to his apartment, he heard Phil clop down the stairs to the garden. Verlin crept close enough to see Phil sitting on Nicky Sue's bench. Phil was drinking from a bottle that glinted in the dim light and smoking cannablis. He wanted to tell Phil to get off that bench -- his bench. The man was trespassing.

But something in the air prompted Verlin to keep his mouth shut. He comforted himself with the knowledge that he now possessed some of Phil's treasures. He knew Phil's car had been hurt and hidden in the garage. Phil might be trespassing, but he,

Verlin, had the upper hand for once.

After spying on Phil for awhile, Verlin made his way back to the carriage house so he could make his diary entry before he got too sleepy.

* * * * *

When the big black man appeared in the garden early the next morning, not dressed like a cop but acting like one, Verlin was puzzled but pleased. Now Phil would have to get off Nicky Sue's bench . . . Verlin's bench. Maybe Phil would get a ticket for trespassing.

But neither man paid any attention to him.

24

Too Many Kangols
Wednesday, April 26, 2006

When the hit-and-run Prius sped away, Matt Bearsall wanted to follow it to see who it belonged to, but there was a man down. First things first. He pulled within a few yards of the biker lying on the curb of Spyglass Lane and walked over to see if he could find a pulse. He did, but it was faint. Though the man wasn't moving, he made a faint groaning sound from time to time. There was blood on the curb. Matt was afraid to move the man for fear of a spinal injury.

On a pre-paid mobile phone, Matt dialed 911 to report a hit-and-run bike accident with injuries. Though he was asked to stay on the line, he turned off his phone, got back into his car, made a u-turn in the street, and worked his way back to the highway to Marco.

The second call he placed was to the emergency number he'd been given for the campaign staff. He was told McBride was in D.C., not returning until Thursday night.

Finally, he called Tom Lawton.

"Matt, it's damn near midnight. This better be good."

"It's good and it's bad. The Russian I was tailing just got hit by a car less than a mile from McBride's house. I called 911 to alert the authorities. We've got to talk to McBride immediately."

"By the Russian, do you mean McBride's driver?"

"Yes. I couldn't see the number on the license plate but the car that clipped him was a blue Prius that I tailed from near Beaudry Hall. The driver was wearing a kangol, but I was never in a position to see the driver's face, so I can't say who was at the wheel."

"Kangol. Are we talking about the flat cap Samuel L. Jackson wears? Kind of a modified beret?"

"That's a kangol."

"You don't think the driver you saw with the kangol was Phil? That's his signature headwear if I'm not mistaken."

"I don't know who it was. I saw Alexie get picked up by a black Cadillac across from Jerry Lee's carriage gate. Because the windows are tinted, I couldn't see the driver clearly, but I assumed the kangol I spotted in the Cadillac meant it was Phil. The Cadillac drove to a public park, idled awhile, then dropped the Russian back at his bike. When I saw a Prius follow the biker, out of curiosity I followed along. As I said, I assumed the driver of the Cadillac was Phil, but when I saw the kangol in the Prius, I wasn't sure who it was or what had happened. There was no time for Phil to change cars, though, so it had to be two different people."

"Do we know if Jerry Lee or Phil owns a Prius?"

"No, but I'm going to find out."

"What are you going to tell the cops?"

"If I were still at the scene, I'd tell the truth. I saw a blue Prius, couldn't read the license plate or see the driver's face. From half a block behind, I saw the Prius speed up and then the biker go flying to the curb, but since I wasn't in front, I didn't see the direct impact."

"If you were still at the scene?"

"I left after I called 911. I'm on my way back to Marco now. I don't want to explain why I was tailing the Russian or who wanted him tailed. Besides, I wasn't in a position to see the car clip the biker or the face of the Prius driver, and I couldn't make out the license plate. It's foggy and dark, and I was half a block behind. All I can really say for sure is I saw too many kangols in one night."

Tom chuckled. "The Case of Too Many Kangols. That's a

new one." He cleared his throat. "Some way, I'll find McBride ASAP and talk to you tomorrow morning. This is going to be complicated."

"I'll pick you up at six tomorrow morning."

"Where are we going?"

"Beaudry Hall. By the way, brother, the next time you're tracing assets in the Caymans or chasing drug-runners in Jamaica, something simple like that, remember me, will you?"

"Matt, you know you love this stuff."

Matt harrumphed, turned off his phone, and drove home with troubled feelings. When he was a cop, he hated people who witnessed an accident and then melted into the crowd before they could be identified and questioned. In those days, citizens who didn't want to be "involved" were, in his mind, the scum of the earth. Now he was one of them, except that at least he'd called 911 to get the man some help.

Before reaching the island, he detoured to an RV park, got out a tire iron, smashed the fifteen-dollar Virgin mobile that had been activated with a ten-dollar card, wiped it clean of prints, and discarded it in a public trash basket. Tomorrow morning, using a fake name again and paying cash, he'd buy a stash of them at Best Buy.

25

Swear
Thursday, April 27, 2006

When Phil woke in Nike's garden Thursday morning, a little before sunrise, he leapt off his bench in fright, immediately wishing he'd stayed still. He clutched his head in pain. Light, movement, the sickening sweet smell of jasmine -- everything nauseated him. Especially the sight of the large black man standing near the statue, glaring at him. Verlin, running his hands down the front of his trousers and muttering to himself, stood a few yards back.

"Who the hell are you?" He switched his eyes to the troll. "Who is he, Verlin?"

Matt held out his hand. "Matt Bearsall. I'd like to take a look at your Prius."

Refusing the proffered hand, Phil barked, "I'm not selling."

So you do have a Prius, you dumb ass. "I'm not buying. I'd just like to take a look at it."

"You're not taking a look at anything, so get your black ass out of here before I call the cops."

Matt gave Phil a bemused look. *Why do Hollywood types, the diversity crowd, always notice race first? I've known Tom for ten years and the only time we ever discussed race is when he asked me why I wear sunscreen and I asked him why he didn't. Oh, and that time we were in a bar after a great collar, watching some pretentious retro thing on the overhead TV, and simultaneously remarked how much we hated Las Vegas and the Rat Pack. I told him Samy Davis, Junior was crap, and he told me Peter Lawford was the same.*

Matt brought his thoughts back to the garden. In a perfectly even tone, he said, "You don't want to think like that."

Phil wanted to sit down before he fell down but he couldn't risk losing the advantage of standing man-to-man with the stranger. "Why the hell not?"

"Because, if I leave, the cops will come with a warrant, that's why." Matt was bluffing, of course, but Phil had no clue.

"Warrant?" Phil was outraged. "Why would they do that?"

"Your hands are shaking. You have a bad night?"

"None of your business."

Matt took a step in Phil's direction and sniffed the air. "I think I smell something. Funny cigarettes, maybe."

"Stick to the subject."

"Have it your way. A blue Prius was involved in a hit-and-run accident last night. If it wasn't your car, now's the chance to prove it."

"I didn't drive the Prius last night. And I don't have to prove anything to anybody."

"Did your wife drive it?"

"She's not my wife."

"Whatever she is, did she drive the Prius last night?"

"No."

"You're sure?"

"I'm sure. She was asleep when I got home."

"Got home from where?"

"None of your fucking business."

"I'll give you thirty seconds to reconsider. But remember this, Phil Coker. Once I leave this place, I'm not coming back alone. Your fate is in your hands."

"Give me time to take a shower."

"Absolutely not. You go in that house" -- pointing up at the veranda -- "I'm out of here. You'll look back on this as the worst decision you ever made. Other than losing out to Michael Douglas."

Phil winced. Unable to keep his footing, he fell back on the bench, then with alarm watched Matt spin on his heel and start walking away.

"Wait a minute, asshole."

Matt turned and without pausing closed the few yards between him and Phil. He grabbed the neck of Phil's t-shirt. "You ever use that language with me again, Mr. Coker, and you'll be spitting teeth over that far wall from right where you're sitting."

Phil was in no shape for a physical altercation. Seething, he got up, shook himself, and started walking down the slate path around the side of the house in the direction of the garages. He turned and signaled Matt to follow him. Punching numbers into a keypad, he opened the third door from the left. "There it is. Look as long as you want." He turned to leave. "When you get done, close the door and get the hell out of here."

"If you have an ounce of self-preservation, you're staying right where you are. I want to see the front of the car."

The car was snugged up against the back wall of the garage, the passenger side less than a foot from the side wall. Matt squeezed his way around to the passenger side. "Can you turn on the overhead light?"

Phil flipped a switch. The right front fender was crumpled, the headlight broken, the passenger side mirror hanging at a crazy angle. After snapping a few pictures on his camera phone, Matt made his way to the driver's side, took out a flashlight, and laid down on the brick floor. He looked around for a few seconds. "Something's caught near the right front tire, can't see what it is. You might want to check it out for yourself."

Phil hesitated before he walked to the front of the car. Being so thin, the space wasn't as tight a fit for him as for Matt. "What the hell?" he yelled. He ran his hand over the crumpled fender. Turning to look at Matt, he continued in high volume. "Who did this to my car?"

"A driver wearing a kangol hit a guy near Port Royal. Killed him, in fact."

"When?"

"Man, you don't listen well. Last night."

"The driver was wearing a kangol?"

"Just like the one you were wearing last night."

"Yeah, but whoever was driving a Prius wearing that kind of hat last night wasn't me."

"I saw a picture of you in New Orleans, helping out the Katrina victims, handing out t-shirts as I remember. You were wearing the same kind of hat as Brad Pitt. Same two-day stubble too, looking like you were making a movie or something."

Phil slammed his fist on the back bumper. "I wasn't in this car last night."

"Maybe I'd believe you if you said where you were."

"Jerry Lee told me to go to Marco Island to pick up a case of wine from a dealer who wanted the whole thing kept secret. I took her Cadillac."

"Show me the wine and the receipt and maybe I'll believe you."

Phil put his hand on his head. "I never found the address."

"So no one can vouch for you, and you have neither the wine nor the receipt to back up your story."

"It's no story. It's the truth." He held up his hand. "Swear."

"You're a man of your word, I'm sure, but maybe the cops won't be as gullible as me."

"You keep mentioning the cops. I'm sick of hearing about them."

"You haven't asked who got killed."

"Somebody got killed?"

"That's what I said. A cyclist on an expensive bike. I keep mentioning the cops because they kind of want to get to the bottom of it, you know? They're unreasonable like that."

"You look like a cop."

"I was. Now I'm doing other things." Matt kept his eyes on Phil's. "You might be interested in the identity of the guy on the bike."

"I doubt it."

"McBride's driver."

Phil looked like Matt had landed a physical blow. "Alex?"

"You know him then."

Phil looked flustered. "No. I've seen him. Ferrin or somebody must have mentioned his name."

"Sure about that?"

"About what?"

"Not knowing him."

"Swear."

"Man, you do a lot of swearing. You taking oaths on the Bible or your mother's grave or what?"

Ignoring the taunt, Phil looked at his car. "I'm going to have to get that fixed."

"I'd wait on that, my boy, until you hear from McBride's office."

"Why?"

"Somebody's in a whole lot of trouble. Don't take any action until you know the consequences."

"I need to talk to Jerry Lee."

At that moment, Tom Lawton walked out of the front door on the veranda and bounded down the steps. Niall, the butler, stared at the men a few seconds, then slammed the door.

"What are you doing here, Tom?" Phil asked, his forehead creased in worry, his eyes swiveling back and forth between the two men.

Matt looked at Tom. "Coker here wants to take a shower. Is it OK now?"

"First, I want to see the car." He squeezed into the space between the passenger side and the wall. After a few seconds, he said, "No surprise, I guess." He looked at Phil. "What a mess. Does Jerry Lee ever drive this thing?"

"Sometimes."

"So if we find her prints on the wheel or the driver's door, no surprise, huh?"

Phil shook his head. "You think she drove it last night?"

Tom ignored the question. "She ever borrow one of your hats?"

"She hates them."

"So that's a negative?"

Something clicked in Phil's head. "Hating them doesn't mean she never wears them. One year she gave a Halloween party and we dressed like each other."

The picture of Phil in drag made both Matt and Tom suppress a smile.

Tom looked at his watch. "Exactly ninety minutes from now, I suggest you check in with McBride at his home office."

"Suggest?"

"Strongly suggest. That'll give you time to take a shower, get caught up on your domestic situation. You and Jerry Lee might have a few things to discuss. You'll know then whether your life is worth living."

As Matt and Tom walked to Matt's car, parked on the street just outside the entrance to Beaudry Hall, Phil yelled, "What the fuck does that mean?"

Neither man looked back or answered. Before Matt started the engine, the two men glanced at each other and smiled. Matt pointed at Tom. "That part about switching identities on Halloween . . . ."

"I know what you're thinking, Matt. But you're going to have to shave that mustache."

"And you're going to have to lose ten pounds, maybe work out a little, put a little curl in that wave you've got going on up there."

"Somehow I think your mustache, my hair, and the weight difference might be the least of our problems."

They glanced at each other again and started laughing. They laughed so hard Matt could hardly see the road. Then they drove to the white Italian palazzo in Port Royal to debrief McBride, who'd taken the red eye in, and wait for the Joker, as they now referred to the actor they both thought of as a monumental twit.

26

Dead Man
Thursday, April 27, 2006

When Jerry Lee stepped out of the shower, her eyes still clouded by water, her hair dripping, she saw Phil standing in the doorway to her dressing room, looking like the Grand Inquisitor. He was holding a plastic bottle of Aquafina in one hand and the black kangol she'd worn the night before in the other. She'd prepared for this.

"I found this bottle of water in my car this morning."

"So?"

"I don't drink water. Ever. And this hat, oddly enough, has a couple of long blond hairs attached to the inside."

"Are you confessing you've been somewhere with a blonde?"

"You took my car last night. You wore this hat. You sent me to Marco so I'd be out of the way."

"Well, aren't you the detective."

"You followed Alex and killed him."

"As I said . . . ."

He strode toward her, dropping both items on the floor, and grabbed her upper arms so hard she felt her blood pounding, as if his fists were blood pressure cuffs. She kicked him with her bare foot and tried to twist away. He laughed. Then he pushed his face within inches of hers. His hazel eyes looked demonic. "You black-hearted bitch."

She twisted again. Her arms hurt like hell and she bruised easily. Thin as Phil was, she was thinner and older. In a physical struggle, she'd lose. She wasn't yet scared but the thought that he might be capable of real harm tickled the back of her brain. She hadn't prepared for this.

"If you don't let go, I'm going to scream. Niall will be here in seconds."

"That English fag? He's as afraid of me as you are."

"Please, Shugah, you're really hurting me." She started to crumple. "Let me get dressed. We'll talk."

He pulled her upright, let go of her arms, and gave her a contemptuous little shove. "I should just go to the constabulary."

She couldn't help it. She laughed derisively. "The *constabulary*? Are there normal people on the planet you live on?"

He stood just outside her closet, glaring at her, while she pulled on a pair of shorts and a sleeveless t-shirt. She looked down at her arms, which were red and already darkening with finger-shaped bruises. The blood-thinners she took ensured the bruises would last. She wanted Niall and Maria to see them. She'd call Poppy and make sure she saw them too. Maybe she'd call the damn constabulary herself. Or maybe not. She'd had a rough enough time with that stupid detective.

When they returned to the sitting room outside their bedroom, Jerry Lee signaled Maria to bring up a pot of coffee and another of tea, plus a plate of croissants, grapes, and crisp bacon. Once Maria left, they got down to the domestic business of accusations, denials, and epithets.

"I just spent a half hour with a big black son-of-a-bitch who looks like Denzel."

"And I spent the same amount of time with a big white son-of-a-bitch who looks like Bill Pullman."

In ordinary circumstances, they would have laughed and drifted into entertaining trivialities, caustic observations of everyone they envied and therefore loathed. But these circumstances weren't ordinary.

"You drove the Prius last night. You wore my hat."

"So what?"

"You killed a guy."

"I did?" She tried to sound bored.

"That's what Denzel told me."

"Good. Who did I kill, by the way?"

"Ferrin's driver. Alex Abrams."

"The guy in spandex riding a bike?"

"That was Alex."

"How come you were meeting him on the sly?"

"I wasn't. You're so full of shit . . . ."

"Don't lie, Phil. I saw you drop him off at his bike. Verlin saw him too, for weeks, every Wednesday night."

Phil closed his eyes, slumping in his chair. "He was my connection to Goldstein."

"Why did you need a connection to that old socialist? I thought he was your personal friend, you didn't need a go-between." She sipped her tea, watching him like a hawk that had spied a sick rabbit in the weeds.

"That's the way Goldstein wanted it. You ever hear of plausible deniability?"

She shook her head.

"Me neither till I made *Silver Back*. But that was his reasoning."

"So what was Alex up to, working for Goldstein *and* my son-in-law?"

"Getting dirt on him. Which wasn't hard."

"What dirt? Ferrin's clean as a whistle, according to Poppy."

"Everybody's got secrets, stuff they don't wanna cop to. Anyway, when I figured out what Alex was up to, I pretended to go along. You know what a double agent is?"

"Who doesn't? Somebody who plays for both sides but only one side knows the truth."

"That's what I am. I do my best to keep McBride informed of the spies around him."

"That's what he'll tell me if I ask? Or would he tell me you're spying on him for someone else's benefit? Goldstein's, for example."

"You aren't going to ask Ferrin anything if you know what's

good for you. This game is way above your head."

She chose to ignore the taunt. "Why would Goldstein agree to back your picture if you're really working for Ferrin instead of him?"

"He doesn't know I'm a double agent. That's the point of being a double agent. My loyalty lies with you, but I'll never let him know that."

"But he's agreed to back your new picture, right?"

"We're getting there. We've met a few times, done a lot of talking. He gave me those Nauman pictures. But I haven't seen a dime yet."

"You didn't tell Goldstein about Poppy's miscarriage, did you?"

He gave her an exaggerated look of innocence. "I haven't been able to tell him much of anything yet. That's why I haven't seen any hard cash."

"You're sure you didn't tell him about the miscarriage?"

"What do you think I am? I know how much you love that girl of yours."

"No, you don't. You have no idea."

"Oh, my sweet Southern belle, I think I do."

"Tell me."

"You killed poor old Jonah when he put his foot down about the pageants. You killed her boyfriend and then gave your precious daughter something to get rid of the baby. You abducted Nicky Sue and killed her so Poppy would have a better chance to win the pageant. A few days ago you tried to kill Molly because you're still angry she snatched the title from Poppy."

"You're guessing. You have no proof whatsoever."

"Sure I'm guessing, but tell me I'm wrong."

Jerry Lee just smiled.

"But you're right about one thing, my dear girl. I have no proof of anything. And I'm not about to try to find any, so there's no reason for you to kill me. All I want is some dirt on Ferrin."

Catching his contradiction -- he was secretly trolling for dirt on Ferrin, just as she assumed -- Jerry Lee hid her feelings about that slip of the tongue as best she could. "I'd never kill you, Shugah. No matter what you did. Especially if you take me with you tomorrow to Goldstein's place in Napa. I want to meet some of your friends, see how wine is made, hear the details about the new picture."

Suddenly, Phil looked at his watch and stood up. "I'm late."

"Late for what?"

"Your son-in-law wants to talk to me."

"I'll go with you."

"I don't think so."

"What are you going to tell him?"

"The truth about who was driving the Prius last night." He bared his teeth in the semblance of a smile. "Unless, of course, you agree to put up a few million for the picture."

"You're blackmailing me."

"Damn right, sister. I get a couple million from you, I make up some story about getting hit in a parking lot and take you to Napa."

Jerry Lee clutched her chest.

"And don't go swooning on me like some delicate Victorian girl. You fool no one with that act." He waited for her to answer. "So what's it going to be? A few million for my picture, or the truth about what you did?"

She pretended to give in. "You'll take me to the premiere, the Oscars?"

"No one else."

She nodded. "I'll go right to the bank. Then I'll start packing."

She watched him walk out of the sitting room, losing sight of him only when he reached the magnificent curving stairway to the second floor. He descended without looking back. She rubbed her sore arms, recalling his demonic eyes. Who did he think he was kidding with that story about being a double agent for Ferrin? Alex was the double agent, taking Phil's slander to his real boss. In the meeting with Ferrin, Phil would throw her under the bus without a thought, do anything to save himself. Who knows, he might return and kill her in a fit of temper.

She'd already have killed him if he didn't owe her so much money. Her best hope that he'd repay her had always been the prospect of a comeback. But now she strongly suspected there would be no comeback. If Goldstein hadn't "gone hard" yet, he wasn't serious about a picture. He was serious about destroying her son-in-law and thus her daughter. Every fiber of her being told her that Phil was the leaker.

She walked to the window and watched Phil back her Cadillac out of the garage. She had no intention of going to the bank but she was going to take care of business. She was going to Napa. Verlin would know exactly what she needed to take with her to give a special glass of wine a special kick.

Phil was a dead man.

27

Jackwagon
Thursday, April 27, 2006

Phil had never been in Ferrin's wine room before. "I didn't know you had a place like this, man. Why've you been hiding it?" He passed his hand over the cool, polished stone wall, then surveyed the well-designed room with an artist's eye. "What'd you do, import the whole thing in a crate from Italy?"

"Have a seat over there, Phil."

Phil stood his ground, angry at being told what to do, not getting his questions answered, having his flattery rejected. "First, let me pick out a wine. Talk to me like a gentleman."

"I'm going to talk to you all right, but there isn't going to be any wine today. This is business." Ferrin once more gestured to a bar-height leather director's chair, one of a set of four lined up two-by-two on either side of a long, high pine table.

Phil spun on his heel when he heard footsteps, narrowing his eyes at the sight of Tom and Matt striding into the room. "What are they doing here?"

"We need to talk. You're not going to keep standing like you're in charge, so sit down like a gentleman -- speaking of gentlemen -- and shut the fuck up."

When Phil opened his mouth to protest, Ferrin held up his hand with his cell phone in it. "You don't cooperate in every possible way, you're going to be talking to the police. I'm not a

Hollywood director. I don't take shit from jackwagons like you. I'm going to tell you how to play this scene, then you're going to play it my way, and there'll be only one take. No screwing around. Got it?"

"For a holier-than-thou politician . . . ."

He didn't get a chance to finish. Ferrin hit him square in the mouth. Phil went down on the cold stone floor, screaming like a girl, holding his bloody lip. "Hey!"

Ferrin pulled him up by his skinny arms and set him on his feet. "Sit down before I hurt you." He found a towel so Phil could blot the blood on his mouth. "I'm going to turn on a recorder. Any objections?"

"I'll say you hit me."

"I don't think so, rat-face. You're going to tell me what the hell you've been up to."

Phil sat down, trying not to look scared. Ferrin took the chair opposite him. Tom sat on Ferrin's right, Matt across from him to Phil's left. "I haven't been up to anything."

Ferrin turned on the recorder. "You killed a man last night. My driver, no less."

Phil eyed the recorder with alarm. "You got the wrong person, man. It wasn't me driving the Prius."

"Who was it then?"

"Jerry Lee."

Ferrin already knew that was probably true. Matt told him that Phil's surprise at finding his car damaged seemed genuine. "How do you know that? She say so?"

"Nah. I found her hair in my hat, her water bottle in the car. I don't drink water and I don't have long blond hair. As you can see."

"Where were you last night?"

He looked at Matt. "I told Denzel here that I drove the Cadillac to Marco to pick up some wine from a dealer at his house, only I never found the address."

"Got any proof of that?"

"No."

"Where were you before you drove to Marco?"

"At the house."

"You didn't pick up Alexie and drive to a public park?"

Phil glanced at Matt, who was smiling, then at Ferrin, who was impassive. "Why would I do that? Man, you must be smoking something better than I can get my hands on."

Matt spoke for the first time. "I doubt anybody smokes something better than you do."

"I think you did pick him up," Ferrin said. "What's your connection with Alexie?"

"I told you, I don't have any. I don't know the man."

"What's your connection with Goldstein? Other than the obvious."

"He directed the Viet Nam picture that made me famous. I was nominated for an Oscar for that, you know. Then came *Silver Back* . . . ."

Ferrin cut him off. "That's the obvious connection, but I don't think it's the only one. Did you know Alexie used to work for Goldstein?"

"Well . . . ."

Ferrin sat back and rubbed his chin. "Why'd you tell Alexie about Poppy's miscarriage?"

"I didn't. I'd never. I told Jerry Lee the same thing, knowing how much she loves her daughter."

"But you don't love me and you need money. So you told Alexie who told Goldstein, isn't that it?"

"Think anything you want."

"How much did Goldstein pay you for that wretched little secret?"

"Nothing."

"You get paid anything, you better start paying back my mother-in-law or I'll tear you a new one."

Phil couldn't help a little whining. "The papers said he's paying me millions, but he's not. He gave me some of his old funk art, but that's it so far. The movie is a straight up deal, doesn't have anything to do with Poppy's secrets. Virgil likes my idea for a screenplay. If he can find some more backers, or if I can find some money-men, I'll make a blockbuster for him. Then I'll have enough money to repay Jerry Lee." Phil smiled scornfully. "Why are you so interested in Jerry Lee's money? Expecting to inherit it someday?"

"You stand up, you piece of shit, and I'll put you on the floor again for that one."

"Just saying." Though still defiant, Phil's voice was little more than a whisper.

"Do you realize that instead of paying you for the slander about Poppy, which he made good use of to wound me, Goldstein slipped Mullett a couple million dollars?"

Phil's eyes narrowed. "You shitting me?"

Ferrin let the information sink in. "Tell me this, Joker. If you didn't run over Alexie, Jerry Lee must have. But why would she want to kill him?" He stared Phil down. "Unless she figured out he was the conduit for the secrets you told him about Poppy."

"That's a question for her, wouldn't you say?"

"That's my question for you."

"The only thing she told me was that she and Verlin watched me pick up Alex at the carriage gate."

"So you were lying about not knowing my Russian driver?"

Phil did his best to look suave and relaxed, pushing his chair back a little, crossing one ankle over the other knee. "Mind if I smoke?"

Ferrin pushed a ceramic ashtray toward him. "Help yourself. Mind if the rest of us smoke cigars?" Without waiting for an answer, he extracted three cigars from a humidor at his end of the table and distributed two to Tom and Matt.

"I don't think cigar smoke is recommended in a wine cellar, Ferrin." Phil was miffed at not being offered a cigar but was too proud to ask for one.

"I don't think selling family secrets to a left-wing nutcase is good for your health, Phil."

"What do you mean by that?"

"If Jerry Lee killed Alexie based on nothing more than

147

suspicion that you were using him as a conduit to Goldstein for Poppy's secrets, what do you think she'll do to you?"

Phil sat up and looked at the tape recorder. "Do you know how many people your mother-in-law has killed? Jonah, Dewey, and Nicky Sue. A few days ago she tried to kill that writer, Molly Something, merely because she's still seething about how Poppy got cheated out of the Miss South Carolina title."

"So if you turn up dead, we'll know where to look."

Phil snapped his head in Ferrin's direction. "I'm . . . I'm not going to turn up dead. She actually said she'd never kill me. To seal the deal, I'm taking her to Napa tomorrow to meet Goldstein at his Napa estate."

"What do you two have to discuss?"

"Nothing about you, that's for sure. We're going to do some planning for the picture."

"Why'd you mention that you wouldn't be talking about me? You two discussed me a lot in the past, have you?"

"Man, it's no secret Virgil hates your guts. Nothing personal. He just hates hypocrites like you. He wants a revolution in the streets, you want one through the churches, and never the twain shall meet."

"I don't want any kind of revolution, much less one through the churches, but that's beside the point. I want to hear it in your own words. You traded Poppy's past for a future with Goldstein, isn't that it?"

Phil nodded.

"Speak up."

"If that's the way you want to put it, I suppose so."

"Why?"

"My chance for a comeback," Phil whined. "I'm not political, man. I've never even registered to vote."

"What else have you told the Czarist butt-licker about me?"

"Nothing."

"Why is that?"

"Don't know anything."

"You got that right." Ferrin turned off the recorder. "Have

you touched the Prius?"

"No, if you mean getting it fixed. Denzel here said to wait till I heard from you."

"Leave it alone until we see what happens." Ferrin slid back his chair and stood up. "You're free to go."

"Am I going to be hearing from the cops?"

"No."

"There weren't any witnesses?"

"There was one, but Denzel's not talking."

Matt smiled. Tom laughed outright.

Phil looked at Matt. "You knew all along what you'd find on that car this morning, who was driving?"

Matt cocked his head noncommittally.

"Just remember, Phil," Ferrin continued, "you have no alibi, it was your car that hit Alexie, you had the personal connection with the victim, and the witness -- the only witness -- saw the driver wearing your kangol."

Phil stood up, pretending not to be worried. "The three of you are smart. Good-looking too. I bet the camera loves you. You lose this election, Ferrin, I'll write a screenplay for all of you. Make you famous."

"I'm not losing the election, Joker. And, if I were you, I wouldn't spend a lot of time dreaming up screenplays from now on. I think you're already the star in one and somebody who doesn't like you very much wrote it. This time, you'll be lucky to get out alive."

28

Scandal
Thursday, April 27, 2006

After Phil left, the three men returned to Ferrin's office to discuss strategy. The local paper was laid out on Ferrin's desk, open to the third page. He read the article aloud:

LOCAL POLITICIAN'S DRIVER KILLED IN HIT-AND-RUN

Late Wednesday night, Alex Abrams, 32, was struck by a vehicle while riding his bicycle on Spyglass Lane, about a mile from the home of his employer, U.S. Rep. Ferrin McBride (R), the 14th District's Congressman. Abrams, who died a few hours later of his injuries without regaining consciousness, served as a driver for McBride, who is running for reelection in a heated contest with Myron Mullett, Collier County's former Commissioner. The authorities were notified of the accident by an anonymous tip to 911. A spokesman for the McBride campaign said that they first learned of the accident from the morning news but would cooperate fully in whatever investigation was undertaken.

An autopsy will be conducted. The police are trying to locate any witnesses to the hit-and-run accident. Spencer Tibault, a spokesman for the Naples Police Department,

said the vehicle that struck Abrams was apparently a small blue sedan, given the color and height of paint markings on the Micargi Road Racer the victim was riding, but declined to provide any other identifying information. Police are setting up a tip line; callers will be able to remain anonymous.

"Apparently the police know nothing other than that a small blue sedan might have been involved, which won't get them far." Ferrin looked at Matt. "So what do we do?"

"What we should do and what you want to do are probably two different things."

Tom spoke up. "We could call in an anonymous tip about the car's location. There's a downside to that, however. We can't be sure the Prius we saw in Jerry Lee's garage is the one that hit the Russian since neither Coker nor Jerry Lee admits to anything and Matt, for reasons we all understand, couldn't follow the Prius after the accident. If we're wrong in our hunch, we'd be subjecting Jerry Lee and Coker to the unnecessary inconvenience and humiliation of being investigated. Whatever the investigation yields, it's bad publicity for you. On the other hand, Coker's Prius probably is the right car and, for reasons we can't disclose, we think that Jerry Lee was probably driving. But, no matter what we say, the police are likely to focus on Coker. With no alibi for his whereabouts last night, Coker is likely to be sweated a lot and, since he was essentially a double agent for Goldstein, that's not entirely a bad thing from our point of view."

"Terrible publicity," Ferrin said.

Matt again: "Coker's leaving in the morning with Jerry Lee. The car's in the garage, so unless Coker can somehow get it fixed before he leaves for California without someone getting suspicious, it'll be all right for a few days while we decide what to do. Something's caught under the front passenger axle. Might be a piece of the Russian's bike."

Ferrin looked at the ceiling. "The police can't get in Beaudry Hall without a warrant. But no judge is going to issue a warrant against a celebrity or his girlfriend based on an anonymous tip without substantial and credible backup evidence."

"I'm sure the police are going to want to talk to you, since Alexie was your driver, so be prepared," Tom said.

"Since I wasn't present at the scene of the accident, all I'd have to tell them would be rank hearsay. I officially know nothing, and that's the way it's going to stay."

Matt leaned forward. "What do you think about the Joker's accusations that Jerry Lee killed -- how many people?" He ticked them off on his fingers. "Her husband, her daughter's boyfriend, her daughter's pageant rival, plus an attempt on the life of the woman she thinks stole her daughter's crown. If I can still count, that's three and a half."

Ferrin laughed derisively. "Without hard facts, I don't believe Coker." He paused. "But if the proof turned up, I wouldn't die of shock, given how protective my mother-in-law is of her daughter. For now, I'm putting Coker's accusations aside as pure spite and self-preservation." Ferrin got up and paced behind his desk. "I don't like the idea of a second anonymous tip about the car's location because even if Jerry Lee is only questioned as a witness, my campaign comes to a screeching halt."

Matt gave Tom a look that said "I knew it," then directed himself to Ferrin. "Given my decision to report the accident and then leave, I think we're locked into staying quiet, at least for awhile. I sure as hell don't want to explain to Mullett's campaign what I was doing near midnight on Spyglass Lane following their inside man as he bicycled home. So I'm in agreement with keeping quiet for awhile. What do you think, Tom?"

But Tom was distracted. He was pointing at the TV screen, tuned to a local news station with the sound off. "Turn that sound up, would you, Ferrin? The banner scrolling along the bottom just mentioned Mullett and the camera's showing an overhead shot of a parking lot."

Ferrin grabbed the remote and brought the sound up.

" . . . ran over her husband's mistress, not once, but twice, with her Navigator, as the security footage shows. It happened around seven this morning. Mrs. Mullett's teen-age daughter was in the car, screaming for her mother to stop. Mullett, watching the assault from the back door of the hotel, never moved to help his mistress or stop his wife. When Mrs. Mullett's Navigator finally came to a halt, Mullett was hustled into a black SUV, which appeared out of nowhere and sped away to an unknown destination. LuAnn Mullett, a chiropractor, has been taken into custody. This station, which has repeatedly contacted Mullett's office for a statement, informs us that Harley Wangle will hold a press conference later today." The screen changed to a sultry studio photograph of an attractive young red-head revealing impressive cleavage. "The victim has been identified as Muffy Wayne, a twenty-four-year-old aspiring actress. She was hired six months ago by the campaign as a scheduling assistant to Wangle." The picture changed again to a scene of Mullett speaking before a large crowd of supporters. Muffy Wayne, wearing tortoise shell sunglasses and a fetching straw hat, was standing a few feet behind him, holding his jacket. "She frequently traveled with Mullett. Now she's dead."

Ferrin turned the sound down and laughed. "The stars are in alignment, the sun's still rising, and the moon arcs across the sky every night. Everything's right with the world. Myron Mullett, the proud owner of a weird growth on his chin and a stringy comb-over -- a man so ugly a toad wouldn't touch him -- has been caught in a sex scandal."

Ferrin sat back down, steepling his hands. "Here's how I see things. Matt called in the accident immediately so if Alexie could be saved, he would have been. Nobody associated with this campaign endangered anybody's life. There's no point in tipping the authorities to Coker's blue Prius because we don't know of any forensic evidence linking his car to the bicycle and since we don't know for sure who was driving, we unnecessarily subject at least one person to the humiliation of being questioned. Coker was double-crossing me and did everything he could to kill my campaign and wound my wife with a fabricated story, so if the shadow of suspicion somehow falls on him, so be it. Nobody will weep for Coker. Both Alexie and Coker are in cahoots with

Goldstein, the arch-enemy of politicians like me. Goldstein's goal is to strip us of all our civil liberties and overturn the Constitution with a socialist dictatorship. But Goldstein's guy is now embroiled in a sex scandal. For the good of the country, we're keeping quiet about Alexie."

Both Matt and Tom sat stock still, marveling at Ferrin's rationalization for why saving his own ass was good for the country. Both were equally uncomfortable with their own satisfaction in knowing they wouldn't have to change the course set by Matt when he made a split-second decision to avoid being identified as a witness.

"Think about it," Ferrin resumed, "Mullett's scandal is going to occupy the media for weeks. If his campaign implodes, there will be no time for the liberals to put up a viable candidate and I'll win the contest in a landslide. Better that I be elected with my reputation intact than with my reputation unfairly besmirched by my crazy mother-in-law."

Ferrin got up, grabbed a putter, and walked toward the terrace. "So you two have any comments?"

Tom and Matt swiveled their chairs toward Treasure Cove. Tom gestured for Matt to speak up.

"I can go along with that strategy, Ferrin, but if you really want to quell any suspicion, we should consider getting that Prius fixed while Coker's in California. I wouldn't take it to a dealership or independent repair shop. I'd have someone fix it right where it sits."

"You know a guy who can do that?"

"Of course."

"I'll think about it, but for now I say no. What about you, Tom?"

"I think you need to keep an eye on your mother-in-law and do a thorough audit of your employees to make sure there are no other Goldstein moles."

"Good advice." Ferrin turned his attention back to Matt. "Has Wangle called you yet?"

Matt pulled his good mobile phone from his pocket and

checked it. "No. He'll be a little too busy for me today, but since he mentioned Alex as a valuable mole when we first talked, I have no doubt I'll hear from him. I'm going to need some little unfortunate tidbit from your past to keep Wangle thinking I'm with Mullett."

There was a pause while Ferrin returned to his desk and sat there a few minutes, tapping his pencil on a pad of paper. "How about this? When I was a student at Indiana University, I wrote a political science paper praising the U.N., which I now think -- upon mature, sane reflection -- should be kicked out of New York and stripped of all U.S. money. Publication of that stupid paper will supposedly embarrass me." He smiled triumphantly. "But when I'm forced to respond to that juvenile paper, I'll take the opportunity to talk about international matters -- currency, defense, balance of trade, that sort of thing. I'll have an assistant get you that tomorrow."

"Mullett's campaign, by the way, is paying for Doris and me to attend the fund-raiser starring Verbena Cross. I'm supposed to dig up some dirt on her too."

Tom laughed. "There's plenty but it's all been dug up by *The National Enquirer*. Wangle must know that."

"I told him it was stupid to mess with Goldstein's daughter."

Ferrin looked at his watch. "I have a meeting in ten minutes downtown. Are we agreed we'll leave the Prius alone for now, see what happens?"

Matt and Tom nodded.

When Matt and Tom were pulling out of McBride's estate, they were somber. "I definitely need a beer," Matt said. Tom seconded that emotion. They drove to their favorite dark and aromatic sports bar frequented by cops, firemen, and a few local sport nuts, where they inexplicably decided to taste a shot glass of every beer on tap. During a long, rambling conversation, they agreed on three things: marriage was good, politics was bad, and no true-blue red-blooded American could really, seriously, genuinely like Guinness stout.

29

The Really Rich Are Really Different
Friday, April 28, 2006

From the backseat of the Escalade provided by their hosts, Jerry Lee watched the Napa Valley scenery roll by, enchanted by the mountains in the distance, the rolling green hills, the manicured rows of grapevines. She'd never been in Napa before. Occasionally she spotted an isolated house amidst the lush greenery. She knew grapes weren't grown in the city, but still she was surprised by how rural the area was. The narrow, winding roads said it all. How long had it been since she'd really been in the country? Especially very wealthy country, unlike the foothills of the Smokies where she grew up. Napa Valley looked like a movie set, every estate a Potemkin village.

When she turned to say something to Phil about how Hollywood refugees made everything look like a movie set, she found him slumped in the corner, snoring. He told her he'd busted his lip stumbling over a rock at McBride's house. She doubted it. He lied so much about the big things, why not the little ones as well?

The driver announced they were passing Francis Ford Coppola's winery and park, a vast estate studded with imposing buildings. She frowned at how commercial it looked. She hoped for something very different up ahead, something glamorous but cozy. Jerry Lee could not describe what she hoped to see, but she'd know it when she saw it.

Less than ten minutes later, they pulled into a long winding lane leading to the heart of Virgil Goldstein's estate. Mid-point they stopped at a gate outside a small gray guardhouse. When the driver waved to the guard, the gate opened and they proceeded another half mile.

As she'd hoped, this estate was smaller, less intimidating than the Coppola extravaganza, but still very grand. The long two-story rambler with a Western-style veranda across the front was perfect. Off to one side and back about two hundred yards was a cluster of cottages, also clad in weathered gray wood, partially screened from the main house by a little grove of fruit trees. In the distance, Jerry Lee could see another cluster of larger buildings surrounding a bandshell, again built of weathered gray wood. At the base of a small rise a quarter of a mile to the north loomed a huge metal barn in a nest of smaller buildings where she supposed the wine was made. The vast green lawns, the vegetable and herb gardens near the cottages, and the neat gravel lanes had been manicured within an inch of their lives.

A young woman wearing black capris and a white blouse directed the driver to one of three cottages, where a very tan young man dressed in black bermudas and a white polo shirt was sitting in a golf cart, waiting for them. When the Escalade stopped, he got up, introduced himself as Skip, and began carrying their bags into the cottage.

Before he left, Skip told them they were expected at the main house at seven for a reception, followed by an *al fresco* dinner with their hosts and a number of other special guests. Dress was casual. He winked. "All you have to bring is your most entertaining conversation."

Jerry Lee frowned. She had no idea what California casual might mean or what comprised entertaining conversation in Napa Valley, but she wasn't about to humble herself enough to ask a young servant who was so impertinent as to wink at her.

Meanwhile, Skip said they could use the golf cart parked under the carport to tour the estate. They were welcome, for instance, to visit the pavilion, where their hosts' movie and stage memorabilia were displayed, or if they wanted to see the winery, they could do that as well. If they could find Virgil's Grotto, a private, hidden wine bar that looked like a cave, they could sample some of the estate's wines. Skip assured them they'd find everything they needed in the guesthouse, but in case they didn't, just dial "0" on the phone in the kitchenette and he would do what he could.

Before he left, he handed them a map of the estate. "You'll see that every gravel lane has a name taken from one of Virgil's movies. You might want to study the map a few minutes before you set out, but if you get lost, there are emergency telephone posts at the intersections and a couple of security guards with dogs roam the estate often enough you won't be lost long."

Glancing at the map, Jerry Lee frowned again. Their cottage was located on The Ho Chi Minh Trail, a coincidence that would please Phil, though the name was patently silly for such a civilized place. Standing in the doorway of the cottage, she looked up in time to see Skip drive silently away in his own golf cart. She stared in his direction until he was long out of sight.

She was out of her element. Despite reading magazines like *Palm Beach Illustrated* and *Art and Antiques*, she had no idea people -- especially the über-rich who viewed themselves as anti-imperialist revolutionaries -- lived such royal lives, so important they didn't even personally greet their guests. The really rich were really different. They must assume they'd always be the elite, the oligarchy, no matter what political system rose up around them. Phil often told her how naïve she was, how she really didn't know the world the way she thought she did. For the first time, she suspected he was right.

Waiting inside the cottage was a young woman who looked like a model and introduced herself, in an Eastern European accent, as Sophia. She was already unpacking their cases, carefully hanging their garments in separate closets and arranging toiletries in the bathroom where the his-and-her sinks and showers were separated by a water closet with a bidet. She tucked their jewelry cases and "delicates," as Marilyn Monroe used to call them, in vintage oak chests, and even lined up their shoes on raked closet shelves.

"I'll return while you're at dinner, ma'am, to turn down the bed. Do you need anything pressed or steamed?"

Jerry Lee's brain locked up. She might need something pressed if only she knew what her hostess would be wearing that night at dinner. She'd planned to wear silver sequined palazzo pants and a fitted black silk embroidered tunic, both by Naeem Khan, with Giuseppe Zanotti studded sandals, but now wondered if that would be too dressy. It was a little warm for long sleeves, but she had to cover the bruises on her arms, so what choice did she have? With a sigh, she pointed to the Naeem Khan outfit. "Thank you. Perhaps you could steam these."

"And your husband's clothes?"

Jerry Lee looked around. Phil had disappeared. "I don't think so."

She left Sophia to her work and returned to the sitting room, where she found a bottle of white wine in an ice bucket and half a dozen crystal stems. She opened the bottle, poured herself a half glass of wine, and went out to the veranda, where she found Phil sitting in a chair. She walked to the railing, turned her back to the scenery, and smiled at him.

"Just think, Phil, you might have had all this if you'd not gotten fired from *The Belly of the Beast* or won that part you screen-tested for in *The Midnight Caller.*"

He shot her a murderous look. "I'll get it yet."

"Better late than never, is that what you're thinking?"

"That's what I'm thinking."

"What are you wearing tonight?"

"Who gives a flying fuck what I'm wearing? I'll wear anything I damn well please."

"Perhaps a change of mood and language would make things go better."

"Don't tell me what to wear or say."

"You want some wine, by the way? It's good."

"Virgil makes crap wine, hugely over-priced, and you know it. Bank managers and car salesmen love it because it's called Virgil's

Running Dog. It's the zingy label that convinces them that if they shell out the big bucks and pretend they scorn the capitalist system they've embraced, they'll suck down a little Hollywood cool with the vinegar."

"It's not vinegar. It's really good."

"Then get me a glass."

She got up. "Saying please once in awhile wouldn't hurt, you know."

"Please," he said scornfully.

When she returned with his wine, she sat down. "So what's the plan, Shugah, other than dinner?"

Phil looked at his watch. "I'm meeting the running dog himself in a half hour. By dinnertime I'll know what's what. You do anything you want till then."

"Thanks for nothing. What am I supposed to do all alone in this place?"

He ignored her plea. "Has anybody told you who's going to be here?"

"No."

"Slade Winters and his newest wife, a hot Korean chick he met in Cannes while still married to his third wife. Her name is Bong Cha."

Jerry Lee laughed. "You're not serious. Bong Cha? Sounds like marijuana from Thailand."

"A very popular name in Korea, I'm told, so be careful. Slade's a powerhouse at Creative Artists. If he makes fun of the A-list stars he represents, don't fall into the trap. Praise them to the skies.

"Then there's Baron von der Wettin, a moneybags who may or may not be a baron but claims he's a distant cousin of Prince Albert, whose real surname was Wettin. He's so rich nobody ever questions him. They just bow and kiss his hand if they can't get all the way down to his fat ass. He doesn't like to be called Baron, by the way. Call him Hump."

"Hump?"

"For Humphrey. His partner, a young Colombian who still looks like a teenager, is named Sergio."

"Should I write this down?"

"Memorize it. So far we have Slade and Bong Cha, Hump and Sergio -- a talent agent, a billionaire, and two hotties.

"Finally there's Verbena, Virgil and Ellen's darling daughter, the celebrity." He made quotes in the air around the word celebrity. "She's here with her fiancé, Bordon Settle, known to intimates as Wank. Don't ask. Any outsider who calls him Bordon and claims to be a close friend isn't . . . although Verbena never calls him by anything but his real name." He stubbed his cigarette out on the porch floor. "Which isn't his real name. I think it was Dwayne before it was Bordon."

"Is Phil Coker your real name?"

He glared at her. "You bet your ass it is."

"Okay, okay, I'm just asking. But don't you think we need nicknames to keep up with the Joneses? Buzz and Bets or something like that."

"Not ridiculous enough for the Left Coast." There was a hint of a smile on the corner of his lips.

" And why the quotes? Verbena is definitely a celebrity."

"If she weren't Virgil's daughter, she'd be flipping burgers somewhere God lost his shoes. I loathe people who inherit their good fortune."

"You also loathe people who make it on merit."

"Merit, schmerit. Everything's connections."

"You didn't have any when you started."

"I have raw talent. Then I got connections."

"Then you lost them."

He glared at her. "You know how to bring a guy down, you know that?"

"Speaking of connections, I'm beginning to feel like a peasant who should have stayed at home."

"Well, that's appropriate, don't you think? You *are* a peasant."

"And you aren't?" She was thinking a man born in a dusty little Nevada town, where God actually did lose his shoes, of parents who lived above their drab general store had no occasion for pride. "I don't know what to talk about so I'm entertaining or what to wear so I look chic but casual."

Phil smiled broadly for the first time that day. His lip was still a mess, but his old lady's confession of being out of her league made him happy. "Wear something simple, preferably white and loose, and don't talk unless somebody asks you a question, and then say as little as possible. Follow-up with a flattering but pointless question, like 'What's your favorite hotel in Cannes?' That'll lead to a half-hour discussion you don't have to contribute to. People out here get fat on flattering, pointless questions."

He got up and stretched. "How's my lip look?"

"Bad. You're going to need a better story than the one you gave me to make it seem heroic instead of pitiful."

"I have one ready." He walked down the couple of steps to the ground. "I'm taking the golf cart, so you're on your own. Have fun."

Jerry Lee got up too and reentered the cottage. She knew she should go easy on the wine but she couldn't help herself. She'd brought nothing white and loose to wear. Why couldn't Phil have passed on that little bit of wisdom before they left Naples? No flattering but pointless questions came to mind. He could have suggested a few useful questions or conversational tidbits on the plane instead of pretending to sleep so he wouldn't have to talk to her.

How could she have been so deluded as to look forward to this miserable experience? She was used to feeling rich and superior. She wasn't used to feeling provincial and unimportant. She supported a washed-up actor so she'd have a companion, not so she'd be alone.

Before pouring herself another glass of wine, she found Sophia and told her, in her coldest voice, that everything -- every last item in their suitcases -- needed to be steamed after all.

Then she returned to the porch with the open bottle of wine. Every time the image of that biker in spandex popped into her mind, she pushed it down with the help of another sip of wine. She hated blood. She hated collateral damage to property. Herbs were so much neater.

Then, wondering what celebrity Annie Leibovitz had shot nude this time, she opened the May issue of *Vanity Fair.*

30

Disappointment
Friday, April 28, 2006

The instant Jerry Lee walked with Phil into the Goldsteins' main house, she hated herself. Phil was dressed in a Stalin t-shirt under a safari jacket with sagging pockets, linen trousers that looked unpressed the minute he put them on, and trendy backless sneakers. He fit in perfectly. She, on the other hand, wearing an expensive formal evening outfit, looked ridiculously overdressed. The other women, who apparently shared the same stylist, were wearing narrow white capris, asymmetrical jersey tops exposing one shoulder, and Jimmy Choo sandals. Bong Cha was set apart by a gauzy scarf draped around her long neck.

Ellen, Broadway star and hostess extraordinaire, didn't help matters. "Oh, you're wearing my friend Naeem Khan. Do you know him? Girls, doesn't she look pretty?"

Jerry Lee knew she didn't look pretty, despite Verbena's warm smile. Bong Cha's contemptuous glance gave the game away: she looked clueless. Humiliated, Jerry Lee acknowledged she hadn't met Mr. Khan but, in a burst of inspiration, asked a flattering, pointless question. "How do you know him?"

While Ellen chattered on about meeting his parents in India and entertaining Naeem at their New York pied-à-terre, Jerry Lee surveyed the huge room they were in. Situated at the back of the house with a view of the vineyards, it was part of a long wing used for entertaining. From the front, the house had looked large but not overwhelming. Once inside, Jerry Lee realized the house was the size of a small hotel. The room they were in was a fooler too, its bright modern décor and huge windows so different from the house's weathered gray facade.

She rather liked the modern furniture, the casual arrangements allowing many little groups to form for private conversation. But the art was something else, depicting threatening faces, hammers in upraised arms, street violence. The worst was a dark mural that ran along one wall, the kind of Thirties stylized worker's art that gave her nightmares.

When she was introduced to Virgil, she was shocked. He was shorter than she was, pudgy-soft, with mean eyes. His face was pock-marked, his stringy hair dyed much too dark for his age. The beard probably concealed sagging jowls. She recoiled at the touch of his puffy hand. How did Ellen, so tall and willowy, so poised, so classically beautiful, so well-spoken, bring herself to sleep with this hairy troglodyte?

"I hope you had a good meeting with Phil," she said.

"All my meetings are good." He laughed so loudly she jumped. It was as if somebody had shoved a bullhorn against her ear and shouted into it. "Good for me anyway." Still bellowing, he patted her shoulder. "Don't you worry about that old man of yours. He's still got the stuff." He leered at her, lowering his voice to a whisper. "Where'd he find a good-looking broad like you, may I ask? Were you in one of his films?"

I'm not a broad and I was never a bit-part, D-list actress, you acne-scarred lump of hog fat. At least her truthful answer would give her some caché. "We met in a Chelsea art gallery. I was buying a Jim Dine picture."

"Oh, Jim Dine. He's so over." Without warning, he grasped her upper arm, the back of his puffy hand pressing against her breast, and led her to the mural that frightened her. "Now this is art."

"I don't recognize it."

"You shouldn't recognize the piece, but you do recognize

Diego Rivera's style, don't you?"

Who the hell is Diego Rivera? A dishwasher? A landscaper? She nodded, unwilling one more time to admit to a shocking lack of knowledge, but more humiliation was coming.

"Well, it's not Diego Rivera." He laughed at her discomfort, giving her breast a little bump. "But, don't feel bad, it's in his style, Social Realism. It's about the oppression of the worker through urbanization and industrialization." For five minutes that seemed like an hour, he led her through the pictorials of various forms of worker oppression. "Diego, you know, was a Marxist. He married that uni-brow artist, what was her name?"

Jerry Lee wasn't venturing another word. She stood stock still.

He snapped his fingers and laughed. "Frida Kahlo. That's the gal. You know her?"

"Where does she live?"

This time he laughed so hard and so loud he almost blew out her eardrum. "Good one, Janie. Frida hasn't been doing much but rolling in her grave for years. Now I've got to see to my other guests." He bumped her breast again before unhanding her.

Jerry Lee was so angry she was shaking. He'd copped a feel. He'd made fun of her. He'd called her by the wrong name, a ploy that up till now had been exclusively hers. When a waiter walked by, she grabbed a glass of wine and tried to find Phil.

He was yukking it up with Verbena, who was pretending to be entranced by some story he was telling. Jerry Lee noted with disapproval how thin Verbena's body was, what could be seen of it beneath her flowing top. Verbena looked like an undeveloped pre-pubescent girl. Why did the richest Jews want to look like Dachau survivors? When they got rich from banking or investing or movie-making or whatever they did, why did they idolize oppressed workers and support unions? She knew lots of rich people were like that, but why the Jews, God's chosen people? She was so confused she was dizzy.

She only got more confused. During dinner her host waxed on and on about the importance of sustainable farming for maintaining a small carbon footprint: saving water, recycling manure, altering plant genes to produce drought-resistant grapes, minimizing the use of non-renewable resources. Ellen pointed out that all the food was organic and most was locally grown, some harvested from their own land.

Yet, so far as Jerry Lee could see, the estate was like a small city, using all kinds of non-renewable resources. Lights blazed everywhere. The vineyards were irrigated. Farm machinery, cars, pickups, SUVs, all sucked gasoline. Golf carts pulled electricity, as did the ubiquitous air-conditioning. The enormous swimming pool and the party-size jacuzzi were heated. What on earth were these people talking about?

They were sitting at a long table in the loveliest garden setting she'd ever seen, coddled by a platoon of servants. Long, white scrim hung between pillars, fluttering in the breeze. Illuminated grape clusters, half-hidden in the trees, cast flattering light and shadow. The gravel underfoot had been finely sieved and raked with a dinner fork. The huge vintage tablecloth had been pressed without a crease. Soft jazz, barely audible, hung in the air. Lovely food scents produced by a large kitchen staff delighted the nose. The Goldstein estate's carbon footprint was surely the size of Rhode Island's.

She looked down at her plate in dismay. If only the unfamiliar dishes were as good as they smelled. She pushed her food around, trying to make it appear that some had gone into her stomach. She'd never liked lamb in any form. The mashed eggplant had a baby-food texture and tasted of Middle-Eastern spices. She didn't know how to deconstruct the steamed artichoke. Dates did nothing for grilled carrots. She could have told them that nothing did anything for grilled carrots. The lentils were dry and tasteless. The olives were so spicy they burned her mouth. At least the tabouleh was edible, though to her taste it didn't have enough parsley. She was so hungry she filled up on it anyway, supplementing it with millet bread and olive oil, longing for a pat of creamery fresh butter. As she watched Hump and Virgil eat and eat like pigs getting ready for the slaughter, she wondered whatever happened to grilled shrimp, rice pilaf, and a good green salad? She was so disappointed with the dinner she was tempted to ask.

She could have hugged Verbena when she urged her father to find another subject of conversation. The talk inexplicably turned to children. Ellen recalled her favorite anecdote about giving birth to Verbena, how Virgil stepped right through the crotch of his pants in his excitement, hurrying to get her to the hospital, a story that seemed to make Verbena uncomfortable.

Hump bragged about the careers of his son and daughter, good-looking marketing geniuses, frequently photographed for luxury magazines, the products of his youthful marriage to a fashion designer. Sergio, who looked no more gay than Rock Hudson in Jerry Lee's favorite Doris Day movies, admitted he had no children, sounding neither apologetic nor wistful, nor even embarrassed at the question.

Slade made jokes about having fathered seven children with three different wives.

Wank said that by having no children he knew of, he'd made up for Slade's profligacy. Verbena said she kind of wanted a child once upon a time but was too old to start now.

When Jerry Lee started to brag about Poppy, Phil cut her off before she got to the Miss South Carolina pageant, saying he'd made several children but fortunately none of them ever saw the light of day.

His callousness was too much even for this crowd, except for Bong Cha, who made an approving noise. Flashing a ring set with a diamond the size of a quarter, she declaimed her disapproval of bringing children into this rotten, over-populated, stinking hot world. "You Westerners use up everything, you have too much. You melt the icebergs. Your children wear Nikes so the children in Brazil go barefoot." Or at least that's what Jerry Lee thought she heard through the accent.

Jerry Lee wanted to challenge the Korean woman's logic. Did wearing her Jimmy Choo sandals mean some refugee in the Sudan was going barefoot? Did eating roast lamb mean some poor wretch in a North Korean prison was starving? But she was too cowed by her earlier humiliations, too deadened by wine, to make the effort or risk the consequences.

Fortunately, Bong Cha's dispiriting observations prompted Ellen to declare dinner over, time to move to the fire pit. The night was chilly, after all. Ellen offered her female guests white Pashmina shawls, which she told them to keep. Jerry Lee suspected the gesture was less about generosity than sanitation.

It turned out that no topic was immune from politics. They ended the night pretending to be ordinary people, roasting DeBrand marshmallows. "The *Wall Street Journal* declared these to be the best marshmallows in the country," Ellen said. "I have to order them on-line, which I do by the case." The group roasted their pricey, precious marshmallows on willow sticks, but without the merriment, the spontaneous silliness, the friendly banter of truly ordinary people for whom roasted marshmallows were a treat.

When the men began discussing Phil's proposed movie, *Rear Action*, Jerry Lee's ears pricked up. Having rejected a liqueur in favor of a double espresso, she was doing her best to recover sobriety. But unless she missed something, the talk wasn't about making a movie at all. It was about how stupid both Bushes were, how Rumsfeld should have been hanged instead of fired, and why the first Gulf War either should never have been waged or should have been doggedly pursued until Baghdad was reduced to dust and rubble. One or the other.

Jerry Lee's heart was heavy. There seemed to be no definite plan for actually making the movie. No money seemed to be changing hands. She could sense no warmth between Phil and Virgil, no suggestion that the famed director/producer so admired his bad-boy actor friend he'd lay out a small fortune to back a picture about a forgotten war. She studied Phil. He was uncommonly subdued, the way he was when denied something he desperately wanted. He'd been that way all day. When he returned from his afternoon meeting with the running dog, he'd refused to say anything other than "Let it go."

And that meant Phil, the traitor, would always be a drain on her. If she could not forgive him, now was the time to cut her losses.

31

The Late Phil Coker
Friday, April 28, 2006

Jerry Lee and Phil returned to their cottage in silence. Fortunately, the cottage's bar was well-stocked. In a large pitcher she mixed tequila, Cointreau, and lime juice. Though it was her own recipe, she pretended it was Jack Kerouac's favorite, since he loved Mexico so much. Phil liked the idea of drinking what his favorite beat poet drank.

She plopped ice cubes into short glasses, added a lime wedge to Phil's so the glasses couldn't be confused, poured the tequila concoction over the ice, and took the glasses to the veranda, where Phil was smoking and staring at the full moon.

She kissed his forehead and handed him a drink. "How about a Jack Kerouac for the road?"

He pushed it away, growling that he wanted the tequila straight, but the hint of a smile hovered at the corners of his mouth. Unmoved by his petulance, Jerry Lee set his glass down on the table between them and began sipping hers.

After a few minutes, she asked him whether he liked the dinner.

"I liked the lamb but almost nothing else." Absent-mindedly, he took a swallow of Jack Kerouac.

"I didn't like anything but the bread and salad. Why couldn't they have served something simple, like grilled shrimp? I was so irritated I was this close to saying something."

He laughed. "Good thing you didn't, peasant girl. You'd have embarrassed yourself. Jews don't eat shellfish."

"My friend Goldie does."

"Then she's not kosher."

"Was that a kosher meal?"

"Unless you could see the kitchen, you wouldn't know."

He held out his glass for a refill. When she returned, he asked her if she'd caught that silly bit about how Virgil put his foot through the crotch of his pants in his hurry to get Ellen to the hospital.

"I thought it was funny."

"Verbena isn't their daughter. Ellen never had a baby."

"What are you talking about? Verbena looks like a clone of her mother, except thinner."

"Virgil's sterile as a mule. The rumor is he had mumps as a boy."

"Who is Verbena then?"

"Who knows? The rumor is that Ellen's sister had the baby for them. Whatever the case, they love Verbena as much as they would their own child. Maybe more. She's the pride of their life."

"So, if Virgil's sterile, Ellen doesn't have to sleep with him. I wondered how she managed that."

"You're confused, peasant girl. The old goat isn't impotent. He's just sterile. There's a difference, you know."

"The old goat copped a feel." She told him about listening to him blather on about the imitation Diego Rivera mural, all the while he held on to her arm with the back of his hand pressed against her breast. She was hoping Phil would be incensed.

Instead, he laughed. "That Virgil -- what a *poseur*. In his conference room, he has a bunch of Salvador Dalí paintings. Everybody knows they're probably fakes, but he can't admit he was had."

"He asked where we met. I told him about buying that Jim Dine picture in New York ... to which he responded that Jim Dine is *so* over."

"He was just letting you know you're an amateur collector and he wasn't impressed."

"Did you know he gave Mullett's campaign a lot of money right after that magazine article about Poppy appeared?"

"How do you know that?"

I didn't until just now, you drug-addled traitor. I was just guessing. "Everybody knows that. So how much has he given you as an advance to make the new movie?"

"We haven't worked that out yet, but it'll happen. He loves the idea for the script. He raves about it. Hump likes it too."

"Just so I'm clear. He hasn't signed anything or advanced any money yet. Is that right?"

"No." He looked up at the moon. "But he will. I can feel it in my bones. I'm very intuitive, you know." He turned his seductive gaze on her. "Where's your patience, old girl? These things take time."

"I know they do." She picked up their empty glasses. "How about one more for the road?"

In the kitchenette, she poured the last of the tequila drink into Phil's glass and then stirred in the contents of her old nitro prescription, which through time and jostling in her purse had been reduced to powder, though it hadn't yet expired. Fortunately, the attack she'd faked after Molly's accident had provided her with the excuse for a new prescription, which was safely in her toiletry bag in the bathroom. The powder from a dozen or so tablets should do it. She waited until the nitro dissolved, then added a another lime quarter and refilled her own glass with seltzer.

As she watched Phil drink his last Jack Kerouac, she felt a little wistful. She'd miss these late night gossips. She'd probably never again find another famous man to be her companion. At her age, it was unlikely she'd ever again enjoy a lover as accomplished as he was. What man would take the time to select wine for her cellar? How boring it would be to attend art openings without him.

She waited a couple of hours. She was pretty sure he was dead long before she got up to check his pulse. Satisfied, she went inside to put on her nightgown, mess up her hair and the bed. She rearranged the toiletries in her half of the bathroom suite, then laid her open purse on the coffee table in the sitting room as if Phil had rifled it to find the nitro. She placed Phil's fingers around the old prescription bottle and then dropped it, uncapped, next to Phil's almost-empty glass. It rolled onto the floor. Perfect. Then, as if she'd just woken up to find her beloved companion slumped in his chair on the porch, she dialed 0 on the kitchenette phone. Keeping firmly in mind the losses she'd just suffered, she managed to sound distressed without coming across like the overwrought, unintelligible spouses who called 911 pretending their loved ones had been murdered by an intruder.

She should have been an actress herself. She knew she'd have been much more successful than the late Phil Coker.

32

Schadenfreude
Friday, April 28, 2006

When Bernie finished doing background checks on three candidates for the position of chief accountant at a local law firm, she discovered that one of them was a registered sex offender who'd forgotten to disclose that little fact. She shook her head at the evil she ran across every day. She then turned her attention once again to Alexie Abramova to see if she could supplement the file she'd already given Tom.

The succession of photos she found on line showed a young man in the mid-nineties with a bad haircut and a fairly normal young body becoming five years later a hippie with long hair and a handlebar mustache and then finally a muscle-man with a goatee and a shaved head. His bad teeth and crooked smile ensured that he never looked completely American. His puffy eyes were small and dark. His head and nose were bulbous, like Nikita Khrushchev's.

He had not, as one of the papers said, come to America on a claim of amnesty. Alexie Abramova was born of Russian parents in Bishkek, the capital city of Kyrgyzstan, which had been a republic of the old Soviet Union but obtained independence in 1991. At the age of 21, he emigrated to the United States on a student visa, supposedly to enroll at Westwood College in Los Angeles to pursue an associate's degree in criminal justice. She could find no record that he ever registered.

Then he applied for asylum. His claim, if true, was plausible. As Christians in a Muslim-dominated country, his parents were being persecuted, denied jobs, burned out of their house, threatened by their neighbors. They'd been loyal Communists, part of an elite ruling group, but when the republic became independent, they lost their jobs working for the government. As the Muslims grew more powerful, the Christians faced more and more oppression. Claiming to be a member of the Russian Orthodox church, Alexie feared persecution too, imprisonment, possibly even execution if he were deported back to Kyrgyzstan. Or so he claimed. But his green card expired and he never applied for citizenship. Yet, on April 26, the day he was killed, he was still in the country, apparently without facing any immigration problems.

Bernie looked at a copy of the American passport provided to McBride's staff. The passport stated that "Alex Abrams" was born in Columbus, Ohio on August 19, 1974. To get that passport, he must have had some sophisticated, high-powered help getting through the State Department, which if it had looked, would have spotted everything she'd found and more. Or the State Department hadn't issued the passport at all. From the photocopy on her desk, Bernie couldn't tell how good a fake it was -- if it was a fake.

She found nothing new about Alex's work for people associated with the Soros Documentary Fund. She did uncover three new tidbits, however. He was a member of the Service Employees International Union, having joined during a brief stint as a waiter. He, or somebody who looked just like him, was spotted with Michael Moore, possibly as a bodyguard, during the making of *SiCKO*. And Alex had been arrested twice in San Francisco for lewd behavior during gay pride parades. A snapshot of him in black leather revealed far more about his assets than anybody wanted to know. Bernie grimaced. She was gay but not an exhibitionist or activist.

She sat back, puzzled. The claim of asylum because of Muslim persecution was plausible, but it didn't match up with The Soros Fund's "documentaries" about how there is no jihad, no radical Islamists, no war on terror, no persecution of Christians. Where did Alexie get the money to emigrate from a poor country where his parents were jobless and being persecuted? If he was part of a persecuted Christian minority, why did he work for Soros, who denied that any such persecution was taking place anywhere in the world? Why hadn't he followed through on his claim of persecution to get citizenship?

Bernie then turned her attention to LuAnn Mullett, whose bond had been set at a million dollars and whose troubles made the McBride campaign almost giddy. She searched for the word that fluttered at the back of her brain. *Schadenfreude* or something like that. She googled Wikipedia. That was it. A German word meaning pleasure derived from the misfortune of others. She didn't feel it herself, but then she wasn't a politician.

LuAnn Julia Bloodworth was born in Athens, Georgia in 1957, making her three years older than her husband. Her father Gerald, was a dentist. Her mother, Shirley, was his hygienist before marrying him and having five children in quick succession. LuAnn was the oldest child. The only parent still alive was Shirley, a resident of Mullett Village at Naples. The youngest Bloodworth child, born with Down's Syndrome, had died many years ago but LuAnn's other siblings still lived in Athens.

A 1979 graduate of Palmer College of Chiropractic in Port Orange, LuAnn was childless and divorced when she met Myron Mullett, who'd sought her help for a leg problem. At that time he was the director of one of his father's many nursing homes. They subsequently married and had three children, two boys, now both in college, and a girl, Megan, a senior in high school. A few years after they were married, Mullett ran for County Commissioner, a post he'd held until a few years ago.

Four years ago, LuAnn pleaded guilty to a DUI charge and later entered rehab. There had been no arrests since then. The only unusual thing Bernie could uncover was that the Mullett home was in Fort Myers, where LuAnn still practiced, but her husband claimed their villa in Naples as his primary residence. His office was also in Naples. So they'd been living apart.

LuAnn was a woman with regular features, a little overweight, dressed very plainly. Myron, on the other hand, was downright ugly, a stray strand of hair always hanging over his forehead, his lips blubbery and wet. A large dark wen marred his chin. They didn't look like a couple.

Bernie sat back again to contemplate her findings. LuAnn seemed to have led an unremarkable life, a little spotty here and there, a few bad choices, but whose life wasn't spotted with a few bad choices? How did a woman with the discipline to become a successful chiropractor while raising three apparently normal children become so enraged as to run over her husband's mistress, not once but twice, while her daughter screamed in the passenger seat and her husband watched from the sidelines?

Schadenfreude might be the mood of the entertainment and news culture that ruled the day, but it wasn't for Bernie. This was a sad story, heart-breaking for so many. No doubt it was grist for Molly's mill -- if, that is, she could untangle herself from whatever conflicts of interest might have settled around her shoulders like an industrial strength spider web now that she was an apologist for Poppy McBride.

33

Butterfly Pin
Saturday , April 29, 2006

On Saturday, Molly, Lily, and Sara joined Poppy for an early breakfast at the Port Royal Beach Club. Their husbands had an early tee time. Dressed in summery clothes, the women looked to an outsider like a flock of brightly plumed birds twittering about nothing more important than good nesting sights and conveniently located bird-feeders. And for awhile that was true.

The murder of Muffy Wayne, though, was such a hot topic that they couldn't avoid it. To a woman, they felt sorrier for LuAnn than either Myron or his mistress. Their pity was mixed with dark humor.

"Just think," Sara said, barely suppressing a smile. "If Muffy had married Myron, she'd be Muffy Mullett."

"A trendy variation on the Brazilian wax job, the Mullett Muff is preferred by politicians everywhere," Lily said, unable to keep from laughing.

"LuAnn clearly ran over the wrong person," Molly said. "Myron would be so much handsomer with tire marks on his face, that ugly wen on his chin flattened. Don't you think he looks like he just dropped a bite of sausage on himself? Every time I see him, I want to wipe the sausage off his face."

But the real subject of their meeting was Molly's first background piece on Poppy, published on Friday and focusing on her humble upbringing -- "a puff piece," according to Mullett's campaign.

"Your wonderful article has taken some of the heat off me, Molly. It wasn't too fawning, I think, though there's nothing wrong with a little fawning." She laughed. "But you have to admit that LuAnn Mullett and her Navigator have pushed me right under the radar. Now if you could just arrange for Harley Wangle to rob a liquor store or something, you wouldn't have to write another word to help the campaign."

Not until their plates had been cleared away and the waiter had left did Molly confess her concerns. "Your story is endearing, Poppy, and I'm honored to tell it. But from what I've discovered, there's a boogeyman lurking in the corner holding a grenade, and it might be Verlin. If Dewey's and Nicky Sue's disappearances weren't innocent, he might know why."

"Tell me again why you think they might not be innocent."

"Dewey's car was found in the pond at the mortuary where you grew up. That's pretty odd. Why in that location? Why was it abandoned? What happened to him? His mother told Tom that she thinks her son just walked away from the crisis of your pregnancy, but Jerry Lee admits she told him he was never going to marry you. Maybe she decided to enforce that decree. What if he didn't just walk away?"

"But there was no body in the car."

"It's somewhere, we know that, either living or dead. Where is it? If he's alive, it's pretty strange no one has heard from him since then. If he's dead, my money is on the person who put the car in the pond.

"Next, you mysteriously have a miscarriage that almost kills you. Verlin gave you tea just before you laid down for a nap. He knows a lot about herbs, so maybe there was something in the tea. The emergency room doctor admitted to Tom that Verlin whispered a word that sounded like 'Texas' but might have been '*Taxus*,' short for *Taxus baccata*, an herb that is used as an abortifacient and that Verlin mentioned to Lily. The miscarriage, according to what Jerry Lee told Tom, was 'convenient.'"

"Convenient? It almost killed me."

Molly didn't want to lose her train of thought. "Next, Nicky Sue, your roommate, goes missing. She would have won the pageant if she'd been present the next day. We know how much your mother wanted you to win. She might have thought that getting Nicky Sue out of the way would ensure that. Think about it. She's never forgiven me for being crowned, so maybe, just maybe, my accident on the veranda wasn't an accident.

"And then there's poor old Paul Rossetti, living under a cloud all these years, the last person to see Nicky Sue . . . except for two people in a vintage Impala that fits the description of the one your mother preserved from Jonah's collection. She denied Verlin knows how to drive, but you know better, and for some reason he loves that car so much she let him keep it. Paul saw two heads in the car before your roommate got in. Maybe Verlin was driving, with Jerry Lee in the passenger seat, the night Nicky Sue was walking back to the hotel alone, never to be heard from again."

She stopped, out of breath. "What do you think?"

All eyes were on Poppy, whose eyes were red and watery. "If Jerry Lee did what you imply, she's a monster."

Molly took her friend's hand. "Honestly, Poppy, at this stage I'm not implying anything. I'm just stating facts and trying to make sense of them. My point is that if someone else gets hold of these same facts, they're going to put the worst possible interpretation on them, and we already know someone has at least one or two facts about your miscarriage. It's in your interest to find out what the right interpretation is before someone else does."

"So what do we do?"

"Jerry Lee's out of town. She'd deny everything anyway, as she's already done with respect to Dewey. But Verlin seems to have been present at a lot of dark events. He might not have understood everything he saw, but wouldn't it be wise to find out what he knows? I'm afraid that all the good work we're doing with these background pieces will be for naught if . . . ."

"You don't have to spell it out. Maybe the best thing is simply to show up unannounced. Lily has a book for Verlin anyway, so that's the pretext for us all to go."

When they mounted the stairs at Beaudry Hall and rang the bell, Niall answered. Unsmiling, he claimed the house was unfit to be seen while a professional cleaning company readied it for the fund-raiser. He did not invite them in, instead suggesting they walk around to the back. Verlin might be anywhere, but they might want to start with the stone potting shed.

Poppy rolled her eyes at Niall's insolence but declined to make an issue of it. They found Verlin, who was indeed in the potting shed. On a wooden table, he'd laid out the contents of a Mason jar, this time not buttons but belt buckles, barrettes, broaches, money clips, cuff links, a necklace, coins, a pendant carved with the Mayan calendar, and many other items. The treasures were sorted into clusters that made no sense to anyone but Verlin, who was bending over one of them with a magnifying glass.

Lily stood in the doorway, waiting for him to notice her and be invited in. When he looked up, she held out a book. "I've returned with the book I promised, Verlin. May we come in?" She turned to reveal her friends.

"All of you?"

"If you don't mind."

"Okay." In a familiar gesture, he wiped his hands down the legs of his overalls.

When he spotted Molly, he hastily found the Leo ankle bracelet and slipped it into his pocket. She might want it back.

Poppy walked over to hug him. "How's my favorite uncle?"

"Am I your favorite?"

"Yes, of course," she answered, not mentioning the obvious, that he was her only uncle.

Lily handed Verlin the book she'd bought him.

He read the title and author aloud. "*A Guide to Deadly Herbs*, by Julie Gomez."

"I want you to know it wasn't easy to get that book, Verlin. It was written more than five years ago and everywhere I checked it was out of stock. The Silvermans had to search for a second-hand copy." She gently took the book from his hands and opened it.

"You'll notice that besides photographs it has a lot of charming hand-drawn illustrations. Do you like it?"

"Yes." He took her hand. "But I already know all about deadly herbs."

"I guessed that. But I thought you might find it helpful anyway so you don't grind up the wrong ones."

He walked her closer to the table. "I like looking at pretty things."

"You have quite a collection."

"They're mine now."

Poppy walked over to the table and began scanning the items. When she spotted a sparkly butterfly pin, she picked it up. "This looks exactly like the one I lent to Nicky Sue. She was going to wear it in the evening gown competition." She looked at her uncle. "I don't remember her returning it to me."

"It's mine now."

"You can keep it, Verlin, but where did you find it?"

He pointed in the direction of the carriage house. "In the Impala."

"How did it get there, for heaven's sake?"

"Nicky Sue left it."

"When? When was she ever in the Impala?"

He realized he should stop talking now, but he was in the company of friends and he was lonely. He hardly ever got to say what was on his mind. Because Jerry Lee was gone, she couldn't suddenly appear around a corner to shut him up. He wanted the women, who seemed to be entertained by what he had to say, to stay awhile longer. He ran his hands down the legs of his overalls. "The night we picked her up."

"We? Who's we?"

"Your mother and me."

Molly perked up her ears. "At the pageant in Greenville?"

Instead of answering, Verlin walked over to the tall cupboard and picked through a stack of little notebooks with paperboard covers and curled wire spines. Finding the one he wanted, he opened it up.

"May I?" Poppy asked.

Verlin handed her the notebook. "It's my diary."

She stared at the page in disbelief. "But I don't understand a thing here. What language do you write in? It's certainly not English."

"My own."

"I recognize some Latin words. Some symbols, some stuff that looks like hieroglyphics."

"Cuneiform, the Hebrew alphabet, and runes too. Did you know that when the Hebrews were slaves in Egypt, they didn't write the same way as their masters? The Hebrews already had a real alphabet."

"How do you know that?"

"I watch an archaeologist on cable who knows all about the Hebrews and Egyptians."

"Where'd you learn all these forms of writing?"

He smiled proudly. "Some from books, some I make up. I'm alone a lot, you know. And I don't like people knowing my business. I tried invisible ink, but then I couldn't read it either."

"So why did you pull out this book?"

He took it back, flipped a few pages, and stopped at one where he began to read. "'Greenville. Year 5750.'"

Poppy interrupted. "What do you mean, year 5750?"

"Hebrew calendar. I like that calendar because it's in lunar months. Good for gardeners, you know."

"What year in our calendar was 5750?"

"1989," Verlin answered without hesitation. He resumed reading. "'My sister and I picked up Nicky Sue on a street around 10:30. Then we drove to a motel, where Jerry Lee and Nicky Sue got out. Then Jerry Lee made me leave and drive back to Charleston all alone that night.'" He looked up. "I never saw Nicky Sue again. But I know where she is."

"You do? Where she'd go?"

"She didn't go anywhere. She's in the statue, like I said."

"The Nike statue? You've said that for years, but nobody knows what you're talking about."

He stayed silent.

"Will you take us there?"

He took Poppy's hand. When they got to Nike's garden, he pointed at the long marble plinth. "She's in there."

"You mean she's dead?"

"I think so. She never comes out."

"But she can't be in there. It's solid stone."

He shook his head vigorously. "It's hollow." He walked to the back of the base and pointed. "See where that big piece is set in? It can be removed."

"Her body or her ashes are in there?"

"Her body."

Poppy looked at her friends with horror, but Verlin wasn't done.

"See the *Datura stramonium*?" He looked over his glasses. "Angel's Trumpet? That's what Jerry Lee took with her that night when we picked Nicky Sue up."

"A bouquet of flowers?"

He shook his head vigorously. "Powder. Jerry Lee put it in a simple syrup, made lemonade out of it."

"What's it do?"

"Gives you visions."

"Hallucinations, you mean?"

"If you don't take too much."

"What if you take too much?"

"You die."

Poppy sat down on the bench. "Is Dewey here?"

Verlin cast his eyes toward a far corner of the garden.

"He is, isn't he? Take me there."

He took her hand. After she rose, he led her to the herb garden, Molly, Lily and Sara bringing up the rear. Then he walked over to the bronze statue and ran his hand over its snout, which was shiny. "I rub it for luck. He's the pig."

"What do you mean, he's the pig?"

"Jerry Lee gave Dewey's ashes to the artist, said to add them to the metal when it was cast."

"Why?"

"So he'd always be with us." He paused and smiled. "I heard somebody found his car in the pond. I always liked that car, hated pushing it into the pond."

"You did that?"

He looked very proud. "Did they find the stick I used on the accelerator so I wouldn't have to drive it in?"

"I don't know."

Molly spoke up. "What did Jerry Lee give him?"

"The *Datura stramonium*. She tried it first on Dewey, but for him she put it in Coke. He liked Cokes. She just wanted him to stay away from her daughter." He smiled at his niece. "You," he added as if it wasn't clear who Jerry Lee's daughter was.

Poppy looked at her friends, then back at her uncle. "Tell me, Verlin, who else is in the garden?"

"Your dad. Jonah's in the mausoleum."

"I know that. But at least he died naturally."

Verlin stared at her, saying nothing.

"Oh, please don't tell me. Did he have any . . . ?" She searched for words. "Did he have any help from Jerry Lee?"

"A little. He was going to stop you from doing pageants. She didn't want him to suffer."

"What help did she give him?"

"*Cicuta virosa* . Water hemlock. She had me grind up the roots. It took about fifteen minutes before he started having seizures, but she used so much he died pretty quick. Jerry Lee and his assistant laid him on an embalming table. He didn't last long after that."

"They didn't call an ambulance?"

He shrugged and took off his glasses, wiping them on his sleeve. "Can't remember. He did suffer, though."

"Oh, God help us all." Poppy looked at her friends in disbelief.

Verlin wasn't done. "You were almost here with Jonah, you know."

"What do you mean by that?" Poppy's eyes were wild.

"*Taxus baccata*. That's what got rid of the baby, only she gave you too much. I didn't know she was going to do that. Otherwise,

I wouldn't have given you the tea. I'd have made her hand it to you."

Poppy looked around as if she'd just found herself in a charnel house with a lunatic. "What do we do now?"

Lily took her arm. "I think we get out of here."

Poppy turned to Verlin. "Don't tell Jerry Lee you told us this." *She'll kill you too if she finds out.*

"It's in my diary."

"Does she know you keep a diary?"

"Probably." He remembered mentioning it that night they were watching the biker outside the carriage gate. "But she couldn't read it anyway. Do you want to go back to the shed? I have Dewey's belt buckle. It's brass with a horse on it. I have Jonah's . . . ."

"Verlin, stop talking, put that stuff away and don't show anybody else. Not ever." She looked at Lily. "Clearly he didn't need that book you found."

"I'm so sorry. I never bought a worse gift in my life. I thought it would help him *avoid* . . . ."

Poppy gave her friend a sympathetic look. "I know what you intended. You couldn't know. None of us could." She turned to Verlin. "Did you ever tell any of this to anyone else?"

"Not what I told you."

"Why not?"

"Nobody ever asked."

Molly took Poppy's other arm. "Sweetie, I really think it's time to go."

Poppy looked at Verlin with a mixture of pity and distaste. "Go back to the shed, Verlin. We have to go now. Put all that stuff away, hide it. And don't tell a soul what you told us. Wipe it out of your mind. Okay?"

Verlin put his glasses back on. "Okay." He looked accusingly at Molly. "Then I'll trim the hedges where that lady broke some of them."

Molly said, *sotto voce*, "At least your mother didn't put anything in those sticky buns. I ate two of them without a second thought."

"Never eat or drink anything in this house," Poppy warned. "Don't go near a railing if Jerry Lee's nearby. Don't tell her I'm pregnant. Don't beat me at anything, not even tennis." She took a deep breath. "I'm going to carve a warning under the sign for Beaudry Hall -- No Dogs, but Beware of Owner, Enter at Your Own Risk."

"I think we have to either change the venue for the fund-raiser or make sure Jerry Lee isn't here," Lily said.

"Or have somebody follow my mother like a hawk." Poppy laughed weakly. "If she opens an oven, push her in. Isn't that what Hansel and Gretel did to the old witch? Tell you the truth, I'm ready to do it myself."

34

Speak of the Old Witch
Saturday, April 29, 2006

Before the women reached Port Royal, Poppy's cell phone rang. She rolled her eyes when she saw the screen. "Speak of the old witch."

She let it ring a second time before answering. "How was the party last night?"

"Terrible. I'll tell you about it later, in detail. You're going to like Verbena, but the rest of them are nothing special. The food was gross."

"I'm sorry to hear that."

"Anyway, the reason I'm calling is that Phil died last night."

Poppy gasped, both at the dreadful news and her mother's matter-of-fact tone, opening with her assessment of the party rather than the sudden death of her partner. She switched to the speaker phone and looked at Lily, who was driving.

"Phil died? How?"

"Heart attack maybe, but we won't know for sure until an autopsy is done. It looks like he might have taken some nitro out of my purse."

"How do you know that?"

"The nitro bottle was uncapped and had rolled onto the porch floor. His fingerprints are on it."

"You can see his fingerprints?"

"No," Jerry Lee said impatiently to cover her mistake. "I'm presuming."

"You didn't see him take it?"

"I'd gone to bed. He must have sat outside on the porch awhile."

"If he was having an attack, why didn't he wake you up? He had enough time to find your nitro, after all. He could have asked you to call 911."

"You'd have to ask him, Poppy. I was asleep and I'm not a mind-reader."

"I'm shocked. And sorry. Are you all right?"

"No, I'm not all right, Poppy. What do you think? I'm stranded out here, all alone, and these are not the friendliest people in the world. Ellen and Verbena left for the airport without even coming to the cottage first. They're going to Savannah for the premiere of her new movie."

"So what are you going to do?"

"The police have asked me to stay around for a few days. They're coming back this afternoon to talk to me. The Goldsteins have had the decency to let me stay in the cottage for awhile . . . which is the least they can do, don't you think? It happened on their watch, after all."

"What do you mean, their watch?"

"Don't get smart. I can barely think straight, so if my words don't come out right, forgive me." Her tone was sarcastic. "It happened in their guest cottage, that's what I mean. They have a responsibility to take care of me."

"No, they don't, Jerry Lee. But I'm glad they are taking care of you."

"Am I on the speaker phone?"

"Yes, you are."

"Is anybody else there?"

"No." Poppy grimaced against the lie. "I'm driving, that's all. I don't want to hold the phone."

"Before I come home, I'm going to spend a week at The Fairmont Sonoma Mission Inn and Spa. I've already booked it.

Have you ever heard of it?"

"No, but I know Sonoma's near Napa."

"Thermal mineral waters, five-star food, the works. I have to get away from Virgil, who's the only one still here, besides the servants. He copped a feel at the party last night, so I've got to stay out of sight. Besides, I'm entitled to a little get-away, don't you think?"

"You said Phil took your nitro. Did he take it all? Do I need to call your doctor so he can send you another prescription?"

"Luckily, Phil only found my old prescription, and, yes, he took it all, every last grain. My new one was in the bathroom."

"Did you say grain? What do you mean, grain?"

"The pills had disintegrated into powder."

"How many pills disintegrated into powder?"

About eleven, you nosy girl. "I have no idea."

"Did he take all the powder?"

"Looks like it, the fool."

"Why didn't you throw the powdery stuff away if you already had a new prescription with you?"

"Good heavens, Poppy, I didn't have time yesterday to think about things like my nitro prescriptions. I had to pack in a few hours."

"This is so sudden it's hard to believe."

"Phil and I had such a nice little gossip last night. I'm going to miss that. Did you know Verbena isn't really the Goldsteins' daughter?"

Lily's head snapped around. "How does she know that?" she mouthed.

"How do you know that?"

"Phil says Virgil's been sterile from childhood when he got the mumps. That's the rumor, anyway. Ellen's sister had the baby for them. Hard to believe, let me tell you, because Verbena looks exactly like her mother. She's not as snooty as Ellen, but they look alike. In fact, they look more alike than you and I do."

I suppose it's too much to hope I was adopted. "Do you know what Phil wanted in the way of a funeral?"

"No, but I'll think about that at the spa. He was from Nevada, you know, some place called Dusty Crossroads or something." She laughed. "I'll send his body there, I think. Let him rest with his parents."

"You don't want him in Florida?" She turned to look at Molly and Sara in the backseat. "In the garden, perhaps, with all the others?"

"In the mausoleum, you mean? No. That's for family. That's where I'll be someday, along with Verlin. You and Ferrin too, unless he'd prefer Indiana."

"Well, let's not rush things."

"I've got to go. My breakfast is being delivered. I ordered crab bennies and fruit. I'm hoping breakfast is better than dinner was."

"What time is it there?"

"Eight o'clock."

"When did Phil die?"

"Who knows? Some time before I found him around two in the morning."

"Why didn't you call me right away?"

"Oh, for goodness' sake, Poppy. Why should I disturb you so early? It won't bring him back."

"You don't sound very sad, Jerry Lee."

"I'm old, remember. I've seen a lot of death. You get used to it."

Poppy rolled her eyes. "I bet you do."

"What's that supposed to mean?"

"Nothing. So what do we do about the fund-raiser?"

"You can have it at Beaudry Hall anyway. I'm generous that way. Make sure Ferrin knows that."

"We're . . . I mean, *I'm* just on my way to talk to him. Where should we send flowers?"

"Don't waste your money. Besides, I have no idea when Phil's body will be released or where the memorial service, if there is one, will take place."

"Be careful what you say to the police."

"Why?"

"It's just a general rule. If they think there was anything suspicious about his death, you're the one going to be sitting under the hot lights in a windowless room."

"There wasn't anything suspicious, Poppy. You and your friends watch too many crime shows. He drank too many Jack Kerouacs, then he took too much nitro and died, that's all."

"If you say so."

"I'll call you when I get to the spa."

"You do that, Jerry Lee." Poppy flipped her phone shut.

She looked at Lily, then turned to look at Molly and Sara in the backseat. "Did she kill the poor guy or not?"

"How does she know his fingerprints are on the nitro vial? That's my first question. How does she know he took too much nitro, that's my second question," Molly said. "And if he was having a heart attack, why didn't he call 911 or wake her up? That's my third. Fourth, why did she have two nitro prescriptions with her? Don't most people throw out the old one? I have more questions if you want to hear them."

"Oh, God help us. Ferrin's going to have a fit."

35

War Movie, Schwar Movie
Saturday, April 29, 2006

On Saturday night, the Lawtons, the Bancrofts, and the Standardts reached The Marshall House in Savannah just before the free wine reception closed on the main floor. Given how little time they'd had after the women's rendezvous with Verlin and Poppy at Beaudry Hall, it was a good thing Lily had booked a charter jet. She was thankful her first husband's contract on it hadn't yet expired.

They shamelessly took two glasses of wine each, plus plates of crackers, cheese and grapes, to the second floor, where they briefly admired their beautiful high-ceilinged rooms and then crawled through the enormous windows onto the long veranda. "I had no idea we'd have to hoist ourselves up a couple of feet to get out on the veranda," Sara said. "I thought you could just step through the window."

"We'll work off a little of this cheese that way," Bob said, helping Tom and Carl to put a couple of round tables together and find six wrought iron chairs.

Molly walked over to the veranda rail. "It's interesting, looking down at Broughton Street. We're across from the Casbah Moroccan Restaurant, which I think is still open." She wiggled her hips. "Anyone interested in watching belly dancers during dinner?" There was a chorus of groans behind her. "No? Then come watch the busses and bums with me. Lots of those and totally free." She whirled around, pretending to stagger. "Did I hear Jerry Lee behind me?"

They laughed. There were only two other people on the veranda at the far end, a fortyish couple, occupying the same rocking chair, so physically interested in each other they wouldn't have noticed a five-alarm fire.

The six friends collectively breathed a sigh of relief. Finally, they were free to talk about Phil Coker's death without anyone overhearing them. After discussing that awhile, adding many speculative details to what the women had learned from Jerry Lee's call to Poppy, they reached a consensus: the superannuated rebel had passed his expiration date and Jerry Lee had tossed him out like curdled milk. The means seemed obvious: She'd shaken some nitro powder into his tequila.

"His blood pressure would have fallen into the pits," Bob observed. "He might not have felt a thing other than that he was passing out."

"What will the autopsy reveal?" Tom asked.

"Well, didn't you say he had heart problems, at least according to Jerry Lee? The autopsy might show a damaged heart but not what we really want to know . . . whether the man took the nitro voluntarily."

What they couldn't reach a consensus on was the motive. Molly bet it was because he leaked the abortion story. Sara thought it was because Jerry Lee Beaudry was tired of supporting him. Lily was convinced it was because Coker didn't get the movie deal that might have saved his hash. Tom thought an unmitigated prat like Coker had been asking for it for years and was surprised it hadn't happened earlier. After Bob and Carl glanced at each other, they spoke in chorus. "Because she could."

They moved on to Harley Wangle's press conference the day before. Commissioner Mullett was not having an affair with Muffy Wayne, Wangle insisted. She'd been dating a member of the campaign staff but not Mullett. There was more to the story than the security tapes showed, so the public shouldn't rush to judgment.

LuAnn never meant to kill anyone. Knowing Mrs. Mullett as they all did, they didn't believe she was aiming her Navigator at the staffer but in a moment of rage just drove around blindly, unfortunately striking Miss Wayne twice. Yes, Wangle conceded, the second impact crushing the girl's chest made it look like a deliberate homicide, but looks are sometimes deceiving. Mullett stood by his wife, whom he loved and had always been faithful to. The Mullett family asked for privacy while they dealt with their grief.

Unable to resist a campaign plug even in the midst of tragedy, Wangle thanked the police for their timely arrival at the scene, saying he hoped people understood now why funding their pensions was so important. In response to a question, Wangle assured the public that, despite the tragedy, Mullett would be honoring his scheduled appearances.

"Not a word of condolence to Muffy Wayne's family," Carl observed. "That's what I noticed. If the Mullett family is dealing with grief, think what the Wayne family is dealing with."

"Do you really think Mullett's supporters will abandon him, though?" Lily asked. "Somehow, I can't see the left-wingers swinging over to Ferrin just because Mullett was getting it on with a staffer. Remember Clinton? Liberals only condemn affairs when the politician is conservative and therefore can be excoriated as a hypocrite."

Bob laughed. "I think his backers will high-five him for finding someone who'd sleep with him."

The women giggled their agreement. "Our sentiments exactly," Sara said.

It was dark and they were on their second glass of wine when Tom got a call on his cell phone. He looked at the screen and then his friends. "It's Verbena," he said, getting to his feet. "Should I step away?"

"No, no. Stay here. Put her on speaker." Molly bounced in her chair with eagerness.

Tom sat back down. "Verbena, how's it going?"

"Are you in Savannah yet?"

"We are. I have you on speaker so everybody can participate."

"Everybody? Are the McBrides with you?"

"No. Just the three couples you knew about."

"Well, hi, everybody," Verbena said in her signature throaty voice.

The women chorused their hellos.

"We've checked in," Tom resumed, "and are listening to sirens and drinking wine on the veranda." He caught Lily's frown at the mention of sirens. "The rooms are great, by the way, and the veranda allows us a breath of fresh air, so thanks for making the hotel arrangements. Where are you?"

"At The Ballastone Inn on East Oglethorpe, a very short distance from you. No sirens, but we have history and wine and plenty of antebellum atmosphere. This place was built in 1838 and, though it was first a grand residence and then a boarding house and so on, it's a very exclusive bed-and-breakfast now, with just sixteen rooms. Paul Newman stayed here and raved about it, so you get the idea. My co-star . . . Cree Kahane, remember him, Tom? You met him on the set. As always, he brought an entourage: wife, children ranging in age from fifteen to two, parents, nannies, driver, maybe a couple people from his fan club, meaning he booked every room except mine and Bordon's, my mother's, and a third reserved for Dad. Until an hour ago, the hallways were a little kid-noisy because Cree and Theresa embrace the latest parenting techniques, which are all about self-expression."

"Virgil's not here yet?"

"No. He's flying in tomorrow. He never, ever cooperates, has to do everything by himself on his own unfathomable schedule. Even though I'm over forty, he pretends he and Mom have to fly separately for my sake so I won't be an orphan. Before I forget, I want to remind you that you're all invited to the after-party tomorrow." They reviewed details about the location, the arrangements to get them in, the dress code, and the time the limo would pick them up.

"Be forewarned that security's going to be very tight and the lines will be long and slow, so I've arranged for the limo service to get you to the Jepson Center about ninety minutes early. I'm really sorry about how long you're going to have to wait, but there's nothing I can do about it. I've been getting death threats."

"From whom?"

"Mostly far-left wingnuts, anonymous bloggers living in their parents' basements and snarfing Cheetos. They're angry that I'm appearing at that fund-raiser you invited me to. My little stunt seems to have stirred up a hornet's nest. *The Huffington Post* is all over my tush on this one because apparently everything Goldstein belongs to them. They're calling for a boycott of the premiere, though I'm told there have been no cancellations. Maybe, Tom, you and I could talk at the after-party for a few minutes about security at the fund-raiser."

"I'll make sure I'm available."

"Did you hear that Phil Coker died last night at Mom and Dad's house? In a guest cottage, but still."

"We heard. The McBride campaign is trying to stay on top of it, since Coker lived with his mother-in-law. So, what's the story?"

"Heart attack, according to that woman he brought. What's her name again?"

"Jerry Lee Beaudry."

"That's it. Why she called our staff instead of 911 is beyond me. We didn't know Hollywood's Bad Boy had heart problems, so it was a shock for someone his age to pop off like that. Privately, Mom wonders if he wasn't on cocaine again, but you didn't hear it from me."

"What's Coker's death do to your dad's plans to make his war movie?"

She laughed. "War movie, schwar movie. Nothing whatsoever. There were no plans. Dad never bought any rights or made an advance on a script, which Coker hadn't written yet anyway, or made commitments of any kind. Dad met with Coker Friday but said all he did was compliment him on the pitch and make a few vague promises. When Coker couldn't get a contract from Dad, he did a little acting out, but that just made Dad dig in his heels. As I told you before, that whole thing in *Rolling Stone* was a big PR balloon, either a charade on my dad's part or wishful thinking on Coker's."

"Did Jerry Lee know that?"

"I have no idea. Neither she nor Coker said much at dinner. He was morose and bitter . . . which gave rise to Mom's suspicions that he'd fallen into his old druggie patterns. His overdressed companion mostly just pushed her food around as if it were hog slop." They heard Bordon Settle's voice in the background. "Sorry to cut this short, Tom, but Bordon says it's time to go down to the courtyard for a nightcap and a cigarette. I'm glad you're here. Sleep tight and see you tomorrow."

Bob reentered his and Sara's room to find the cigar case, portable liquor bar, and huge cans of mixed nuts he'd brought for just this contingency. Tom and Carl both went in search of ice. The women emptied ashtrays and generally straightened up. They had a lot to talk and laugh about and the night was young. They didn't want to lose their buzz.

When they were all settled again, the men with brandies, the women with Kahlúa, Molly mentioned another death. "So tell us, Tom, what you know about Ferrin's driver. Was it just an accident or something else?" She laughed. "I assume his death has nothing to do with Jerry Lee."

He looked around. The frisky couple at the end of the veranda had disappeared. He decided it was safe to tell the story. "You might be wrong about that. The driver, Alexie Abramova, a Russian immigrant, had worked for various far-left organizations, including a Soros group that funded some of the documentaries Goldstein made. He was here illegally, but somebody was protecting him, somebody pretty powerful. Phil was meeting Ferrin's driver every week. He admitted he was passing on Poppy's secrets through Alexie in exchange for a movie deal with Goldstein. There's no question, by the way, but that Phil knew about the miscarriage. Though millions of dollars made their way to Mullett, Phil hadn't yet gotten any money or commitments as payment for his inside information, and Verbena, as you heard, seems pretty sure he never was going to get any, at least not a movie deal. Phil seemed genuinely surprised when Ferrin told him about Goldstein's generous contribution to Mullett's campaign. No doubt that's why he made his most recent trip to California, to demand some money. What we don't know for sure is how much Jerry Lee had figured out about Phil's double-dealing."

"Even if she only had a suspicion he hurt her beloved daughter, Phil's life was in danger," Molly said.

"This is all off the record, by the way."

Everybody nodded. "So was Jerry Lee driving the blue sedan mentioned in the papers?" Lily asked.

"Not just a blue sedan but most likely Phil's blue Prius. Somebody wearing a kangol like Phil's was at the wheel. But Phil, we think, was in Jerry Lee's Cadillac on a fool's errand to Marco that night."

"So it was probably Jerry Lee driving. Did we overlook another motive for Phil's death then?" Sara asked. "Revenge."

"Well, Molly hazarded her guess that Jerry Lee killed him because he was the leaker. That's revenge, I suppose."

"Jerry Lee's been very clever." Molly again. "Can anything be proved?"

"Not easily. There's not enough forensic evidence to give confidence to a prosecutor to risk his career on a trial or convince a skeptical jury that circumstantial evidence is as real as forensic evidence when the crime was committed without witnesses. I'm amazed how often juries think any doubt is reasonable. In a perfect world, prosecutors would be brave enough to charge Jerry Lee and juries would be intelligent enough to convict her. But in a perfect world, of course, she wouldn't be murdering anyone."

"Speaking of witnesses," Molly said, "as we learned this morning, Verlin was a witness to some of the old deaths."

"But can you imagine what would happen to him on cross-examination?"

"I know, I know, but somehow Jerry Lee's got to be stopped," Molly rejoined. "In less than a week she's taken out the Russian and the washed-up actor who lived with her. And I swear she deliberately pushed me over that railing. Poppy said I just missed a stake that could have impaled me." She shivered. "The old witch wanted to kill me, I'm sure. My elbow is still stiff and you can feel the bone chip."

"It's a big problem for Ferrin. The last thing he needs is to have his mother-in-law arrested for murder."

"Thank goodness she won't be at Beaudry Hall for the fund-raiser," Lily said.

"Maybe the medical examiner in California will find something," Tom said, accepting a cigar from Bob. "For now, I think he's our best hope."

36

A Mad World

Sunday, April 30, 2006

Since they wouldn't have to be ready for the premiere until just before five o'clock Sunday afternoon, and since their husbands had already reserved a tee time at a nearby golf club, Lily, Sara, and Molly decided they were going to use the scant hours they had to see something of historic Savannah. But what?

"Bonaventure Cemetery," Molly said, "since that's the place the movie is named for."

"Don't you think tons of people here for the premiere will have the same idea?" Sara asked. "I fear it'll be too crowded. Besides, we'd have to book a driver and I bet this weekend everybody's booked."

"I always wanted to see the Mercer-Williams house where *Midnight in the Garden of Good and Evil* was set," Lily said, flipping through a copy of *Savannah Scene*. "It's on Bull Street, only a few blocks from here. We can walk, see some of the squares that have made Savannah famous, eat lunch at the Gryphon Tea Room, also on Bull."

"But first, we're going to church," Sara insisted. "I suggest either the Cathedral of Saint John the Baptist or the First African Baptist Church."

They ended their church-going, historic house tour, and walk-about at Leopold's Ice Cream, a short distance from The Marshall

House, tired and ready for a nap.

When they gathered late that afternoon in the lobby of the hotel to wait for the limousine Verbena had hired for them, the six friends looked like a flock of birds with the genders reversed, the males sporting the sober colors of classic tuxedos, the females gaudy in colorful gowns and jewels.

"This is so much fun," Molly said, swishing the skirt of her long emerald-green gown and adjusting its matching stole. "I've hardly worn a long gown since my beauty queen days."

"Will I finally get to meet Verbena?" Lily asked teasingly of her husband. "You know, the movie star *The National Enquirer* swore you were going to marry?"

"If I were a litigious man, I've have sued their socks off for that."

She kissed his cheek. "Oh, well, it all came out right in the end. But I'm serious. Will I meet Verbena?"

"At the after-party we'll meet everybody, I promise. This will be a night to remember."

Tom spoke more than he knew. The night went normally enough at first. Limos choked the narrow streets. Pushy photographers and screaming fans lined the ropes along the red carpet. Television commentators pulled the big stars aside to ask them how they felt and who they were wearing. Ushers herded clots of dissatisfied celebrities to their assigned seats, few of which met their occupants' ideas of their own importance. Twenty minutes late, after the stragglers were finally seated, Verbena and Cree appeared on stage with the director to introduce *Bonaventure Blues.*

The movie was dark and thrilling. It ended with the well-deserved death of the villainous stalker husband -- played by Cree, his hair dyed dark brown and sporting a sinister goatee -- and the triumph of his abused wife -- Verbena, who despite having placed herself in harm's way over and over, mercifully survived to make her ill-advised way through life another day, this time in possession of her husband's wealth and a new boyfriend so stoic he might have been a piece of wood.

"That story line hit just a little too close to home. The clueless wife, the rich, dark-hearted husband," Lily said as the lights came up.

"Ah, but you'd never run around a cemetery in the dark like the inmate of a lunatic asylum or leave the bathroom door unlocked while taking a bath," Tom laughed, hugging his wife to his side. "And I think I'm much handsomer and more emotive than the movie boyfriend, don't you? Besides, I'm built for comfort."

By the time the six friends got into the after-party, they were ravenous, but getting near the food and snagging a glass of Cristal Rose took every wile they possessed. It was going to take time to break through the clutch of fans surrounding the stars of the movie, giving the women a chance to scrutinize the apparel of the guests. The most memorable was one of the film's supporting actresses, Tish Winebottom, a curvy woman wearing a black gown by Azzedine Alaïa. The arrow cutouts on the back revealed her derriere down to the thigh.

"Ah," Molly said, giggling, "a girl needs a lot of cheek to wear that."

"Are we sure her name isn't Tush Barebottom?" Sara whispered, suppressing a laugh.

As promised, more than an hour after the party started, they finally got to meet Cree and Theresa, Virgil and Ellen, and then Verbena and Bordon. Verbena had just stretched to kiss Tom's cheek when he noticed something behind her. Suddenly they were both on the floor in a heap as a man threw a glass at Verbena's head, yelling "Here's to the polar bears, you global-warming denier." The glass struck a woman behind Tom, who screamed. Something that did not smell like wine splashed several guests. Before he could end his tirade, the glass-thrower was quickly subdued and Verbena hustled out of the room. She signaled for Tom to follow.

Having reached Verbena's limousine, jostled by men with big shoulders and firearms at their waist, Tom leaned in to hear what Verbena wanted to tell him. She was shaking. "Thanks, Tom."

"Are you going to be all right?"

She nodded. "But I know Dad isn't."

"Me either," Bordon added.

"I'll call you tomorrow, but I think I'm going to have to send Gi in my place to Naples."

"I understand."

"Tell everyone I'm sorry."

"Be safe."

"In this mad world? I'll do my best."

Tom watched the limousine pull away, then returned to the Jepson Center in search of his wife and friends. He had to shoulder his way through a sea of frightened, chattering guests flowing toward the door.

When Tom found Lily, he drew her aside. "She's so scared she's sending Gi to McBride's fund-raiser."

"That's not good."

"Don't tell anybody for awhile. Let me think about it."

"I won't. By the way, what's Verbena have to do with global warming?"

"I have no idea."

"Who have you told that Gi is Verbena's twin?"

"Nobody but you."

Tom's friends were aware that Verbena wasn't the Goldsteins' blood daughter, but only Lily knew that Gi was Verbena's identical twin, both born to an unmarried Tennessee teen-ager over forty years ago. Verbena was lucky, having been adopted by the Goldsteins and thereafter living the life of Hollywood royalty. Gi, on the other hand, had not been so fortunate, until, that is, she was hired to be her sister's double without acknowledgement of their blood bond. The surgery Lily's first husband had performed on Gi ensured that all the superficial differences caused by their very different lives had been erased. Verbena and Gi were now mirror images of each other.

When a couple of years ago Gi began stalking her twin after finding their birth records, the secret of Verbena's true parentage might have been blown but for Tom's intervention after he found Gi. At his unorthodox suggestion, in return for not attempting to get DNA evidence of her twinship, Gi had been offered a well-paid position as Verbena's body double so long as she took her medication and kept her mouth shut about family secrets. The strategy seemed to have worked.

Now, Tom was presented with a conundrum. He had no idea whether to tell McBride the truth or not. The "celebrity" he was about to meet wasn't Verbena but her twin. What had Verbena said about his having a priest's secrets? She was right. If he clued McBride in as to who Gi really was, he'd be betraying his actress-client's secret about the identity of her body double and thus the true parentage of both. If he didn't, something was sure to go wrong, and in that event, he'd incur the wrath of two important clients, one a famous actress, the other a powerful politician.

He only had a few days to decide what to do. Thank God he had Lily to confide in.

37

The Birdcage

Wednesday, May 3, 2006

Simon Diodorus was beside himself with excitement. In three hours, he would move from Lily's office to Beaudry Hall. In four hours, the sound and lighting technicians would arrive there. In five hours, the florists would work their magic. In six hours, the caterers would take over the kitchen and start setting up their stations in the garden. In seven hours, the videographer and serving staff would arrive. A half hour later, there would be a security sweep, and a few minutes after that he'd meet Verbena Cross for the first time. And, finally, in eight hours, the guests at McBride's fund-raiser would start arriving, bussed from a church that had generously allowed the campaign to park guest cars in its parking lot in exchange for a modest contribution to the building fund.

Simon wasn't in charge of everything but he thought he was. The weight of the world was on his narrow shoulders.

Lily gazed at her agitated assistant as once more he reviewed his checklist. "Simon, if you don't take a Valium and go home to catch a nap, I'm going to have to knock you out myself. You're making me crazy."

"Oh, I couldn't. Last night I watched *Front Page News*. That just got me all revved up to meet Verbena."

Lily unconsciously passed a hand over her face, as if hiding secret knowledge. Tom had decided, with her approval, that he had to tell Ferrin and Poppy that Gi Greer would be appearing in Verbena's place, but no one else could know about the deception other than the Bancrofts and the Standardts, and then even those three couples wouldn't know Gi was actually Verbena's blood twin. Lily was afraid that with Simon's sharp eye, he just might give the deception away, if only inadvertently.

"Remember, Simon, Verbena doesn't look now like she did all those years ago. She's much thinner. Her nose is narrower at the tip, straighter at the bridge, her teeth capped, her lips plumped. Although she's fifteen years older, all frown lines and signs of aging have been removed. Her hair is lighter and her breasts bigger. Want more?"

"No. But tell me again what she wore to the premiere."

"I'm told it was vintage Dior, royal blue satin, strapless, draped and pleated to give her a little padding. No jewelry except for diamond chandeliers from Cartier and a huge rock on her left hand. She looked like a twelve-year-old famine survivor playing dress up."

"That's harsh."

"You're right. She's pretty and actually very nice. She talked a long time to us Saturday night when she must have had better things to do."

"Speaking of weight, my dear, I think you've gained a little."

"Thanks ever so much for noticing."

"I don't mean . . . ."

"It's okay. I'm back to a size eight now, and Tom loves it. I'm thrilled to get to eat again."

"The good doctor didn't like normal-sized women, did he?"

"No. What a fool I was to try to change everything to suit a man. Hair, weight, the things I did all day, the car I drove, the clothes I wore." Lily didn't like talking about her first husband. "Anyway, back to Verbena. After Tom rescued her from the crazed bomb-thrower, she comped our hotel rooms."

"But it wasn't a bomb."

"Just a champagne glass, but it cut up the poor woman it hit.

Because it was filled with urine, I hear she's had to undergo a regimen of antibiotics."

"Oh, that's so gross."

"I know."

Simon brightened. "What did you wear?"

She threw a tissue at him. "What do you think I wore? The gown you picked out."

"The strapless Donatella Versace with the silver pleated bodice and the tight skirt in ivory with sexy ruching on one side of the slit. I can just see you in it."

"Yes, but I had to have my tailor sew the split skirt together almost down to my knees so people wouldn't be able to tell if I was a natural blonde or not."

"You didn't!"

"I did."

He laughed. "If I were a woman, I'd wear Donatella every day."

"You'd be broke in a week, Simon. Be glad you're a man."

"Where's Verbena staying?"

"At Beaudry Hall."

"All alone?"

"Well, no. Jerry Lee is out of of town, but Niall and Maria are there to take care of her. Niall lives in the garrett and I understand Maria is staying the night. Verbena is used to mansions, so this way she'll have one all to herself, maybe without quite as many servants as she's accustomed to." *What I can't tell you, my dear Simon, is that it's really Gi who's coming and she isn't used to mansions at all, but telling you would be like telling the world.*

"Is she making a speech?"

"No, no, and no. She's just going to mingle. I've suggested that you escort her so she's never alone. Of course, there will be plainclothes men everywhere; you'll know them when they talk into their wrists."

"Me!" He clapped his hand over his heart. "I get to escort her?"

"You do -- if you want to, that is. I didn't commit you to

anything."

"Make sure there are lots of pictures of me and her." He jumped up and did a little jig. "Why didn't you tell me sooner? I could have lived off that anticipation for a week."

"Because you'd have lived off it for a week, that's why."

"What should I talk to her about?"

"First, the don'ts. Don't talk about her family or politics or religion or anything serious or personal."

He looked insulted. "I wouldn't anyway. I don't like those subjects."

"Now the do-s. Talk to her about clothes, jewelry, makeup, perfume, all the light and easy girly stuff."

"I can do that all night."

"I know you can. But remember, this is business, not a game."

"Enlighten me, madame."

"Don't monopolize her. Let her meet the guests. Don't let anybody take up too much of her time. Make sure she doesn't get stuck with a bore. If somebody asks something embarrassing or probing, politely change the subject. Make sure she mingles, meets everybody. That's what people are paying for . . . a lot of them, anyway. Can you play it straight?"

"What do you mean, straight? I haven't liked that word since I was eight years old."

"I mean, can you pretend to be a straight guy? We want people to think you really are her escort, so if some sleazy guy tries something, you can throw those shoulders back and scare them off with rugged manliness."

"But I don't look anything like Bordon. And everybody knows who I am."

"I know that. Just be a little less obvious. The political world likes to sort people into the known categories of male and female."

He threw his shoulders back and pretended to walk like a dude.

"Oh, God," Lily said, laughing. "You need to watch that movie, what was it?"

"*The Birdcage*?"

"That one. Don't imitate Nathan Lane. Try to be like Dustin Hoffman."

"Girl, you are so confused. You're thinking of Robin Williams. I know, I know. They're both short and a little chunky. I can see we're going to have to schedule a movie night."

"Speaking of movie nights, when's my media room going to be finished? How about the kitchen? The laundry room?"

He shot her a mock scowl. "I'm leaving now, just like you said. I'm going to take a Valium, get some rest, take a shower, and put on my Armani blazer. I'll be at Beaudry Hall before the technicians get there. Do you know what Verbena's wearing?"

"I don't."

"If you find out, call me. I'll wear a pocket handkerchief that matches her dress so we'll look like a couple."

"I'm sure she'd be flattered."

"What perfume does she wear? I don't want to splash on a cologne that will clash with hers."

"I have no idea, Simon."

"Are you going to be all right without me for a few hours?"

"There's always a hitch, but we've planned this thing to a fare-thee-well. I'll survive for the next couple of hours without you, Simon. I think."

"Are you wearing the blue and gold print Roberto Cavalli dress?"

"Of course, Yoda."

"Just remember. Don't wear matching shoes. That's so yesterday. Wear the fuchsia Alberta Ferretti's. And don't carry a bag."

"That violates two rules of my Midwestern upbringing, you know." She waved him toward the door. "Just get to Beaudry Hall bright-eyed and bushy-tailed."

He wiggled his backside. "I'm always bushy-tailed." He whirled around. "Sorry. I suppose dudes don't do that."

"No, they don't, Simon. Go home and practice thinking like Jeff Bridges."

"You mean walking like him."

She narrowed her eyes. "I mean thinking. Which encompasses not just walking but laughing, talking, drinking, joking, gesturing, eating . . . the whole shebang. For one night."

"Should I bring you a salad?"

Lily stood up. "Simon."

"I'm going, I'm going. Love you."

She blew him a kiss as he sashayed out the door.

38

Vesta
Wednesday, May 3, 2006

The fund-raiser was a great success, but there were the usual minor hitches. At least twenty couples forgot their invitations. There were gate-crashers who weren't willing to pay but were equally unhappy to be turned away. One of the lamp stands fell over and would have killed a woman if her husband hadn't caught it. The raw bar was so crowded guests could be heard kvetching about the lines. A waiter jostled by a slightly inebriated guest dropped an entire tray of champagne flutes. The caterer ran out of jumbo shrimp.

Still, the party was festive and noisy. The garden looked magnificent. Soft light flattered the women in colorful spring dresses. Laughter floated like a peculiar kind of folk music in the air.

Jerry Lee, dressed in black, watched the party from her darkened bedroom, the curtains closed, allowing only an arrow-slit aperture for viewing the festivity. She felt like the doyenne of a medieval castle, spying on invaders camped at the base of her castle walls. She was ready.

When her beloved daughter ordered her not to return until after the fund-raiser was over, Jerry Lee pretended she had no intention of leaving the spa. She'd booked a week's stay, after all, and she needed the rest. But the order infuriated her.

Poppy had said several other things to alarm her. *Don't you want Phil in the garden with all the others?* What others did she have in mind? Surely she didn't know about Dewey and Nicky Sue. Or did she? *I'll bet you're not sad because you're used to death.* Well, at her age, she was used to death, but why that accusatory tone? Where was the sympathy? *Be careful what you say to the police.* Did her daughter think there was something to lie about? a reason for them to be suspicious?

She'd let that annoying conversation roll around in her head while she relaxed on the massage table and luxuriated in mineral baths. Her daughter wasn't going to use insinuation to stop her from getting revenge on the Goldsteins. In a pact with the devil, Phil had harmed her daughter, but if he'd gotten the millions the devil promised him, that would have ameliorated her grievance. Both Phil and Verbena would have been safe, at least for awhile. It was all the Goldsteins' fault that she was once again living on the financial edge, without a man in her bed, sitting all alone in the dark instead of hosting a party in her own garden.

When Poppy asked if Verbena could stay at the house the night of the fund-raiser, Jerry Lee had been inclined to say no just because she could but on second thought realized the arrangement might suit her perfectly. So Verbena had been installed in the green room, the largest and most luxurious of her guest bedrooms, the one with the biggest closet, a balcony overlooking the gardens, and the rain-shower in the spa-like bathroom.

Only Niall and Maria knew she was back. Hours ago she'd had a tray of food and wine delivered to her room, together with newspapers and Sophie Kinsella's *The Undomestic Goddess.* Her door wouldn't have to open even once before morning. It was double-locked, and when the security detail appeared, Niall claimed he didn't have the keys. Only Jerry Lee did and she was in California.

She'd used her old nitro on Phil, but she'd left behind the foxglove Verlin had prepared. At the last minute, she decided not to take it to Napa because she was afraid nosy TSA types would find it in her luggage and confuse it with a controlled substance. From the conversation around the fire pit at the Goldstein estate, she learned that it was Verbena's habit to drink hot Constant Comment tea before she went to sleep, sometimes combining it with Ambien and a little fresh fruit.

That gave her an idea. Before she left California, she called Verlin and told him to find the Constant Comment tea tin in the pantry, take it to his potting shed, bag the foxglove with Constant Comment and some rose hips, and reattach the original tags. Then he was to throw all the untouched bags away and return the tin with only the two new special bags to the pantry. It was important that Niall know nothing about the super-charged, high-octane tea. She made Verlin repeat the instructions.

When he'd done that, he asked, "Who's it for?"

"Verbena Cross. She'll be staying at the house Wednesday night."

"Verbena. Is she *Verbena officinalis?* That was the herb used to staunch Jesus' wounds, you know. She must be really special."

"Verlin. Focus. I'm going to call Niall and tell him to serve the tea in my best Limoges teapot, together with some English digestive biscuits and fresh raspberries on the Venetian tray."

"I can tell him that."

"I'm afraid that's too much for you to remember. I want you to concentrate on the tea."

He was hurt. "I don't have a problem remembering things."

Frankly, I hope that's not true. Some things are best forgotten. "I won't see you for a few more days at least. Are you okay all alone?"

I haven't been alone. Those nice women were here. "I'm okay."

Now everything was set. She was a little bored. Keeping her room dark meant she couldn't read unless she hid herself in her windowless dressing room, and she couldn't turn on the television lest the flickering light give her away, so there was nothing to do but wait in the dark. She heard Ferrin's silly speech to his guests through the filter of her closed window, catching only a few words here and there, but she knew by heart the clichés he'd be throwing around: fiscal responsibility, our founding values, the traditional family, offshore drilling. The man's rich baritone voice and self-assured delivery grated on her nerves. How could Poppy stand such a boring, self-righteous man?

She was a patient woman. She watched and waited from her lair, smiling to herself. If the Goldsteins seduced Phil into harming her daughter, then it was only fair they repay her in the same currency. Like fools, they'd given the boulder a little push down the hill and now it was gathering speed. It wouldn't come to rest until it had crushed their beloved daughter.

Her heart fluttered a little, but she recognized it as the anticipatory thrill of exerting her will on an intractable and fractious world. If Nicky Sue was Nike, she was Vesta, the Roman goddess of hearth and home. It was in her last will and testament that a bronze statue of Vesta would stand guard at the gate to the mausoleum once she joined her family in the afterlife. There she would exert her maternal power once again, this time eternally, unhindered by the feckless, unworthy mortals she'd been burdened with for almost seventy years.

39

Without the Drama
Wednesday, May 3, 2006

Once again, the Bancrofts and Standardts, together with Simon, were gathered on Tom and Lily's patio to deconstruct an event, this time the McBride fund-raiser. The full moon revealed that the patio was almost finished, and a new umbrella table and chairs had been installed. Though the outdoor kitchen was still under construction, at least it had a roof and a refrigerator. Tom poured chilled wine for everybody, a Chinon rosé from the Loire Valley that Lily was testing for the parents of brides wanting to serve fifteen-dollar instead of thirty-dollar vino to thirsty, undiscriminating guests.

After everyone had toasted the patio improvements, Lily announced that she wanted her guests' opinion on the wine. "I need to find something modestly priced for weddings. The vintner sold it to me as 'vivacious and charming.' So what do you think?"

The laughing evaluations poured in so fast she could hardly sort them out. Tom's, as always, was her favorite. "Frisky but accessible, subtle notes of a summer shower with a long rainy finish."

He winked at his wife. "Actually, Lily, it's delicious, even if it is too pink for a man to be seen drinking. If your clients serve this to men, they'd better use wineglasses the color of beer."

Simon was uncharacteristically immune to the silliness. He looked pouty.

"Did you enjoy yourself, Yoda?" Lily smiled, hoping to raise his spirits and anticipating a little gushing.

"I did. But I was underwhelmed."

"Really? Why?"

"Verbena's so quiet. I thought she'd be much livelier. I asked her about the Stella McCartney show because *W* photographed her in the front row, but she acted like she couldn't remember. And that dress she was wearing! An old stone-gray Sonia Rykiel, I think. I can't make myself like that designers's bushy red hair and ridiculous bangs so I never recommend her clothes to my clients."

"I was surprised to see your friends the Spanopouloses there. I'd have thought a rich plaintiff's lawyer like Niko, a prominent member of the trial bar, was a liberal."

"Nee-Nee explained to me that Niko gives to both parties just in case."

"In case of what?"

"You never know who's going to win, she said. He likes to be friends with everybody in power. And Niko thinks McBride is going to win because LuAnn ran over that poor girl in the parking lot."

"Well, I thought Verbena did a pretty good job," Lily said. Everyone but Simon smiled at their secret knowledge that the woman he thought was Verbena was actually an impostor.

"You told me she looks emaciated, but she doesn't." Simon sounded aggrieved. "Thin, but not like -- what'd you call it? A famine survivor."

"That was a terrible exaggeration, and it was mean of me to say it. If she looked heavier than you expected, maybe it was the dress she was wearing."

Simon shook his head, unconvinced.

"Okay. How about this to cheer you up?" Lily said. "We're all invited for brunch tomorrow morning with the McBrides before they take Verbena to the airport. You too, Simon. I think Poppy wants some advice on clothes."

"Really? I'd love that. Get her out of those beige suits and pearls. She has pretty legs, needs to show them off with some spiky heels, if you ask me."

"Speaking of clothes, the washer-dryer combo you ordered is awful."

Simon grew a little huffy. "It's from Sweden and looks great. It's gotten all kinds of awards for earth-friendly design."

"But the washing machine doesn't even hold a beach towel, it uses almost no water so nothing's really clean, and I can't figure out the cycles."

"It's green, good for the environment."

"I want it to be good for my clothes, not for the polar bears, and I want it to hold more than one towel at a time. So I'm asking that you return it as soon as possible and get something from Sears, something intuitively simple and sturdy as a truck, something so American that it actually works."

"You want me to find some linens while I'm at Sears?" He pretended to choke on the name of the store. "They're really cheap, you know."

Lily realized from his bitchy tone that she'd made a mistake. She should have conveyed her criticism of the super-chic washer-dryer combo in private. Simon was sensitive that way. Patting the arm of her chair, she said, "But we love this outdoor furniture. Very comfortable. You really have an eye."

The conversation turned to the headaches of construction, back to the rosé from the Loire Valley, which tasted more vivacious and charming with each glass, and then to the garden party again. The fund-raiser, they concluded as they finally got up to leave, had been just as exciting as the premiere of *Bonaventure Blues* but mercifully without the drama of an attack on Verbena.

40

Silver Pillbox
Wednesday, May 3, 2006

Verlin sat on the steps of the mausoleum for hours, first watching the party, then the cleanup. After the last of the catering staff left, and then *Lilium* and her little assistant drove away, he returned to the mausoleum. He turned his eyes to the balcony off his sister's best guest bedroom, where he knew Verbena Cross, the famous actress, was spending the night. She came out to the balcony, wearing a soft, flowing caftan, and smoked a cigarette. He could tell from the smell it wasn't a special cigarette. That surprised him. He thought all actors liked cannablis. Everyday, he learned something new.

When he saw the lights go off in her room shortly before Niall's dormer window went dark, he waited another hour, finally daring to smoke his own special cigarette. Then he made his way to the side door to the garage, unlocked it, and carefully made his way upstairs to the bedroom floor. He listened at the woman's door. No sound. Then he tested the knob. It wasn't locked.

He let himself into the bedroom. This time he was wearing only ankle socks so that there would be no noise. Fortunately, the woman hadn't pulled her curtains, so a little light entered the room. He waited until his eyes adjusted.

He could see that she was lying flat on her back, wearing a white eye mask. It gleamed like satin. He couldn't hear her breathing. She must sleep very quietly. He knew that Jerry Lee and Phil both snored, and once or twice he'd awakened himself with a snort. This woman was not only special because of her flower name but because she slept so quietly, like one of those princesses in the fairy tales Jerry Lee used to read to Poppy. He knew princesses were different. They could feel a pea under the mattress.

He crept into her bathroom. A little nightlight illuminated the granite counter, where Verbena had dumped her jewelry. Without touching anything, he scanned the various items, in search of a really good souvenir, perhaps something shaped like a flower. But he was disappointed.

He looked at the little bronze clutch awhile, debating whether he dared open it. He stretched out his hand toward it, as if pulled by a magnet. He had to know what was inside.

He carefully snapped it open and, laying a plush pink hand towel on the granite, shook out the contents. He picked up each item. A little silver bubble pack of four pills read "Paxil." He put that aside, together with a tube of lipstick and a used tissue. Finally, he found something interesting: a tiny silver pillbox, the lid engraved with fancy, scrolly letters he couldn't read in the dim light. He hoped the letters might be the princess' initials. He pressed the miniature button and the hinged lid sprang open. Inside were a dozen or so tiny yellow pills. Aspirin? He wasn't sure. He dumped out the pills on the towel, closed the beautiful little empty box, and slipped it into his pocket. He left the clutch gaping, the contents scattered about with the pills, as if Verbena had dumped everything out herself.

Before he left the bedroom, he once more gazed at the sleeping woman. She hadn't moved. *She's the beautiful sleeping princess, poisoned by her jealous step-mother, waiting for a handsome prince to revive her. I'm glad I saw her this way.*

Back in his apartment above the carriage house, Verlin gazed at the pill box, entranced. He'd never found anything like it before. The whole day was different because, until just now, he'd never dared slip into his sister's house knowing someone was in there --

other than Niall, of course.

He made a triumphant entry in his diary, marked by a drawing of a flowering verbena, before turning off his bedside lamp.

Part Three

"Indeed the safest road to Hell is the gradual one --
the gentle slope, soft underfoot, without sudden
turnings, without milestones, without signposts."

From "Our Mission Statement," Screwtape speaking,
in Paved with Good Intentions, C.S. Lewis

For it is shameful even to mention what the
disobedient do in secret. But everything exposed
by the light becomes visible, for it is
light that makes everything visible.

Ephesians 5: 12 - 14

41

Twisted Hearts and Juicy Couture
Thursday, May 4, 2006

By ten on Thursday morning, Lily, Molly, Sara, and Simon have already drunk a pot of coffee at the McBride palazzo. They are waiting for the woman Simon knows as Verbena to arrive for a farewell brunch. Their husbands are not present, all having pleaded early appointments. For an hour the conversation has been lively enough, but it has suddenly dropped off as they begin to fret about the busy day ahead. The women, seated around a table on the terrace, look as if they've suddenly been afflicted *en masse* with restless leg syndrome.

Simon, who hates silence, is telling his favorite audience how he asked Verbena if she knew Goldie Hawn was a Jewish Buddhist. What did she think of that? He'd heard Buddhists didn't even believe in God. Then how could anybody be both Jewish and Buddhist?

Lily frowned. "Simon, you weren't supposed to bring up personal subjects, like religion."

"I didn't think that was a question about religion exactly. More like a chance to dish about a rival. Anyway, Verbena said she was a Buddhist too and wanted more than anything to meet the Dalai Lama. Then I asked what she thought about Goldie's performance in *The First Wives' Club*, sort of hoping for a bitchy response. But do you know what she said?"

The women shook their heads.

"'Goldie was great, better than Verbena in *Front Page News.'* Those were her exact words. She talked about herself . . . ." He threw up his hands. "She talked about herself in the third person. Why do famous people do that?" He looked around at the smiling women. Molly was actually giggling. "Anybody, anybody?"

"Perhaps you've got it all wrong," Poppy said, choking back a laugh. *Obviously, it was a slip of the tongue by a body double who hasn't yet mastered her craft.*

Lily spoke up. "Perhaps Verbena was just being modest, willing to admit the actress she's often compared with is in truth better, as her critics often say."

Before Simon could respond, Shelly, Poppy's assistant, signaled her boss from the doorway to join her in the house. A business-like woman in her thirties, Shelly's face normally conveyed no emotion, having been botoxed into immobility by her own importance. This time, however, she looked puzzled.

Once they were inside the house, Shelly whispered, "Walter says Niall didn't answer the door. So far as he can see, only the housekeeper is there. He's talking about Maria, I presume."

"Walter?"

"Ferrin's new driver."

"You say Walter didn't see Niall or pick up Verbena?"

"No. Maria said Miss Cross is not answering a knock on her door, which is locked."

Just as she was conveying that news, the doorbell rang. Both Poppy and Shelly made their way to the front of the house. Poppy could not believe her eyes.

"Jerry Lee, what are you doing here?"

"It's good to see you too," the older woman said in an irritated tone. She was wearing a black Twisted Heart track suit, richly embellished with pink heart appliques and rhinestones, and carrying a giant pink Juicy Couture duffel, her uniform for flying. Her hair was tousled, her makeup smudged. Jerry Lee's bloodshot, watery eyes were magnified by black-rimmed glasses, which she only wore when she couldn't get her contacts in. "What a welcome, Poppy!

I took the red-eye in, so I haven't slept, and this is the reception I get. Thanks for nothing."

"I thought you were staying at the spa a few more days."

"Niall picked me up at the airport," she said, as if that explained everything.

"Why'd you come here instead of going home first?"

"To make sure I have the all-clear to enter my own house," she said, sounding aggrieved, as if anybody could have stopped her from doing whatever she wanted. "I hope the garden's been cleaned up." She shifted the duffel to her other hand. "This is heavy. Are you going to let me in or not?"

"Sorry, of course. We're waiting for Verbena."

"Why?"

"We're giving her a farewell brunch before Ferrin's new driver takes her to the airport, but she's late."

"She's still at my house?"

"Yes."

"Does she deserve all that? A brunch in her honor?"

"Yes, she does. She was a big draw for the fund-raiser, very gracious all night. But Shelly just told me that Maria's all alone at the house and can't get Verbena to answer her bedroom door."

"The silly woman's probably in the shower, using up all my best bath soap and every ounce of hot water. Did you know I bought her verbena-scented soap in honor of her name? Verbena and lemon." She brushed her hair out of her eyes. "And of course Maria's all alone at the house. As you can see for yourself, Niall had to pick me up at the airport."

You had time and the presence of mind to buy verbena-scented soap before you left for California but not to dump a dangerous old nitro prescription? "We're all out on the terrace. Why don't you join us? You know everyone, I think."

"Remind me of their names."

"Molly, Lily, Sara and Simon. Go on out there. I've got to call Maria."

"Don't let anybody break down the door if it's locked, that's all I ask. I've suffered enough without having my house wrecked."

"Who has the keys to the guest bedroom?"

"I do." She set her duffel on a chair and began removing things -- a pink satin eye-mask, a neck pillow, a makeup bag, a white Pashmina shawl, a bottle of Evian water, a hardback book, and a package of tissues -- before she found her keys. "Here they are. Tell Niall to go back now, run upstairs and see what Verbena is up to. I'll stay here because I want to hear all about the party."

After seeing Niall off, Poppy returned to the terrace, where she noticed with irritation that her mother had taken the chair she'd vacated at the table. "I sent Niall to Beaudry Hall to see what's happened to Verbena. As you can see, my mother has surprised us." *And is acting like the guest of honor.*

"What did you tell Niall?" Jerry Lee asked.

"I told him if he had to, to kick in the bedroom door. Maybe she fell in the shower or something."

"Don't you dare tell him any such thing." Jerry Lee's face was red with anger. "I found that precious door in a *brocante* in St. Rémy-de-Provence. It cost a fortune to ship it home, and it's one-of-a-kind." She turned to her daughter's guests. "I have so much to tell you about the Goldsteins."

After listening for fifteen minutes about the glories of the Goldstein estate, Simon was beside himself. He wanted to hear about the tragedy that was in all the papers. What really happened to Phil Coker? He wanted a blow-by-blow account. "So, have you heard from the authorities what really happened to your husband?"

She shot him a frown. "He wasn't my husband -- what's your name again?"

"Simon."

"Well, Simon, he left everything to me as if we were married, that I know for sure, but I suspect he had so many debts I won't get a thing."

That wasn't my question, you self-absorbed dingbat. "Did he have a heart attack? That's what the papers are speculating."

"I suspect the medical examiner will find he had a damaged heart, so my bet is, it was a heart attack. He'd had angina attacks all the years I knew him. Poor man."

"Was it sudden, so sudden nobody could call 911?"

"Yes, young man, it was sudden. At least that's what I assume. I was asleep when it happened. Imagine my shock when I found him."

"Is the memorial service really going to be at the Staples Center?"

"Good heavens, no. Honestly, where do rumors like that get started? It's going to be at a funeral home, just a little private memorial on Saturday. He offended so many people, I doubt we'll fill the room. I'm flying back for that, of course, since he had no family."

"Where will he be buried?" Simon asked.

"I've directed that he be cremated after the service. I'll bring his ashes to Beaudry Hall and put up some kind of statue in his honor."

"I thought you were going to send his body to his hometown in Nevada," Poppy said.

"I've changed my mind. You have to take a bus and a mule just to get to the little Podunk town he grew up in. At my age, that's just too strenuous a journey, so I'll keep him with me."

"A statue of what?" Simon asked.

Jerry Lee dabbed her eyes. "Peter Pan, maybe. He never grew up. You had to live with him to know that."

Lily looked at Poppy. "Anything from Niall?"

"No," Poppy said, checking her cell phone again. "Total radio silence. Strange, isn't it?"

Lily stood up. "I hate to leave you like this, but Simon and I have a wedding on Saturday and we've got to get going."

"Let's just hope it's all some kind of comedy of errors," Sara said, standing up too. "Call us, won't you, Poppy, when you hear what's happened? And give Verbena our best."

Poppy shot Molly a beseeching look. "Any chance you can stay awhile?" *I don't want to be alone with my mother. If something's gone wrong at Beaudry Hall, it's bound to involve Jerry Lee and I don't want to spend my day trying to untangle the mess all by myself.*

"Tell you what, Poppy," Molly answered, as if reading her

friend's mind. "Why don't we take your mother home together so she can make sure that Verbena's okay and her precious door hasn't been kicked in."

"Girls!" Jerry Lee was furious. "Have some respect. You're talking about me as if I weren't here. I'll go home when I'm damn well ready. I'll wait for Niall."

Poppy made an exasperated sound. "I'm speaking to a PTA group in two hours, so you can't stay here. You look like you need to take a shower and get some rest anyway, and I need time to pull myself together."

Over Jerry Lee's protests, Poppy hustled Jerry Lee into Molly's Lexus SUV.

42

No Good Deed Goes Unpunished
Thursday, May 4, 2006

Niall must have been watching for them because before the women could ring the bell, he opened the door, looking perfectly normal. He addressed Jerry Lee as if no one else was present. "I've taken your cases to your room, madam."

"Where's Verbena?" Poppy asked impatiently, moving to the staircase and looking upward.

"She's not here."

"What do you mean she's not here? Where is she?"

"When I got here, I went upstairs. The door was locked, just as Maria said, so I knocked and then used the key."

"And?"

"She was in bed. I couldn't tell whether she was asleep or . . . ." He didn't complete the thought. "I called her name and touched her shoulder, but she was unresponsive. I came back downstairs and called an ambulance. They took her away."

"Why didn't you answer my calls?"

"I had other things to take care of."

Poppy stared at the butler, so rigid in his suit he might have been standing in a gale-force wind, straining to stay on his feet. Fear filled her chest like indigestion.

"Is she alive?"

"I believe so." He told her the EMTs hadn't answered his

question about where they were taking the woman. He heard them arguing about the location of the nearest emergency room.

Poppy sat down on a step, her head in her hands. "This is a nightmare. Verbena was unresponsive but is alive, she was taken away, yet you don't know where she is."

Molly was racing up the stairs. "What room was she in?"

"Take a right, second door on the left. The green room."

A few seconds later, Molly appeared at the head of the stairs. "Empty except for her suitcase. Her clothes are scattered everywhere. The shower is dry. A bunch of pills are scattered on the counter in the bathroom."

Niall looked aggrieved at having been doubted. "Of course Miss Cross isn't there. And if clothes and pills are scattered around, well, that's to be expected. Maria hasn't had time to clean up yet. We've been a little preoccupied."

"Well, tell her to do it now," Jerry Lee snapped. "I should never have agreed to let that actress stay here. No good deed goes unpunished." She headed for the sitting room off the kitchen. "I need some tea. Girls, do you care to join me?"

Poppy lost it. "Stop where you are, Jerry Lee. Are you insane, Niall? An unresponsive woman leaves this house in an ambulance and you don't bother to find out where she's being taken?" With effort, she stopped screaming. "Don't touch anything upstairs. Not one thing. Leave the pills where they are. Did you let anyone in last night after the party?"

"Of course not."

"Have you called the police?"

"No. I believe the 911 operator will make that decision."

"Well, I want you to call them right now. How do you even know . . . ?"

Before she could find the right words for her fear that the EMTs were part of a political plot to harm Verbena for her support of a conservative candidate -- a plot by persons who had no idea Verbena had sent her body double to Naples -- several uniformed police were at the door of Beaudry Hall.

Poppy's nightmare had only just begun.

43

Gallows Humor
Thursday, May 4, 2006

Early Thursday evening, Tom and Matt were once more seated in Ferrin's wine room, which doubled as the McBrides' safe room and had been swept for bugs before they entered. The two heavy, reinforced doors on either end of the room were closed, a plainclothes man standing outside each. Ferrin read the newspaper article aloud. One more reading, and they'd know it by heart.

HOLLYWOOD ACTRESS DIES AFTER MCBRIDE FUND-RAISER

Verbena Cross, 44, was found dead Thursday morning after a fund-raiser for U.S. Rep. Ferrin McBride, Republican candidate for a second term in the House of Representatives. Miss Cross, the daughter of Virgil Goldstein, an award-winning director of left-wing docudramas, and Ellen Matter, a highly acclaimed Broadway actress, was Hollywood royalty. On April 30, her latest picture, *Bonaventure Blues,* **premiered in historic Savannah, where many scenes were shot. Though Miss Cross was renowned for her comedic talent and frequently compared to Goldie Hawn and Meg Ryan, in the new film -- a chick-flick thriller -- she plays an abused wife in fear of her life.**

The film opened to mixed reviews.

Niall Kilcommon, butler for Jerry Lee Beaudry, called 911 Thursday morning when he found Miss Cross unresponsive in a guest bedroom at Beaudry Hall. She was to have returned to her Malibu estate around noon after appearing Wednesday night at a fund-raiser in support of Rep. Ferrin McBride. Once Miss Cross' support of the 14th District's incumbent Congressman was announced, the number of supporters eager to pay two thousand dollars each to attend the Naples fund-raiser reportedly rose from a few hundred to more than five hundred.

[Note: Harley Wangle, press chief for Commissioner Myron Mullett, running on the Democratic ticket for the 14th District's Congressional seat, observed that the big-ticket, super-exclusive fund-raiser proves that McBride's constituency comprises the privileged classes whose only real interest is protection of the wealth they accumulated at the expense of the under-privileged. He noted that attendees at the exclusive McBride "garden party" were the kind of white elitists who drive gas-guzzling SUVs, live in gated communities, and hire immigrants as servants, all the while agitating against amnesty for undocumented aliens. For more on the heated Congressional campaign, turn to p. 3, col. 1.]

As publicity mounted for Miss Cross' appearance at McBride's fund-raiser, so reportedly did the death threats from bloggers who viewed her as a traitor to her father's liberal causes. Security for the highly anticipated event was tight, especially in light of an incident at the premiere in Savannah. At a party in the Jepson Center following the screening of the film, an environmental activist threw a champagne glass at the actress, not intending to kill her "but only humiliate her. Wake her up to global warming." The activist, Tony Pericone, is in custody. Unfortunately, the glass, which was discovered to be filled with urine, injured one of the guests, who had to be treated not only for cuts and bruises but for potential infection. Miss Cross' fiancé, Bordon Settle, who is very protective of the actress, saw the activist raise his arm in time to prevent injury to her.

Wes Dingly, a spokesman for the local Medical Examiner's office, said that neither the time nor the cause of Miss Cross' death can be determined until the autopsy has been completed but acknowledged that there were no obvious external injuries. Despite the well-documented death threats against the actress and the assault in Savannah, foul play is not suspected. Dingly refused to speculate about whether Miss Cross, who on several occasions underwent rehabilitation for drug addiction, had died of a drug overdose. This paper has learned from an anonymous source that pills were found scattered in the bathroom Miss Cross was using.

Beaudry Hall, where Miss Cross' body was found, is the stately home of Jerry Lee Beaudry and the late Phil Coker, Hollywood's notorious Bad Boy who died unexpectedly of a heart attack last week at the Goldsteins' Napa Valley estate, where he and Mrs. Beaudry were guests. A private memorial service for Mr. Coker is set for Saturday in Los Angeles. Mrs. Beaudry, famous for her spectacular gardens, which were featured several years ago in *Garden Design,* was still in California on the night of McBride's fund-raiser but had generously allowed her gardens to be used for the party rather than forcing a last-minute change of venue.

Mrs. Beaudry, who didn't return to Naples until Thursday morning, told this reporter that she was "shocked and saddened" to learn of the death of Miss Cross, whom she'd met for the first time at the Goldstein estate. "She was a lovely woman, very sweet. I was concerned about her weight, of course, but otherwise she appeared to be healthy." Mrs. Beaudry added that she wished she could have attended her son-in-law's fund-raiser Wednesday night but was unavoidably detained in California because of Mr. Coker's death. An avid student of Greek and Roman mythology, Mrs. Beaudry said that "Nemesis seems to be following my family around these days." (Nemesis is the goddess of righteous anger whose purpose is to see that good and evil are justly paid.)

Mrs. Beaudry's metaphor is apt. Tragedy has indeed stalked Rep. McBride. His driver, Alex Abrams, was killed in a hit-and-run accident on April 26 in Port Royal. The police investigation is on-going but no suspect has been identified. Two days later Phil Coker, his mother-in-law's companion, died suddenly at the home of the Goldsteins in Napa. According to Mrs. Beaudry, he died of a heart attack, though the Medical Examiner's report has not yet been made public. Now Miss Cross, the daughter of the Goldsteins and the headliner for McBride's fund-raiser on May 3, is dead of causes undetermined at the time this paper went to press.

A spokesman for Rep. McBride extended his condolences to the family of his guest. Rep. McBride and his wife will temporarily suspend all campaign appearances.

Ferrin put down the paper. He offered Tom and Matt cigars, then lit one of his own. "Well, Tom, I guess it's a good thing Verbena's fiancé protected her from that crazy activist."

"If I've learned anything, it's that you can only believe half of what you read in the papers."

Matt slapped his friend on the back. "He's much too modest to seek glory for saving a celebrity."

"And how about my indiscreet mother-in-law running off at the mouth to a reporter on a sensitive subject?" Ferrin asked. "That quote about Nemesis is pure theatrics. I think the real name of the goddess of retributive justice is Jerry Lee Grubbs Beaudry." He looked at Tom. "What do you think the chances are that Gi Greer's death will become a police matter?"

"Just a dark hunch, but I'd guess the chances are pretty good. We know the victim isn't Verbena Cross, or even just her body double, but her identical twin. The chance that she died of natural causes seems pretty slim. We have no reason to believe Gi was ever a drug addict, although she took antidepressants as a condition of her employment. I don't know what pills were found in the bathroom, but we know she had to take some pills. Maybe she did overdose. But maybe she didn't. If she didn't, we have to consider poison. She was staying in the house of a poisoner, after all."

Ferrin scratched his head. "The puzzle then becomes how the poison was administered since the poisoner wasn't present."

"Are we sure of that?"

Ferrin gave Tom an inquiring look.

"I mean, are we sure that Jerry Lee was actually out of town Wednesday night?"

"That's her story, and it seems credible. As your wife no doubt told you, Tom, she showed up here this morning, straight from the airport, having been picked up by Niall. She was wearing what Poppy tells me is her flying uniform and looking like she'd spent the night on a plane. But . . . ."

"But what?" Tom prompted.

"But, you've made me think. Jerry Lee gave no reasonable explanation for why she cut short her stay at a spa in Sonoma. When Poppy pressed her, Jerry Lee acted as if her reason was obvious: She had to return to get suitable clothes for Coker's memorial service. But isn't it equally obvious that that excuse makes no sense? She has to turn right around and fly back to California tomorrow. Why didn't she just ask Niall or Poppy to overnight a black suit to California, thus saving a long and expensive plane ride? Or hire a car to take her to San Francisco, where she could buy a new one?"

"It might be a good idea to be sure she really caught that redeye last night," Tom said.

"Check into that, would you?"

"I've spent my professional life being paranoid, but tell me, Ferrin. Why would your mother-in-law want to harm Verbena . . . that is, the woman she thought was Verbena? She only met her once and she told our wives she liked her. She told the reporter the same thing essentially."

Ferrin closed his eyes a second. "To get back at Goldstein for being the conduit for the abortion story?"

Tom cocked his head. "That would be true only if she knew Goldstein was the man behind the curtain who got the abortion story from Alexie and fed it to the Canadian reporter. We suspect she guessed that, but we don't know for sure."

Matt spoke up. "Are there any results on Coker's autopsy yet?"

"Jerry Lee told my wife that the autopsy showed he had a damaged heart, exacerbated by an overdose of nitroglycerin and a boatload of alcohol. Since no report's been issued yet, I don't know how she knows that, but it doesn't sound off the wall. I suspect the old reprobate damaged his heart with years of drug abuse, and I don't doubt for a minute he drank too much that night. But . . . ."

"But what?"

"The overdose of nitro is puzzling, don't you think? Doesn't every heart patient know how much nitro to take so they don't kill themselves?"

Tom again. "In my presence, Jerry Lee taunted him about angina attacks, and he didn't deny them, just said he didn't want people to know. He even lied, he said, on an insurance form for Goldstein. But what I never heard was whether he had a prescription for nitro. If he did, why did he take Jerry Lee's instead of his own? If he didn't, was that because his doctor didn't think it was important he have one? Because his heart problems weren't that bad or what?"

Ferrin glanced at the notes Matt was making. "There's another fact for you guys to establish."

"Did the police search the room that Gi/Verbena was staying in at Beaudry Hall?" Matt asked.

"They did. They couldn't get a search warrant that quickly, but Jerry Lee gave them permission to search the whole house if they wanted to. Poppy said she didn't hesitate, didn't follow them around, didn't act nervous at all."

"And they found . . . what?"

"I don't know." Ferrin rubbed his eyes. "With Jerry Lee's permission, they bagged the woman's possessions and left without comment. Without Jerry Lee's permission, they also took her best Limoges teapot, the tea cup, a fruit bowl, and the Venetian tray, which Poppy says has infuriated her mother."

"They must not have found any identification for Gi Greer because otherwise the paper would surely be reporting her death, not Verbena's." Tom rubbed his chin. "Where do you suppose her driver's license, insurance card, or plane ticket went?"

Having no answer, Ferrin got up and began to pace. "What do you think the Goldsteins are going to do now? To paraphrase Mark Twain, the news of their daughter's death is much exaggerated."

"I think the fit is going to hit the Shan," Matt said.

"And the Shan's going to make sure a few other people have fits too," Tom said. "Verbena told me in Savannah that she wasn't going to tell her father she was sending her twin in her place, so if Goldstein didn't hear the story first from Verbena, there might have been a few minutes of confusion and anguish in Napa."

"Have you talked to Verbena yet?"

"I have, very briefly. She was shocked, of course, and seemed sorrowful to lose Gi."

"She isn't worried that somebody will dig into the true identity of her double?"

"Probably. But for the moment, I suspect she's just thanking her lucky stars she didn't come to Naples."

"Why? Because she's guessed it wasn't an overdose and she was the real object of someone's wrath?"

"Like us, she probably thinks it's at least possible that somebody carried out a death threat directed at her. And she might be a tad worried that somebody, like *The National Enquirer,* will dig into the background of her double, especially because Gi Greer looked suspiciously more identical to Verbena than body doubles normally do."

"So what will Virgil do? Or Verbena?"

"If I were advising them? Stick with the story that they made up a couple years ago. Yes, Gi Greer, looked a lot like Verbena, but they weren't related and it's just one of those remarkable accidents of nature. Very few people know the truth, and they won't be talking. Since to my knowledge no DNA tests were ever done, even the most persistent investigative reporter may come up empty."

Ferrin sat down again. "You know the hell of it? The publicity about Verbena's double will probably be good for that mediocre picture she made, you wait and see. The Hollywood machine will roar into overdrive with stories about the perils of being a famous actress: the death threats, the constant scrutiny, the need for a body double. It'll be the Princess Diana story all over again." He put his head in his hands. "Meanwhile, I, who had nothing to do with the death of anyone tangentially associated with me -- not Alexie, not Coker, not Verbena's sister -- am caught in a whirlpool of suspicion about why tragedy is dogging me like Nemesis. How do I get my campaign back on track?"

"Well," Matt said. "LuAnn Mullett's out on bail. I hear through the grapevine -- meaning Harley -- that she might plead temporary insanity. Maybe she'll get her Navigator back and, in between cracking wonky backs, hunt down another of her husband's wonky chickies."

They laughed. Gallows humor.

"By the way, Matt, what's going on with Harley Wangle?"

"We met early this morning before we knew about the death that has grabbed all the headlines. I gave him a little rundown on the fund-raiser. Even though Doris and I were present at Beaudry Hall, he's still going to pound the theme of how Republicans are an all-white cabal intent on retaining their power no matter what. They're just pretending they support a constitutional republic. I told him I saw a lot of Cubans and other Hispanics, Asians, and blacks, even some gays there. He asked me how they could possibly vote any way but Democratic."

Ferrin smiled for the first time that day. "Really? I reviewed the list of supporters carefully and shook hands with everyone. Most of my supporters are business people. No matter what color you are, if you're making a payroll, you don't like confiscatory taxes, burdensome regulations, or expensive energy."

Before he could comment further, Ferrin's pager buzzed.

After checking it, he looked at the two men. "My wife insists on seeing me this second. She's right outside the door."

When Poppy entered, she was carrying a book. "You'll never believe what I found."

Ferrin took the book and opened to the title page. "*Toxic Bachelors* by Danielle Steele." He smiled. "You trying to tell me something?"

"Notice the book marks?"

He pulled them out. Each was half a boarding pass.

"Read them."

"They're dated May 3, Seat 2A, from Los Angeles to Dallas, Seat 3B from Dallas to Fort Myers." He looked up.

"My mother didn't come back today. She came back the morning of the fund-raiser."

"God, you're right. Where did you find her boarding passes?"

"She had to search for her keys in the duffel she was carrying this morning so that Niall could get into Gi's bedroom. The things she had to remove to find the keys she piled on the hall table. In our hurry to get to Beaudry Hall, I didn't make sure she put her stuff back in her duffel. I just found the mess. These boarding passes are Jerry Lee's."

"So Nemesis didn't return today. She returned yesterday."

There was a long silence. Poppy took a chair beside her husband.

"So where was she Wednesday night?" Poppy asked, breaking the silence. "Not at Beaudry Hall. There was a thorough security sweep. I know because Niall complained about it."

Without responding, Ferrin punched in the number of his security chief and put him on speaker. He abruptly asked, "Baxter, can you tell me with certainty that Beaudry Hall was swept clean Wednesday?'

"It was."

"Nothing overlooked?"

"The only room we couldn't get into was the master suite. We didn't overlook it, but the butler said it was double-locked and he didn't have the keys. He said Mrs. Beaudry always locked it when she was away because of the jewelry and furs in there. From the hallway, the suite appeared dark and quiet, so instead of kicking the door down or finding a locksmith, which we didn't have time for, we let it go."

"I'll get back to you." Ferrin flipped his phone shut and looked at Tom. "I think it's time to round up the usual suspects."

"Jerry Lee and Verlin?" Tom asked.

Ferrin nodded. "Plus, in this case, her butler and her housekeeper."

44

Trick-Cyclists
Thursday, May 4, 2006

Leaving Tom and Matt on the patio, where they were discussing Jerry Lee's secret trip from Los Angeles, Lily hurried to the front door and greeted Doris Bearsall with a hug. "Doris. I haven't seen you . . . ."

"Since last night. Until then, I hadn't seen you since the Fourth of July two years ago on your birthday."

"Sorry we didn't get a chance to talk last night, but I wasn't really a guest. I was on duty until the last dog left."

She walked Doris to the kitchen. "It was nice of you to drive up here all alone on such short notice. Well, actually, no notice at all, I suspect. By the way, with that haircut, you look like Lena Horne."

Doris laughed, touching her hair. "If only I could sing the way she did. Anyway, I was happy to drive up here. Matt said he and Tom were going to have a drink at your house instead of going to their favorite bar and I could come up if I wanted. When you've been married forty years to a man with unpredictable hours, that's an offer you can't refuse." She held out a glass jug. "I brought mint juleps. That's what I was going to give Matt when he got home, so I just brought it along. If you have something else planned . . . ."

"I don't. Tom and Matt have started on beer and pretzels and will probably walk that road the rest of the evening, but mint juleps sound perfect to me. All I can offer is cheese and crackers, plus some fancy Italian olives. I'd heat up some mini-quiches for us, but as you can see, my kitchen isn't finished and I still don't have an oven."

They talked awhile about the hassles of construction, trading war stories, before joining their husbands on the patio. As Lily expected, the men were still talking about the meeting they'd just had with Ferrin.

Both men stood up when the women approached. "Doris, you're the perfect person to weigh in on our meandering discussion about human nature," Tom said. "We need your input here."

"I told him," Matt said, "that you have a master's in psychology."

Doris made a face at her husband. "Maybe on some planet that makes me an expert, but not here." She turned to Lily with a self-deprecating smile. "I never practiced as a clinical psychologist. Mostly, whatever psychology I might have practiced on my husband, children and students came from experience, not from textbooks. In that sense, all women are psychologists, aren't they?"

Lily returned her smile. "I'll add that credential to my resumé."

"We've reached the point in our discussion," Tom continued, "where we're not being practical. We're just talking through our beer about why Jerry Lee Beaudry did what she did. You know about her, right?"

"Some," she said, glancing at Matt, unsure how much she was supposed to reveal of what she'd heard. "I know she's McBride's mother-in-law, and her partner, that creepy actor I never liked, just died in California. I'd heard about her fabulous gardens before I saw them last night. And today I read that Verbena Cross, whom I met for the first time last night, was found dead in her house this morning. That's about it."

"Well, let me fill in the picture. She's our suspect in a string of murders. All of them seem to have something to do with being a very protective mother. Poppy's her only child. Poppy's childhood was spent preparing for beauty pageants under Jerry Lee's direction. Jerry Lee even ran a little school to train pageant contestants.

Poppy, of course, was her prize pupil but through a fluke lost out to Molly Standardt, whom you've met a couple of times. You can tell how much Jerry Lee adores her daughter by the shrine to her pageant days, which I'm told is set up in a little alcove off of Jerry Lee's bedroom."

"A shrine? Or a pagan alter? She claims her child is her idol, but I suspect the real idol is her own maternal ambition." Doris smiled. "Shrines, pagan alters, and idols never work out well."

"You're going to have to explain that one," Matt said.

"One of the ten commandments given to Moses is not to worship idols, even your own children."

"I'm not sure I ever fully understood that commandment," Tom said.

"Most people don't bother to think about it. Most of us worship something other than God. Money's the big one, but there are other idols -- family, power, career, possessions, fame. The most popular pagan cause these days is earth-worship, saving the planet, as if worship of the creation instead of the Creator is virtuous. In Jerry Lee's case, you might think her idol is her daughter, but to me it sounds like she worships herself." She took a sip of her mint julep. "But I've gotten sidetracked. You say she's a suspect in a string of murders?"

Tom recounted Jerry Lee's suspected poisoning of her husband, her daughter's boyfriend, and her daughter's pageant rival.

"So we have a theme here," Doris said. "Anybody who threatened Poppy's success as a beauty queen was killed, always with herbs. Was Jerry Lee ever treated as a suspect or charged with a crime?"

"No. And I've left out one incident, half a murder, you might say. Verlin says Poppy's teen-age miscarriage was caused by an abortifacient herb that Jerry Lee put in her tea before she took a nap. The tea almost killed her, but she recovered and resumed her pageant competitions without her good-girl reputation being tainted."

"To me, that just proves the obvious: that Jerry Lee's real object of worship is her own ambition since she was willing to risk her daughter's life for it."

"So the first three deaths were all about her? Not about protecting her daughter?"

"That's the way it looks to me."

"Well, almost twenty years pass, apparently without incident. Then we have three deaths in a week."

"You're leaving out Jerry Lee's attempt on Molly," Lily interjected. She turned to Doris. "You've met Molly a couple of times. Remember, she won the Miss South Carolina pageant that Jerry Lee expected Poppy to win once her rival was eliminated. Jerry Lee falsely accused Molly of leaking the abortion story about Poppy. Recently, Molly fell from the veranda on the second floor of Beaudry Hall. Jerry Lee was pretending to have a cardiac episode and fell against Molly, who's pretty sure she was deliberately pushed over the veranda railing."

"I saw her last night, so she obviously recovered."

"Yes, very lucky fall."

Tom resumed the story. "The next three deaths are all once again connected, however tenuously, to Jerry Lee. Ferrin McBride's driver, Alexie Abramova, is killed in a hit-and-run. Matt sees the accident. By a process of elimination, he determines that Jerry Lee was driving the blue Prius that hit the man. After that we discovered Abramova was an illegal immigrant who worked for ultra-liberals like Virgil Goldstein, Verbena Cross' father, gathering dirt on McBride. He was the conduit for the false abortion story between Coker and Goldstein."

"Did Jerry Lee know that?"

"We have no direct proof of that, but she found out Coker was meeting Abramova and must have at least suspected he leaked the abortion story in return for a movie deal to revive his career. Whether she knew a lot or a little, we know Jerry Lee was following the Russian the night he died and used Coker's car to kill him.

"Then comes Phil Coker. He gives the abortion story to Abramova, who gives it to Goldstein, who in turns feeds it to a reporter, who twists it just a quarter turn for her article on right-wing political wives. A miscarriage becomes an abortion. But

Goldstein's money goes to Myron Mullett, not to Coker. Coker was surprised when he learned that. Verbena told me her father gave Coker some art but not any money.

"Coker's latest trip to California was probably to get the money he was promised, or at least a commitment to make his war movie. Verbena, however, said there was no movie deal and never would be. Jerry Lee must have learned that, or at least sensed it. Her flashy partner had betrayed Poppy for nothing. The night of a dinner party at the Goldstein estate, Coker is drinking a tequila drink. Jerry Lee goes to bed. In the night Coker, who has some kind of heart condition, finds her nitro and takes too much of it. Is that the way it really happened, or did she give his tequila drink a little boost before she went to bed?"

"Neither of the two murders you've described involve herbs."

"No. The hit-and-run is unusually direct. But the nitro is a lot like a poisonous herb, wouldn't you say? In neither case does she literally have to touch her victim, and both were done in secret without witnesses ... or so she thought with Abramova. In the case of the nitro, it's almost impossible to know how it was administered, and in the case of the hit-and-run, she disguised herself as Coker and drove his car."

"I'm guessing that Verbena's death is the next one you're going to talk about."

"First of all, Verbena didn't die."

"She didn't? Her death is in all the papers."

"Like some famous people, Verbena had a body double, in this case named Margaret 'Gi' Greer, who looked exactly like her, a little heavier perhaps, but otherwise identical." Tom omitted the fact that Gi was Verbena's blood twin. "Because of the incident in Savannah and the death threats, Verbena sent Gi to the fund-raiser. You met Gi, not Verbena, at the party, and last night she stayed at Beaudry Hall. Now she's dead."

"What's the body double's death got to do with Jerry Lee? The papers said Mrs. Beaudry was in California, and I didn't see her last night. I was hoping to meet the woman whose gardens are so famous."

It was Matt's turn. "Turns out, Jerry Lee might have been hiding in the master suite, which was locked, so it wasn't checked during the security sweep. Poppy just found her boarding passes, so we know Jerry Lee flew back the day before she said she did. Jerry Lee could have been hiding in the house. We know that the police took custody of a teapot in the woman's room. There might have been something in the tea."

"How does Jerry Lee know so much about herbs?"

"I don't know," Tom answered, "but she has help from her brother Verlin."

"What's he like?"

"An idiot savant," Lily said. "Jerry Lee calls him simple."

"Don't forget," Tom interjected, "she sometimes calls him a troll."

"True. He's a very strange little man who knows all the Latin names of everything and keeps a diary written in his own language. He grows and dries herbs and grinds them up, hanging them from the rafters of a little potting shed. He has peculiar ideas about where the souls of dead people and animals go. He thinks they're in the objects he collects, objects linked to the victims. From meeting him, I suspect he has some sort of autism."

"He doesn't know right from wrong?"

"I'm not sure. He's very forthright about having given herbs to Jerry Lee that he knows could kill people -- and did kill them. He just seems more entranced by the power of herbs than concerned about the consequences."

"So tell us, Doris. What's a psychologist say about Jerry Lee's character?" Tom asked.

"Remember, I'm not a practicing psychologist. I've just read enough to be dangerous. My guess is that the secular world of psychologists and psychiatrists would classify her at best as a sociopath, at worst as a psychopath. By the way, do you happen to know what the Brits call psychiatrists? If you ever watched *Jewel in the Crown*, you heard it there."

All three shook their heads.

"Trick-cyclists. I love that term, don't you? It's so descriptive of the skepticism most of share about the so-called science of psychology, which often seems to defy common sense and always eschews moral judgment. To many people, psychiatrists' expertise isn't scientific at all; it looks more like an illusion, meant to trick us into accepting their esoteric knowledge, as if it actually explained something rather than just describing it. Really, they're just spinning their wheels, like a cyclist on a treadmill . . . or so it seems. Think of all the times they recommend parole for a murderer or rapist who returns to society only to murder or rape again. Or recall the spectacle of two different psychiatrists testifying in court, one claiming the defendant was insane at the time of the crime, the other denying that claim."

"What's a sociopath?" Tom asked.

Doris took a deep breath and shut her eyes. "A person who has little regard for the life of others, typically from childhood. Often they start by abusing animals and graduate to abusing and manipulating people. They don't show remorse. On the surface, they're charming, but their emotions are shallow. They lie a lot. Many are narcissistic."

"And what's a psychopath?"

Doris laughed. "In a nutshell . . . so to speak? A really abnormal sociopath, often violent, lacking all empathy. I've heard them called 'intraspecies predators.'"

"Are they born that way, or do they learn to be abnormal?"

"One of my professors said sociopaths fall into two categories: some are driven by genetic factors, others by their environment. He had a long list of causes -- or excuses, depending on your point of view. A defect from birth, perhaps a badly wired brain. A chemical deficiency. An abusive -- or permissive --childhood. A life of unrelenting bad luck or bullying. A compelling addiction. The absence of a father. The presence of a mother who drank too much while pregnant. A lack of self-esteem, or the opposite, exaggerated self-love."

"That's a long list," Lily mused. "And very confusing, since opposite conditions can produce the same result."

"The list goes on and on, but to me it explains very little

because many people share the same problems, yet they aren't all anti-social. Most don't become addicts or murderers. Secular labels describe events without explaining why one abused person murders and another doesn't."

"Are you hinting there are better labels than secular?"

"Perhaps I am." Doris gave Tom and Lily a searching look. "Pardon me for being so personal, but are you two Christians?"

"Yes. We both are," Lily said.

"Well, then, I'm not throwing pearls before swine, a practice I've learned through hard experience to avoid. My reference is not the textbooks I studied at Spellman but the Bible. Remember the Mary Magdalene story? The real one, I mean, not the slanderous tale made up by her misogynist detractors in the early church. She was demon-possessed. Christ drove the demons out. Then she became his devoted follower. In the Old Testament, as well as the New, there's no mention of mental illness. People who act abnormally are said to be possessed by demons, utterly overcome by evil, controlled by satanic spirits. The devil, we know, roars around like a lion devouring the vulnerable. The apostle Paul calls iniquity, meaning Satan, a mystery."

"In what way do people act who give themselves over to evil? Other than the obvious act we all recognize as evil."

"There's a good picture in the Gospel of Mark of a demonically possessed man named Legion, because he's possessed by thousands of evil spirits. He lives among the tombs, meaning he's obsessed by death. He separates himself from those who could help him. He cuts himself with stones and breaks the restraints people put on him. Many people who give themselves over to evil are loners and love darkness. They might consult psychics who claim to talk to the dead, join cults, or become hit men."

"If evil is a mystery, what does it really explain?" Tom asked.

"Realizing it's a mystery keeps us humble. And acknowledging there is evil in the world keeps us from excusing bad behavior as if it involved no free choice. Satan's greatest victory occurs when we deny that he exists."

"And who is vulnerable to demons?"

"From the secular point of view, anyone with traits that match those on the psycho-trade's list. But from the Christian point of view? Those who don't know God or his Son. Those who don't arm themselves with his Word or walk in his ways. Those who don't get on their knees, confess their sins, and seek forgiveness and redemption. That's the only way we can resist the devil and choose good over evil. It's a constant battle for all of us."

"So you think Jerry Lee is possessed in the way Mary Magdalene was?"

"Yes. She's possessed in the sense of giving herself over to evil. God warns us that once we reject him repeatedly and thoroughly, he hands us over to our sin. That's possession. At least that's my view."

"Possession makes it sound like the person has no choice."

"We always have free will to choose good over evil. In the story Mark tells, Legion seeks out Christ and the demons are driven out into a herd of pigs."

"I never heard anyone say those things before," Tom said. "When Lily and I were first getting to know each other, she asked me how a person recognized Satan or his demons. At the time, I was surprised to hear anyone talk about the old dragon as if he were real."

"I'm a little embarrassed at saying what I did. It's not exactly casual conversation." She patted her husband's arm. "Matt, tell them I don't usually go off like this."

He put his arm around his wife. "I enjoyed every minute of it."

She looked at Tom and Lily. "If you weren't Christians, I'd have said nothing because non-believers would view me as mad, deserving of less sympathy than they accord sociopaths. In fact, I know how non-believers think, because in college I fell away from my faith."

"I did too," Lily said.

"Well, then, you recognize the experience. I saw God through their eyes: either not existing at all, or frighteningly judgmental and therefore a hindrance to enjoying life. I didn't want to think evil existed either. If neither God nor Satan existed, I was freer to do what I wanted and make my own rules.

"But eventually, like you, I got back to God. I accepted that I was sinful. My bad acts are sins of disobedience, violations of God's law. There is no excuse for them. Jerry Lee probably doesn't know God or respect his law. And her acts are so vicious and self-serving, so often repeated, we see them as evil, not merely the sin we're all guilty of."

"So it's useless to speculate about what in Jerry Lee's background caused her to murder so many people, is that what you're saying?" Tom asked.

"No. I didn't mean to suggest that. All of us like mysteries and want to solve them. Furthermore, it's human nature to talk about the failings of others. It helps us identify the same failings and vulnerabilities in ourselves. For instance, I'd bet Jerry Lee and her brother Verlin poisoned animals when they were little children."

"That I don't know," Tom said.

"And Jerry Lee uses poison because the secrecy of it means she's unlikely to be caught. She can maintain the facade of an upright woman, a loving mother. Sociopaths typically have an exaggerated sense of self."

"Interesting."

"And I'll bet she had a mother who either paid very little attention to her or demeaned her."

"Good guess," Tom said. "Nicky Sue's mother told Molly that Jerry Lee's mother was mean and uneducated, treated badly by her own step-mother. Jerry Lee left home as soon as she could and got married very young."

"So, when Jerry Lee becomes a mother, she lives vicariously through her daughter. To her, any action is justified to remove impediments to her daughter's success. What she never admits is that her fulsome mother's love is nothing but a cover for her own narcissism."

"Aren't we all a little narcissistic?" Lily asked.

"We are. We're all a little in love with ourselves. We're supposed to love God more than ourselves, but even believers have trouble with that commandment. Still, some of us restrain our self-love better than others. The heroic soldier throws himself on a grenade to protect his comrades. Mothers and fathers send their kids to college instead of funding their own retirement accounts. Doctors give up thriving practices to treat wretches in some stinking refugee camp on the other side of the world."

"Jerry Lee's the grenade-thrower, not the heroic soldier," Matt said.

"What hope is there for her, Doris?" Lily asked, pouring the last little bit of the mint juleps into their glasses.

"Her only hope, I think, is confession. She should accept her punishment here under the laws of Caesar, then make her peace with God if she wants to avoid the second death that comes to non-believers."

"But how realistic is that, my dear?" Matt asked, patting her hand. "She seems to have done unusually well for a serial murderer. Criminals who want to be caught usually make some obvious mistake, but she doesn't seem to have made any. And, as you said, she kills in very secretive, remote, calculated ways."

"But criminals get careless, especially when they don't get caught. Isn't that what you always tell me?" She gave her husband a searching look until he nodded affirmatively.

"And where there's a lot of circumstantial evidence and very little forensic evidence, don't you always say a confession is critical to prosecution?"

"Have I done that much pontificating?" Matt asked.

Doris gave her husband a teasing look. "Maybe not pontificating, but you've taught me a lot. Anyway, if Jerry Lee was foolish enough to make up that elaborate charade about returning a day later than she really did and leave her boarding passes where her daughter could find them, then she made other mistakes. And there's one mistake she seems to have made repeatedly."

"What's that?" Lily asked.

"Verlin. He's simple, she says, yet he's some kind of genius with herbs and he seems to have been connected with at least the old murders. You said he keeps a diary, so there's a record.

Maybe he's connected to the latest deaths too, at least to Coker and Verbena's double. The old murders are truly cold cases and would be very hard to take to trial, but the latest ones are still hot. Verlin might be the key to finding the detail that will get Jerry Lee to confess. Then, using that, get Poppy to confront her mother, maybe wearing a wire."

"You know police work very well, Doris," Tom said. "That's pretty much our plan, though it's good to hear someone like you confirm its wisdom."

Doris stood up. "It's getting late and we've got to go. I hope we haven't overstayed our welcome."

"Of course not," Lily exclaimed. "This is our favorite entertainment, sitting outside under the stars, imbibing a few spirits, gossiping together. We often solve the world's problems, though nobody knows it but us."

"But I want to say something before we leave," Doris said. "You know what I enjoyed most about this evening?"

"No, what?"

"I was comfortable saying what's on my heart. I get so tired of watching my words, concealing my beliefs, wearing a mask in a politically correct world." She picked up her purse. "Political correctness is the arch enemy of wisdom."

They toasted to spirits and stars, tearing off masks, searching out wisdom, and saying what was on their hearts.

45

Dueling Albatrosses
Thursday, May 4, 2006

While the Lawtons and the Bearsalls were discussing her mother, Poppy was doing the same with her husband in Port Royal. They were sitting side by side on lounge chairs on a balcony at the back of the house, screened by a plantation of up-lit palm trees, separated from their neighbors by an acre of land. The sounds of a neighbor's party had died away, giving way to the insistent call of tree frogs. The McBrides might have been ensconced in a luxury suite at an island resort, it was so peaceful and private. It felt remote from real life.

But it wasn't. Poppy was crying. "What are we going to do? She's a monster."

"We'll wait for the autopsy results. If Jerry Lee put something in that woman's tea, then we'll know. And so will the police."

"I saw the tags hanging out of the teapot. It was just Constant Comment."

"Well, then, something else happened. I'm told she may have had a heart condition she kept under wraps."

"A heart condition? How convenient for Jerry Lee. Like Phil Coker and my father and God knows who else?"

"Maybe Gi was on drugs and killed herself." Ferrin rubbed his chin. "Actually, that's a real possibility. Tom told me she's on anti-depressants. He hinted at worse psychological problems than

255

that, so maybe she was taking other medications as well."

"Well, we can only hope it was an accident."

"Because?"

"I'm afraid my mother might have done something. You know, I'd like to kill her myself," Poppy whispered. "If the only person she ever murdered was my father, who really loved me, that would be too much. But she actually almost killed me too. Dewey, Nicky Sue . . . where does it end?"

"You know you don't want to kill her, darling. Then you'd be just like her. Your heart would fill to the top with poison."

"My heart *is* filled to the top with poison. Horrible images burst, unbidden, into my brain: she spontaneously combusts, she falls down a forgotten well, she accidentally poisons herself."

"I've had a few of the same thoughts myself."

"If she ever suspects Verlin said what he did to me and my friends, she'd kill him too." She suddenly sat up. "Oh, my God, we've got to get him out of there."

"Well, not tonight, so relax. I'm not prepared for a midnight raid. Besides, what would we do with him? He's as dangerous as she is. I don't want him anywhere near our daughter."

"You're right. Emma thinks he's the coolest uncle ever. She's at that rebellious stage where everybody's cool except us. She'd have no defense at all."

"I'm meeting tomorrow with Tom and Matt. If they don't have a plan ready, then we'll create one. I give you my word, your mother's finished as Nemesis."

"When it all comes out, your campaign's going to be in tatters."

"Maybe, maybe not. Mullett and I have dueling family albatrosses. His albatross is a wife who killed his mistress. Mine is my mother-in-law who apparently kills because she can. What's worse, do you think?" He mimed weighing lead weights. Left hand: "Homicidal wife and pulchritudinous mistress." Right hand: "Homicidal mother-in-law." He let his left hand drop to the floor. "Wife and mistress, I think."

Poppy giggled a little hysterically. "Do you think we could get Jerry Lee committed?"

"Not without revealing what we suspect, and your mother would resist every step of the way. So far, all we have is speculation."

"We could lock her in our safe room, let her drink herself to death."

Now Ferrin laughed too. "It'd take too long and keep me from drinking my own wine. But you've floated the germ of a good idea, my love. She's got a very fancy wine room of her own. How about that for a prison? Or how about the mausoleum? It's got a gate at one end, so there'll be plenty of air, and she'll be with her loved ones. She can keep an eye on her precious herb garden and have the time to design her own death monument."

"She's already done that, you know. I've seen her will. She's going to be Vesta in bronze, guarding the mausoleum."

"You're kidding. Who's Vesta?"

"The Roman goddess of hearth, home and family." Poppy giggled. "A virgin, no less. Remember the Vestal Virgins? My mother thinks she's some kind of goddess."

"Goddess -- I can see that, I suppose, if you're looking in a fun-house mirror. But she can't think she's some kind of virgin, can she? And on what planet is killing your own husband and almost killing your daughter considered protective of hearth, home, and family?"

"There's a surreal aspect to all of this, just like the fairy tales I hated as a girl. Despite my protests, Jerry Lee read them to me anyway. As a result, I'm still terrified of wolves and trolls. The impossible task of picking up every grain of sand before morning, or spinning straw into gold, makes life seem pointless and daunting. I'm still fearful of towers, caves, and enclosures of every kind."

Suddenly, on the verge of hysteria, Poppy giggled through her tears. "Charming cottages now hold no attraction because I imagine there's a cannibal witch living inside, waiting to shove me into an oven. Somebody gave me a beautiful coffee table book once featuring country cottages. You know what I did with it?"

"No."

"The next day I drove over to Beaudry Hall and gave it to Uncle Verlin."

"He loved it, I imagine."

"He did. The worst fairy tale of all is Little Red Riding Hood. She finds the wolf in bed, pretending to be the very grandmother he ate. That's my discovery in reverse. My mother's in bed, having consumed the wolf and now glares at the world through lupine eyes."

"But don't fairy tales usually come out all right in the end?"

She nodded, hiccuping on tears. "This one won't, I suppose."

"No, it won't. I expect it's going to come out very badly for everyone."

"What will you do if you have to withdraw from the race?"

"Go back to the family business. Seamus wants me back anyway now that we're developing properties in the South."

"I always hated Washington."

"I don't like it that much myself, to tell you the truth. But I have the sense the nation is thundering down a path toward the edge of a cliff, and I'd like the chance to help turn the nation around."

"How can you forgive me?"

"Forgive you for what?"

"My youthful indiscretion, proclaimed to the whole world in a popular women's magazine. My rambling speech at the pageant, which the ladies on The View have run at least twice, to a spiteful running commentary from Joy Behar. My mother's alliance with a disreputable actor. Her life-long killing spree. In some countries, you'd be justified in killing me for the sake of your honor."

"That's a country I don't want to live in, and you know it. Besides, you didn't blow up this ill wind all by yourself. If it weren't for my political ambitions, we could deal with our problems privately instead of squirming under the gaze of self-righteous people who hate us."

"I wish I could see into the future, know how this all comes out."

"No, you don't, Poppy. There's a reason we can't see into the future. The only thing we'd ever be fixated on would be our own death."

"Speaking of that, Jerry Lee said I'm going to be occupying a niche in her mausoleum someday, but you might want to go back to Indiana."

Ferrin laughed grimly. "I never was good enough for her, was I? Even in death, I'll be somebody you shouldn't have married. Well, we're both staying right here in Naples. Together." He put his arm around his wife.

She strangled on something between a laugh and a sob. "Do you think I should confront the old witch about what we know?"

"Not yet. Let's allow a few things to play out first. Then we'll make our decision."

46

On the Side of the Angels
Friday, May 5, 2006

Friday morning, Harley Wangle was gleeful. Matt sensed he was in the mood to chat. "You look rested, Harley. What's your secret?" Out of habit Matt was surreptitiously eyeing Harley's messy desk, his wrinkled suit, the pile of boxes which seemed never to change. Had the Marines taught the man nothing about organization?

"I'm not rested yet, but I'm going to get the chance in a few hours. That gleam in my eye is anticipation. The wife and I are taking a few days this weekend, driving to Panama City with our new Airstream. We just bought a Ford Expedition to pull it. You ever drive one of those things? Like a luxury tank. You're high up off the road. It's got power to spare, it's a dream to drive. Roomy enough for a big family. Everybody should have one."

Matt smiled. "How's that go over with your boss? He's always preaching that fossil fuels are bad and hybrids are good. Gas taxes should be higher to discourage unnecessary driving. Americans gobble up more than their fair share of the world's energy . . . ."

Harley cut him off, showing no embarrassment at all. "You remember what LuAnn was driving? A Navigator. Myron can't say anything to me about an Expedition."

"So who's supposed to buy the hybrids?"

"Working Americans. Myron affectionately calls them 'the

proles.' We give them enough tax breaks, tighten the fuel standards so the auto makers have nothing to sell but battery-powered boxes, the proles will have no choice but to buy what we want them to buy. We have to wean them away from the gas-guzzlers. First make hybrids chic so the prole is just dying to get his butt into one. Then subsidize a price cut with tax credits and have the government guarantee low-interest loans."

"So you don't really mean everyone should have an Expedition or Navigator. Just people like you and Mullett."

"And you too," Harley said generously. "My heart's in the right place, you know. It's just that we have to reduce greenhouse gas emissions somehow. When we get down to the nut-cutting, some people are going to feel more pain than others. Remember that old slogan, a chicken in every pot? Well, I'd like to say an Expedition or Navigator in every garage, but it won't work. Some people will be able to have them, some people won't. People on the other side of the political divide think the free market ought to determine who gets what, but smart people like Myron know that's inefficient and unfair. Better to let some neutral bureaucrat lay down a few rules. What do you drive, by the way?"

"For everyday? I wish I had a new Expedition or Navigator. No scruples about owning one at all. But all I have is a five-year-old Honda CR-V I bought used. It's got dents and scrapes and it's broken in. It'll carry a small elephant and never needs repairs."

Harley frowned. "A foreign-made car." He wagged his finger. "Around here that's a no-no."

"Why? You know about Honda's Ohio assembly plants, right?"

Clearly, Harley didn't, but he wasn't about to back down. "Are they unionized?"

"I don't know. I think I've heard they aren't."

"Well, that's a problem. Without unions, workers would be working 70-hour weeks and being laid off every time management caught a cold. We can't let that happen."

But Honda doesn't do that. "I suppose the union dues come in handy too at election time."

"That they do. Myron wants a change in the law that makes it easier to form a union. Anybody mentions Walmart, for instance -- Myron almost has a stroke. He either wants them unionized or put out of business. You ever go in one of those stores?"

"A few times."

"Watch the people who shop there sometime." Harley wrinkled his nose. "Really, you don't want to touch the carts. I swear, every third shopper is carrying food stamps and some awful disease. They hang out of their dago-t's like wrestlers that have gone to fat -- and that's just the women." He laughed heartily at his own wit.

"But they're our voters, aren't they? The union workers, the poor, the minorities."

"True, but so are the Neiman-Marcus customers if they have any heart and can find enough ways to shelter taxes. You'd be surprised how rich Democrats are these days. I know how they think. The wife prefers Needless-Markup, let me tell you." He laughed, pleased he had a wife like that and could afford to indulge her.

Harley abruptly checked his watch. "I'm enjoying this, but the day's getting away from us." He picked up a folder and waved it. "This U.N. paper is priceless."

"Glad to hear it."

"Did you know McBride's on the Appropriations Committee? They decide what taxpayer money the U.N. gets. A lot of our voters are going to be surprised he's been quietly trying to sandbag that noble organization, cut its budget, even take away its tax breaks. Can you imagine? Everybody knows the trend is toward world government. Economics, energy, unions, banking -- everything's global now. Without the U.N., everything would be chaos."

"Don't mean to quibble, but isn't the world in chaos now?"

"It would be a lot worse without the U.N. In a couple of days, Myron's speaking before the Council on Foreign Relations. He's going to praise the United Nations to the skies, talk about how John Bolton's the worst U.N. ambassador ever. The bigwigs in the party are going to make sure the Senate doesn't confirm him later this year. We need soft diplomacy, negotiation, deals, not big mustaches and bombast. Myron will cut McBride off at the knees."

"Myron's writing that speech himself?"

"Of course not. We have researchers, speechwriters, all kinds of people for that kind of thing. Besides, Goldstein's sent us a lot of stuff. He's a big help on international relations. He's friends with Soros, you know. Al Gore too."

"I'll be watching for the news reports."

Harley rolled back in his chair. "You do that. Speaking of news reports, could we have asked for anything better than the last week's headlines?"

"Which ones?"

"Deaths connected with McBride. I don't know how we've gotten this lucky, but Myron must be on the side of the angels."

"What angels would that be?" Matt asked, careful to keep his face expressionless.

"Maybe not angels plural. Just one, the angel of death. What was it McBride's mother-in-law said about Lady Nematode following him around?"

"I read that article too. She mentioned Nemesis, as I remember. Female, but neither a lady nor a worm."

"That's it. Nesemenis. That's what the old battle-axe said. Three in a row," he said, holding up three fingers. He counted them as if playing little piggy went to market. "Alex, Ferrin's driver. Coker, Ferrin's would-be father-in-law. Verbena, Ferrin's headliner. What's the theme here? Ferrin and death." He winked at Matt. "You didn't by chance take me a little too seriously and off the actress yourself, did you?"

Matt bristled but before he could speak, Harley held up his hand. "Now, don't take that the wrong way. I'm just kidding around. So what's Ferrin the trailer-park king going to do?"

"Let the police do their work. Coker had heart problems, but he kept them under wraps, so the story that he had a heart attack doesn't sound unreasonable. The Medical Examiner's report should be out soon. As for the actress that just died, I hear she was taking some pretty heavy medications for depression, so maybe it was an accidental overdose. As for Alex -- I don't think there's been much progress on the accident investigation." A light bulb flashed in Matt's head. Always keep the other guy off balance, put him on the defensive. "You guys wouldn't have had anything to do with that bicycle accident, I suppose, since he was Ferrin's driver and his death embarrasses the opposition. Any of you drive a small blue sedan?"

"No. Absolutely not. What made you think anybody here would want to take Alex out?"

"I hear through the grapevine he was playing a double-game with Coker."

"Which grapevine?"

"He hung out at sports gyms and gay clubs. The word is that with a few beers, he spilled his guts."

"What was the double-game?"

"Feeding Coker a few secrets about our man Mullett to pass on to the trailer-park king."

"Wanna give me an example?"

"Sure. Somehow, before LuAnn took out your assistant in the hotel parking lot, the McBride campaign found out that Myron had other girlfriends before her, always staffers so nobody would notice they were hanging around. Your opponents were about to leak a few names to the press when LuAnn took matters into her own hands and garnered her own headlines."

"Our voters don't care as much about that kind of thing as McBride imagines."

"True. But if campaign funds were misused -- well that would be different, wouldn't it? Pretty girls with big salaries who don't do much real work. Secret trips. Lavish gifts. That sort of thing riles everybody." Matt watched Harley's face as a number of emotions played across it like storm clouds scudding through a spring sky.

"I appreciate the warning, brother. You think Alex fed that stuff to Coker?"

"Maybe. How else would McBride know? Unless you've got another ringer in your midst."

"You hear any names?"

"Names of who? Girls or ringers?"

"Girls."

"Maybe, but I don't know how accurate they are," Matt said. "I didn't memorize them, but I'd probably recognize them if I heard them."

"That's a bummer."

Matt snapped his fingers, as if he'd just had a brilliant idea. "If you whisper them to me, I'll tell you if I've heard them before. Then you'll know if there's any substance to the scuttlebutt. Our opponents get the names wrong, the grenade'll blow up in their faces because you'll be way ahead of the scandal. I think that would be very satisfactory, don't you?"

"I hate to say the names out loud. I'm superstitious that way. Just naming something makes it more real than it should be."

"Write the names on a piece of paper. I'll look at it and give it back so it never leaves this office."

Harley tore off a page from a note stack and began to write.

Matt watched, transfixed. He'd been shooting in the dark about the other girlfriends. Having no facts, he simply acted on a hunch derived from long professional experience with transgressors of every description. Philanderers who got away with it once were just like murderers and armed robbers who got away with it once: they did it again.

When Harley handed the paper to Matt, he said, "Recognize any of these?"

Matt pretended to be thinking when he was really just memorizing three names. Before he handed the paper back, he glanced at the printed legend in the corner of the note. A stylized donkey carried a little sign in its huge teeth reading "Mull it over." He looked at Harley. "Is a mull-it-over like a comb-over?"

"Clever, huh? That was Muffy's idea. She liked puns on Myron's name. She also thought he should do something about his hair." Harley patted his curls. "His hair isn't thick like ours. Myron's almost bald on top. Just between you, me, and the lamp post, Myron's getting hair plugs. He slips into a clinic late at night, through the back door, so nobody sees him. Muffy had a lot of clever ideas. We miss her already."

"I'll bet you do."

"So you recognize any of those names?" Harley tore the note to shreds and let the mess flutter every which way, some into his overflowing wastebasket, some onto the floor.

"All of them."

"Crap." Harley took out a handkerchief and wiped his forehead. "Myron's going to shit himself blind. How do you suppose Alex found out?"

"That's something you might want to look into. As I said, it may mean there's somebody else hiding in the weeds, pretending to be a loyal staffer."

Harley scribbled another note on his planner before looking up. The to-do list was growing. "Back to McBride. Is there anything we can pin on him?"

"You mean with regard to the deaths?"

"Yeah."

"I don't think so. But you might want to ask Goldstein why Verbena uses a body double."

"She has a double?"

Matt nodded.

"Lots of famous people have doubles," Harley said dismissively.

"I'll let you in on a little secret, Harley. McBride's headliner wasn't Verbena, but her double. Goldstein knows who she is. Everybody who met the woman Wednesday night at the fund-raiser thought she was the real deal. If I didn't know better, I'd think she was Verbena's actual blood twin."

"Are you telling me the dead woman isn't Verbena?"

"That's what I'm telling you, though you didn't hear it from me. I suspect the woman's real identity will be in all the papers in a matter of hours. The delay in identifying her is puzzling."

"Puzzling how? Didn't she have identification on her?"

"Apparently not. I was at the fund-raiser, so I know what the woman looked like. She's so much the spitting image of Verbena Cross, if I were the Medical Examiner, I wouldn't suspect anything either. He was told the dead woman is Verbena, she looks like the pictures he's seen of Verbena, so he doesn't worry that no identification was found with her body. In my mind, only an identical twin, a blood sister, could cause that much confusion."

Harley's mouth twisted into something between surprise and triumph. "We could float a little rumor that Verbena sent her twin to Naples, and McBride pulled a fast one on his supporters, who just might want their money back for being defrauded. Claim that's the way the jerk is in everything -- talks a good game while fooling the folks with a little three-card monte. Plenty of reporters who'll take it as the God's truth, not even check with anybody."

"Not a bad idea." *You put out a story that Verbena has a blood twin, Goldstein will personally fly down here, without needing a plane, and strangle you.* "That'll get some headlines."

Harley pushed himself away from his desk and, clutching his knee, struggled to his feet. "Got a little arthur-itis. Sitting's hell on it. So's standing, unfortunately. Anyway, thanks for all the help, brother."

Matt stood up and shook the proffered hand. "You've got a busy day, I'm sure." He glanced at the many notes Harley had scribbled in his planner. "You're going to deserve that weekend getaway to Panama City."

"I'm starting to think I might have to postpone it."

Matt couldn't help it. Once he reached the parking lot, he laughed out loud. Before he started the engine, he found a pad of paper and wrote down three names, plus a note about Mullett's upcoming speech to the Council on Foreign Relations.

47

I Love Mysteries
Friday May 5, 2006

Early Friday morning, Jerry Lee was already on the second leg of her flight back to Los Angeles for Phil's memorial service when she got a call from her daughter. She checked her watch, a diamond-encrusted Baume et Mercier Phil had given her the Christmas after he came to live with her. When a few weeks later she found the charge on her American Express card, she gently called his attention to it. He slapped her butt and made a joke about paying her back, double, when he got the supporting actor's part he'd auditioned for in Goldstein's latest picture about corrupt cops. She believed him then. Besides, she was so caught up in the fresh glamor of living with a younger man with a famous Hollywood name that she was prepared to overlook all offenses, big and little. She was looking forward to a brilliant life. He hadn't taken her to Hollywood for the audition, but he promised the next trip he made out there, she'd be with him. Of course, he hadn't snagged the part he wanted and never paid her back.

"What are you doing, Poppy, calling this early?" It was 8:30 in the morning, Florida time. She hadn't moved her watch back yet.

"We've got to to talk."

"It's hard to hear. Wait till I get to the hotel."

"Where are you?"

Jerry Lee looked out the window. "I'm not sure. Looks like a lot of mountains down there."

"What? Are you on a plane?"

"I'm on my way to Los Angeles. I switched to an earlier flight. Fortunately, a first-class seat was still available. Phil's agent planned the memorial service, but he has a few questions for me, asked me to come out early. I told him I'm not paying a thing. Phil had an insurance policy to cover his final expenses. I've done my part just paying the premiums. If Phil's agent thinks a memorial service is so important, then he can just arrange everything himself and find the money. I have the policy with me. It was in my safe."

"Didn't the police ask you to stay around until Gi -- that is, Verbena's autopsy was done?"

"Did they? I don't remember. In any case, they didn't *order* me to stay. I told Niall the police don't need a search warrant to go back to the house, so I can't imagine what else they could possibly need from me. I don't know anything."

Before Poppy could protest, Jerry Lee thought of something else. "I should never have let my house be used the way you did. If it gets around that somebody died there, I'll never be able to sell it. It'll be tainted forever."

"Are you planning to sell?"

"Not if your husband makes a success of Spy Run. It's all on his shoulders. He's going to owe me big time if it turns out to be a mess."

"Where are you staying out there?"

"I booked a bungalow at The Beverly Hills Hotel. Dominick Dunne used to write about meeting Nancy Reagan and Betsey Bloomingdale there for lunch. Maybe I'll run into him. Wouldn't that be fun? Maybe he'll write something about me in *Vanity Fair.* I deserve a little recognition . . . all I've been through."

"If you run into Dominick Dunne, I'd advise you to skedaddle the other way. He's an investigative journalist, you know. He might start looking to find out whether you put that nitro in Phil's drink."

Jerry Lee laughed. "There were no witnesses."

"What do you mean? No witnesses to what?"

Jerry Lee realized how her words could be taken. "I mean, he was alone. Whatever he did, nobody saw it. Even me."

"Where were you Wednesday night, by the way?"

"Remind me of the date."

Poppy had to keep herself from screaming. "I saw your boarding passes. You were back in Naples Wednesday, not Thursday."

"Where'd you find them?"

"In that Danielle Steele bodice-ripper you were reading."

"I wondered where it went. What did you do with the boarding passes?"

"They're in my hand. I'm looking at them. Where were you the night of the fund-raiser?"

"I stayed with Goldie. Why don't you throw those passes away?"

"Goldie Wasserstein?"

"What other Goldie do I know?" Jerry Lee made a mental note to call Goldie right away, warn her what to say.

"Why?"

"I needed some comfort."

"Why the charade about returning Thursday morning?"

Jerry Lee let all her irritation bubble to the surface. Her tone was a mixture of sarcasm and self-pity. "Because I knew you were busy with that overbearing husband of yours, and I didn't want to be alone. When you lose your husband, you'll understand. And I didn't want to insult you by preferring to be with a friend rather than my own daughter. Sometimes talking to a woman your own age is better than talking to your own child."

"You sure you weren't in your own bedroom Wednesday night with the lights off and the door locked?"

"Now why would I do something that creepy?"

"You swear to me you had nothing to do with that poor woman's death?"

"I'm going to hang up if you keep talking like that."

"Don't hang up."

"Hold on." Jerry Lee signaled a flight attendant, holding up her empty wine glass for a refill.

"I'm back. Where were we?"

"Trying to find out where you were Wednesday night. I take it Niall will tell the same story you just did."

"It's not a story. And leave Niall out of this. Where I was Wednesday night has nothing whatsoever to do with Verbena's death. She was a druggie, wasn't she? She'd checked herself into some fancy detox clinic more than once. She was probably back on pain-killers, took too much."

There was silence on the phone. Finally Poppy spoke. "You realize, don't you, that the woman everybody thought was Verbena was somebody else? She wasn't Verbena."

Jerry Lee clutched her chest. "What do you mean, she wasn't Verbena?"

"Verbena had so many death threats she sent her body double. She'd been attacked at the premiere of her new movie. Virgil didn't want her to come to Naples, but Verbena didn't want to spoil all our plans, so she sent her double."

"So Virgil was willing to endanger another woman to save his daughter?"

"I guess you could put it that way. The woman looked so much like Verbena -- identical really -- that nobody suspected a thing."

Jerry Lee had so many other questions she hardly knew which one to pose next, but as she always did, she played offense as long as she could. "You mean your husband advertised the presence of a famous actress to boost the price of admission? What are his supporters going to think when they find out they were tricked?"

Poppy was exasperated. "That's the least of our problems."

"Do you think the woman was Verbena's twin sister if they looked that much alike?"

"No. I think it's just one of those accidents of nature."

"What's the double's name?"

"It'll be in the papers soon enough, so I guess it's okay to tell you. Gi Greer."

"You mean Margaret Greer?"

"How do you know that?"

"Let me think." Jerry Lee did her best given her lack of sleep and two glasses of breakfast wine. "Verbena must have mentioned her when the people at the Goldsteins' party started talking about how hard it is to be famous. Poor them." She laughed scornfully to cover her lie. She'd never heard about a double named Margaret Greer, though she'd seen the unfamiliar name a few hours ago in her own home. "If Goldstein-the-toad comes to the memorial service, I'm going to confront him."

"I'd be very careful if I were you. He's not likely to be in a good mood. There's more to this story than you know."

"How do *you* know who the woman is? Did the police find her driver's license or something?" Jerry Lee knew they hadn't. All the shredded documents were in her purse, in a little plastic baggy, to be disposed of in a trash bin at LAX. When she'd glanced at the driver's license, she thought Verbena was using a fake name to throw off the paparazzi. She realized now how stupid that assumption was. Verbena's appearance at the fund-raiser had been heavily advertised. What good would a fake name have been, even for traveling?

She was reminded of Phil's taunt about how naïve she was. Her heart sank further when she realized that by the time she retrieved the woman's papers, it was too late anyway, even if she'd known the woman was Verbena Cross' double. At four in the morning, Margaret Greer was already dead.

"Strangely, Jerry Lee, they didn't find anything. No driver's license or insurance card or even her return plane ticket. Her billfold still had money in it, but no credit cards, nothing to identify her. Something must have happened to them, because she couldn't have gotten on a plane to Fort Myers without them. But I can't tell you right now how I know the body isn't Verbena's."

With bravado, Jerry Lee purred, "I love mysteries, don't you?"

"No, I don't. I've always hated them."

"You want to know what I'm wearing to the service?"

Poppy sighed. "Not especially."

"My Isabel Marant leather jacket over a Calvin Klein sheath, both black, Dior pumps, no stockings. I'll look like I'm in mourning but a little edgy, the way Phil would want me to look. I forgot my Chanel bag, so I'm going to have to buy one this afternoon. Maybe Prada for a change."

"I don't think he cares any longer what you look like, do you?"

"You don't think he's watching us now from some place up above?"

"I doubt very much he's up above anything, but wherever he is, he's surely glad he's left this vale of tears. It's safer that way."

48

A Cheap Suit
Friday, May 5, 2006

Niall folded like a cheap suit.

When Tom and Matt appeared at Beaudry Hall mid-morning on Friday to ask Niall a few questions, they were wearing sidearms in holsters under their sports coats. The day was a little warm for sports coats, even for the unlined ones they'd selected. Anyone with an eye knew what caused the bulge on the left side of their chests.

"Niall Kilcommon?" Tom asked, knowing full well who he was. "I'm Tom Lawton. This is my partner Matt Bearsall. We've met before."

Niall tipped his head a fraction of an inch in acknowledgement. "What can I do for you gentlemen?"

"We'd like to talk to you about Mrs. Beaudry."

He drew himself up stiffly. "I never talk about my employer."

"We'd like you to step outside a minute."

"Did Ferrin send you?"

"Yes."

Niall glanced toward the street. "Anybody passing by could see us."

"Then take us to the back porch." Matt's voice was patient.

"You mean the veranda?"

Matt shut his eyes in frustration, but he was still patient. "The back veranda then. If you're concerned about being seen, take us through the house."

"May I ask the occasion for the visit?"

"No."

For a few seconds, Niall looked like he was going to stand his ground, but then, without a word, opened the door wider and allowed the men to enter the house. When the trio reached the back of the house, Niall gestured toward chairs in the sitting room off the kitchen. "Perhaps this room would be more private."

"Perhaps it would," Tom said.

"Would you like coffee? Maria's gone home, but I can make it for you."

"No thanks." Tom took out a notepad. "We're only going to be here a few minutes if you cooperate. Please, have a seat."

Niall sat on the edge of a chair. "What am I supposed to cooperate about?"

"You asked if Ferrin sent us. He just wants to be sure there's nothing suspicious about the death of Miss Cross."

Niall tipped his head a fraction of an inch, saying nothing.

"By the way, how's Phil's car?"

"Somebody came out and repaired it while Mrs. Beaudry and Mr. Coker were in California."

"You allowed that?"

"Of course. Mr. Coker called to make sure I should expect the man. If you want to have a look, I have the code to the garage."

"No need."

Niall abruptly rose and walked to the kitchen, opened a drawer, removed something, and returned to the sitting room. "The repairman found this under the car. I understand it was attached to an axle. We have no use for it, but it may be of interest to you."

Matt examined the mangled piece of metal, then showed it to Tom. "It's part of the bike, I'll bet." He chuckled. "You can't trust anybody to do a good job these days. I suspect Coker wouldn't have wanted this kept."

Tom smiled at Niall. "Did you show this to your employer?"

"You mean Mrs. Beaudry?"

"Yes."

"No. I'm embarrassed to say I forgot."

"For once, that's a virtue,"Tom said. "We want to ask you about something else. How long have you worked for Mrs. Beaudry?"

Niall examined the ceiling. "Eleven years, I believe. Ever since Beaudry Hall was built."

"Are you here on a green card?"

"I'm a naturalized citizen now."

"Do you know why Mrs. Beaudry moved to Naples?"

"To be near her daughter."

"We're confused about something. Maybe you can help us out."

"How?"

"Tell us about picking up Mrs. Beaudry at the airport in Fort Myers."

"You mean this week? It was routine."

"That was Thursday morning, is that right?"

Niall nodded affirmatively.

"You sure it wasn't Wednesday morning?" Matt asked.

Niall closed his eyes, as if picturing a calendar. "So much has happened, the days are running together. I believe it was yesterday. I took her back to the airport very early this morning. She's returning for Mr. Coker's memorial service tomorrow afternoon."

"As you say," Matt interjected, "a lot has happened in a couple days. Perhaps your memory is faulty."

"No. I have an excellent memory."

"Oh, come, man," Matt said, his patience slipping a little. "We all have our little lapses, and as you said, so much has happened it's hard to keep it all straight. Letting the auto repairman in, overseeing the cleaning staff, picking Mrs. Beaudry up in Fort Myers, helping the caterers set up for the fund-raiser, lying to the security guys that you didn't have keys to the master suite, clearing up afterwards, taking a late-night tea tray to your honored guest, driving Mrs. Beaudry to Port Royal Thursday morning as if she'd just arrived in Naples and refusing to return Mrs. McBride's frantic calls, dialing

911 when you returned here and found Miss Cross unresponsive, letting the police bag Miss Cross' possessions, taking Mrs. Beaudry back to Fort Myers." Matt smiled. "With all that going on, it's only natural you'd get confused about something."

"I didn't lie about the keys."

"You didn't?"

"Mrs. Beaudry had them. I didn't."

"So it was only a half-lie. Mrs. Beaudry took all the sets of keys into her room, didn't she? My guess is she sat in the dark and watched the fund-raiser from her window. Would that be about right?"

"Perhaps."

"And let's concede you didn't lie about which day you picked up Mrs. Beaudry in Fort Myers, but you might be mistaken."

"As you said, it's hard to keep the events straight."

"Especially when your employer wants the facts altered just a little. If you need your memory refreshed, you might want to take a look at these," Matt said, proffering Jerry Lee's boarding passes.

Niall glanced at them without taking them. "Now that we've talked, I'm beginning to sort out the days. I think I may have picked her up on Wednesday."

"Why the charade?"

"It wasn't . . . it was just a small thing. Mrs. Beaudry said she had to return to get funeral clothes and find Mr. Coker's will and an insurance policy. But she didn't want to attend the fund-raiser, steal the limelight from her daughter and son-in-law or Miss Cross. However, once it was known she was back, it would look odd, maybe even insulting, if she stayed away, as if she didn't support her son-in-law. So she stayed out of sight until the next day. Then she went to see her daughter because she missed her so much."

"Who made the tea that Miss Cross drank before she went to sleep?"

"I did." Niall looked faintly startled at the sudden change of subject. "Constant Comment with some rose hips added. I added a bowl of raspberries and some English biscuits." He omitted mention of the Ambien.

"Did you take the tray to her room?"

"I did."

"Why did you prepare those exact items? Did Miss Cross specifically request them?"

"No. Mrs. Beaudry told me what the lady's late-night preferences were. She met Miss Cross in California at the estate of her parents. She wanted her guest to be comfortable, so she assigned the best room to her. Mrs. Beaudry instructed me to make her feel like a guest in a luxury hotel."

"Did you put on the tray all the tea or biscuits you had in the house?"

Niall looked puzzled. "No."

"Do you live here?"

"I have a suite on the fourth floor."

"So you were here Wednesday night after the fund-raiser?"

Niall nodded.

"Did anyone try to enter the house after Miss Cross went to bed and you took her tray to her?"

"No. I locked up after the caterers left. The doorbells ring in my rooms on the fourth floor. They didn't ring."

"Your hearing is good?"

"It's excellent."

Like your memory? "Was the alarm system on?"

"Mrs. Beaudry had an alarm system installed years ago but for several years she hasn't paid to arm it."

"Any signs of forced entry?"

"No. I check all the doors every morning."

"Does Verlin have a key to the house?"

"No."

"Did Miss Cross lock her room after you left the tea tray?"

"I wouldn't know. I didn't hear the lock click. But she must have done so eventually because when I went up there yesterday morning at Mrs. McBride's direction, the door was locked."

"Since Mrs. Beaudry was actually in the house Wednesday night and Thursday morning, she might have locked the door to the guest bedroom herself. From the outside. Isn't that right?"

278

"It's theoretically possible, I guess."

Matt stood up, glancing toward the kitchen. "Mind showing us whatever is left of the tea and biscuits?"

Niall hesitated a second before getting to his feet. "They're in the pantry."

The pantry was a large closet with built-in shelves, stuffed with big pots, electric appliances, and foodstuffs in boxes, tins, bottles, cans, and bags. Niall pointed to the tea tin. Matt took out a clean handkerchief and opened it. One tea bag was left. "How many tea bags did you use that night?"

"Two. The pot's rather big. It hasn't been returned to us yet. Mrs. Beaudry has called me several times about that."

Matt put the lid back and set the tin aside. "And the biscuits?"

Niall pointed to another much bigger decorative tin box with a bucolic scene painted on the lid. "Quite a few are left."

"You mentioned something about hips?"

"Rose hips," Niall said with compressed lips. "They're in that burlap bag."

"Do you have authority to turn the tea tin, the biscuit tin, and the bag of hips over to us?"

Niall's face tightened. "Of course I have the authority."

"Do you personally have any concern if these items are examined in a laboratory?"

"For what?"

"Just a precaution. Do you have an unused paper grocery bag?"

"We only have reusable totes. Mr. Coker insisted on that."

"They won't do." Matt turned to Tom. "You want to get a few paper bags from my car? They're in the back."

While Tom was gone, Matt walked over to the granite island. "I have a form here I want you to sign. It says you have authority to turn these specific items over to us and are doing so voluntarily."

"Will you be returning them?"

"Don't hold your breath. Where's Verlin?"

"I haven't seen him this morning, but he'll be somewhere in the gardens. Do you want me to summon him? There's a buzzer that sounds in his apartment and the potting shed."

"No. After I put those items in bags, Tom and I will find him. We need one more thing from you."

"Yes?"

"Your silence. It would be most unwise of you to say a word about this visit to Mrs. Beaudry. Understand?"

"No, I don't understand."

"Sometimes it's best not to. Just take my word for it that staying silent will be good for your health."

Once the paper bags were stowed in the way-back of Matt's Honda, the two men walked around the side of the house to the herb garden in the back corner where they could talk without being overheard. Matt said that if Jerry Lee or Verlin had done anything to the tea or biscuits, he'd bet the ranch that Niall had nothing to do with it and knew nothing about it. Niall seemed to have no idea that the unresponsive woman was anyone other than Verbena Cross and had no suspicions about how she died.

"Still," Tom said, "Niall was willing to lie about the day he picked up Mrs. Beaudry."

"But he thought it was a harmless white lie to avoid embarrassment."

"His lie to the security guys about Mrs. Beaudry being in California and the master suite being empty wasn't so white though, was it?" Tom asked rhetorically.

"What are you thinking, Tom?"

"I'm thinking about Miss Greer's identification papers. If they were scooped up with everything else, why didn't the Medical Examiner know whose body he had? If there were no identification papers, somebody must have taken them. Somebody with keys. Somebody who'd been hiding all night in a room down the hall from Miss Cross' room. Somebody who had access to the guest bedroom and a poisoner's experience killing people secretly."

"I still have a good contact in the Medical Examiner's office," Matt said. "I'll make a call as soon as we're done with Verlin."

49

Tea and Twinkies
Friday, May 5, 2006

Tom and Matt found Verlin in his potting shed. When he saw the men standing in the open doorway, he quickly closed the doors on his cabinet.

"Do you have a few minutes to talk to us?" Tom asked.

Verlin wiped his hands down his trousers. "Not really."

"You're a very smart man, Verlin. You might be the only person who can help us."

Verlin had never been called smart before. He studied the men's faces for signs they were making fun of him, but he couldn't see any. "How?"

"May we come in?"

Verlin nodded.

"We didn't see you at the fund-raiser Wednesday night."

"I was there."

"You were?"

"I sat on the mausoleum steps and watched. Jerry Lee told me I could watch if I stayed in the shadows. She told me to wear something dark and not smoke or make noise."

"Did you see the famous actress who was here?"

"Yes. She was pretty."

"Did you get a chance to meet her after all the guests left?"

"Not exactly."

"What do you mean, not exactly?"

He wiped his hands again on his trousers. "She walked out on her balcony before she went to sleep."

"Where were you that you could see her?"

"You want me to show you?"

"Lead the way."

They walked to the mausoleum. Verlin pointed to the balcony. "She stood there."

"What was she doing?"

"Smoking a cigarette and looking at the moon."

"Do you think she saw you?"

"No. She looked like a princess, waiting for something. In the fairy tales my sister used to read to Poppy, the princess was waiting for a prince."

"Do you think she found him?"

Verlin looked startled.

"I mean," Matt said, " did you see anybody around here after the party?"

"No."

"You didn't say anything to her when she was on the balcony?"

Verlin shook his head. "I waved at her, but she didn't wave back. I don't think she saw me."

"Do you think she'd already drunk the tea Niall prepared for her?"

Verlin had to think about that. "How would I know that?"

"Were her lights on awhile after she left the balcony?"

He shook his head. "When she went back in, her lights went out right away."

"And that was the last you saw her." Tom didn't ask it as a question but as an invitation to talk.

Verlin rubbed his trousers again.

Matt glanced at Tom. They were thinking the same thing. Even the best poker players have a tell. Verlin was nervous about half-truths told through silence.

"It would help us a lot if you told us whatever you know."

"She doesn't move when she sleeps. She sleeps on her back

but she doesn't snore. She wears a white mask over her eyes, like the Lone Ranger." Little by little, Verlin told his visitors about his clandestine visit to her room. "I wanted a souvenir."

"Why?"

"Before people disappear, I find something where their souls can go."

"Would you show us the souvenir?"

"You won't tell Jerry Lee?"

"Don't tell me you're afraid of her," Tom said, patting the little man's shoulder.

"She doesn't know I have a key to the house. She doesn't know about the souvenirs."

"She may never have to know."

They returned to the stone shed. Once Verlin got started explaining his souvenirs, there was no stopping him. The silver pill box, engraved with the initials MAG, had not yet been put in the cabinet. Verlin opened the little box to show it was empty.

Matt pointed at the little box. "Did this contain anything when you found it?"

"Little yellow pills. I dumped them out."

"Why did you dump out the pills?"

"To make room for her soul." The answer was so obvious, his tone was just short of scornful.

"How did you know her soul would need a place to go?"

"The tea."

"Tell us about that."

"Can I show you?"

"Even better."

On a shelf of his cabinet devoted to commercial teas, canned soup, and Twinkies, Verlin removed a little paper bag and dumped out a dozen or so bags of Constant Comment, forming a little heap on a waist-high table. Beside that he placed a small stack of square papers, a tiny spoon, a scissors, a plastic measuring cup, and a stapler. Using a step ladder, he took down a gauze bag from the rafters and placed that beside the heap of teabags.

"What's in that bag?" Matt asked.

"*Digitalis purpurea*."

"English please."

"Foxglove. I grow it in the herb garden. Here's how I did it." He snipped the string at the point of contact with the teabag and, with the tag still attached, laid the string aside. Then he opened the tea bag and carefully shook the contents into the measuring cup. After adding the ground foxglove, he stirred them together. Then he spooned some of the contents onto a fresh tea paper, folded it into an origami envelope, and stapled the string and tag back in place. Like a hypnotist, he dangled his work of art by the tag. "The bag is a little bigger than it was and the string a little shorter, but most people would never notice."

"You've done this before."

"For Jonah. He liked Lipton black tea, mixed with lemonade and crushed ice. He drank pitchers of it every day. And for Poppy that time she went to sleep. She liked peppermint tea, but that herb wasn't *Digitalis purpurea*. That was *Taxus baccata*. I tried to tell the doctor that." He pushed his glasses back on his nose. "I warned my sister that *Mentha pulegium* and *Ruta* were safer."

"*Mentha* what?" Matt asked.

"Pennyroyal and rue. You give a little weak tea made from them for a few days until the baby comes out. Most girls don't die that way."

"Did Niall or Maria know that the teabags for Miss Cross had been altered?"

Verlin shook his head. "I snuck into the pantry to get the tin and then return it."

"Did Jerry Lee know?"

He rubbed his trousers. "She wasn't here."

Matt and Tom exchanged a look. Even Verlin seemed to have been fooled into thinking Jerry Lee was still in California Wednesday night.

"Let me ask another way," Matt said. "Why did you change the teabags?"

"Jerry Lee called me. But I didn't do exactly what she said."

"What do you mean?"

"I made three instead of two to be sure there would be enough. She wanted me to throw away the real bags, but I kept the rest of them so I could make myself tea whenever I want." He pointed to a little hot plate and a tea kettle. "Those are mine. I like tea." He held up the teabag he'd made. "You want this?"

After taking the bag, Matt pointed at the gauze bag of foxglove. "Did Jerry Lee take any of this with her when she and Phil went to California?"

"She was going to but changed her mind."

"Do you know why?"

Verlin shook his head. "I thought maybe Phil was going to be all right."

Matt had a thought. "Where has Mr. Coker's soul gone?"

Without a word, Verlin returned to his cabinet and took out a clean Mason jar with only a few items in the bottom. "He's here." Verlin gently shook out the Scorpio cuff links, the Jimmy Carter campaign button, and the peace pendant.

"All these belonged to Phil Coker?"

Verlin nodded. "Maybe he's in the cuff links." He picked up the campaign button and studied it before showing it to the two men. "Do I look like Jimmy?"

Tom and Matt both laughed. "Now that you point it out, there's a definite resemblance," Tom said. "When did you take these?"

"The night I saw my sister drive away in Phil's car. She was wearing his hat." Verlin walked to his cabinet and took out a little notebook. He turned to the page he wanted. "That was Wednesday."

Matt leaned over to look at the diary. "What language do you write in?"

"Mine."

"How long have you been keeping a diary?"

"Since I learned to write."

"Have you always lived with Jerry Lee?"

"No. Just since I found Ma and Pop dead. Jerry Lee was already married then, so she told me I had to live with her."

Matt exchanged a look with Tom. "So everything's in those notebooks." He returned to the pile of trinkets. "Why did you take these things, Verlin? Did you know Mr. Coker was going to die soon?"

"I never *know*. But sometimes I just have a feeling."

"What gave you the feeling about Phil?"

"On Wednesday night, Jerry Lee didn't wait by the gate to see Phil pick up the biker and then bring him back, the way she promised. She said it was time to do something. She said it in that special voice."

"Special voice?"

Verlin held up his hand, his fingers spread. He counted off five. "Jonah, Dewey, Nicky Sue, the biker, Phil. Each time, in that special voice, she said it was time to do something. And so she did."

After exchanging a look with Matt, Tom asked Verlin if he'd be willing to take a ride to talk to Ferrin, who needed to hear what he had to say.

Verlin almost smiled. "Can I drive the Impala? You two can sit in the back seat. I'll pretend to be Niall."

Tom told him they appreciated the offer, perhaps some other day, but for now it would be more convenient for Matt to drive his Honda.

Verlin, sitting in the passenger seat, ate two packages of Twinkies on the way to Port Royal. Keeping an eye out for Impalas, he spotted one, triumphantly calling the men's attention to it.

50

A Grieving Widow
Friday, May 5, 2006

Jerry Lee put the death of Margaret Greer behind her once she reached her bungalow at The Beverly Hills Hotel. After unpacking, she opened the door to the patio and stood there, her back to the palms, taking in the elegance of the room. It was airy in a way that her own bedroom in Naples was not. She walked over to the four-poster bed to rub the silky tropical hangings between her fingers. Then she tried out a beautiful French chair upholstered in a pink and ivory plaid, pretending an audience of courtiers was waiting just outside the door for admittance to her royal presence, her beplumed but emasculated consort beside her.

It was unfair that she no longer had a consort. If only Phil were here, they could gossip about the glamorous couple -- married, but not to each other -- she'd spotted getting out of an exotic roadster when she exited her taxi. She had asked so little of Phil. If only he'd been loyal and gotten a contract to make *Rear Action,* he'd be alive and she'd have a companionable consort full of sardonic gossip.

Determined to enjoy the last little bit of glamor associated with Phil, even if it was only his memorial service, she shook away the stabs of disappointment that assaulted her in unguarded moments. Having showered and changed into a printed Vera Wang sheath, she walked to the pool and surveyed the crowd. Much too young and firm for her to return in a bathing suit.

She strolled to The Signature Shop, where she took her time examining robes, mugs, beach towels, and bags. Though she admired the sophistication of the black bag embroidered with the hotel's logo in pink, she couldn't resist the pink-and-white striped tote with the black handle and logo. Even the unwashed would recognize it. As an afterthought, she chose a pink beach towel for her granddaughter and pink mugs for Poppy and Ferrin, directing the clerk to send them to her bungalow.

She'd planned to have lunch on the terrace of Bar Nineteen 12, overlooking the pool and gardens, but to her chagrin found it didn't open until five in the afternoon. Feeling a little cheated but making a dinner reservation so she could return, she made her way to The Fountain Coffee Room, where she studied the menu. The Grilled Russian on Rye sounded delicious, but it made her laugh aloud, thinking of the Russian she'd knocked off with Phil's Prius. If only she'd been able to grill him instead of merely smacking him into oblivion! After a debate with herself about taste versus calories, she ordered The Princess Salad, bland but virtuous. There was no debate, though, about a flute of the Veuve Clicquot Ponsardin, Yellow Label. It was neither bland nor virtuous. Instead of pretending to busy herself with her novel, a practice she'd adopted years ago to disguise solitary, friendless lunches as pleasurable choices, she spent her time scanning the crowd for celebrities, but saw nobody she cared about.

A few years ago she and Phil had had lunch in New York at The Russian Tea Room, where they ate the best Chicken Kiev either had ever tasted. As they entered the restaurant, Phil spotted Michael Douglas and Rob Reiner sitting, heads together, in the valuable half-circle booth in front where they could be seen by everybody. Against his better instincts, Phil nodded to them, hesitating a moment in case he'd be invited over. But he wasn't. Though both men glanced in his direction, they looked through him as if he were vapor.

To the sound of laughter from Booth Number One, she and Phil were led to the back of the tea room, where they were seated at a nondescript table inches from other tourists. Once seated, Phil, his little hazel eyes narrowed and his face beet red, ranted against the bad manners and mediocrity of his rival. She'd been embarrassed, afraid the crowds around them, their ears aflame, would laugh at the jealousy and rage in his voice. Finally, a few people recognized Phil and asked him to autograph their menus. Though Phil never introduced her to anyone, despite the strangers' inquiring glances, she appreciated the softening effect of the public attention on Phil's mood.

Time had blurred the rough edges of that experience. At least, it was emotionally charged and involved celebrities and was therefore memorable. She longed for a little emotional charge, for something memorable. Tomorrow she'd get to say a few words about Phil . . . memorable, emotionally charged words. She was prepared.

After two glasses of champagne, Jerry Lee was in a mellow mood for her appointment at La Prairie Spa, where she'd booked a ninety-minute caviar firming facial. For the price, she could have ordered a caviar appetizer at dinner, but rationalized that it was worth five hundred dollars to have glowing skin for tomorrow's service. A makeup artist would give her a new look in the morning. In anticipation of wonderful pictures in all the trades, she had given the front desk a list of newspapers she wanted delivered to her bungalow on Sunday. The articles, perhaps accompanied by flattering pictures of her as the grieving widow (never mind that she wasn't really his widow) would make an important coda to the scrapbook of her years with Phil. Before going to bed, to ensure an appropriate public performance, she would stand in front of a mirror and practice the facial expressions and body language of grieving widows. She especially admired Jackie Kennedy in that respect.

After her facial, feeling drowsy and thirsty, she sat for awhile in the lounge with the other guests, wearing the spa's luxurious pink terry robe, a terry band still holding her hair off her face, drinking sparkling water and staring into space. She knew she was old now, for the well-being that followed ninety minutes of gentle pampering was more satisfying than the sharper, more defined pleasures of either sex or shopping. As she closed her eyes, just on the verge of dozing, her hearing sharpened. From the murmur behind her, she gradually distinguished a theatrical voice. It must be Ellen Matter's, which despite the whisper, carried as if she were projecting to the second balcony in a spacious theater.

"Your father wouldn't even consider it."

"You don't think it's just a little rude to stay away?" Jerry Lee recognized the throaty voice as Verbena's. "Shouldn't he send someone to represent us?"

"Who? Why?"

"Maybe Errol, the producer of *The Ho Chi Minh Trail*. And as for why, just to be polite. He died at Mom's place, for starters. He was Dad's little pet once upon a time."

At the mention of the film's title, Jerry Lee came to full consciousness. The older woman wasn't Ellen. It must be her sister, what was her name? Dorothy something. Verbena's real mother, according to Phil.

"When Phil refused to do a publicity tour for *Silver Back*, Errol washed his hands. So did your father. I told Ellen it was a mistake to invite him and that poor old woman he was living off of, but Virgil was determined to keep up the deception that they were friends and colleagues."

"Do you think I should go?"

"Absolutely not. Virgil put the word out. Anybody who's seen at that memorial service is done in our world."

Jerry Lee was so angry she saw stars. She rose regally out of her chair and turned to stare at the woman. When neither Verbena nor her mother-aunt looked up, Jerry Lee stalked over.

"Excuse me. I'm Jerry Lee Beaudry, Phil Coker's widow." With her mouth but not her eyes, she smiled at Verbena. "We met a week ago at your parents' estate in Napa."

Verbena politely stood up. "This is my aunt Dorothy Salzman."

When Dorothy showed no sign of standing or extending a greeting of any kind, Jerry Lee waved her hand as if in blessing and said, "Please, stay seated. I couldn't help overhearing your remarks about the service tomorrow."

Verbena, to her credit, flushed, but before she could say a word, Dorothy spoke sharply. "It was a private conversation."

"I understand. Mothers and daughters have much to talk about, don't they?"

There was a moment of silence. "What on earth are you talking about?"

Jerry Lee put her finger to her lips. "Your little secret is safe with me, Dorothy. But I'm afraid the fact that Verbena's twin died at my house will soon hit the papers, no matter how hard we all try to keep it hush-hush."

Dorothy stood up. "Do you have any idea what you're saying? It's slander, plain and simple. Or who you're dealing with?"

Verbena patted her aunt's arm. "I'm sure Mrs. Beaudry will be discreet."

Dorothy's blazing eyes were so fierce that Jerry Lee, immune as she was to other people's feelings, felt her knees grow weak. Without a word, she turned to find her locker and get dressed.

Once she reached her bungalow, Jerry Lee sat frozen with horror in that lovely pink and ivory chair for a half hour, wondering what the punishment was for poking a dragon. In her experience, once the dragon had been poked, it had better be slain, so she called a reporter in Naples, an old friend always on the lookout for the inside scoop.

Despite feeling she had the upper hand, her nervous tension didn't dissipate, even with an entire bottle of Veuve Clicquot. She canceled her reservation at Bar Nineteen 12, instead ordering dinner in her bungalow, a savory meal she barely touched.

She was very nearly dozing in her chair when her cell phone rang. It was *The National Enquirer*. She talked a long time to the reporter, grateful for the attention. Then she called Goldie Wasserstein.

That night, she dreamed she was standing behind a podium under a spotlight, naked from the waist up.

51

A World of Hurt
Saturday, May 6, 2006

By Saturday, the Naples reporter had her scoop.

VERBENA CROSS ALIVE!

Verbena Cross is alive. No, it isn't a miracle of resurrection. It's a case of mistaken identity.

U.S. Rep. Ferrin McBride drew a big crowd at his Wednesday fund-raiser when he announced that Verbena Cross, the famous Hollywood actress, would appear in support of his campaign. The announcement was a surprise because Miss Cross' father, Virgil Goldstein, is an internationally famous liberal who makes controversial films critical of the defense and economic policies of the United States. His films are often made in collaboration with organizations funded by George Soros, Al Gore, Michael Moore, and other activists who would never support the positions advocated by Ferrin McBride, a right-wing conservative.

But it was not Verbena Cross who appeared at McBride's fund-raiser, which was held in the famous gardens of Beaudry Hall, the Naples estate of McBride's mother-in-law, Jerry Lee Beaudry. It was Miss Cross' body double, a woman who began appearing as Miss Cross at various events several years ago. Until today, it was not known that the body double was actually her identical twin sister, Margaret Greer, whose existence has been a secret for almost all of the the forty-five years of the sisters' lives.

McBride supporters came out of the woodwork by the hundreds when Verbena Cross announced her support of the conservative incumbent in defiance of her famously liberal father. Though McBride's supporters were curious about the actress' unexpected political views, the woman who attracted so many McBride supporters reportedly said nothing political at all. "I'm here to lend moral support to Poppy McBride, who has been unfairly characterized as a hypocrite due to a youthful indiscretion," she said.

Simon Diodorus, a young man about town often seen in the company of Arachne Spanopoulos at fashion shows and charity balls, escorted Margaret Greer at the fundraiser. "Now that I've heard the woman I escorted wasn't Verbena Cross, I realize I should have put two and two together," he said. "Though she was very nice, she seemed to know less than I did about the real Verbena. That should have been a clue."

Upon learning that the deceased "celebrity" was not Miss Cross but her heretofore unacknowledged twin, Harley Wangle, the press chief for Commissioner Myron Mullett, McBride's Democratic challenger, expressed disgust at the deception. "McBride supporters now know that their candidate is up to his old tricks. We wouldn't be surprised if there's a suit for fraud. No one told the people who paid two thousand dollars apiece that the 'celebrity' they were going to meet was not Miss Cross but her twin sister."

Asked how he learned of the deception, Wangle said with a smile that an outraged McBride supporter who felt duped had tipped him off to expect a surprise announcement about the woman's identity.

The woman who died at Beaudry Hall has been

identified as Margaret Greer. Little is known about her life up until two years ago, when she first began appearing at certain events in place of Verbena Cross, not then known to be her twin sister.

Mrs. Beaudry, the owner of Beaudry Hall where the McBride fund-raiser was held and where Miss Greer died, was reached yesterday in California as she prepared for the memorial service of her long-time companion, actor Phil Coker, who recently died of a heart attack. [See P. 3, Col. 1, for more on the unexpected death of Phil Coker and the memorial service to be held this afternoon in Los Angeles.] She confirmed Mr. Wangle's surprise disclosure that Miss Greer is Verbena Cross' twin sister. "When Phil and I recently visited the Goldsteins at their Napa Valley estate, he told me that Verbena's real mother is Ellen Matter's sister, Dorothy Salzman, whom I happened to see today at La Prairie [the luxurious spa at The Beverly Hills Hotel, where Mrs. Beaudry is staying while in California]. What I didn't know until a few hours ago is that Verbena had an identical twin." Mrs. Beaudry refused to divulge the identity of her source that Verbena Cross and Margaret Greer were twins.

Ellen Matter is Goldstein's wife, the well-known Broadway actress, and Dorothy Salzman is her sister. Until now, Miss Cross was believed to be the Goldsteins' own daughter and only child, but Coker told his companion that Goldstein had been unable to have children ever since contracting mumps as a boy. Mrs. Salzman was the twins' surrogate mother. When asked why Ellen Matter would not have chosen to carry the babies herself, Mrs. Beaudry said she didn't know but perhaps she didn't want to interrupt her career or ruin her figure. She also didn't know why the Goldsteins didn't keep both twins. This paper has not been able to confirm either Wangle's disclosure or Coker's allegations as reported by Mrs. Beaudry. Coker is thought to be credible because he was an intimate friend of the Goldsteins for many years. Previously unknown, and never trained as an actor, Coker catapulted to stardom when he appeared as Private Ron Cutter in Goldstein's award-winning movie, *The Ho Chi Minh Trail.* That film was shot shortly after Miss Cross' birth. The movie, which won Goldstein an Oscar as Best Director and Coker an Oscar nomination as Best Actor, was widely credited for influencing President Lyndon Baines Johnson to end the unpopular war in Viet Nam.

Coker later made *Silver Back*, a movie also directed by Goldstein based on a novel whose title was a pun. The movie depicted two intertwined wars: the slaughter of mountain gorillas (silver backs) by an African dictator modeled on Idi Amin, and the European exploitation of African silver mines to fund internal strife in East Africa. Coker had recently visited Goldstein and his wife at their Napa Valley estate to discuss production of *Rear Action,* a script Coker wrote about the first Gulf War. Though Goldstein did not respond to inquiries, Junald al-Rashid, a spokesman for Truth-To-Power, one of Goldstein's production companies, issued a statement, which reads in part: "Bush 41, a tool of the Saudi Arabian royals, was all about protecting Kuwaiti oil to benefit the United States. Saddam Hussein was merely an excuse for the Bush Administration's Middle Eastern crusade against Muslims. Phil Coker courageously decided to set the record straight, but before he could do that, he died suddenly -- under mysterious circumstances, we might add. He had many enemies in the current Republican Administration."

A source at the local Medical Examiner's office said no identification for Miss Greer was found with her body and that the office did not realize she was anyone other than Verbena Cross until someone called in an anonymous tip. Calls to representatives of Virgil Goldstein, Ellen Matter, Verbena Cross, and Dorothy Salzman have not been returned.

Ferrin put down the paper and looked at Poppy across the breakfast table. "I think your mother is in a world of hurt. Tom called me this morning to remind me that Margaret Greer was not just Verbena's double but her identical twin. It was a jealously guarded secret known only to a very few people, but with your mother's foolish mouth, now everybody knows."

"Well, Harley Wangle is just as culpable, isn't he? In fact, wasn't he the first to announce that the women were twins?"

"I think Goldstein is going to blame my people, don't you?"

"You're right. Does that mean Goldstein will go crazy?"

"He'll deploy every weapon in his arsenal to destroy the woman who told the world his beloved daughter isn't really his blood."

"Given human nature, he may be even angrier that his infertility has been disclosed to the world."

What neither Ferrin nor Poppy knew, because they avoided the tabloids, was that *The National Enquirer* had just published an even bigger story, founded on a stronger basis in fact, about the Goldsteins' domestic deception.

52

Cuckoo in the Nest
Saturday, May 6, 2006

On Saturday morning, Lily and Tom were trying out the new seating area on a second dock they'd had constructed just for viewing the Gulf of Mexico. Their boat, a 28' Bayliner, was tied up at an adjoining dock. Simon had furnished the viewing dock with white cushioned benches, low tables, and modern lamp stands. A plexiglass shield sheltered them from the northwest winds.

They had spread out several newspapers. While Ferrin was reading the local paper to Poppy in Port Royal, Lily read *The National Enquirer* to Tom.

CUCKOO IN THE NEST

Ever since she was born, Verbena Cross has been heralded as Hollywood royalty, the daughter of Virgil Goldstein, the internationally famous director and producer of highly regarded but controversial films, and Ellen Matter, the Broadway actress. Both have won numerous awards for their work.

Miss Cross, who looks like a clone of her elegant mother, is often said to have inherited her thespian talent as well. It turns out that Miss Cross inherited nothing from either parent. She's the cuckoo in the nest: beautiful

and talented, to be sure, but the chick isn't the Goldsteins' chick.

The Goldsteins' deception was carefully orchestrated right from the start. When Verbena was born on February 3, 1961, the Goldsteins allowed *Vanity Fair* to publish the first pictures of their new baby daughter. A full-page studio portrait featured Virgil and Ellen with the week-old baby in a royal pose reminiscent of Princess Grace and Prince Rainier gazing adoringly at their first child, Caroline.

A full-page montage of snapshots lowered the pretentiousness a few notches while buttressing the story that the baby was actually born to the Goldsteins: Ellen Matter, heavily pregnant on the arm of her husband at a black-tie event, wearing a two-piece black faille maternity suit in the style of the day. Ellen, sitting up in a hospital bed, cradling her new daughter against her lacy bosom. Ellen and Virgil, silhouetted as they rushed early in the morning, before first light, into an emergency room door at the back of Cedars Sinai, as if evading the paparazzi. Virgil, in jeans, pushing a cart full of purchases outside an upscale baby store. Ellen, looking as if she'd lost all the baby weight in a day, at a baby shower given by her sister Dorothy Salzman two weeks after the birth of the baby.

The *Vanity Fair* article, as well as the Goldsteins' official press release, reported that Verbena, weighing 6 pounds 14 ounces and 21" long, was born at Cedars Sinai in West Hollywood at 6:30 in the morning on Friday, February 3, 1961. She was named Verbena Rachel Goldstein. (When Verbena turned eighteen, she legally changed her name to Verbena Cross, a move which reportedly angered her father.)

In reality, the Goldsteins' daughter was born Baby Girl One Paggott in a Catholic home for unwed mothers near Piney Flats, Tennessee. She was Baby Girl One because Baby Girl Two, her identical twin sister, was born a few minutes later. They were actually born on Wednesday,

February 1, not on Friday, February 3. Verbena's mother was not Ellen Matter but Norma Paggott, an unmarried teen-ager. Verbena's father was not Virgil Goldstein but reportedly a Viet Nam veteran who worked for Norma Paggott's father, owner of a small feed store in Tennessee. Baby Girl One was adopted by the Goldsteins, named Verbena, and taken to Hollywood to live in a mansion. Baby Girl Two was adopted by Edith and Cyrus Digger, named Margaret Ann, and taken to Florida to live in a trailer. Just as Verbena changed her surname to Cross when she was eighteen, Margaret changed her surname to Greer when she married at nineteen.

For many years, Verbena Cross reportedly did not know she was adopted or had a twin sister, but when someone began stalking her, the truth came to light in a most surprising way. Verbena hired a Naples, Florida detective, Thomas U. Lawton, who discovered that her "stalker" was none other than Margaret "Gi" Greer, her identical twin. Greer's communications with her sister had become more and more threatening as the years passed, culminating in a break-in where Greer left a threatening note signed "Venus Cross" and stole several items of memorabilia. It turned out, however, that Greer wanted nothing more than to establish a family connection.

Lawton was briefly linked romantically with Miss Cross during the shooting of her latest film, *Bonaventure Blues*. Since then Lawton has married the widow of a surgeon with a dubious past and Cross is currently engaged to actor Bordon Settle. Both Lawton and Verbena Cross deny they had an affair. Eventually, Lawton persuaded his client to hire Gi Greer as her body double. Cross agreed upon condition that Greer attend weekly sessions with a reputable psychiatrist, maintain a regimen of appropriate medications for depression, and never try to confirm their blood connection. Though some Hollywood insiders knew that Cross often sent Greer to events she could not attend, no one seemed to suspect that the woman who looked so remarkably like Cross was not merely her body double but her identical twin sister. Reportedly, no DNA tests were ever performed to verify the blood ties between the sisters.

The family secret that Verbena Cross was adopted and had an identical twin who was adopted separately might never have been outed but for the unexpected and still unexplained death of Greer in Naples after appearing at a fund-raiser for U.S. Rep. Ferrin McBride (R), who is running as the incumbent in a tight race for Congress in Florida's 14th District. Various sources close to Goldstein suggest that Cross, at the urging of her worried father, sent her twin in her place because of the attack she suffered from an environmental activist at the premiere of her movie in Savannah only a few days earlier. Miss Cross started receiving death threats when she announced that she would appear on behalf of Rep. McBride. After the premiere, she and her fiancé Bordon Settle flew to Anguilla in search of peace and safety.

On Miss Cross' web site, we found this explanation for supporting Rep. McBride. "Tom [Lawton] told me my father was helping out Ferrin's opponent, possibly by twisting the story of a miscarriage into an abortion. I don't like lies. Though I don't support a ban on abortions, I felt sorry for Poppy [McBride], whom I haven't met yet but have heard good things about, because a secret from her youth had been unfairly exposed and twisted. I knew how I'd feel if the real story of my birth had been published for all the world to hear. Now, of course, my secrets have been published, so I really know how bad Poppy feels."

After the fund-raiser, Greer stayed at Beaudry Hall, the home of McBride's mother-in-law, Jerry Lee Beaudry. [See article on p. 5 about the death of Phil Coker, the actor who lived with Mrs. Beaudry.] When Niall Kilcommon, Mrs. Beaudry's butler, discovered the woman to be unresponsive in a guest bedroom on the morning of Thursday, May 4, he identified her to emergency personnel as Verbena Cross. No identification papers were discovered with the body, which reportedly showed no signs of physical trauma. The mistake in identity was not discovered until the Medical Examiner's office received an anonymous tip that the dead woman was actually Margaret Greer. The butler, who has been questioned by authorities, apparently knew nothing of the subterfuge.

Though the Medical Examiner has not issued a report establishing a cause of death for Greer, knowledgeable sources report that she was on a regimen of anti-depressants, as well as medication to control bipolar disorder and a genetic heart defect. Those same sources speculate that Greer may have died after consuming too much alcohol in combination with her medications. Doubt has been cast on that theory, however. Simon Diodorus, a "walker" for the socialite Arachne Spanopoulos, escorted Greer at the fund-raiser. He told this paper that he never left her side and at most she consumed one glass of champagne during all the hours he was with her. An insider at the Medical Examiner's office maintains that another anonymous tipster alleges that Greer might have been the victim of digitalis poisoning.

Shortly before going to press, this paper learned that Mrs. Beaudry, who did not appear at her son-in-law's fund-raiser and who claimed to have been in California on May 3, was actually back in Florida that day. Reached at The Beverly Hills Hotel, where she is currently staying, Mrs. Beaudry admitted she returned a day earlier than she first claimed. "I was there simply to get funeral clothes and find Phil's will and insurance policies. I didn't stay at Beaudry Hall. I didn't want to up-stage my son-in-law or his special guest by announcing a last-minute appearance at the fund-raiser. Neither did I want to appear to be avoiding Ferrin as if I didn't support him in his campaign. So I stayed out of sight with my old friend Goldie Wasserstein. We played mahjong and ate sponge cake." Mrs. Wasserstein did not return calls seeking confirmation of Mrs. Beaudry's claim.

Though Verbena Cross can no longer lay claim to being Hollywood royalty, her latest film, *Bonaventure Blues*, which opened to a disappointing box office and a scathing review in *The New York Times*, has been pulling in large crowds ever since Cross was attacked in Savannah. The publicity about her secret identical twin is likely to make the movie a cult film, especially among support groups for abused women and adopted children seeking their birth parents.

"Who are all the anonymous tipsters, do you think?" Lily asked, laying the paper aside.

"You'll never guess."

Lily studied the horizon. "Not Verlin. Not Niall. Not Goldie. So who?"

"Ferrin himself."

She bolted upright. "You're kidding."

"He wants his mother-in-law stopped without having to go to the authorities himself."

"Wouldn't it look better if he fingered her openly?"

"I think so, you think so . . . but he doesn't. He'll keep close tabs on the official investigation, and once it gets to a certain point, he'll offer up Verlin as a witness in exchange for his immunity from prosecution. Verlin's not innocent, of course, but the poor little man probably never understood the full consequences of the poisons he prepared at Jerry Lee's direction. And he knows about every single person who died as a result of posing some kind of obstacle or irritant to his sister. His diary alone is a stellar record of his sister's murderous past."

"If anyone can translate it."

"There's that. As we speak, do you know what Ferrin's doing?"

"Committing harakiri?"

"In a sense, I suppose. He's having the plinth under the Nike statue opened to see if Nicky Sue Darling's body is really there. If there's a body, he'll notify the authorities so they can get a court order to take possession of it. Then, by some means, he'll convey his suspicions about how Jonah died. I don't know whether the poison she fed her husband will still show up in his remains, but it might if the authorities know what they're looking for. He won't have to be exhumed, after all, since he's occupying a shelf in the mausoleum."

"Ever since I saw the mausoleum, I've wondered if that's legal on property that's not an official cemetery."

"I hadn't thought of that, but now that you bring it up, it probably isn't."

"And Ferrin's explanation for looking for Nicky Sue at this particular date will be what?"

Tom poured himself another cup of coffee. "I don't know if he's thought that far ahead. I suppose he'll be frank about what we've just learned from Verlin -- in exchange for getting him immunity."

"Won't these revelations ruin his career?"

"Probably." He smiled ruefully. "Unless LuAnn Mullett kills again."

"She won't unless Myron had more than one fling."

"Which, you won't be surprised to learn, he did. Matt got the names of three other inamoratas from Harley Wangle, who had no idea who he was really talking to." Tom told her how Matt got the information out of Harley.

"So Matt wangled the goods out of Wangle," Lily said, laughing. "You'd think the names alone -- Wangle, Mullett, Muffy -- would warn voters off."

"I doubt that true-believing liberals think that way."

Lily tapped the tabloid she'd just set aside. "You know what I most dislike about this piece?"

Tom smiled. "I think I can guess."

"'Lawton was briefly linked romantically with Miss Cross during the shooting of her latest film, *Bonaventure Blues*.' That bit of libel still makes me furious."

"Or how about describing you as the widow of a surgeon

with a dubious past?"

"Very restrained, when you think about it," she said. "His past was a little worse than dubious, don't you think?"

"If the story about a romance with Verbena wasn't so far off the mark as to be monumentally stupid, I'd be furious too. But as it is, I'm so happy now I just can't muster much anger."

"Meanwhile, *we're* happy, but Poppy's going to have a nervous breakdown, don't you think?"

"Maybe you should go see her with Molly. She's going to need every woman friend she ever had." Tom stood up. "Meanwhile, I have a meeting in forty-five minutes with Ferrin."

53

The Destiny of Every Man
Saturday, May 6, 2006

Jerry Lee was not at all satisfied with Phil's memorial service. It was dispiriting and boring, fit for a pauper, not a prince. The service was short on specifics about the deceased and his almost-widow. Phil's agent, Morty Zeller, had refused to publicize the event and invited only a few old colleagues and putative friends.

When Jerry Lee stepped out of the limousine she'd hired for the occasion, there was no one to greet her other than the funeral director. Taking his arm as if she were an honored guest, she walked regally past the tabloid photographers, head held high, dry eyes hidden behind oversized Jackie-O sunglasses.

When they reached a room called The Rose Cottage -- such a silly euphemism, she thought -- she shook off her escort and stood at the back of the room a minute, counting the rows of chairs. Ten rows, ten seats in each, but not every seat was occupied, so less than a hundred people were present. Almost all the guests were older men in business attire. Pitiful. She was most annoyed that hardly anyone turned to look at her.

She reached the front of the room a couple minutes before the service was to start. Every seat in the front row was occupied, none left open for her. Furious, she stood beside Morty, who had an aisle seat, glaring at the back of his head, unwilling to move until he acknowledged her and somebody gave up his seat. When Morty kept his head turned away from her, she finally tapped him on the shoulder as if pounding a nail into his flesh. He stood up then, said hello without embracing her, and nodded to a man who got up and walked to the second row. Jerry Lee sat down in Morty's seat on the aisle before he could object. Shaking his head, he moved to the vacated chair a few places away. She wriggled in her chair, which was too hard and straight-backed for any comfort. It was nothing but a faux-gilt folding chair. So déclassé! What was Morty thinking? She should have paid more attention to his plans.

There were no religious artifacts at the front of the room, no cross, no candlesticks, no banners, no alter. That was fitting, perhaps, for an avowed atheist, but still it seemed cold, as if everyone simply assumed Phil Coker had been consigned to the dark outer reaches of the universe where the Bible said there was weeping, wailing, and gnashing of teeth.

Beside the dais, on a plain wooden easel, was propped a large photograph of Phil at age twenty-five or so, a backlit black-and-white studio portrait that made him look ordinary and well-behaved. He was wearing a suit and a dress shirt open at the neck. His hair was longer in those days but it was very neat. A car salesman, perhaps, or a bank manager, on his way to have a drink with his buddies after a long day of work in an office. So not like the Phil she knew.

On the other side of the dais was a closed bronze coffin draped with a blanket of pale lavender mums. Who had provided the flowers? She'd forgotten all about such niceties. If she'd thought of flowers, or been willing to provide them, she'd have chosen something more exotic and colorful, like Phil himself. And why wasn't the coffin open? He wasn't to be cremated until after the service, so she was sure he was in there. She'd hoped to see his face one last time. Everyone should want to see him one last time.

As the funeral director introduced an old man wearing a purple vestment, she deliberately ignored both men, instead discreetly surveying the rest of the room. The décor was embarrassingly overdone with gilt and baroque touches, yet worn and out of date. The Rose Cottage was hardly more fashionable than the stuffy, very proper suburban mortuaries Jonah had operated in South Carolina twenty years ago. Only one official videographer was allowed inside, though without Morty's knowledge, another photographer was seated at the back, passed off as a friend of Jerry Lee's.

The old man in the purple vestment was bald and pudgy with sad eyes, his voice practically a whisper. His swollen nose and red-veined cheeks suggested a long struggle with church wine. He looked clinically depressed. Morty had told her earlier that he was a defrocked Catholic priest who had married his life-long housekeeper and finally acknowledged his only child, a young man who still used his mother's surname and now operated a car dealership in Oregon. The priest's wife, a shapeless, graying mouse of a woman, played piano accompaniment to the one and only hymn they sang, *No Tears in Heaven*.

Jerry Lee, who did not recognize the melody, choked on the words. When the mourners came to "The angel messenger of death, has gently borne away, a dear companion from our side, to realms of endless days," she put down the printed program and leaned over to glare at Morty, who assiduously ignored her. Dear companion indeed! Phil had betrayed her mercilessly and left an estate so deeply in debt that unless Morty could capitalize on his client posthumously, making him into a money-making idol like Elvis, she'd never see a penny to reimburse her for the years of providing her ungrateful consort with cars, vacations, wine, clothes, and art.

She had persuaded Morty to allow her to read a homily, and when after she listened to a number of brief eulogies from men she didn't recognize and the old priest gave her a nod, she tucked her sunglasses into her new Prada purse and rose. She took her time walking to the dais, where she placed on the podium Jonah's dog-eared Bible and a pair of reading glasses. With the aid of a bookmark, she opened to Ecclesiastes Chapter 7 and paused, taking her time to scan the small group of mourners. She waited to speak until their full attention was turned to her.

"Phil Coker was not a Christian. He didn't believe in God at all." She dabbed at her dry eyes with a lacy silk handkerchief, letting her words sink in. She shook herself, as if shaking off fears for her late companion's soul. "When I was asked to read a homily, I wasn't sure it would be appropriate to read from the Bible. Perhaps, I thought, something from one of his screenplays would be more fitting. But then I prayed about it and was led by the Lord to the book of Ecclesiastes, Chapter 7, the first four verses." She slipped on a pair of black and gold Christian Dior reading glasses.

**"A good name is better than fine perfume,
and the day of death better than the day of birth.
It is better to go to a house of mourning
than to go to a house of feasting,
for death is the destiny of every man;
the living should take this to heart.
Sorrow is better than laughter,
because a sad face is good for the heart.
The heart of the wise is in the house of mourning,
but the heart of fools is in the house of pleasure."**

She removed her glasses and put them on the podium. "I am not a Bible scholar." In fact, she wasn't sure she understood the passage she'd just read. Did the poet really mean mourning was better than feasting? She had no damned idea. She smiled at her audience. "But then I would be surprised if anyone here was a Bible scholar either." Still smiling, she waited for a murmur of acknowledgment, a nod or a grin from anyone at all, but there was only silence. Instead of looking relaxed and ready for a rousing speech, her audience looked frozen, as if waiting for the hand of God to smite her. The old priest, who was sitting on a folding chair at the far end of the dais, kept his eyes on his program as if memorizing it.

As she had once trained her students to do -- princesses-of-this and queens-of-that at Crowning Glory, her Charleston school for pageant contestants -- she searched for one receptive face. Her little princesses, as she called them, were trained to direct their answer to a kind face when a pretentious judge asked them a question to which they could not possibly form an intelligible answer. Finding one kind face in a hostile crowd could soothe a girl's fears, transforming incoherent thoughts into a charming and heart-felt response. But among the hundred or so mourners, all suddenly seemed busy with their programs or their BlackBerrys.

Only Morty Zeller actually looked back at her, so, though she was angry with him, she focused on his shiny forehead and wary eyes, silently willing him to sympathize with her. "Phil once had a good name, but he lost it trying to be a rebel, the Bad Boy of Hollywood. By visiting the Goldsteins . . . who I notice did not bother to attend . . . he was trying to regain it by making a movie exposing the dubious motives of powerful people. Unfortunately, before he could accomplish anything other than more empty promises from the man who made him a star and then abandoned him like a dog, Phil was suddenly felled with a heart attack. The hand of God struck him like lightning in the night."

Again, she dabbed at her eyes, careful to avoid touching her mascara. She nodded, almost imperceptibly, at the photographer she'd hired to get some good pictures of her.

When, after the flash, her eyes had once again adjusted to the twilit gloom of The Rose Cottage, she resumed. "Phil preferred feasting to mourning, but then don't we all? He valued his good name more than fine perfume, which is more than can be said for many in Hollywood, even the women." Not even a knowing snicker. "He preferred laughter to sorrow, telling people he offended that if they had no sense of humor, then they might want to relinquish the space they were taking up on this crowded earth." She paused again for some sign of agreement but none came, even from Morty, who looked puzzled. "Phil hated mourning and sad faces. He was a fool for pleasure. He believed that however disappointing life was, it should be lived to the fullest. But then again, aren't we all fools for pleasure?" Dead silence. Her rhetoric was getting her nowhere.

"But if Phil were here, he might well applaud the author of Ecclesiastes in at least one respect, for the day of his death was in fact better for him than the day of his birth."

She looked up from her notes, so shaken with anger at the chilly reception she was getting that for a split second she pictured picking up a gun and mowing every last one of her enemies down, leaving a room full of dead bodies, the walls splattered with blood. The vision made her dizzy.

She couldn't help herself. The dam was bursting. She had to say what was in her heart. She abandoned her notes, and without showing any sign of anger other than narrowed eyes and a tight mouth, she spit out her curse. "Phil made many of you rich and famous, yet I see no tears for him, or for me, in this dreadful place." She slowed the cadence of her words so each was a sentence in itself. "I wish you all a day of death that yields more pleasure than your day of birth."

Finally, she got the response she sought. Heads snapped to attention. A collective gasp filled the room. The mourners looked like they wanted to bolt from the room.

Satisfied at last, she closed the Bible with a thump, creasing the pages, and stood there a moment, glaring at the room full of chastened strangers. She wished she was Jim Jones. She'd invite them to a funeral lunch and serve them Kool-Aid so they'd expire in front of her.

Then, carrying the Bible and her reading glasses, she returned to her front-row aisle seat, picked up her new Prada bag, and paused a few seconds to adjust her Isabel Marant jacket so everyone would notice how chic and slim she was. Then, head held high, she marched out of the funeral home to the limousine waiting for her near the front door.

Her personal photographer hurried after her. Before getting in, while the driver held the back door open, she posed for another picture, and before the limousine pulled away, she waited until the photographer approached her window, whereupon she posed for yet another snapshot, all alone in the back seat, looking forlorn as a widow should.

She couldn't wait to read the next day's papers. People the world over would be moved by her loyalty to Phil Coker. They'd be astonished at her understanding of Scripture, her profound insights into human nature expressed in noble words, her courage in the face of heartless rejection.

She'd be famous, she knew it.

54

Playing Chess with the Devil
Saturday, May 6, 2006

Luis Gonzalez, a third-generation Hispanic-American, had been a prosecutor in the Homicide Unit of the Office of the State Attorney, Twentieth Judicial Circuit of Florida, for over twenty years. Both Tom and Matt knew him from their years in the Naples Police Department, and Ferrin had conferred with him several times when he was Florida's Attorney-General. Once he heard the name Ferrin McBride, Gonzalez agreed, no questions asked, to meet the three men in his Fort Myers home on Saturday at noon for a private discussion of a serious matter.

Gonzalez' wife, Patty, a muscular blonde dressed in tennis whites, greeted them at the door and ushered them into a wood-paneled room at the front of the house. Gonzalez, also dressed in tennis whites, stood to welcome them, then offered them seats in a corner of his office furnished with a sectional sofa and twin Eames chairs. After some greetings and small talk, and upon learning that the Gonzalezes had a tennis date in an hour and a half, Ferrin got down to business. "As you probably know, I'm running as the incumbent Representative for the 14th Congressional District."

Gonzalez, whose only ambition was to be the best prosecutor in Florida, had merry eyes, as if somebody had just told him a really funny joke. His eyes crinkled at the unnecessary introduction. "My wife, bless her heart, is a political junkie, so she's been following the campaign and keeping me current. Me? I prefer sports. When you deal with violence all day, the last thing you need to do is turn on the evening news or follow any politics other than in the office. The violence of sports is so much cleaner." He laughed heartily at his own wit.

Ferrin's laugh was less hearty. "I'm starting to think that way myself, Luis. What I have to say will probably shock you."

"Try me."

"I think my mother-in-law, Jerry Lee Beaudry, may have had something to do with the death of Margaret Greer, who appeared at my fund-raiser a week and a half ago. The poor woman died of something, apparently in her sleep, while a guest at Beaudry Hall."

Gonzalez, who had been lounging in his chair, straightened. "Your own mother-in-law? I think there's a bad joke there."

"No joke, I'm afraid. As you can imagine, I'm very reluctant to be doing this, but I've come to the conclusion that I have no choice."

"Didn't I read somewhere that Mrs. Beaudry was in California when you threw that big party in Naples?"

"You did. But if you'd read *The National Enquirer*, a tabloid I'm sure you don't check out very often, you'd have learned that she admitted she was actually in Naples that night, and I have her boarding passes to prove it."

"How did the woman die?"

"Jerry Lee's brother says she told him to prepare teabags composed of a commercial tea mixed with an herb called foxglove, which contains digitalis. The tea was served to Miss Greer at bedtime. The victim may have had a heart condition that exacerbated the effects of the herb. I understand there are postmortem tests for that, and I believe the Medical Examiner has been tipped off to the possibility of digitalis poisoning." Ferrin did not reveal that someone from his office, at his direction, had called in the tip after Matt and Tom talked to Verlin and watched his teabag demonstration.

"So, let me get this straight. Jerry Lee, as you call her, didn't prepare the tea. Did she serve it to the woman?"

"No. Niall Kilcommon, Jerry Lee's butler, did, but I doubt very much that he had any idea there was anything wrong with the teabags. They looked so normal no one who wasn't looking for a problem would have noticed any difference. My friends here watched Verlin prepare a poisoned teabag, and we have both that one and a third that was leftover from the original preparation."

"So what was Jerry Lee's part in all this?"

"She told her brother to prepare the teabags and separately told the butler to serve it to Miss Greer after the fund-raiser. Her brother -- whose name, by the way, is Verlin Grubbs -- said she called him with the instructions. He assumed she was in California when she called, and she may have been. The butler says much the same thing."

"What was the motive? Did Jerry Lee know this Miss Greer?"

"No. Jerry Lee thought the woman was Verbena Cross. She's the famous actress who decided to appear at my fund-raiser, not because she agrees with my politics, but because she felt sorry for the false abortion story about my wife. I don't know for certain why my mother-in-law had it in for Verbena Cross, but my best guess is that killing her was a handy way to hurt Virgil Goldstein, her father." Ferrin then explained the complicated connection between Goldstein and the *Marie Claire* abortion story and Verbena Cross' use of a body double.

"Proof of motive isn't necessary to prosecute a homicide, of course," Gonzalez said, "but juries don't like to convict without understanding motive, and telling that story coherently would be a challenge."

"Agreed. As an experienced prosecutor myself, I sympathize. But there's more. This wouldn't be the first time Jerry Lee killed someone . . . perhaps I should say, allegedly killed someone. We're here to tell you that Verlin Grubbs claims that the body of a young woman is interred in a statue in Jerry Lee's garden at Beaudry Hall, a young woman who may also have been killed with an herb poison. We had the plinth opened this morning. We discovered the plinth really is hollow, as Verlin claimed, and there is a skeletonized body inside. We left it untouched and closed up the plinth. Verlin claims that Jerry Lee also poisoned her husband, Jonah Beaudry, who is interred in a mausoleum at Beaudry Hall, and an old boyfriend of my wife's, whose ashes were mixed into metal cast into a pig statue."

At Gonzalez' startled look, Ferrin waved his hand. "Don't ask. More about the pig statue later. Plus, I have reason to believe that the late Phil Coker may not have taken nitro for a heart condition voluntarily. You probably heard he died recently in California, and as we speak my mother-in-law is attending his memorial service in Los Angeles."

"Where did the alleged murders of the girl, the boyfriend, and the husband take place?"

"Two near Charleston, South Carolina, and one in Greenville, all about twenty years ago, give or take a few years in each case."

"And Phil Coker?"

"In California at the Napa Valley estate of Virgil Goldstein."

"If those crimes in Charleston and Greenville actually occurred, they're out of my jurisdiction and the evidence is so circumstantial and so old, there's nothing I can do. Even the Phil Coker case is out of my jurisdiction unless we could prove she planned it in Florida."

"I know that. I tell you about them only so you know what kind of person we're dealing with here. And even if none of the old acts can be prosecuted, they establish a pattern of homicidal activity that a judge might allow to come before a jury. She has to be stopped."

"And the only recent act in my jurisdiction is the death of the actress' body double?"

"No. I was getting to that. There's one other. Do you recall that my driver, Alexie Abramova, a Russian immigrant, was killed recently in a hit-and-run? The police surmised he was struck by a blue sedan."

Gonzalez' eyes widened. "You know who did it?"

"Not for sure," Tom interjected. "But Phil Coker drove a blue Prius. Jerry Lee's butler told Matt and me that somebody had been by to repair it while Coker was in California. We haven't verified that yet, but the butler gave us a piece of metal the repairman found attached to an axle. It might be part of the racing bike Abramova was riding when he got hit."

"There'll be a few chain-of-custody problems with that, but it's something." Gonzalez cleared his throat. "Was Phil driving the night of the hit-and-run?"

"Either he was, or Jerry Lee was. We have reason to believe it was Jerry Lee."

"Who is 'we'?"

Matt spoke up. "I called 911 after the accident. I never saw the face of the driver because I was always behind the Prius, but Phil was driving Jerry Lee's Cadillac that night and admitted to it on tape. I therefore surmise that it was Jerry Lee driving the Prius, but if she drove it before on other occasions, which I'm sure she'd claim, then her fingerprints in the Prius wouldn't prove she drove that night."

"Why were you following the Prius?"

"I didn't start out following the Prius. I started out following Alex Abrams because Harley Wangle suggested he was a double-agent, pretending to be loyal to Ferrin but really working for Mullett. I saw Phil pick Abrams up in Jerry Lee's Cadillac, drive to a public park, idle awhile, then drop Abrams off opposite the carriage gate at Beaudry Hall. When I saw a blue Prius leave the curb and follow the biker, I decided to see what that was all about. At that time I wasn't sure who was driving, or even who the car belonged to, and I sure as hell didn't expect to witness a hit-and-run. It wasn't until the next morning I deduced that the Prius belonged to Coker, and Jerry Lee must have been driving."

Gonzalez closed his eyes in thought. When he opened them, he fixed on Ferrin. "I can surmise why you're here, but you tell me in your own words."

Ferrin held up three fingers, turning each down seriatim as he ticked off his reasons. "One, I want you to know privately about my suspicions and tell us what you think. Your office might not be willing to prosecute the Greer case because it's largely circumstantial and rests primarily on the testimony of Verlin, a most unusual witness. The hit-and-run case isn't much better. If that's your analysis, then there's no point in stirring things up further. In that case, you can be assured I will act in whatever way the law allows to limit Jerry Lee's freedom.

"Two, if you agree with my construction of events, I would like Jerry Lee to be investigated at least for the homicides of Margaret Greer and Alex Abrams. They both occurred in this jurisdiction, they're recent, and the evidence is at least as good as in any other of her homicidal acts . . . though I think it would be worthwhile to look at the other deaths as well so that you grasp the pattern.

"And three, I'd like Jerry Lee's brother to be given immunity as a witness. He's a little odd, autistic perhaps, a genius with herbal concoctions, completely under his sister's sway. He has very bizarre views about death. For a multitude of reasons, I don't think he ever understood the lethal consequences or the moral implications of what she asked him to do. To me, the proof of that is his openness about admitting his part in the poisonings. He's kept a daily diary for almost all of his life, complete with dates, names, places, and herbal concoctions, implicating not only Jerry Lee but himself as well. His memory is excellent, and his responses are startlingly direct. And speaking not as a former prosecutor but as a loving husband, I don't want my wife to lose her uncle, whom she's always adored despite his many peculiarities. She's going to lose her mother, and that's going to be hideous enough."

"But he's dangerous too."

"Agreed. He may need to be institutionalized to be sure he doesn't unknowingly poison someone else. There are humane ways to accomplish that. But he'd never survive prison."

"You're not expecting a response today."

"No, I'm not."

"Off the top of my head, I'd say the State Attorney isn't going to be inclined to prosecute unless your mother-in-law confesses."

"Which she won't do. To my knowledge, she's never breathed a word to anyone, even to her daughter. You could put her on the rack and she might scream out a few curses but no confession, so bringing her in for an interview would yield very little. She'd ask for an attorney anyway. At the most, she might turn on Verlin if cornered because he prepared the concoctions and there's no proof that she rather than he administered the poisons. In the case of Miss Greer, it's his word against hers that she ordered the preparation."

"What about wiring Verlin?"

Ferrin glanced at Tom and Matt. Tom spoke up. "Given his limitations, I don't think that would work. He'd never understand what he was supposed to ask or do."

"I agree," Matt said. "He'd be so proud of wearing a wire, he'd show it to her."

Gonzalez sighed. "Horrible thing to ask, but what about wiring your wife?"

Ferrin looked up at the ceiling with pained eyes. "I'll ask her."

"You're a brave man, Ferrin." Gonzalez, surreptitiously glancing at his watch, stood up.

"No, I'm not," Ferrin said, standing up too. "I'm a man who finds himself playing chess with the devil, and I'm pretty sure I'm going to lose."

55

Pinkie Swear
Sunday, May 7, 2006

Jerry Lee reached Beaudry Hall on Sunday night. She was not a happy woman. No one had called to congratulate her on the forceful speech she made at Phil's memorial service. Morty Zeller did not apologize for anything, neither the low-key nature of the service, which might have been fitting for a plumber but not for Phil Coker, nor his failure to treat her, Jerry Lee Beaudry, Phil's fascinating and generous partner, like a grieving widow and honored guest. The *Los Angeles Times* carried no picture of her in the Sunday edition.

Niall picked her up at the Fort Myers airport, but he was unusually quiet on the ride home. After he'd carried her bags to her room and served her a tray of wine and a grilled ham-and-cheese panini in the sitting room, he informed her that he was giving her two weeks' notice. He was returning to Ireland. He also informed her that Maria seemed to have extended her vacation indefinitely; she wasn't returning calls.

"I'm fresh from a funeral, Niall. Why are you doing this to me? Now, of all times? You've been with me forever."

"It's time for me to go home," he replied.

"Why is it time now?"

Niall murmured something she couldn't hear.

"But I'll be all alone. May I remind you that Phil's dead," she said, dabbing at her dry eyes. "I can't manage alone."

"You're a very efficient woman, madam. You'll manage just fine."

"Please. Won't you sit down a minute?"

Niall sat on the edge of a chair, stiff as a poker, his mouth stitched shut.

"What have you heard about our guest who died in her bed?"

"With your help, they identified her as Miss Cross' twin sister, her body double."

"With my help?" She clutched her chest.

"I have the local papers for you to read." He nodded in the direction of a table against the window, where there was a small stack of newspapers. "You're quoted as claiming Miss Cross had a twin nobody knew about."

"Do the authorities know how she died?"

"Not to my knowledge."

She sat in silence a few moments, fury growing in her like mushrooms in manure. "I suggest you leave immediately. But before you do, would you ask Verlin to come in?"

Niall stood up. "Should I prepare him a tray too?"

She looked at her watch. "No. I'm sure he's already heated up some canned soup for supper. But you can offer him a glass of wine." Wine was a rare treat for Verlin. "Then go." She glared at her butler. "Get out of here," she commanded, as if it were her idea that he leave her employ.

Twenty minutes later, when Verlin entered, he looked nervous.

"Tell me what you've been up to, Verlin."

"Nothing."

"Why are you fidgeting?"

"I want to go back to my room."

"Maybe the wine will calm you down."

"I don't like visitors."

"Have you had visitors?"

"Those big men were here. They asked me questions about that pretty woman who was here for Poppy's party."

"You mean the fund-raiser?"

He nodded. "*That* party."

"What kind of questions?"

"About tea. Then some men came back yesterday morning and opened up the Nike statue."

Jerry Lee looked stunned. "What did they find?"

"Nothing. They closed it up again."

"How did they know there might be something in there?"

Verlin looked down to hide his eyes from his sister's hard gaze. "I don't know."

"Are you sure you didn't tell them?"

Verlin struggled to remember the men's warning. He wasn't supposed to tell anyone about the visit or the men opening up the plinth. "Maybe I just dreamed it."

"Have you been having bad dreams?"

"Sometimes. I'm out of cannablis, you know," he added, as if that was the reason for the bad dreams.

"Well, why don't you get some more?"

"Phil gave me the cigarettes. He's gone."

"He won't be coming back, Verlin."

"I know. But I want more cigarettes."

Jerry Lee stood up. "Let's have a look in the freezer." She walked to the pantry, where a small stand-alone freezer was tucked under a counter beside a wine cooler. "I can't bend over without my back killing me. Look for a Stouffer's beef-and-noodles dinner box."

Verlin found what he was looking for. Inside was a baggy of herbs.

"That's what Phil smoked. I don't know where he got it. He had some papers and a little machine in the wine room downstairs. Before you go back to your apartment, if you want to, go down and find the stuff so you can roll your own. Take it all to the potting shed. Put the pot in a gauze bag and hang it from the rafters so it isn't noticeable, and put the cigarette papers with the tea papers. Hide the machine anywhere you can. Until the bag is empty, you can have a cigarette every night."

"Really? Then what? Should I try growing some *Cannabis*

sativa in the herb garden?"

"We'll see."

They returned to the sitting room, where Verlin drank his entire glass of wine in one draft. "Verlin. That isn't the way to drink wine. You're supposed to sip it."

"Sorry," he said, holding out his glass for a refill.

"Go into the kitchen and pour it yourself. Niall has gone to bed and Maria's not coming back. In fact, Niall is leaving tomorrow."

"You're going to live here all alone?"

"Well, I thought about asking if you wanted to move into Niall's apartment on the fourth floor."

"No."

"No? Why not?"

"I like my apartment."

"But I don't want to live in this mausoleum all alone."

Verlin looked confused. "Mausoleum?" He looked around, as if spying out dead bodies.

"Just an expression, Verlin. But think how cozy we could be if you're up in the garrett. We could cook together in the evening."

"But won't you find another Niall?"

"I'm not sure I can afford that. You can serve me like we used to do when we were kids. We'd play house, remember? You were always my servant."

Verlin's face became animated. "I liked that game. Except when you hit me if I didn't understand what you wanted or move fast enough."

"I promise not to hit you."

"You won't poison me the way you did Annie?" Annie was their older sister.

Jerry Lee laughed. "How about making a pinkie swear neither of us will poison the other?" She held out her pinkie. Verlin got up from his chair, wiped his hands down his trousers, and walked over to his sister to link pinkies.

"Pinkie swear," they said in unison. Jerry Lee laughed so hard her eyes flooded with tears. Verlin looked nervous.

"So how about it, Verlin?" she asked when he'd returned from the kitchen with the bottle of wine. "Why don't we celebrate our new living arrangement soon? We'll make dinner together, invite Poppy over. You want to see Poppy, don't you?"

"You bet. I love Poppy. She's very special. What should we make for her?"

"How about fried chicken? We can make some special brownies for dessert if you'll let me use a little of that herb."

Verlin had put the plastic baggy of pot on a table beside his chair but now picked it up possessively. "No."

Jerry Lee appeared to give in. "Oh, well, it was just a thought. But what I would like you to bring me tomorrow morning is some pennyroyal and verbena. I want to make some bath oil for myself."

"Do you want me to make it?"

Jerry Lee lounged back on her sofa. "No. I want to play around a little myself with various essential oils and food color. I need a hobby now that Phil's gone." As if in afterthought, she made one final request. "Oh, and a couple of castor bean seeds, if you don't mind."

Verlin looked nervous. "I don't like to handle them. What are you going to do with them?"

"Use gloves then. I'm just going to put them in some potpourri."

"But they don't smell good."

"Listen, you damn troll. Stop thinking, and do as I say. Then forget everything I ever told you to do. Wipe it right out of your memory bank."

At his injured look, she softened her voice. She often called him a troll in the presence of others, but she'd never slipped and said it to his face before. "Just do as I say. We always get along better that way."

As Verlin returned to his potting shed, he couldn't get the word "troll" out of his head. He knew from the years of listening to his sister read fairy tales to Poppy that trolls were ugly little dwarves, often very naughty, living under bridges and in forests. But he wasn't a dwarf, nor especially ugly. He didn't live under a bridge and he never deliberately did anything naughty. So why did she call him a troll? Whatever the reason, he was sure it wasn't good.

56

Fried Chicken and Castor Beans
Tuesday, May 9, 2006

Tuesday, May 9, was Emma Jocelyn McBride's eleventh birthday. She was a studious girl, more interested in the debating club than the cheerleading squad, but otherwise was normal. She fell asleep with her cellphone in her hand. She showed early promise as a shoe collector. And she had just begun to be deeply ashamed of her mother and father.

As the only child of prosperous, loving parents whose discipline was rare and gentle, Emma had no idea how good her life really was. She just knew her parents were *so* boring, whereas her flamboyant grandmother Jerry Lee and her eccentric uncle Verlin were cool. When she announced to Poppy and Ferrin that they were celebrating her eleventh birthday at Beaudry Hall with a fried chicken dinner, Poppy had only three questions.

"Don't you want a birthday party with your friends?" Emma's face was scornful. Of course she did, but the party had to be on the weekend, at the country club pool, with neither parent anywhere in sight, except to pick up her and her guests when it was time to start the sleepover.

"Won't you be bored at Beaudry Hall?" Emma, showing just a smidgeon of doubt on that subject, rallied to the defense of Beaudry Hall. No. Verlin would take her to the potting shed and let her sort through his treasures, then to the carriage house to let her sit in the driver's seat of the Impala. After that, they'd stroll through the gardens, Verlin reciting Latin names as if he were some sort of mad genius. Grams would take her to her dressing room to try on shoes and costume jewelry.

"Well, don't you want to save Grams from the work of cooking dinner? We could have pizza delivered or get take-out Chinese." Emma was patient with her foolish mother. No. She loved southern-fried chicken, just the way Grams made it.

Poppy was both relieved and anxious. Relieved because she'd agreed to wear a wire but had not yet been brave enough to propose a fixed time for a meeting with her mother and uncle. A birthday dinner at Beaudry Hall was the perfect opening. And anxious because she was afraid of eating or drinking anything either of those strange practitioners of the black arts might prepare. She would have to watch the preparations from beginning to end.

Fortunately, Emma insisted on arriving at Beaudry Hall at four o'clock, right after school, so she and Verlin would have ample time in the potting shed, carriage house, and gardens. Ferrin did not accompany them, promising them that if his schedule allowed, he'd arrive around seven, but in any case not later than ten.

Wearing a thick, quilted Mandarin-style jacket to conceal the wire, in case Jerry Lee insisted on hugging her, Poppy looked a bit strange, she knew, but what else could she do? While Jerry Lee cooked dinner -- fresh chicken marinated in buttermilk, then floured and fried in lard -- Poppy sat at the granite island on a bar chair, sipping a Coke out of a glass bottle, the only drink she would accept because she could pry the bottle top off herself. She listened to her mother's unending complaints about Niall's retirement, Maria's disappearance, and Phil's memorial service, mostly responding with innocuous phrases like "Oh, wow" or "No kidding" or "That's awful" as the occasion required. She was so preoccupied with how to get her mother to confess to murder that she hardly heard what her mother was saying.

Just before the meal was ready to be served -- mashed potatoes, peas in butter sauce, biscuits, and fried chicken -- Jerry Lee asked her daughter to make the gravy because suddenly she was very tired.

"Your heart giving you a problem?"

"No. I'm almost seventy, remember? I just need to sit down a minute. I was going to mix up a pitcher of mint juleps, but I don't have the energy."

"I'll do it if you have the ingredients."

"The simple syrup and mint leaves are in the refrigerator. The bourbon's right here."

Poppy wouldn't have drunk anything mixed by Jerry Lee or Verlin, so she was more than happy to prepare a pitcher of strong drink. She needed the bourbon.

After dinner, Emma opened her gifts: from Jerry Lee, a matched set of luggage in pink from The Signature Shop at The Beverly Hills Hotel, and ostensibly from Verlin, a set of pink luggage tags. Emma then begged to be taken to the dressing room upstairs. Jerry Lee uncharacteristically said she was too tired, too full of birthday cake, to go up with her. "You go on up there, Emma. Try on anything you want. Just don't take anything without asking."

After a few minutes of inconsequential chatter, mostly about how Jerry Lee had told Niall to leave immediately so as not to prolong the torture and Verlin was going to move into the fourth floor garrett, where he'd have his own big-screen television, Poppy started on her mission.

"Jerry Lee, I have to decide whether to send Emma to summer Bible school."

"It won't hurt her."

"Do you believe in God?"

"What a silly question. Of course."

"What's He like, do you think?"

"Well, he's not the thundering god of judgment from the Old Testament, the way Jonah thought. He's love. That's all. Just love."

"So He forgives all of us no matter what we do while here on earth?"

"Yes. There's no hell, just heaven."

"So there's no justice after this? No one gets punished for their lack of faith or their bad deeds, is that what you're saying?"

Jerry Lee's face grew tight with suppressed anger. "What's justice?"

"I should think it's about righting wrongs, to start with. You said Nemesis was following Ferrin around. She's the goddess that balances good and evil. I don't believe in goddesses, by the way, but if Nemesis exists in your mind, why not the Old Testament God of judgment as well?

"Everybody goes to heaven because everybody does wrong and has to be forgiven."

"So it doesn't matter if we believe in God or not?" Poppy was stupefied by her mother's world view but realized for the first time how Jerry Lee justified her hideous actions. "There's no accountability. Is that what you're saying? Because if that's what you're saying, then why bother sending Emma to Bible camp?" Poppy knew there many reasons to send her daughter to Bible camp, but she had to test her mother. What world view allowed her to murder people without remorse?

"It doesn't matter, frankly, whether you do or don't. But if Emma wants to go, it won't hurt her."

Poppy couldn't let the subject go. "So it doesn't matter if we do something really terrible here. We don't need to confess our sins or atone for them. No matter what we do, we still go to heaven, sit in the holy presence of Jesus through eternity."

They had moved to the sitting room, Jerry Lee, as always, taking the green sofa. "Mind if I lie down, rest my weary bones? If we're going to have a discussion this boring, I need to relax."

"I didn't realize it was boring to talk about life and death."

"I like this conversation," Verlin said. "I know where dead people's souls are."

"I know you do, Verlin." Poppy didn't want to hear his explanation again. Before he could wade into muddy waters, Poppy directed her inquiry back to her mother. She had to know if Verlin had told the truth about the water hemlock in her father's afternoon drink. "So if you killed Dad, it doesn't affect your eternal fate. You don't need to confess what you did or worry about what happens when you die, is that it? You don't need to pay for what you did?"

Jerry Lee opened one baleful eye. "What in hell are you talking about?"

"I'm talking about the water hemlock."

"*Cicuta virosa*,"Verlin interjected helpfully.

"How do you know about that?" Jerry Lee sat up, her hard gaze switching from her daughter to her brother like a cop with a searchlight spotting a fugitive in the weeds.

"Why did you do it?"

"I didn't. Verlin gave him a lemonade slush."

"With water hemlock in it?"

"I don't know. I had nothing to do with it."

"That makes no sense. Why would Verlin want Dad dead?"

Jerry Lee turned to Verlin. "Why did you want him dead?"

Verlin looked panicked. "I didn't."

"But *you* did," Poppy said to Jerry Lee, "because he was going to put an end to my pageant career, wasn't he? My pageant career meant more to you than to me or anyone else."

"Do you realize, my ungrateful daughter, that if Jonah had gotten his way, you wouldn't have been in the Miss South Carolina pageant and Ferrin McBride would therefore never have known a thing about you?"

Poppy ignored that taunt. "What about Phil? Did you add the nitro to his drink?"

"That's pure speculation."

"But you did, didn't you? That's why you didn't throw away the old nitro after you got a renewal."

"Maybe, maybe not. But if I did give it to him, he deserved it. He betrayed me. He took my money and lied about repaying me. He gave that horrible abortion story to your husband's driver, who gave it to Goldstein, who gave it to a reporter. If I died this minute, you'd inherit very little money, you know, all because of Phil's profligacy. Everything I've ever done was to protect you."

"Dewey and Nicky Sue too?"

"*Datura stramonium*,"Verlin said helpfully.

"Dewey and Nicky Sue were obstacles. I loved you so much,

wanted so much success for you, it would have killed me if you failed or had to drop out. I couldn't let anybody get away with killing my dream."

"Loved? Wanted? Past tense?"

She sighed dramatically. "Just an expression, Poppy. You're still the reason I live."

"Why would it have killed *you* if *I* failed? Why was it *your* dream that was so important?"

"We worked hard for that dream, both of us. You're the only good thing in my life."

Poppy put her head in her hands at the *non sequitur*. "Did you know Nicky Sue's body has been discovered in your garden?"

"Verlin told me that the plinth had been opened but not that anything had been found." She shot a furious look at Verlin. "Who, by the way, gave anybody permission to dig in my garden?"

"I did," Poppy said. "But that's not the point."

"The only thing that body proves is that I wanted to give the poor girl a decent burial."

"Did you bump off Ferrin's driver?"

Jerry Lee shuddered. "I might have tapped him with Phil's car."

"Why?"

"I wasn't sure. I didn't even know his name. Verlin pointed out that Phil had been secretly meeting him. I suspected the guy was the conduit to Goldstein. As it turns out, my suspicions were justified because Phil confessed."

"And then there's poor Margaret Greer, Verbena's sister. Why her?"

"*Digitalis purpurea*," Verlin interjected.

Neither woman responded to him.

Jerry Lee drained her glass. "I thought she was Verbena until it was too late."

"So you *were* in this house the night of the fund-raiser."

"Nobody can prove that except maybe Niall or Maria, and they're both gone."

Poppy's eyes opened wide with fear. "What did you do to

them?"

"For God's sake, Poppy, I didn't do anything to them. Maria left the day after the fund-raiser and won't return calls. I fired Niall and he went back to Ireland."

"Did you take the dead woman's identification papers?"

"How else do you think I found out it wasn't Verbena?"

"But why, Jerry Lee? Why kill a woman you thought was Verbena?"

"Revenge, my girl. Her father hurt you with that abortion story, so he hurt me too. I wanted to hurt him in kind."

"Your killing his daughter wasn't quite the same thing as his libeling me. You went way beyond a tooth for a tooth. His sin was words that harmed me. Yours was poison that killed the woman you thought was his daughter."

"Don't throw that old shibboleth in my face. An eye for an eye, a tooth for a tooth. Phew," she spit. "I say, that old desert tribe didn't know what it was saying. Bring a knife to the party, I'll bring a gun."

Verlin looked puzzled. "You never used knives or guns, did you?"

"Just another expression." With teeth bared, Jerry Lee smiled at Verlin. "Have you been talking to Poppy about our secrets?"

Verlin simultaneously shook his head vigorously and rubbed his hands on his knees.

"Has he?" she asked Poppy.

"No." Poppy was a bad liar.

Jerry Lee, looking skeptical, got up and went to the kitchen. Poppy, hawk-eyed, watched as her mother mixed another pitcher of mint juleps, using the same bottles of bourbon and simple syrup and the same bunch of mint leaves she had used to make the first pitcher. At that moment, Emma returned wearing an armload of her grandmother's bracelets. "Look, Grams. I like all these."

"Come in here, darling." Emma did as she was told, laying her forearm on the granite island to display the bracelets.

Poppy, watching from the sitting room, decided to load the three empty tumblers on a tray and take them to the kitchen for refills.

Jerry Lee, smiling at her daughter as the tray was set down, said, "You'll notice that these aren't all costume bracelets. She has an eye, doesn't she? Takes after me." Patting Emma's head, she suggested that she go sit on the sofa and they'd examine the treasures in better light. When Poppy made a move to refresh the tumblers, Jerry Lee shooed her away. "That's enough. I'll do this."

As Poppy reluctantly returned to her chair by the fireplace, unaware that turning her back to her mother for a few seconds was a matter of life and death, Jerry Lee called out a question to Verlin. "Where are those special cigarettes of yours? I think we need one for each of us."

Verlin obediently stood up and reached into his pants pocket, pulling out a little silver case. "One for each?" His tone was doleful. He didn't like sharing his cigarettes.

"What do you mean, 'special cigarettes?'" Poppy asked.

"Phil's cannablis."

"I'll pass," she said sharply. She'd never smoked pot in her life and wasn't about to start now.

"Suit yourself," Jerry Lee said, returning with the tray of refreshed drinks, placing one on a table next to Poppy, handing one to Verlin, and then carrying the third, still on the tray, to a table beside the sofa.

As Verlin surveyed the room, not listening to the women's chatter about the bracelets Emma had confiscated, the hair on the back of his neck suddenly stood to attention. Something was going on. He could feel it in the air. The way Jerry Lee said "That's enough" was like scary music introducing the shower scene in *Psycho*. He looked at the three tumblers. Each looked slightly different, though they purportedly contained the same concoction. Poppy's had mint leaves muddled in the bottom and one fresh mint leaf folded over the rim. All the mint leaves in Jerry Lee's were muddled at the bottom, none folded on the rim, and her drink had a swizzle stick. His own tumbler also contained a swizzle stick but had two fresh sprigs of mint leaves sticking from the top. What did it mean? Which glass was which?

Jerry Lee was very clever the way she made sure her intended victim got the special, high-octane drink but no one else did. To allay suspicion, she always made sure everyone drank the same concoction, but the drink with the special additive was always marked in some subtle way. That's how their older sister had not realized the significance of an extra marshmallow in her cup of cocoa. But in this case which drink was marked with what?

He was suddenly afraid for Poppy. She'd asked very strange questions. She was too warmly dressed for this time of year. All evening she'd watched her mother like a mongoose watching a snake. Her voice had been unusually serious, sometimes breaking a little, as if on the verge of hysteria. She'd gotten Jerry Lee to talk about a lot of mysterious deaths she wasn't supposed to know about. Was Poppy marked for death as a result of knowing too much?

He knew a lot too, of course, but he'd known a lot for years without anything bad happening, and Jerry Lee couldn't have managed to get rid of so many people without his help. Besides, she had invited him to move into the house to keep her company, which she surely wouldn't do if she were about to get rid of him.

His musings were interrupted when the doorbell rang and Jerry Lee got up to answer it. Poppy said, "I'll go with you. It's probably Ferrin."

Once the women disappeared around the corner, Verlin got up and switched his drink with Poppy's. He reasoned that Poppy was the person in danger because only her tumbler was missing a swizzle stick. He then took the swizzle stick from the drink that had been his and put it in the drink that had been Poppy's. He was just considering whether he should exchange the drink he was now holding with Jerry Lee's or simply avoid drinking it altogether when the group returned to the sitting room and he had to pretend he'd been up to nothing.

He sat down again on the edge of his chair, rubbing his trouser legs over and over. He was very troubled. He wished, when she asked, that he'd never given his sister the pennyroyal, a member of the mint family called *mentha pulegium,* very hard to grow in Florida soil. He should have known it wasn't meant to scent some bath oil. It smelled so strongly of spearmint, only mint juleps would mask its smell. But it wasn't lethal in small doses, so why bother with it?

Then he remembered the castor bean seeds she'd also demanded. Just a couple, she said. In a far corner of the garden, he grew the plant, *Ricinus communis*, distantly related to the poinsettia, for its decorative qualities, but he was always wary of it. He knew it was the deadliest plant poison on earth. One little seed could kill a child, as Jerry Lee well knew. He wouldn't even let Emma touch it when they toured the gardens.

His eyes moving anxiously from one tumbler to another, he wondered if he dared to gather up all the drinks and pour them down the drain. But an action like that was so out of character for him, so hard to explain and so ridiculous if he was wrong, that he couldn't move. Surely his sister wouldn't risk somebody's instant death.

Lost in worrisome thoughts, frantic that he might have misread the tumblers, Verlin heard nothing of the conversation once Ferrin had settled in. Verlin loved his niece. He'd gladly die in her place. Nevertheless, he placed his hand over his own drink to make sure he didn't absent-mindedly take a sip while studiously watching the others. When Poppy took a sip of her drink, his hand involuntarily shot out as if to stop her, but no one noticed his strange gesture, and he said nothing.

Not until Poppy suddenly began to sweat profusely and gasp for breath did he realize his innocent but deadly mistake. Jerry Lee had meant for him, not her daughter, to die.

57

Twists and Turns
Tuesday, May 23, 2006

I never wrote a more difficult piece in my life. I'm so emotionally close to Poppy McBride, the key player in Jerry Lee's drama, I have no hope of the Mount Olympus point of view required of news reporters. Therefore, I have decided to break my assignment from *The Naples Daily News* into two sections. The first part will convey the facts as I know them, with illuminating background details I've gleaned from my interviews and a minimum of commentary. The second part will be my frankly personal reaction to Jerry Lee's story.

I am fortunate to have ready access to everyone, including Jerry Lee, who had refused to say anything for the first few days after her arrest. Finally, Ferrin persuaded her to plead guilty to avoid the horrors of a trial, the burden on Poppy, and the death penalty. She would have to give a full confession to get such a deal. She, in turn, demanded that she be able to talk to a writer of her choice while awaiting sentencing. The prosecutor agreed on the further condition that Jerry Lee could not benefit financially from her story.

Oddly enough, Jerry Lee chose me, Molly Standardt, as her confidante. She gave no explanation for her unexpected choice, though she hinted at the reason. She wants her life to be made into a movie, and now that *Gilt Trip* is under contract to a Hollywood studio, she thinks I may be the person who can get that done. She expects the movie to depict her rise from rags to riches, her maternal love for her only daughter, and her uncommon skill as a poisoner, a portrait only she could see as flattering. As you will see, Jerry Lee gives me far more credit than I deserve. There are others in a much better position than I am to ensure a movie is made about her, but it won't be the portrait she wants.

The night of May 9, I stayed all night with Poppy in the ICU, praying for my friend's recovery, and I returned to the hospital every day after that for at least an hour, sometimes more. Only yesterday did the doctors tell Ferrin, who had suspended his campaign and spent most of every day with his wife, that Poppy would make a full recovery.

Things might have turned out so much worse. If Ferrin hadn't been present when Poppy sipped the tainted mint julep, there might have been no level head at Beaudry Hall to make an immediate 911 call. If Verlin hadn't unhesitatingly owned up to the castor bean seeds and the mistaken switch of tumblers, the emergency room doctor might not have known what he was dealing with. If Poppy had taken more than the tiniest sip of the tainted mint julep, she might have died at Beaudry Hall.

As it was, Poppy's life balanced for two weeks on a knife edge, for the hospital wasn't prepared for the ingestion of *Ricinus communis*, a natural poison readily available but rarely used. Fortunately, the fact that Poppy had been wearing a wire that night helped the police sort things out as to the relative culpability of Jerry Lee and Verlin.

I know my readers will be as interested as I am in Jerry Lee's background. What led her to murder so many people? How did she evade detection for over twenty years? How did she know so much about poisonous herbs? Was she remorseful?

The day I spent at the jail interviewing Jerry Lee about her past was riveting. Just as Poppy had always maintained, Jerry Lee's claims to an aristocratic past were bogus. She admitted there are no old Beaudry family recipes: not for Southern-fried chicken or cheese straws, not for mint juleps, not for anything. The Grubbs are not related to the Draytons. When I showed Jerry Lee the pictures I'd taken a few miles from Little Gap of the shack she grew up in, Jerry Lee covered her eyes.

"Is that the right house?" I asked. "I'm sure it looks different now."

"Yes," she whispered. It was the first sign of shame I ever saw in her. And the only one.

"So let's start at the beginning. Where and when were you born, Jerry Lee?"

"August 13, 1937 in Pigeon Run, South Carolina, in the foothills of the Smokies. At home."

"Were you the oldest child?"

"No. Annie June was a year older. Verlin Dootz came five years after I was born."

"Tell me about your mother."

"Her name was Stella, Stella Mae Dootz before she was married. She married Pop when she was fifteen to get away from her step-mother, who beat and starved her. At least that's what Ma claimed, though she didn't talk about her early life much. She was taken out of school in the third grade to take care of her step-sisters and -brothers."

"Was she a good mother to you?"

"Not especially. She might have been in the right circumstances, but she was too beaten down, had too many kids and too little money. She often worked in the fields with Pop. Sometimes when he was too drunk to go to work, she did his job for him. She could milk cows, drive a truck, do everything Pop could do. And she was a great gardener."

"She was?"

"If we didn't grow vegetables and can them ourselves, we would have starved in the winter. We picked up the bruised apples that fell in our neighbor's yard so Ma could make applesauce. She grew herbs too. Medicinal herbs. She made a few pennies on the side selling them to people. She knew what to use for a fever, a headache, that kind of thing."

"Is that where you and Verlin learned about herbs?"

337

"It is. Verlin took to gardening right away. He bundled and dried the herbs. The shack we grew up in was awful, but it always smelled good. Ma used to joke that Verlin was born with a hoe in his hands and his nose in a flower."

"Tell me about your father. You said he was too drunk to work sometimes."

"His name was Alf. Strange, I don't even know if it was short for something. His folks took him out of school in the eighth grade. He was a mean son-of-a-bitch. Good-looking, I'll say that, and he could seem charming when he wanted something, but mean as the day is long."

"Betty Darling said her husband hated to see the Grubbs come into his Texaco station because they stole things. Was she telling the truth?"

"I didn't steal anything. Maybe Pa did. The only job he could ever get was being a farmhand. He was a good worker when he was sober."

"Was he a good father?"

"No. He was surly, swore a lot, threw things when he was mad, beat Ma half to death every once in a while, and beat all us kids too. I hated him."

"Tell me about Annie June."

"She was twelve when she died, but I don't want to talk about her."

"Why?"

"I regret what happened."

"You regret what hap- . . . you mean you had something to do with her death?"

Jerry Lee sighed. A look almost of fear passed across her face like a scudding cloud. "I might as well get it off my chest. It can't do any harm now. She was the first person Verlin and I killed."

I felt like I'd been shot. "Your sister? You two killed your own sister?"

"She borrowed my favorite scarf and tore it on a nail. Then she denied the whole thing, but I knew better."

"What did you do?"

338

"Ma and Pop had left that night after it got dark to steal logs from a neighbor's wood pile. It was very cold that winter, and the fire had almost gone out in the wood stove. While they were gone, I made cocoa so we could warm up. A few months earlier, Verlin had ground up some castor bean seeds and fed them to a stray dog to see what would happen. The dog died, so I decided to put just a pinch of the ground seeds into Annie's cup of cocoa, just to make her sick. Punish her, you know? But I must have put too much in because she died."

"Did anybody call the police?"

"No. There weren't any police in Pigeon Run, and we didn't have a phone. I suppose somebody could have tried to get hold of the Sheriff. But Pop, of course, had his reasons for not wanting to talk to the Sheriff. Fortunately, Annie had been sickly from birth with a cough that never went away, so everybody thought it was just a natural death."

"How did you feel after Annie died?"

Jerry Lee looked off into space. "I never thought about that before. I don't remember feeling much of anything then. As I remember, a little fear for awhile. But when nothing happened, I felt vindicated. Triumphant. I taught her a lesson."

I willed my heart to slow down. "What were you like as a girl?" *Besides being a murderer.*

"I was pretty. I studied hard. I was popular with the boys, flirty but not wild, if you know what I mean. Pardon me if I sound like I'm bragging, but from an early age, I had a flair for transforming hand-me-down clothes into stylish creations. I'd change the hemlines, take in the seams, cut off sleeves, add buttons I found, sew on appliques cut out of felt squares, use scarves as belts when I could find them. I learned to curl my hair using juice cans I found in the dump. I was pretty resourceful in escaping the squalor."

"You had no money to buy anything for yourself?"

"Some. I was about ten when I started begging people for jobs. For a dollar a day, I de-tasseled corn in the summer. I babysat. I candled eggs for the hatchery. A neighbor gave me a bicycle so

I could deliver groceries and get to my jobs without walking for miles. I never earned more than twenty-five cents an hour at any job I did, but it was something. I had to hide it from Pop, of course. But the money taught me something."

"What?"

"It's good to have money."

"Tell me about Verlin Dootz."

"Ma said he almost killed her being born, it took so long. He weighed thirteen pounds. I think nowadays Ma would have been diagnosed with gestational diabetes. I remember his cry sounded thin, like a bird's. He was never right."

"Was he ever diagnosed with something, maybe autism?"

"No. You think that's what's wrong with him ?"

"Some people might say savantism because he knows so much Latin. Where'd he learn that?"

"Annie June taught him to read. He wasn't allowed to go to school, so she tried to help him at home. Ma had a picture book of herbs with Latin names. For some reason, Verlin took to it, memorizing every Latin word in there."

"Where'd he learn about all the other forms of writing he picked up?"

"I have no idea."

"Or the Hebrew calendar?"

"No idea about that either."

"Has he always kept a diary?"

"He started at about the same time he learned to read and write the alphabet. Nobody paid much attention because we couldn't figure out what he'd written. It looked like nonsense, like word-pictures or something."

"When did Verlin start living with you?"

"I married Jonah when I was seventeen. Verlin stayed behind with Ma and Pop. He was so unhappy Ma said he cried for me every day. One day a few years after I got married Verlin found them dead in the house. It looked like Pop shot Ma and then himself. Nobody knew what to do with Verlin. Jonah said it was my duty to take care of him, so we let him live in the carriage house behind the mortuary."

"How did you meet Jonah?"

Jerry Lee smiled faintly. "I was a senior in high school, jerking sodas in a dimestore in Little Gap. One Saturday in the Spring of 1954, Jonah Beaudry happened to stop there for a cherry Coke and directions to Pigeon Run on his way to visit an old classmate. We got to chatting. I learned he'd been married before, but never had any children. He was thirty-one years old, born and raised in Charleston. I didn't pay much attention to him at first because he was so old. Very plainly dressed, already balding, and a little portly. He was near-sighted, wore clunky glasses I teased him about. But somehow he let me know he had some money. I didn't like the idea of him being a mortician, but I liked the idea of money.

"Anyway, at the end of my shift at the soda fountain, he loaded up my bicycle in his station wagon and drove me home because he was going that way anyway. Though he didn't touch me or anything, I could tell he was smitten with me. Maybe he felt sorry for me too when he saw the shack I lived in. He found an excuse to return the next weekend and then the next weekend after that for the next several months."

"Did he propose the old-fashioned way?"

"No. He was quiet, a little shy. One day in his station wagon after my shift on our way to Pigeon Run, he asked me if I'd like to change my name to Beaudry and live in Charleston. I said, 'Are you proposing?' He said he was. I liked his name a lot better than Grubbs and I'd heard of Charleston but never been there. Before I even answered, he gave me a pearl pendant on a fine gold chain, which I still have."

"Did you answer right away?"

"I didn't think about it for a second. I knew my only escape was to get married and he was as good as any other man I ever met."

"Tell me about the wedding."

"We were married in a simple ceremony, no family or friends, in Little Gap the day after I graduated from high school. He gave me some money to buy a new dress, and I wore the pearl necklace

341

he gave me. We then drove straight to Charleston. Well, not to the city proper, but the suburb where he lived. Even though our home was only the second floor of a funeral home, I was thrilled to have my own place. He let me buy new furniture and taught me to cook."

"He must have been a good businessman."

"He was. He charged fair prices, did what he said he'd do, never cheated anybody. What you saw was what you got from Jonah. He was old school."

"'Old school.' Strangely, that's the same phrase Betty Darling used."

"He worked hard, long hours, but he made time for Poppy and me. People liked him because they could see he sympathized with them, always had a Bible verse to comfort them. He did free services for paupers in the county. He wasn't cheap exactly, but he was careful with his money. He gave me a household allowance; whatever I didn't need for food and clothes, I could keep in my own little savings account. Every year or two, he opened another funeral home in another town."

"You were married a long time before Poppy was born, weren't you?"

"About sixteen years, I think. I didn't want any children, but Jonah did. I never exactly agreed to get pregnant. I just did."

"Was Jonah a good father?"

"He loved Poppy more than anything. More than me, I know that. He taught her how to count using pennies laid out on a coffee table. Then, while I prepared dinner, she would sit on his lap and listen to him read the newspaper. Some evenings they would practice cursive writing on the dining room table. As a result of those fatherly attentions, Poppy could read, write, and count when she started school. After dinner, he'd pour himself a few fingers of bourbon, smoke a good cigar, and tell Poppy stories."

"About what?"

"The Depression. World War II. He had a brother, much older, who was a tail-gunner in the Pacific and died in combat. He also told her Bible stories; her favorite was Noah's ark. They watched Ed Sullivan together."

"Were you a housewife in those days?"

"More than that. I was practically a slave at first, working like the devil, let me tell you. Jonah talked me into assisting with the corpses: dressing them, doing their cosmetics and hair. I found I didn't mind working on dead people. Verlin grew flowers that I arranged for services. I did my own cleaning of our living quarters, laundry, cooking, all the things housewives did in those days. I sewed my own and Poppy's clothes, canned fruits and vegetables, and, like Ma, took medicinal tisanes to neighbors who had fallen ill to soothe their headaches and coughs."

"Pardon me for asking, but you ever poison any of them?"

Jerry Lee looked horrified. "Never. They never did anything to me."

"If Jonah taught Poppy to read and write and told her stories, what kind of time did you spend with her?"

"Every night before bed, I read her a fairy tale. Verlin was allowed to sit in a chair in the corner of the bedroom during the reading. All three of us always drank a cup of cocoa together before lights out."

"Cocoa without castor beans, I assume."

Jerry Lee made a face. "Cynical girl."

I repressed a retort. "When did you start Crowning Glory?"

"Poppy was ten years old. By that time, Jonah had hired assistants to do what I once did, so I was free to do something I always dreamed of, and I had a big savings account. I started the school to train Poppy, but soon other mothers wanted their daughters to be trained for competition in beauty pageants. I rented a space in a strip mall near Charleston. It was big and plain, but I gussied it up with draperies and chandeliers, made it look grand. It was part pageant training, part charm school.

"What I discovered was that I was really training the mothers more than the girls in hair styling, makeup, dress, manners, runway walking, public speaking, and decorum. The girls learned something too, of course. I made all of them develop a talent that would appeal to pageant judges." She gave me a scornful look.

"No fire batons. My graduates had a very high rate of success in pageants, but none more than Poppy, who won contest after contest. I was always aiming for the Miss South Carolina pageant."

She frowned at me. "She should have won, you know. She had beautiful wavy brown hair that brushed her shoulders and thickly lashed blue eyes. Her only flaw was a faintly freckled nose. Her petite figure was perfect. And she sang beautifully, as I'm sure you'll admit. Her range was phenomenal. Jazz, Broadway ditties, folk, country, popular songs, you name it. Do you remember how she sang *Send in the Clowns*? It was so moving one of the judges grew misty-eyed."

"And the rest of us contestants trembled," I said. "As we did when Nicky Sue played *Für Elise*. It's a simple and familiar piece by Beethoven, but it sounded nothing like the exercise some novice pianists make it. It touched the soul."

"That's your memory, not mine."

"Do you ever regret doing what you did?"

"You mean . . . ."

"Killing your sister and husband, Poppy's boyfriend, her rival in Greenville, almost killing Poppy herself. Then killing three more people and pushing me off the veranda."

Jerry Lee looked away for a second. "No," she said in a firm voice.

"You'd do it all again?"

"I didn't say that."

"Why don't you have regrets?"

"I did what was right. I got rid of people who were in my way. Their lives weren't worth much anyway."

"I'm glad to have mine. I think it's worth a lot."

"To you, maybe. Not to me." Jerry Lee paused. "I didn't start out to kill people, you know. The first was an accident of sorts, done when I was very young. Once I realized it didn't haunt me, the next ones were easier."

"How did you kill so many people without being detected until now?"

Jerry Lee looked stunned by the question. "Isn't it obvious?

Nothing ever went wrong before, and I never confessed to anything. Poison is easy to administer and hard to detect. The effects are easily confused with other possible causes of death, which is probably why women have always liked poison."

Well, not all women, you old witch. "Many people find it bizarre that you kept the body of Nicky Sue in the base of the Nike statue and had Dewey's ashes mixed into a bronze pig."

"Bizarre?"

"Worse than that. Macabre."

She shook her head in disgust. "People can twist anything. I was honoring them. If there had been time, I'd have done the same with Phil."

"But you killed them! Then you even went to the trouble of moving Nicky Sue and Dewey from South Carolina to Florida. I don't think they'd have thought they were being honored."

"What are you implying?"

"Well, for one thing, you kept control of the evidence that might have sent you to jail."

"Of course. I think that was smart, don't you?"

I sighed in frustration. "They were trophies, weren't they? You liked remembering what you'd done. You were proud of killing them and getting away with it. Every time you went to the garden, you could gloat."

"I didn't gloat. I made something beautiful out of their lives. I gave them memorials."

"It was their right, not yours, to make something beautiful out of their lives."

"Then they shouldn't have done what they did to me."

To you? My stomach turned over as if a bout of the flu was coming on. "It shocks me that you never breathed a word to anyone about your little hobby, your terrible victories. Most criminals are so full of what they've done they end up telling someone, a close friend, their priest, even a stranger in a bar."

Jerry Lee ran her hands through her hair. "That was the hardest part. A million times I wanted to tell Poppy what I'd done for her, prove how much I loved her. Show her how little she'd have accomplished without me. She wouldn't have been a contender for Miss South Carolina or married Ferrin McBride if I hadn't gotten rid of the baby and taken out Dewey and Nicky Sue. She wouldn't know how to conduct herself as a Congressman's wife if I hadn't trained her in everything from manners to dress when she was a little girl. Virgil Goldstein would never have been punished for hurting her if I hadn't stepped in. But I knew better than to brag about what I'd done. So, at great cost to myself, I didn't tell her anything."

I was speechless.

She closed her eyes a second, then stared at me as if I were undergoing a doctoral examination in forensics. "You're so smart about crime, think of this, Molly Standardt. Are all murders solved?"

"No, of course not."

"How many aren't solved?"

"I have no idea, but I suppose more than actually get solved."

"Who do you think gets away with murder?"

I had to think for a minute. "The lucky ones? The cases where the police are incompetent, witnesses won't come forward, there's no forensic evidence . . . ?"

She cut me off with a derisive snort. "Think again."

She'd already given me the answer. Her answer. "The ones who don't confess."

She nodded. "It takes discipline not to babble about what you've accomplished."

"You make it sound like a good thing, an accomplishment . . . getting away with murder."

"Depends on your point of view. Try standing in my shoes."

I'd rather stand in a burning tar pit. "What do you have to look forward to now?"

"Besides death? Seeing my life made into a movie."

"You think that will happen?"

"If you write a book about me as good as your first one and have the same good luck with selling it and getting it made into a movie, then, yes, I think it will happen."

"What do you want done with the monuments in your famous gardens? The monuments to murder, as *The National Enquirer* now calls them."

"I told Poppy to give them to the City. They'd look lovely in Golden Gate Park."

I don't think that's going to happen, lady. "What do you think is going to happen to Poppy and Ferrin now that you've confessed and the whole world knows what you've done?"

"Ferrin will get out of politics and go to work for Seamus. Poppy will lead a quieter life. That's all."

"Is that what you wanted all along? Politics is beneath you perhaps."

"A lot of things are beneath me."

"And Emma? What will happen to her?"

"She'll get enough money when I die to make her forget the bad things. She'll wear my jewelry with flair."

"You must worry about Verlin."

"Give him a mortar and pestle, hand him some herbs, and he'll entertain himself all day long." She gave me a long look. "Where is he, by the way?"

"Ferrin found him a place in Amish country."

"Not Indiana." She looked like she was about to spit.

"Afraid so. The eastern part of the State. He'll be well supervised but free to garden all day long without getting into trouble."

When the guard rapped her knuckles on the window, I knew the interview was over for that day. I'd been forewarned there was another visitor expected shortly.

58

Street People
June 2006

My investigative report on the murders committed by Jerry Lee has already landed me another book contract. I've tentatively titled the book *Diaries of a Mad Herbalist*. My literary agent, though beside herself with excitement, wants something more lurid, reminiscent of *Mommy Dearest*. The publisher suggests a title that evokes Greek tragedy, perhaps *The Medea Murders,* although to my mind that title is misleading. I'll let her and the publisher fight that battle.

Now I'm trying to finish the coda in which I lay out my personal reaction to the story of Jerry Lee. Here's the draft:

Confession is said to be good for the soul. I cannot judge how good it has been for Jerry Lee's soul, of course, but it is certainly good for the government. The prosecution of difficult cases like this one, resting primarily on circumstantial evidence, obscure motives, old memories, and unreliable witnesses, is notoriously difficult. Prosecutors don't want to risk a losing trial, not just because they value their own careers, but because if better evidence turns up later, double jeopardy prevents a trial that might have put the perpetrator away.

Shortly after I interviewed Jerry Lee, she suffered a mild heart attack, but she recovered and once again resides in a jail cell smaller than her dressing room at Beaudry Hall. Her cell is plainer than a public bathroom, which in a sense it is, since the lidless toilet sits right beside her cot, in full view of the guards. She wears shapeless prison garb. Her hair is gray and lifeless, lacking both tint and professional shaping. Without pencil, her eyebrows are almost nonexistent. There are dark circles under her eyes, deep crevices around her mouth. Her cheeks are sunken. She no longer smells of expensive perfume. The food she's served is not made from old family recipes. There are no gardens to wander in, no monuments to erect. Though arrogant as ever, she now strikes one as foolish and hollow, a pathetic shell of a woman.

Mrs. Beaudry's attorney, Rudd Weaver, a well-known criminal defense lawyer, has at her direction negotiated an agreement that requires a full confession while avoiding a trial, providing immunity to Verlin Grubbs, and saving Jerry Lee from the death penalty. She has agreed to accept a sentence of life in prison without the possibility of parole. At the age of 69, a month shy of her seventieth birthday, she will never taste freedom again.

Jerry Lee's daughter, Poppy McBride, is my good friend. We were once rivals for the Miss South Carolina crown, which in a sense I won by default, though I was not as talented as either Nicky Sue Darling or Poppy Beaudry. Nicky Sue disappeared and Poppy fell apart. You might say I was the last woman standing, twirling fire batons for all I was worth.

Poppy and I renewed our friendship when, at a book-signing, Jerry Lee accused me of leaking a false story that Poppy once had an abortion. At the time of my book-signing, I knew nothing about Poppy's purported abortion nor about the infamous *Marie Claire* article, which I hadn't then seen.

But, all unknowingly, I've nevertheless played my little part in this drama. If Poppy had had any reason to disbelieve my denials of being the leaker and if she hadn't stirred doubt in her mother's mind about who the real culprit was, Jerry Lee might never have thought further about the matter and thus never have realized her own companion, the infamous actor Phil Coker, was the actual source of the libelous story. Jerry Lee might then never have viewed Alexie Abramova, Phil Coker, and Virgil Goldstein as her arch enemies, and thus the deaths of Abramova, Coker, and Greer might not have occurred. In other words, I have, all unknowingly, played a small but crucial walk-on part in the movie of Jerry Lee's life.

Though I have elsewhere provided the facts about the murderer, the herbs, and the motives as I know them, I make no pretense to objectivity about the actors in Jerry Lee's drama. The reader is therefore warned to make of this very personal account whatever she will.

Poppy McBride is broken-hearted and ashamed. Though her mother claims to have performed all of her murderous deeds to protect or avenge her daughter, Poppy shares none of her mother's motives and knew nothing about the poisonings until recently, when a whole lot of information came together through outside sources. Until recently, she hadn't even suspected her mother's part in the very nearly fatal miscarriage she suffered almost twenty years ago. When Poppy was asked by the authorities to try to get her mother to confess to her part in the deaths of so many people and to secretly record the confession, Poppy hesitated, anguished at the very idea of exposing her own mother's dark deeds. But, fearing her mother would continue to hurt others, she overcame her reluctance, at the risk of her own life. "I know there will be people who despise me for exposing my mother. But I fear God more than any criticism that might come my way. She had to be stopped."

Poppy also knew that exposing her mother would likely end her husband's career as the 14th District's Representative to Congress, a post to which Ferrin McBride was first elected two years ago and for which he was vigorously campaigning up until two weeks ago. "Ferrin is completely innocent in all this," Poppy told me. "Still, people might view him as tainted by association with my mother. As a gentleman of the old school, with heartland values, he assures me that we will walk this path together, whatever twists and turns it presents. His sorrow, as well as mine, is reserved for all those my mother injured."

The only visitors Jerry Lee has are her attorney, her daughter, and me -- and a fourth very surprising visitor. That person is another who was injured by the death of Margaret Greer. With the permission of the authorities, Verbena Cross has, incognito, visited Jerry Lee twice. A few days ago, she was entering the jail the same moment I was leaving, and despite the wig, hat, and glasses, I recognized her. She agreed to meet me for coffee afterwards.

We took two chairs in a corner of Starbucks. "I was surprised to see you at the jail, Verbena."

"I was surprised to see you too. Are you writing another book?"

"I am."

"Want to try your hand at a screenplay?"

"About Jerry Lee?"

Removing her dark glasses, Verbena smiled engagingly at me. "That disgusting old woman thought she ruined my life by revealing who Gi really was. I'm determined to make an omelette out of the broken eggs she handed me."

"So you're doing a movie about her life?"

"That's what she thinks."

I involuntarily shivered at that. "What do you mean?" I whispered.

"She thinks the story is about her, and I encourage that delusion so she'll talk freely and sign the papers I want her to sign. No fees, no royalties . . . yada, yada. The movie I want to make, however, is really about Gi and Verlin. You know I've always been interested in street people."

"Somewhere along the way I heard you got an award for a little film you made about them."

"*Crossing the Street Against the Light.* A little indie film I made a couple of years ago."

"But your sister wasn't a street person. Neither was Verlin."

"In a sense, they were. I'm going to honor Gi with a film about her dreadful life and the happy ending I tried to give her. Verlin's life was different, of course. The angle for him is the mistreatment of the mentally challenged. More to the point, his mistreatment at the gnarled old hands of Jerry Lee, his own sister."

I was reluctant to say what was on my mind at that point, but risking nothing gains nothing. "I hesitate to point this out, but if you hadn't sent your sister Gi to Naples in your place, she wouldn't have died."

"True, but that wasn't a foreseeable consequence." Verbena, who had just brushed off an accusation with no sign of guilt, signaled the barista for another low-fat latte. "Jerry Lee thinks this film will show what a devoted mother she was and give her a place in the annals of crime as a highly successful poisoner. I want her to think that. But I intend no such thing. My spin is how the rich manipulate the poor, the orphaned, and the mentally challenged, discarding them like trash."

"Manipulation of the poor and the orphaned? Isn't that what your parents did to Margaret when they adopted only you? They consigned her to a miserable life, separated from her identical twin."

"They couldn't have foreseen that, any more than I could have foreseen that Gi risked death going to Naples."

"Pardon me, but that was precisely why you didn't come here. You were afraid of being killed by the bloggers who'd been making death threats."

"I arranged enough security she should have been all right."

Then you would have been all right too. "When you speak of the rich manipulating the less fortunate, do you mean only Jerry Lee, or do you include your parents and yourself in that evil?"

A flash of doubt passed across Verbena's face. "Mom and Dad didn't manipulate anybody, and I gave Gi the chance of a lifetime."

"Aren't you manipulating Gi and Verlin by the way you're going to characterize them as nothing but helpless, innocent victims?"

"They were helpless, innocent victims."

"So, let me get this straight. The only bad actor in this drama is Jerry Lee. Mind you, I have no sympathy with her whatsoever, but to me the drama looks more complex than you're making it."

"Depends on your point of view, Molly."

"Strangely, you see the world the same way Jerry Lee does. Everything depends on your point of view. That's called moral relativity, I think. Neither of you thinks there is any absolute truth."

"For good reason. There isn't any. The thing is to make up your own life, your own rules. Doesn't everybody see the world that way?"

I decided not to wade into those muddy waters any further. "Your point of view sounds like your father's point of view."

She smiled, apparently unconscious of whitewashing the deeds of her family and herself. "It does, I suppose. But really it's a universal view, an enlightened one. Karma. Karma explains everything. Gi taught me that. She was studying Buddhism, you know."

I studied her face while swallowing the dregs of my coffee. Verbena is beautiful, engaging -- and thoroughly frightening to me. What you see on the outside resembles nothing of what's on the inside. "What happened to the rebellious daughter? The independent woman who felt sorry for Poppy?"

"I *am* independent." She sounded defensive. "I'm rebellious when it suits me. But this story landed in my lap and I'm going to use it. I'm going to acknowledge that Mom and Dad's innocent deception in adopting me while pretending I was their blood daughter had unforeseen consequences. Acknowledging that fact rehabilitates us in the eyes of our detractors."

I fell silent, gathering my thoughts. I wanted to point out that it wasn't noble to confess to a minor sin in the hope of obscuring a bigger one, but before I could say anything further, she said, "The film will give me street cred too. You can't imagine how important that is in Hollywood these days."

"I take it you've found somebody to underwrite it?"

"Dad's backing the film, he likes it so much. So, Molly, are you interested in being part of the team?"

I must have looked shocked.

"I know we don't agree on everything, Molly but I relish a vigorous exchange of views. That's how good films get made."

So long as you win, girl. I know the drill. But I didn't want to insult her or say no right then and there, so, like the coward I am, I dissembled. "Let me think about it."

353

But I've stopped thinking about it. With the success of my first book, I can do what I want. I'll write my own book about Jerry Lee but not Verbena's screenplay.

Epilogue
Nemesis, Karma, Whatever
July 2006

A month after my surprise meeting with Verbena Cross, I was asked to write Jerry Lee's obituary. Her death, which shocked everyone, has been ruled a suicide, but that doesn't end the speculation. How did she get her hands on enough nitroglycerin to kill herself? If somebody slipped her the medication, was their motive to help or hurt her? Why did she kill herself the same way she said she killed Phil Coker?

There are many theories so far, but until the investigation has been completed, we won't know for sure, and I'm unwilling to speculate, other than to recall her prescient comment that Nemesis, the goddess of retributive justice, was stalking her family. Shakespeare might have portrayed Jerry Lee as hoist with her own petard. Verbena Cross thinks of it as karma. Harley Wangle pictures Lady Nematode worming her way into Jerry Lee's life. Some probably think of it simply as fate.

I don't know how to think about it. Maybe the sins of a mother being visited on her daughter, back through Jerry Lee and then Stella Mae until we reach Eve.

The only clue we have about what was in Jerry Lee's mind is her suicide note, written in very pretty handwriting but not signed: "This life isn't fit for a lady. I wish I'd drunk from Poppy's glass instead of her. The regret of my life is that I didn't do it that night. I'm ready to join the pantheon of goddesses, stand guard over my family forever. That's all I ever wanted: to be a good mother."

Meanwhile, the bitter campaign for Congressman from the 14th District trundles on. Neither Rep. Ferrin McBride nor Commissioner Myron Mullett has dropped out, though both, at various times, have had to suspend their campaigns because of serious family scandals. Fund-raising for both is said to have dropped off precipitously, and neither man has garnered the endorsements he sought.

There is good reason for this depressing turn of events. The scandals see-saw back and forth between the candidates. Just when we think one of the men must surely have sunk to the bottom of the polls after a horrifying revelation, the other man suffers the equivalent fate.

For instance, no sooner had Jerry Lee confessed to a string of murders than it became known that Myron Mullett had many other mistresses before Muffy Wayne.

The candidates' press aides battle it out in public. Harley Wangle, Mullett's press secretary, points out that Jerry Lee Beaudry made the record books as a peculiar kind of serial killer, the most prolific female poisoner ever known in Florida. "Ferrin McBride had to know what his mother-in-law was up to. He looked the other way, that's all. He didn't want the scandal. He'll do anything to win, even cover up murder."

McBride's press aide counters with, "If Myron Mullett can't be trusted to keep his marriage vows, why would anyone trust him to keep his campaign promises? Obviously, he misuses campaign funds for his personal peccadilloes, so shouldn't we expect him to misuse tax revenues for the benefit of his political cronies?"

And so it goes, an exchange of fusillades that never ends. We'll just have to wait and see whether the voters feel more comfortable with a man whose wife allegedly ran over his lover -- not once, but twice -- or a man whose mother-in-law killed, or tried to kill, everybody who stood in the way of her own mad ambition.

Maybe, just maybe, the voters will eschew guilt by association, instead basing their decision on policy and character. I'm not holding my breath.

Made in the USA
Lexington, KY
02 June 2012